"Dear Dr. Braddock:

As everyone knows, these are difficult economic times for all of us, especially those who were not blessed by God as you have been with such a well-paying profession.

We know that you live at 208 Marcus Lane South. We know Marie and Esther. They could both die.

God wants us to share with the less fortunate. We know you go to the big church on Walnut and leave Esther for choir practice on Thursday afternoons at four. Sometimes children die or disappear.

Marie would be easy to kill.

A man in your position can afford to give two thousand dollars a month. Cut down on donations to the church. Our man from Doraville will call you. He has a toothache. Pay him the money or those pretty faces are in the grave. Two thousand dollars, cash only.

Doctors who go to the police have dead children. I hope you are a wise man, Dr. Braddock. God bless you."

MIND-SET

SIGNET

 ONYX

THRILLING SUSPENSE!

☐ **RUNNING DEAD by Robert Coram.** Tony the Dreamer was a master terrorist and sexual psychopath ... a serial killer who combined his bloody business with perverted pleasures. Homicide Detective Jeremiah Buie was a legend of lethal efficiency. He would—and did—do anything to get his man. The killer and the cop—they were worthy of each other. The only question was: which of them was better at the hard-ball game they played for keeps?   (175565—$5.99)

☐ **STRANGLEHOLD by Edward Hess.** The all-too-real horror keeps mounting, as a cunning killer, with the reflexes of a cougar and an agenda of evil beyond basic blood lust, is countering FBI special agents Martin Walsh and Dalton Leverick's every move, as he keeps sending his prey, not to the mat, but to the grave.   (179846—$4.99)

☐ **PURSUIT by Zach Adams.** Martin Walsh is the deep-cover FBI agent who usually takes his fight to the enemy. But this time they bring the war to him when they snatch his son in a revenge-driven payback. Walsh, with the help of his partner, strips back layer after layer of a vicious international child-trafficking ring. Nothing short of a sea of blood will stop them.   (180607—$5.50)

☐ **A TIME FOR TREASON by Everett Douglas.** The premier assassin ... the premier target—in a supercharged conspiracy thriller. Scorpion's mission is to kill the President of the United States on behalf of some of the most commanding men in America—and a woman who is even more powerful than they are. But, FBI Special Agent Joel Matheson is hot on his trail.   (179218—$4.99)

☐ **PRAYING FOR SLEEP by Jeffery Deaver.** Michael Hrubek, a dangerously paranoid schizophrenic, has just escaped from a mental hospital for the criminally insane, and he is on a mission to find Lis Atcheson, the woman who identified him as a vicious murderer.   (181468—$5.99)

*Prices slightly higher in Canada

Buy them at your local bookstore or use this convenient coupon for ordering.

PENGUIN USA
P.O. Box 999 — Dept. #17109
Bergenfield, New Jersey 07621

Please send me the books I have checked above.
I am enclosing $_____ (please add $2.00 to cover postage and handling). Send check or money order (no cash or C.O.D.'s) or charge by Mastercard or VISA (with a $15.00 minimum). Prices and numbers are subject to change without notice.

Card #_____ Exp. Date _____
Signature_____
Name_____
Address_____
City _____ State _____ Zip Code _____

For faster service when ordering by credit card call **1-800-253-6476**

Allow a minimum of 4-6 weeks for delivery. This offer is subject to change without notice.

MIND-SET

Paul Doster

A SIGNET BOOK

SIGNET
Published by Penguin Group
Penguin Books USA Inc., 375 Hudson Street,
New York, New York 10014, U.S.A.
Penguin Books Ltd, 27 Wrights Lane,
London W8 5TZ, England
Penguin Books Australia Ltd, Ringwood,
Victoria, Australia
Penguin Books Canada Ltd, 10 Alcorn Avenue,
Toronto, Ontario, Canada M4V 3B2
Penguin Books (N.Z.) Ltd, 182–190 Wairau Road,
Auckland 10, New Zealand

Penguin Books Ltd, Registered Offices:
Harmondsworth, Middlesex, England

First published by Signet, an imprint of Dutton Signet
a division of Penguin Books, USA Inc.

First Printing, February, 1997
10 9 8 7 6 5 4 3 2 1

Copyright © Paul Doster, 1997

All rights reserved

PUBLISHER'S NOTE
This is a work of fiction. Names, characters, places, and incidents either are the
product of the author's imagination or are used fictitiously, and any resemblance to
actual persons, living or dead, events, or locales is entirely coincidental.

If you purchased this book without a cover you should be aware that this book is
stolen property. It was reported as "unsold and destroyed" to the publisher and neither the author nor the publisher has received any payment for this "stripped
book."

For my Joby

I am indebted to Jeff Sargent and Tim Minors for advice on police and legal procedure. Like Simon Braddock, my knowledge of such matters is extremely limited. A special thanks must go to my dental receptionist, Robin Treadwell, a faithful—albeit captive—sounding board during the writing of *Mind-Set*.

1

Macon, Georgia

The Frisbee gleamed in the early evening sun, though daylight-savings time made it appear late afternoon. The Labrador retriever caught the missile in mid-leap, returned, and scrambled away again as the next toss sailed through the still air, not yet heavy with the humidity of summer. It seemed to float forever across the one-way lane, over the median shrubbery, and beyond the lane on the other side. The youngster waited for the return of the large black dog, then walked in the same direction. He never saw the car.

Max knew how to accelerate without squealing his tires on concrete. The heavy automobile impacted the small body, a blow scarcely perceptible inside the vehicle. Max had killed this way before and knew from the sound that the job was done. Whatever feeling he had about murder was itself long since a victim, totally suppressed by habitude.

The evening was suddenly still as the dog crouched with a whimper and waited beside his companion, then pulled closer with his forepaws, licked the white face and waited again.

* * *

Thanksgiving.

The first hint of winter cold drifted through a clear sky, bare trees, and ruffled the thick layer of leaves that covered the scraggly front yard. A child rocked gently in a swing as she watched her baby brother. She was hardly more than a baby herself, yet old enough to tend her charge, who played in a sandbox now almost out of season with its mixture of dry leaves.

"Gobble, gobble," he chirped. His fat fingers walked the small plastic turkey along the wooden edge of the sandbox.

Obie Prather walked toward the girl on the swing. He was a stranger to her, but she knew nothing of strangers. Obie took her quickly and returned to the waiting car. Her protestations were loud but brief.

The baby was now alone with his thoughts. "Gobble, gobble . . . gobble."

Saturday, April 11, ten a.m.

Simon Braddock answered the den telephone. "Dr. Braddock speaking."

"Is this Dr. Braddock?"

"Yes."

"I've got a toothache, Doc."

It was a male voice. Simon hesitated and felt his anger rise. "Have I seen you before?"

"I'm from Doraville, only in Macon for the day. I'll be at your office between one and two."

Doraville. The word triggered rage, but he wouldn't let it show. "Okay. I'll be there."

Simon heard a click at the other end of the line, then traumatic silence.

"Extortion," he whispered to himself. The letter. The phone call. Simon cleared his mind and waited, allowing his emotions and reason a few moments to broach some brilliant new strategy he had not considered. Nothing was forthcoming.

He had expected the call for weeks, yet the sudden reality of the strange voice and the code left him stunned and furious. Familiar images flashed across his mind with renewed force: the twelve-year-old boy, fatal victim of a hit-and-run; the Thanksgiving disappearance of the Lanier girl. Both were children of Macon physicians. Then a doctor himself had died in a traffic accident. Simon didn't know the man, only the name—Bruce Murray. The newspaper had called it mechanical failure.

Simon tried again to clear his mind, to get his bearings. It was as good a day as any. Better. Marie and Esther were in Atlanta and would be late returning. He needed the day to work alone. The business had been rehearsed in his imagination hundreds of times. There was no other way.

The murders of the two children had been intended to create terror, but Simon's native anger went far beyond terror, into an area of savagery that he never tried to analyze but understood only too well from years of controlling that rage. His eccentric nature would never allow extortion. Life, for Simon, was a vague misgiving—genetic or environmental—a shortcoming, an inability to cope. His temperament functioned normally as long as he was in control. Beyond that point lay the cave.

A familiar psychological habit suddenly rose from some hidden place in his soul, pushing past the initial flush and the shudder, forcing across that primitive abyss into the cave. He fought the outrage, but it passed quickly, leaving the serenity of the cave, the anger beyond anger. A lawyer would have labeled it *temporary insanity,* but Simon had no reason to call it anything. He was not likely to describe the cave. Ever. He had once recounted the feeling aloud to himself, but the words had sounded wooden and commonplace. As far back as he could remember, it had been there—the rage, the mental confinement, the anguish. Only the slow passage of time gave relief.

The cave was no pleasant grotto or cool cavern with stalagmites and stalactites surrounding some serene pool of water, but a dull, ghastly prison, aching with reality, a cocoon of rock tapering to a small point of light from the outside. The walls narrowed so that he could never get his face near the peephole. Simon settled strangely, almost pleasantly, into that alien place.

It was time to destroy the letter. For six weeks the letter with no return address had remained in his rolltop, hidden among the bank statements. He had read it repeatedly, holding the single sheet of paper gingerly and with loathing fascination. The computer printout suggested Simon was not the only recipient. He removed the envelope from its pigeonhole for the last time.

Dr. Dr. Braddock:
    As everyone knows, these are difficult economic times for all of us, especially those who were not blessed by God as you have been with such a well-paying profession.
    We know that you live at 208 Marcus Lane South. We know Marie and Esther. They could both die.
    God wants us to share with the less fortunate. We know you go to the big church on Walnut and leave Esther for choir practice on Thursday afternoons at four. Sometimes children die or disappear.
    Marie would be easy to kill.

A man in your position can afford to give two
thousand dollars a month. Cut down on donations to
the church. Our man from Doraville will call you.
He has a toothache. Pay him the money or those
pretty faces are in the grave. Two thousand dollars,
cash only.

Doctors who go to the police have dead children.
I hope you are a wise man, Dr. Braddock. God bless
you.

There was no signature, and the Macon postmark
revealed nothing. The ridiculous, contemptible message would not have been so frightening except for the
death and disappearance of the two local children.
Each time Simon read the letter, it seemed to have a
different effect—annoyance, terror, anger, even a
pathetic kind of amusement. Now the feeling was only
quiet conviction. Simon was in the cave. The patient
with the toothache would die at the hands of one who
would scarcely kill a spider if he could usher it outside
instead. Simon was calm, but the destruction was
savage and imminent.

Old questions clung and weighed in his mind. Were
the letters mailed all at once or one at a time as family
data was collected? Was the extortion citywide or
statewide? Was this collection day for all doctors in
Macon or only for him? Simon recalled a conversation
he had overheard in the hospital john: *So what do you
suggest? ... I don't know. They both went to the
police, and now the kids are gone.* He had not known
the voices—Simon's stints in oral surgery were infre-
quent—and the dialogue had ended abruptly as he sat
in the toilet stall and heard the outer door close. Only
when the letter arrived had the remarks leaped to his
mind, and with appalling significance.

Simon had told no one of the extortion attempt, and nobody had mentioned it to him. He wondered, but not enough to confide his thoughts. He had never been a team player. Not even Marie knew the depth of his solitary disposition. It was an idiosyncrasy Simon hadn't understood himself until his adult years, when a dropping away of arrogance had allowed him to see himself from the outside, without pride or bias. He knew what he was.

He went out into the hazy spring morning and walked toward the back through thick, wet centipede grass. The lot was two lots, actually, deep in the back and separated from neighbors by fences and thick rows of cedars and pines. Esther's trampoline stood taut and waiting in the center of the open space. Marie would want to plant her vegetable garden on Good Friday.

He stood at his workshop and burned the letter on the ground, far enough away that Marie wouldn't detect the odor. Simon could never have had an affair. Marie's nose would easily pick up the scent of another woman.

He pictured her narrow face, the thick blond hair, the dimples, the dark, soulful eyes. Esther was also blond, lately tall and gangly, taller than some of the boys her age. She would eventually have her mother's long legs, the kind envied by other women. Simon himself was tall and blondish, agreeable in appearance, he supposed, but he always reckoned that Esther had inherited her mother's exceptional looks.

Toby lay with his head hanging out the doghouse opening and banged his tail a couple of times to acknowledge Simon. The huge, shaggy dog tended to stay in his own yard even though other dogs lived in the neighborhood. Toby was a sheepdog, so they had been told, but had never seen a sheep.

Simon waited until the paper turned to ash, then ground the remains into the wet pine needles and hiked back to the house, leaving a second row of footprints in the dewy lawn. He struggled with the wrought iron gate and stepped up onto the brick patio. Skip would weld the gate if Simon could ever remember to take it to him.

He dialed the den telephone and waited. "Skip, this is your friendly neighborhood dentist. Today is the day . . . yeah, yeah, I know. It'll be between one and two. Wait by the phone because the timing may be critical . . . Don't tell me again. Be ready." He hung up, annoyed at Skip's artless insistence that he was unacquainted with a chop-shop operation. Simon knew better, and a simple phone call would not be incriminating. Skip was safer not knowing details, and he would come through like he always did.

Marie could never have imagined Simon's violent plan or believed him capable of such behavior. She would have been terrified for his safety, physically and legally, which was precisely the reason he hadn't told her. He knew Marie. She would never let it rest. Even in moments of silence they would still be discussing the matter.

He stared into infinity as his mind, unbidden, accessed a childhood memory: the hot Cherry Street sidewalk, the flat tin badge with a new penny set at the center, and the older boys who wheedled and cajoled to see the medallion, then refused to give it back. Injustice was not softened by persuasion, he had thought at the time, but adult behavior would be different.

Simon roused from the daydream. Adult behavior was the same. He wondered if that youthful event had been formative. It didn't matter. His obsessive nature was past change. Unexpected pressure only triggered intractable stubbornness—the greater the pressure, the greater the resistance. Surrender did not exist in the cave.

Simon abruptly felt relief. This was finally the day. He struggled not to think through the business again, for it was unnecessary. He had rehearsed the matter like a dental procedure so all the proper armamentarium would be on the tray.

He walked into the hallway and checked himself in the rectangular mirror. The cotton slacks and pale knit shirt were expensive yet casual, the look of a prosperous young professional on a Saturday morning. He was tall and slender, never a real athlete, but more than a wimp. Simon gazed at his face and was satisfied with his appearance—strong jaw and chin, even features—though he often wished he had Marie's darker skin tone. He was clean-shaven and kept the wavy blond hair above his ears.

He stretched his mouth into a fake smile. "You're rich and successful, but you're crazy," he whispered, watching his narrow lips and listening to the sound of his own voice. "I know," he replied.

Simon returned to the den, the family room and often the dining room as they sat with trays and watched the evening news. He slouched into the large sofa and held the remote, but stared at the blank TV with impatience.

The windows were narrow with diamond-shaped panes of leaded glass that diffused the light against paneled walls and highlighted pine knots under the clear shellac. He and Marie had gathered the fireplace stones from Tobesofkee Creek, then hired a mason to build the hearth and chimney. The bricklayers wouldn't touch the job. There was no escaping Marie's judgment in the den, he realized, even when she wasn't there. The Seth Thomas struck twelve times, but he would skip lunch. The antique clock was a gift from Marie's mother. She was judging him too.

The minutes ticked slowly by. He changed into work shoes. As the time grew short, Simon gave his gear a final check and loaded the van. The Plymouth Voyager was well suited for the task. Marie drove the cream-colored BMW. His was the all-purpose vehicle, a super-duper station wagon, the salesman had called it. She had insisted on dark brown, not the fire engine red on display. Everything had to match the color tones of the house.

Twenty minutes later, Simon stopped behind his office with the opening side of the van at the back door of the building.

He entered his private office and called out to Roberta by name, though he never announced himself on a regular workday. He waited a moment in the silence, staring down the hallway into the eerie half-light. He had often been alone in the building, without the piped-in music and the sound of the compressor.

For weeks a small disposable syringe of Innovar and Anectine had lain hidden in the locked file cabinet along with a sackful of money. Simon tossed the plastic tip into the trash and placed the syringe into his Braves windbreaker pocket, careful not to bend the twenty-two gauge needle. He sat at the desk and felt his fleshy biceps, something he hadn't done in years. Simon was over six feet tall and weighed two hundred pounds. He was casually athletic but hoped his opponent would be smaller.

At 1:15, a sedan drove into the rear parking lot and stopped. Suddenly, a horrifying thought: suppose there were two of them. How could he have planned for six weeks and overlooked that? There would be at least

one other man, but Simon had always imagined they
would be in separate cars. In the case of a real emer-
gency toothache, a woman usually brought a companion, but a man came alone. The extortionists would
want the situation to appear normal. It was too late to
worry about it.

Simon looked through the small pane of glass,
relieved to see that only the driver was walking toward
the rear entrance. He felt the syringe through the thin
jacket material. The stranger banged the back door
rather than following the sign to the front entrance.

Simon opened the door, which led directly into his
private office. "Come in," he said, unsmiling.

The face was pudgy and expressionless. "I'm the
guy from Doraville with a toothache."

"I know. Come on in."

Simon's hope had been in vain; the bagman was
massive, especially through the upper body and shoulders. He had dark, slick hair and wore a white shirt
unbuttoned at the collar. His trousers were half of a
suit, but there was no coat or tie. The tip of a toothpick
stuck from the corner of his mouth. He appeared
relaxed, yet Simon noted sideward glances.

"Here's the money." Simon offered the sack.

The stranger tried a smile that didn't work. "I have
to count it."

They stood facing each other across the desk while
the bagman counted the cash, ever alert to Simon's
proximity.

The telephone chime began to ping, but they both
ignored it. A Saturday afternoon toothache. The caller
eventually gave up.

The heavy odor of aftershave filled the small room
as Simon watched the large hands deal through the
bills. He should have been infuriated to submit to a

stranger in such fashion, yet he eyed the other man with gentleness. He was dead and Simon knew it.

At last the big man straightened and spat the tooth-pick onto the carpet.

"A pleasure doing business with you, Dr. Braddock." There was another forced smile and a certain vocal facade, but the dark eyes revealed cruelty.

They moved together toward the door as Simon returned the smile. "Dentistry is the easy part. Uncle Alton taught me to run a business."

"What?"

Simon gestured to a photograph. His easy compliance had the man off his guard. A glance was enough; the needle sank to its hub into the thick neck.

"What the hell!" The big man slapped at the pain, sending the syringe across the room, but the injection had been made. "What did you do? Are you crazy?" He held the edge of the desk unsteadily and dropped to his knees. "They'll kill your kid!" he said with no pretense in the voice. "We got those others." His eyelids began to droop. "You're a dead man." He slumped to the floor.

The reckless injection had been a calculated risk. If he hit a large vein or artery the guy was dead; otherwise, unconsciousness would result but not instantaneously. There might be a gun, but Simon had planned to control the situation until the drugs took effect.

A pat-down of his victim showed that he had guessed correctly: there was no gun. The bagman's role was a patient with a toothache. If the police were waiting, the extortionist would simply play out his hand—a patient with a toothache. Simon had reasoned right along with the enemy.

He placed the sack of money back into the file drawer, then dialed Skip's number. The line was busy.

Skip Olinger had spent thirty years in the navy and was semiretired. He worked little, skulking around his welding shop mainly to escape his wife and drink beer or whiskey when he had it. Simon had known Skip before dentistry and marriage, and had drunk quite a few beers in the older man's company, ostensibly learning to weld. He still enjoyed Skip more than he did his fellow professionals.

Simon dialed again. "Yeah, it's me, I'm ready . . . Skip, don't give me this! Let me say it for you: I know you don't steal cars and you don't know any guys who run a chop shop. Let me just say, hypothetically, there may be a late-model sedan behind my office with the key in the ignition. It's not hot and I want it to disappear within the next ten minutes down the back way . . . What? . . . How the hell do I know what kind it is? It's brown or black! Who pulls your teeth for free? Who paid your DUI and kept your wife from finding out? This is me, Skip, and I don't have time for this."

Simon slammed the receiver into its cradle but continued to bellow. "Call the guy, Skip. Call the damn guy."

The big man lay on his stomach. Simon checked his breathing, then walked to the front windows of his office and looked about the neighborhood, not surprised to see a car parked down the street where two men waited.

The back of the dental office property was separated from a softball field by a thick hedge of privet and a dirt trail that led to Riverside Drive. The access road was seldom used by an automobile, and yet it was there. Simon dragged his heavy companion out the back door and into the van. He put the sedan's keys into the other car's ignition. His blood and adrenaline were pumping, yet it occurred to him to check the vehicle for more money. This he found rather easily in a plastic trash bag under the driver's seat. He reentered the office and piled the cash in the file cabinet drawer, then locked the file and the back door, and hopped into his van. The bagman lay motionless on the floor. Simon started the engine and cringed that the sound seemed louder than usual.

The van bounced slowly down the rough, rutted alley to Riverside Drive. The attack had gone as planned. Simon glanced in the rearview mirror to see a pickup truck turn from the thoroughfare into the dirt trail. Skip had made the call. Simon didn't know who was in the truck but suspected that their breed was as organized and dangerous as the extortionists. Skip was not one of them, not a criminal, not even dishonest, yet he knew such men.

Simon's destination was a place he had been only once. He drove south out of town, careful to stay within the speed limit. Eventually, he turned from the main highway and followed asphalt county roads, then dirt roads, finally a trail between the scrawny pines. A deer hut and a well shack came into view. Simon had come along before at the urging of a friend and remembered being cold, sleepy, and bored. He was no hunter.

The large tract of land was posted property, but Simon would find no deer hunters here in April. The hut was only an open-air shelter, framed with treated two-by-fours and walled with rough slabs that had never seen a planer. Hunters used the shack to hang and dress deer, hosing off the concrete floor after a kill. There was a roof, but the entrance had no door and the three window openings were without sashes or screens. A power line stretched from the county road and provided lights around a picnic table and barbecue pit.

Simon switched off the engine and stood out on the

brown carpet. Sunlight flickered between the opening clouds and through the tall, dark pines. The woods were motionless and silent. He walked around and pulled open the sliding door. The injection had been a hazard, the dosage utter speculation—enough, Simon hoped, to produce unconsciousness but not death. The big man was still asleep. Simon donned his familiar pale green surgical garb and rubber gloves, and worked quickly, not knowing how long the drugs' effect would last. He nailed a wide slat of one-inch plywood to a window ledge inside the hut, the lower end resting against the concrete floor at a thirty-degree angle. The noise of the hammer was unnerving. Simon held his breath and glanced around through the dark, silent woods.

It took more effort than he had anticipated getting the dead weight of his victim onto the ramp, and Simon began to fear that the movement would wake him. He worked without rest until the bagman was at least tentatively secured to the plywood, his hands bound behind the wooden rack. The wide mailing tape had adequate tensile strength, but the victim began to stir as Simon pulled it tightly across the forehead, matting down his dark hair and eyebrows. Simon jammed bite blocks into the mouth between the upper and lower molars, then continued to wind the tape around the plywood, across the nose and upper lip, and finally over the chin. For several minutes the silence was split by the harsh ripping sound as Simon pulled the sticky tape away from its spool.

At last he leaned against the wall and breathed heavily, admiring his work, exactly as he had pictured it. The would-be extortionist was trussed like a mummy from ankles to neck, his mouth locked painfully open.

Now his eyes were also open, though unfocused. Eventually he tried to speak.

" 'ere am I? 'ha the 'ell are you 'oing?"

Simon was silent and waited for the victim to have his say and discover his predicament.

"Are you 'razy? 'ey'll 'ill your 'ife an' kid!"

At last Simon spoke. "Shut up or I'll hurt you."

His captive fell silent.

"Now I will ask you some questions. Right at this moment there're only two things you need to understand. First, if you refuse to answer, I'll torture you. Second, if you lie to me, I'll torture you, and I know the answers to some of the questions already, so I'll know if you're lying." Simon's tone was eerily calm and pleasant. He waited for his statements to sink in.

"What's your name?"

" 'o hell 'ith you!"

Simon held up the other man's wallet so that he could see it, then removed the driver's license. "What is your name?"

The man closed his eyes and made no answer.

Simon fingered through the box of instruments. The #151 forceps was designed for the extraction of lower anterior teeth, but he often used it for uppers because of the fluted grips and its L shape, which allowed more controlled torque for gentle rotation.

"By the way, this is private property and there's nobody for miles around. You can scream if you like." He placed the forceps grips around the upper right lateral, jammed the tips subgingivally, squeezed the instrument, and rotated the tooth.

The patient screamed with pain. The exposed strips of his face beaded with perspiration, and his eyes watered. "O'ay! O'ay!"

Simon released the tooth. "Okay, what's your name?"

"O'ie 'rather!" he wailed.

"Obie Prather. Good. That's what your license says. Now, Obie. Who sent you? Who's your boss?"

"I 'on't know."

Simon reapplied the forceps, snapped off the crown of the lateral, and dropped it to the concrete.

Obie screamed again.

"That's one, Prather. You've got about twenty-five others. Who's your boss?"

Obie breathed heavily as the sweat ran down his face and neck. " 'y 'rother, 'illard! 'illard sent 'e!"

"Your brother's name is Willard?"

" 'es!"

"Willard Prather?"

" 'es!"

"What's his address?"

" 'hat?"

"His address, Obie. It's a simple question. What's your brother's address?"

" 'e 'ives in 'acon."

Simon held the forceps up to view and snapped the grips together. "The address, Obie."

" 'e 'oves around a 'ot."

Simon wedged a piece of gauze between the central and cuspid to keep Obie from strangling on his own blood. He tapped the forceps sharply against the two centrals. "What's his address, Obie?"

" 'e'll 'ill 'e!"

"Your brother will not kill you. What's his address?"

" 'e'll 'ill 'e!"

Simon deliberately extracted the left central and lateral through Obie's continuous scream. He packed more gauze against the sockets. "What's the address?"

Obie strained against his bonds, his shirt now wet through with sweat. " 'e 'ives . . . 'e 'ives in 'hirley Hills! 'ackson 'prings Road! I 'ont know 'he 'um'er. It's in 'he 'hone 'ook."

"Jackson Springs Road?"

" 'es!"

"Good." Simon picked up a pencil and pad. "Now I want the names and addresses of the two men who were with you today."

Obie moved his eyes toward his tormentor.

"You don't need to understand it, just answer my questions. You'd look and feel much better if you'd cooperated in the first place. I told you I'd torture you. What are the names and addresses?"

"Asa 'ondon an' 'ally 'oles."

"Asa Condon?"

" 'es!"

"Wally Boles?"

" 'oles!"

"Noles?"

" 'es!"

"Wally Noles. Wally. Is that Wallace?"

" 'es!"

"Where do they live?"

"Asa 'ives on 'riar'liff 'oad. 'ally on 'otting'am 'rive."

Simon wrote what he understood. "Did you say Briarcliff Road and Nottingham Drive?"

" 'es."

"They all live in Macon?"

" 'es!"

The chairside manner was beginning to feel natural. "That's a nice neighborhood. How many doctors got the letter?"

"All of 'hem!"

Simon ripped the gauze pads and bite blocks from Obie's mouth. "Okay, what happened to those two kids, the doctors' kids? One was hit by a car and the other disappeared."

Obie took deep breaths and spat blood, then spoke with a hoarse voice that crackled in and out of the falsetto register. "Asa and Wally did it! I never killed anybody! I just work for my brother, Willard. I don't approve of what he does, but I have to make a living." He paused to breathe. "He's the one with money, but he never gives me a dime to take care of the old man," he moaned persuasively. "He's my father, right? What else can I do?"

Simon ignored the arguments. "They murdered two children?"

"Yeah, I think so." Obie started to cry, the tears adding to the perspiration and blood that ran down his face.

"You had nothing to do with it?"

"No, I wouldn't hurt nobody!"

"Describe my daughter."

The question startled Obie. He cut his eyes toward Simon again with a pleading expression.

"Describe my daughter or I'll kill you."

"Her name's Esther, tall, skinny kid, blond hair."

"Where does she go on Thursdays?"

"What?"

"Where does she go on Thursdays?"

"Thursday afternoon at four she goes to singing practice at the church."

Simon nodded. "I'm going to kill you now."

The eyes widened. "Oh, no, no! I wouldn't hurt your little daughter for anything!" The crying had stopped; Obie's voice was quieter.

"I don't believe you, but it doesn't matter. I'm gonna kill you anyway."

The big man wanted composure, but his predicament was far past any pretense of balance. "You don't want to do that!" Obie wailed. "I've known guys who killed people, and believe me, you ain't the type."

This genuinely surprised Simon. "Why would you think that?" He peeled the foil away from a #15 surgical blade and inserted it into the handle.

"Look, we can make a deal. I collected almost a million today!"

"I know. It's in my office."

"A million dollars is nothing. Nothing! We can work together. I'm already skimming from my brother." He forced a smile but paled at Simon's alien, deadly composure.

"I'm gonna kill your brother too. Relax, Obie, it's a sterile blade."

Obie squinted his eyes and cried and begged and urinated.

Simon ignored him as he considered the work. He walked outside the hut and around to the window in order to approach the patient from behind and avoid the spatter of blood, the normal working position for a dentist at the chair. "You're an ugly son of a bitch," Simon said without thinking. It was peculiar to taunt somebody he was about to kill, yet natural, as if it needed to be said.

The cutting edge of the blade was only twelve millimeters, but it was long enough.

Obie was still groaning and crying as Simon reached through the window, jabbed the blade into the neck below the left ear, and made a continuous slice to the same point below the right ear. The blood flowed freely as Obie uttered a long shriek. Simon held the handle nearer its end, inserted the blade into the same incision, and cut as deeply as possible, bumping across the tough fibrous tissue of the larynx, trying to follow the original slice. This time the blood squirted for several feet in two directions and spattered the walls on both sides of the hut.

Obie stopped screaming and began to choke.

Bilateral carotid incisions, Simon thought.

With each heartbeat the blood ejaculated across the floor, decreasing as the pulses became weaker. Obie's life-giving fluid pumped away; he lost consciousness long before the blood pressure dropped to zero.

Simon had lived for thirty-six years without being a murderer; it took only brief seconds to become one. Through some bizarre working of memory he pictured the first time he had made love. Vaginal masturbation was a more accurate description. Obie's life was like the girl's virginity. It was not a thing he could give back.

There was always a chance that somebody would happen upon the scene, another calculated risk, so Simon worked with alacrity. He took a baseball from its cardboard box and held it next to the dead man's mouth. The ball was much too large. Simon held back the lip, broke off the upper teeth and ridge with his hammer, and tried the ball again. It was still too large, but one blow with the hammer was sufficient to drive it into the mouth. *Condyles jammed into temporo-mandibular joints, cartilage crushed, ligaments torn, bilateral mandibular fractures,* Simon noted.

He slit the tape binding Prather's hands behind the ramp, then hammered the plywood from the sill and allowed it to drop to the concrete. The loud cracking sound echoed through the woods. Simon looked about and held his breath.

The next step was ghoulish. He took up an ax to separate the head from the body. The ghastly deed had drifted in his mind for weeks, yet the real thing was far

easier than he had fantasized. The thick plywood provided a solid base. A few short chops and it was done.

Simon leaned on the ax handle to catch his breath
and consider the appalling business. Only moments
before, he and the big man had engaged in civil conversation, more or less.

One last abhorrent deed remained. Simon unzipped
the bagman's fly, extracted the penis, and severed it at
the base. He had imagined this to be disgusting as well,
but found it oddly interesting. In any case, it was part
of the plan. Simon secured the head and penis in separate trash bags and stashed them in the van.

The bloody tape that had bound Obie would be
interred along with the rest of the body. Simon carried
the body so as not to leave drag marks, and buried it a
short distance from the deer hut. The earth was soft,
yet it was tiring work. Simon returned the burial site to
its original appearance, a thick layer of wet leaves covering the floor beneath oaks and sweet gums.

He had brought a hose, but it was not needed since
one was permanently connected to the spigot at the
water tank. He hosed off the shack, the plywood and
concrete. Only when the wooden deathbed and other
gear were stowed inside the van did Simon begin to
breathe easier. He took a long look at the deer hut and
surrounding area to make certain nothing was amiss.

He watched the speed limit with even greater care on
the return trip, but his outward appearance was one of
composure. He went by his office without stopping to
see that the two accomplices had left, then circled the
block and parked behind his building. Obie's sedan
was gone. He locked the van and carried the box with
dental instruments and selected body parts back inside
the building.

Nobody would notice the disposable garment,

bloody gloves, and surgical blade in a trash can that already contained such items. He washed the instruments and left them to be sterilized, then turned his attention to his gruesome companion. Obie was still staring into space and mouthing the baseball, his oily hair matted with blood. The head was already cold and surprisingly heavy. Simon recalled with astonishment the common experience of supporting another person in one's arms—a child, a girlfriend. Few people had held a head. He savored the moment with revulsion and a certain gruesome embarrassment. This was war as it had been practiced for centuries. The victor owned the enemy, to do with as he pleased.

Simon secured the twist tie carefully against leakage, then placed the unlikely shipment into a cardboard container and wedged it in Styrofoam material. When the box was thoroughly sealed, he applied an excess amount of postage, then looked up Prather in the telephone directory. The listing was there: Willard Prather on Jackson Springs Road. Simon printed the name and street number onto a mailing label and stuck it to the package. There was no listing for Wally Noles or Asa Condon.

Simon unlocked the file cabinet and removed the cash. He thought to count it but quickly realized he had neither the time nor inclination. It was nearly a million—so Obie had said. How could they have collected a million dollars in one day at only two thousand per person? Someone must be paying more.

At last Simon sat at the desk, amazed that the plan had gone off without a hitch. It was only five p.m. Marie might be another hour and a half. He would stash the money at Skip's. The head could wait in his own wood shop until Monday when the post office opened. The box wouldn't fit through the package drop, but he would leave it on the floor under the slots rather than pass it over the counter. A postal worker might recall his face. The penis needed to get wrapped and mailed immediately.

Thirty minutes later, Simon stopped by the post office. Mailing a dick had a certain bizarre appeal, witty and outlandish but forever private, not a story to be shared over a few drinks.

He headed for home, a different creature and aware of the strangeness. He whispered as he turned into the driveway: "A murderer lives here." He parked the van in the carport and looked at himself in the rearview mirror. "I know," he replied.

It took three trips to carry the assorted cargo to the wood shop. Toby came out to watch and sniff and collapse again in an awkward heap.

Simon had painted the shop brown to match the house and make the structure admissible, but it was his alone. Nobody else went in there. Mental preparation took over: stash the uncommon package; return the ax to its customary place after checking again for blood; use the table saw to cut the plywood plank into various shapes and toss them onto the woodpile; clean the work shoes and leave them in the shed.

It was done.

Simon walked toward the patio and relished the feel of cool, soft grass against his bare feet. The hazy sky had finally cleared, revealing pale blue. The sun was an orange ball touching the tips of the western pines.

The surgical outfit had covered his own clothes, but Obie's blood and aftershave seemed to cling to his very soul. Simon stripped naked and ran a load in the washer, which was not unusual. Marie would think nothing of it. He took a shower because of her discerning nose and thought of Lady Macbeth as the warm, soapy water washed over his body.

At last he was dressed again and lay barefoot on the den couch, suddenly exhausted, his anger abated. He considered the Saturday afternoon with amazement. What had played in his imagination for weeks had finally come to pass. There had been no way to know if he would carry out the plan, but as the time came, each procedure had fallen logically into place. Now the overall deed stood in his mind, astounding and outrageous, greater than the sum of its steps.

Simon knew it would be difficult to face Marie, even though he was a good actor. The New Jersey state patrol had once stopped him for speeding outside Fort Dix. Simon had fallen into character as if the part were rehearsed: his first sergeant had allowed him off base for an hour to check on his wife. They were having problems. If he got the ticket, the sergeant would be in trouble too. He was in uniform, distraught, almost tearful. The trooper was sympathetic and told him to take it easy on the road.

Lying to Marie would be a different matter.

Suddenly, he heard the car door close. They were back. It was six-thirty P.M.

Simon had a strange feeling of unreality and reluctance as he stepped down into the three-car garage to help with the packages, but he wanted to do the natural thing.

Marie's long legs swung out of the driver's seat. She flashed her bright smile through the healthy glow that neither fatigue nor perspiration would diminish. She kissed him on the lips, and Simon was glad the moment was over, almost surprised she didn't read the gruesome business from his touch alone.

"Did you miss us?" she asked.

He gave a lopsided smile and hoped it looked natural. "Yeah, it's always scary when you clothes hounds stay gone that long. How much of my money did you spend?"

"Everything we bought was on sale. You'll love the things I got for Esther."

"Yeah, everything we got was on sale," the child echoed with pride. Toby sidled into the carport and nuzzled Esther with the shaggy white head.

They piled the sacks and tote bags on the dining room table. "Every store was having Easter sales, and it takes time to try things on." Marie kissed him on the mouth with noisy exaggeration to justify the money spent.

Simon tried to appear interested and make appropriate comments as they showed off their purchases.

Eventually, Marie found the matching Easter bonnets, which they modeled, Esther attempting to imitate her mother's pose. The large straw hats framed their golden faces around mats of tousled blond hair. Marie knew they were devastating. "What did you do today?" she asked.

"Puttered around. Watched the Braves' first home game of the season."

"Who won?"

"They did." Even as he answered, Simon felt a pang of fear and guilt, and realized his error. It was small talk. Marie didn't care who had won and was unlikely to notice a sports page. Devious types and criminals should be more careful.

Esther headed for the trampoline with Toby loping along behind.

Marie started to prepare dinner.

Simon watched the evening news and noted with relief that the Braves had won. Everything else had gone as planned—almost. He had neglected to consider that two bagmen might have come to his office, and then he had mentioned a baseball game he hadn't seen. One hit, two errors, but no damage was done.

Six-thirty P.M.

Asa Condon and Wally Noles stood next to the pay phone and argued about who should make the call. The convenience store parking lot was pitted and littered with trash. Rainwater stood in the larger potholes. Asa was the taller of the two, but their dress was similar—polyester slacks and plaid shirts with wide, flat collars. Both men were sober and frightened, and lost without Obie to tell them what to do. They were normally exhilarated on pickup days, joking and laughing aloud as each of the customers paid off. Now another of the doctors was being uncooperative. Worse than that, Obie was gone and they were responsible for him.

At last they flipped a coin and Asa lost. He dialed the telephone while Wally sucked in his gut to admire his spectator shoes and search about the ground among the flattened bottle caps and pop tops.

Willard Prather answered. "Yeah?"

"There's been a problem."

Willard hesitated. "What happened?"

"We're not sure. Obie's disappeared."

"Hold it. How did he disappear?"

"We don't know. He went into a guy's office, a Dr. Braddock, a dentist, and he never came out again. We waited about twenty-five minutes and then checked the parking lot. Obie's car was gone and the office was locked."

"How the hell could he leave without you seeing the car?"

"The parking lot was behind the building. The car

went down a sort of a dirt trail. We couldn't see it from the street. There was no other way out of there."

"What the hell did I send you with Obie for?"

"To keep an eye on him." There was a long pause. Asa wanted to offer an excuse but knew there was no point.

"What about your collections?"

"The money's gone too." He cringed and waited for the invective. This time it came.

"Goddamn it, Asa! It's a simple job. Next time I send a jackass to do a job, I'll go myself!" It was an old joke, but nobody was laughing. "How much had you collected?"

Asa braced himself. "Almost a million."

"I'm gonna bury you two son of a bitches along with that goddamn dentist! I don't suppose it occurred to you imbeciles to keep the money in the second car." The tone was quiet but angry, obvious Prather was more concerned about the money than his missing brother.

Asa heaved a long sigh in his own defense. "Yeah, we'll do it that way next time."

"A million dollars!" Prather muttered. "Shit! I'll carve it out of your stupid ass!"

Prather slammed the phone into its cradle and sat in a moment of rage, his hand still squeezing the instrument. Now he had to call his Uncle Heinrich and make the report. Asa and Wally didn't know Heinrich Wexler existed—part of the security system. Terror began to mingle with Prather's anger. Heinrich Wexler would not be pleased.

They made passionate love that night, more than the usual kissing and foreplay, so much so that Marie commented on it when they were done. He held and caressed her for quite some time, a thing she always enjoyed and wanted longer than he did, and to which he had often given only perfunctory attention. She dozed off in his arms, physically and psychologically complete.

As Simon lay in the darkness, he understood the reason for his intense lovemaking: what if Marie should be murdered? The terrifying thought made him aware that his need was much more than physical. She and Esther were the only important people in his world, the sole motivation that had evoked the horribly violent and unnatural response to the extortion menace. It was too late to take another course. Asa and Wally would have reported to Willard Prather that Obie had gone into Dr. Braddock's office and had never come out. Obie was gone; the car was gone; the money was gone. Being extorted was a no-win situation. Go to the police and your family is in danger; fight back and your family is still in danger.

He was finally out of the cave, and now his mind fixed with horror on the day's events and the grave jeopardy those events would produce. Simon recalled Marie's question. *What did you do today?* He traced the curve of her body with his fingers while she slept the sleep of the righteous, unaware of the grim fantasies that kept him vigilant.

2

Monday. Eight A.M.

Detective Sergeant Martin Li Dao sat behind the glass enclosure and watched his new partner cross the squad room. She was small, almost petite, with short, straight hair and dark eyebrows—feature for feature, a pleasant face but nothing remarkable. The prettiest thing about her was her name, he thought—Alexandra Sinclair. She was definitely a woman but not overwhelmingly attractive or shapely. Li Dao was glad. He'd never been assigned a woman partner, and wanted to keep his mind on business. Maybe she wouldn't last. Every morning for the past two weeks he had looked about the squad room from his cloistered station and struggled again over the new assignment. He knew every man there, some longer than others. *My partner, the chick!* he reminded himself, to see if the thought was any less repugnant.

She opened the glass door and leaned against the jamb. "We got a dick in the mail. What would you like me to do with it?"

Li Dao stared at her mutely. He felt weak from lack of breakfast and wouldn't be so easily amused. "Have they got any coffee out there, Alex?"

"Coffee. You got it, boss."

"Stop calling me boss."

"Sorry, Lid. Coffee. Here's a note that came with the dick." She dropped it on his desk, turned quickly, and walked away.

Even her movement bothered him. Not enough hips to look like a real woman, he thought, just that perky damn little ass.

Li Dao got up to hang his coat, then loosened his collar and tie and sat again at the desk. His stomach continued to churn. Eventually he resigned himself to the hunger pang and picked up the hand-written note.

Dear Police:

This penis belonged to a scum bag hood named Obie Prather, who has now gone on to his great reward. His last employment was bagman for his brother, Willard, who lives on Jackson Springs Road. They are part of a citywide extortion racket. I've known Willard for years, but this time he's gone too far. If he wants to run a simple scam, that's his business, but I can't stand by and watch innocent people put to death. Willard will be receiving a body part in his mail either tomorrow or Wednesday. I suggest you question him. Ask him about the doctor and the two children of doctors in Macon who died within the year. They were all murdered.

Li Dao knew very well the two children and doctor the letter mentioned. He looked at the back of the note, which was blank, then read it again. The anonymous gift was good news, but it stirred old anguish as well as hope. Li Dao had been in charge of the defunct extortion investigation—a great personal failure.

The Macon police had seen only two extortion threats, letters that were not identical except in the deadly guarantees of physical harm unless there was cooperation. Then came the tragic events involving children of those families—Lanier and Bissett— unlikely coincidences but not much to go on. Only Li Dao had seen the letter received by Dr. Bruce Murray, who was a friend. There were no secrets between old buddies, and Lid had lived with a chilling question: had that very friendship caused Bruce's death? Lid's pursuit of the case had yielded nothing. The normal sources were no help—the street types who never had businesses of their own but always seemed to know everybody else's business. The extortionists were nonexistent. Invisible.

The Macon physicians had been questioned carefully. Make friends with the local doctors, Lieutenant Mimbs had said. Be persuasive, promise protection, get somebody to admit something. Anything. The doctors all had denied any knowledge of extortion. Eventually, Lid's team had been disbanded and the detectives given other assignments.

He read the note again. At last somebody out there wanted to feed information to the police, probably a murderer himself.

Alex returned with the coffee. Now Li Dao was smiling. "Did we really get a prick in the mail?" he asked.

"That's what the lab said it was. Of course, I wouldn't know."

"I'm sure. Fingerprints?"

"On the outside of the package, probably the mail carrier's. Nothing on the inside."

Li Dao took a search warrant pad from his drawer and signed the top form. "I guess the guy wore rubber gloves when he took a leak. Get the house number on Jackson Springs Road, fill out the form, and take it by Judge Gaston's office, but first call the postmaster's office. Find out if they have a package for Prather, what day and approximately what time it will be delivered." He handed her the warrant form.

"Do we want to open the package?" she asked.

"No, I want Prather to open it, but I'd like to be there."

"Do you know the Prathers?"

"Sort of." He waved a hand. "I know who they are."

"You're not coming with me?"

"I think Gaston would enjoy it more hearing the dick story from you."

Alex started to leave, then turned. "It takes so little to make you jolly, Lid. What would you do if you got a tit in the mail?"

He made a gesture as she walked away.

At thirty-two, Alex was the youngest detective on the force, also the newest and the only woman. Lid had first refused the assignment with choice profanity, but Lieutenant Mimbs had been adamant, afraid a younger partner might become involved with Alex in a way that would interfere with the job. Lid had a wife and a teenage son. He was fifty-four years old, more conservative than the younger men, even to the point of always wearing a suit rather than mismatched slacks and jackets. Mimbs wanted her to learn from the best, the most experienced.

By now the squad room was up to full complement, a large, grim room of men and desks lighted by long fluorescent tubes of varying brightness. The suspended ceiling had once been off-white but now showed dark patches from the heating system and splotched panels from water leakage. It had the look and smell of a man's world, not quite the locker room but something akin. The leather holsters provided the only uniform feature of dress, a badge of pride for the novice. Alex's desk stood in the center of this male estate, a post she assumed with a self-assurance and resolve that were hers by nature.

She rode the elevator to the third floor and entered the judge's outer office, a quieter, nicer place than where she spent her working hours. The receptionist looked up and pointed. He was expecting her.

Alex entered a wide, tall, windowless room, heavy with books and the warm, moist odor they had collected over years and now emitted into the still air. Massive shelves lined the walls on two sides. A floor lamp stood next to a worktable, adding its glow to the fluorescent light. On the edge of the judge's desk sat a placard routed from plywood: FORREST GASTON, SUPER JUDGE. The traditional black robe hung on a door to one side. A workroom, not a showroom.

Gaston sat in shirtsleeves and stared at a console. A printer chattered away behind him and covered the sound of her entrance, but this was a man accustomed to having others wait. His face was heavy and drooping. He looked up between rimless glasses and shaggy gray eyebrows.

"You must be Detective Sinclair."

"Yes, sir."

They shook hands.

"Have a seat. Grace tells me you're with Li Dao. How is he? I haven't seen him lately."

"The same as ever, I guess. I've only known him a few weeks."

"How does he like working with a woman?" he growled.

"About as well as he likes anything."

"Yeah, Lid can be grouchy, but he's a good cop and a good man." He looked her pointedly in the eye. "A good man, Ms. Sinclair."

"Everybody calls me Alex."

"Take care of him, Alex. He's not as young as he used to be." There was only a hint of a smile; the pleasantries were concluded. "Now, what have you got for me?"

Alex handed over the affidavit and note. "We got a penis in the mail along with this note."

He looked over his glasses again. "Did you say a penis?"

"Yes, sir. The lab said it was a penis—a male Caucasian penis."

They both smiled and repeated it together. "As opposed to a *female* Caucasian penis."

She nodded. "Lid thought you would enjoy hearing this from me."

His smile faded as he steadied the glasses with two fingers and read the note and affidavit. He finally signed the search warrant, nodding as if he agreed with himself. "I suppose a penis in the mail is probable cause. Will you intercept the other package?"

"No, Lid wants it to be delivered."

"I'm sure Lid has it figured out," he said.

Lid stared out the window and drummed his fingers. He and Bruce Murray had grazed through high school together, frozen in Korea together, fished and sometimes golfed, though neither was any good at it. *Dr.* Bruce Murray had correctly diagnosed what the E.R. had mistaken for intestinal virus, and saved the Li Dao boy's life before the appendix ruptured. The death of Bruce Murray, as well as the loss of the two children, gnawed at Lid's gut with the anger and indignation of a personal attack.

Bruce had been dead almost a year now, mechanical failure the police called it, but Lid knew it was bullshit. He had never revealed to Lieutenant Mimbs the fact that Bruce Murray had gotten the extortion letter, not because he had failed to follow procedure, but rather for fear of losing any chance of retribution. Ignorance was the best policy. If the FBI entered the case, pursuit of Bruce's killer would no longer be his jurisdiction, and the fibbies were not Lid's favorite people. Special agents Presnell and Colish were both pricks, Lid thought, who exuded vanity and condescension because they were FBI, and they operated in Macon far too often for his taste. He called them Walter and Harvey to piss them off.

The brightest feature of the extortion-team effort had come in the meetings with Dr. Rachael Brucker, nick-named variously *hooker*- or *looker*-Brucker by the cops working the doctor scam. Li Dao found the dark and attractive psychiatrist appealing, but unresponsive to flirtation and banter. Still, she impressed Lid with her work, and her ability to outline something technical in layman's terms. Her effort to explain the psychology of duress, however, had not enabled the detectives to overcome the local physicians' fear for their families. Dr. Brucker herself had not received an extortion letter. The gangsters probably associated her with city hall and police work, and they avoided killing cops. Lid considered as well the fact that Brucker had no family, nobody to protect.

Lid found Rachael Brucker appealing in a slightly jaded way—shadows under the eyes, the unkempt auburn hair, and the ubiquitous cigarette. Her breasts and hips were ample, but she was unmarried, probably a lesbo. Lid especially liked her mouth, the way the upper lip started inside her mouth and curved outward. Lid was old enough to be her father, yet he caught himself in moments of undiluted lustful fantasy.

Alex entered the cubicle. The automatic hung low under her left arm, making the leather straps cut into the soft cotton blouse. She assumed the serious manner she thought he liked—her cop look and her cop voice. "The post office has the package. It will be delivered tomorrow around two."

Lid stared vacantly and made no reply.

"Here's the search warrant. Judge Gaston says hello. He told me to look out for you because you're elderly."

Lid brushed the top of his head, riffling thick, dark bristles mixed with gray. He turned and looked at her without smiling. "I'll never understand these doctors," he said. "I know they're scared, but in a year's time you'd think somebody would've given us a lead, even accidentally. Those rich bastards lie better'n crooks."

"I doubt they plan to keep paying forever. Each doc is waiting for one of his pals to come forward."

Lid took the search warrant and looked at the signature but made no comment. "What body part do you think this loony will send Prather?"

"We got the dick. He'll probably mail Prather the balls."

Lid didn't smile.

"It was a big package, twelve by fourteen inches," she continued. "It could be anything, a hand or a foot. It might be the head!" She made a face. "Do you think it could be Obie Prather's head?"

Lid drummed his fingers on the window ledge and squinted into the sunlight. "Why didn't he just dump the rest of the body on Prather's front porch?"

"Okay, let's say he is one of Prather's old buddies.

Maybe he doesn't like him much, likes his brother Obie even less. He hears about the deaths of the two children and knows the Prathers are responsible, decides to do something about it, to set Willard up. He and Obie have an altercation, and Obie gets killed. Maybe it's premeditated. In any case, we get the penis, Prather gets some other body part. The killer wants us to raid the joint and find a hand in the mailbox, maybe stumble into the extortion ring."

Lid shrugged. "Prather's not responsible for what comes in the mail."

"We're detectives. We're supposed to detect." Alex stared at the gray eyes and wanted to have a better explanation, but didn't.

He finally gave her a smile. "You're probably right. Tomorrow when we go over there, don't look shocked no matter what Prather gets in the mail. Be a hard-nosed cop, but let me do the talking. Maybe I'll get him to assault me, break his fucking arm."

"Right after the man finds out his brother is dead, you want to break his arm?"

Lid made eye contact. "If the guy who whacked off the dick is correct, Willard Prather murdered Bruce Murray and those two children."

"We were never positive that Dr. Murray was murdered."

Lid couldn't respond to her remark. She hadn't seen Murray's extortion demand. "Get a couple of extra uniforms," he said. "I don't want to go over there alone."

"I thought we were hard-nosed cops."

"I'm an elderly hard-nosed cop, remember?"

"I'll try to take care of you." She gave him a fake smile and walked out of the cubicle.

At his age, Lid could afford to carry a little extra weight, but he was in good condition and he knew it.

He didn't enjoy the workouts as much as he used to, but endured the routine to maintain a hard body as long as possible. That or the work itself made him demanding and harsh, cruel at times, but it was what he knew. Alex's upbringing was softer, more protected. He hadn't had to look at her file to know that. He knew the type, the open, congenial expression that expected the world to be the same. She was a comedian at heart. He would let her get away with calling him elderly. She enjoyed it. Besides, he leaned on her enough about other things.

He had leaned on his wife, Lucille, too, probably the reason he hadn't seen her or the kid in months. Menopausal pregnancies should all be aborted, he thought. He and Marty had never been close. Now he was fourteen, right at that age when he needed a father most. Lucille also had drifted away, unable to cope with the unpredictable hours and the hard, doleful disposition that Lid had developed in police work over the years. They talked occasionally of divorce but never seemed to get around to it. He could accommodate family only until they interfered with work. The job was everything. He had tried to make her understand— no matter how much a man loves his wife and children, his work is the most important thing. She should have appreciated the honesty but didn't.

Memory of the hit-and-run case, the Bissett youngster, flashed across his mind. What if it had been Marty? Lid jerked the trigger in his mind's eye, Willard Prather the target. Lid had actually done it once, shot a man four times in the chest. He hadn't been counting, but the lab later reported it: four times. The memory was confused as reality had been—a shotgun blast that shook the apartment walls, the terror, the plunging through a doorway to discover two men down, bloody, a third confronting him with a knife. A smoky haze and pungent odor. He pointed his automatic and waited for the stranger to drop the knife. Then he recognized one of the men on the floor—his partner—or what was left of him. Lid fired the weapon until the noise hurt his ears. *The assailant had a knife,* he would put in the report. The second assailant groaned from his position on the floor. Lid fired again but never wanted atonement. Memory of his partner's face had always eased the guilt. Marcus Grier had been his name, husband and father. Lid recalled in remarkable detail the trip to Marc's home to break the news to his wife. The disbelief, the screaming, the tears. She'd had to be sedated.

Lid picked up the phone and dialed and waited.

"Dr. Brucker."

"What are you doing answering your own phone?"

"Li Dao! I've missed you lately. What's on your mind."

"I need to talk to you about a case as soon as you can. Tomorrow or the next day?"

She paused. "What about Wednesday at two?"

"Fine."

"Make it here. I've got a comfortable couch."

"What do we need that for?" he smiled.

"I thought maybe this was confession. You haven't killed anybody today, have you, Lid?"

"The day's not over, Brucker." He hung up deliberately before she could respond. Lid knew how to flirt but seldom bothered. Why was he trying to be cute? She was a lesbian; he was married.

Alex was a trifle butch herself. A fuller mouth and larger breasts would be an improvement, but he wouldn't wish for it, for the sake of the job. Brucker was another matter. She wasn't his partner. His wife had moved out; they were practically divorced. He would meet with Brucker Wednesday to talk about a penis, then segue into ... whatever. Lid groaned. Sexual fantasy was a waste of time. Concentrate on the job. The cops had gotten a chicken neck in the mail; Prather would get wing or a drumstick. Go over there and shoot the guy.

His telephone line began to blink, a reminder that all the old interest would start up again. Word would spread quickly, the department brass, the fat dwarf of a mayor, everybody wanting to know how the extortion case was going, when to expect arrests. He would let Alex run interference.

Tony Romano stuck his head in the cubicle door and offered to show Li Dao the dick.

Simon Braddock never went in to the office before nine, but dragged out of bed and had his first coffee while Marie made breakfast. They usually fell back into the sack for thirty passionate minutes after one or the other delivered Esther to school.

This particular Monday, Simon had gotten up earlier than usual. By the time Marie reached the kitchen, he had shaved, showered, dressed, and hiked to the street to get the newspaper. He made an unaccustomed side trip to the post office, which he would say was to pick up a *Constitution,* but Marie didn't ask.

Simon sat at the heavy oak table, already dressed— mist brown suit, white shirt, tie. There would be no sex that morning.

The aroma of sizzling bacon filled the Braddock kitchen. Early spring sunlight streamed in the doorway through dining room windows, brighter and more alive than the gray half-light of winter. Simon nibbled his toast and apple jelly and appeared to leaf calmly through the *Macon Telegraph,* while his mind replayed a dream fragment: wood, glass, and flesh ripping across the bright kitchen, leaving bloody holes in the opposite wall. TV and movies had made the scene familiar. Now it was a private image that dangled in his mind with loathsome persistency and made swallowing difficult.

Marie ate from the stove. She loved her huge kitchen. Cooking appliances and cabinets molded together. The sink was under the windows facing west. In the center of the room stood an island counter with another sink. Above that, a heavy bracket dangled with copper and stainless steel. Antique utensils filled the spaces above the cabinets—coffee mills, slicers, old pewter, and the like.

Esther sat in her accustomed place and said little at this early hour, but hummed, as she always did when the food was savory. She was an eight-year-old version of her mother with finer, lighter hair and skin more pale.

At last Simon kissed Esther good-bye and watched her walk with her mother out the carport door. In that appalling moment Simon knew he was not in control. He heard the car start out, that precious invisible genetic thread stretching away as far as Esther might go. *They'll kill your kid!* Obie Prather had said. It was a bizarre, deadly game of chicken, when to flinch, when to confess the whole business and whisk them away to a place of safety.

Thirty minutes later, he kissed Marie and left for work as on a thousand other ordinary mornings. His terror and astonishment were oddly mixed with remorse for being deceitful to his wife.

Simon drove slowly and tried to admire the Yoshino cherries that draped the edge of the street with lacy white. The landscaped median made a statement:

exclusive neighborhood. Each new house that was built vied with the others for size and elegance. He and Marie had insisted on dark brick, leaded glass, and slate roof.

Simon jerked himself back to reality as the danger to Marie and Esther suddenly weighed with appalling heaviness. There was no way to protect them without providing an explanation. Nana's was an ideal safe house but not a suggestion he was likely to make. Marie knew he disliked dealing with her side of the family, and was already jealous of the time she and Esther spent with her mother.

The penis would arrive earlier than the head to alert the police and give them time to plan. Prather wouldn't attack until he had all the facts. By then he would be in jail. The rationale did little to deter images of the worst scenario.

Simon drove the interstate for several miles, then switched over to Riverside Drive, heavy with Monday traffic and slowed by the lights. He got to the office without incident, in the usual twenty to twenty-five minutes.

Roberta had patients waiting in three chairs. As the receptionist, she spent her days at the front, commanding the business office and waiting room, dealing with patients, insurance forms, and telephone calls all at the same time. Roberta was twenty-nine, small and brown-eyed. Her eyes were her most expressive feature, able to plead or demand as needed. She affected rimless glasses that lent an intellectual look.

There were four other employees, three assistants and a hygienist. Isobel and Emily were older and had husbands and children. Julie was the baby of the three assistants, the youngest, unmarried. Anita was the hygienist and a bitch. Simon put up with her because she was near retirement and hygienists were hard to come by. Every day at quitting time, the girls agreed on the next day's outfit—today it was blue and white stripes. Anita wore what she damn well pleased.

Roberta had known her boss longer than the others and picked up on his moods quickly. Simon's quiet, eccentric temperament appealed to her sense of humor and made the day interesting. She stood in the doorway and waited as Simon pulled on a lab coat.

"Mrs. Crulitz just walked in," she said. "She still has a sore spot when she tries to eat."

"Tell her to stop eating." Simon smiled briefly. "Put her in the yellow room."

"Judy Claymore called. She's collecting for that new house for unwed mothers, hitting all the professionals. What do you want me to tell her?"

"Tell her not to get knocked up," he replied with a look.

Roberta was pleased. She made a face and walked away.

Simon knew he was safe. He could say anything to Roberta. She was an employee and knew to mind her own business. Not so with his wife. Marie would scrutinize his every reflection, sift and weigh and make recommendations. Murder was a bizarre venture, vastly coloring one's view of ordinary activity. Simon abruptly found it difficult to take Brenda Crulitz's sore mouth seriously.

He drifted through his Monday appointments with only vague awareness, making monosyllabic responses when possible. At lunch he stayed at his desk and ate three candy bars and drank a Coke. The phone pinged away incessantly. They would call back.

Thoughts of the penis, the head, and the mail delivery pushed themselves into his mind throughout

the day, yet he had no desire to see Prather open his
mail. Simon's interest was devoid of ironic fascination.
It was a military decision only, a done deed.

In late afternoon the last patient left. Simon called
Marie. She reeled off the day's highlights: Esther's
class was taking a field trip; her teacher thought she
was talented, suggested art lessons; Ollie had a bad
knee and wouldn't be by that week; she had gone gro-
cery shopping. He would be home in an hour, he told
her. Simon inquired casually about Esther. She had
spent the afternoon down the street with friends but
was back now.

He hung up and suddenly remembered the dream:
Mr. Rabbit and Mr. Squirrel watching the decapitation
with chagrin. Simon hated the way his dream had
drawn characters from Esther's old books, his grisly
deed tainting the most innocent recesses. In that peculiar way of dreams, Simon had known he was
dreaming, but woke in stark, breathless terror and
understood how animals could smell fear. The moment
was not followed by the usual relief—he was still a
murderer.

Quitting time. Roberta stuck her head in the door to
say she was leaving, bright and breezy, no longer interested in the mood game.

Simon sat in silence, his feet propped on the corner of
his desk, the very spot where he had jabbed the heavy
needle into Obie Prather. He was exhausted but seemed
to notice it only now, alone, able to relax the mole-
cules and cells and synapses that made up the visible
essence of Simon Braddock. In spite of the apprehension, the obsession, the floating unreality, Simon never
wondered why he had carried out the murder. He'd had
to do it.

* * *

Alex Sinclair drove homeward through a headache and mental fatigue, stymied, withdrawn. The relationship with Lid bore heavily on her mind and held the pain at a point of exquisite dull throb. The assignment was three weeks old, but she wasn't accepted. Each day was becoming a struggle to understand her partner. She had liked the assignment at first. Working with Li Dao meant escape from the piddling stuff, bad checks and domestic squabbles. Lid got the good cases. Then she discovered the generation gap. He probably still referred to women as *dames*. And there were other problems. His wife had left him. One of his oldest buddies had just been murdered.

Judge Gaston had called him a good man, she remembered. He had said it twice. Lid didn't smoke or drink, not more than any other cop. Every man on the squad was tough, but it was more than that. Lid had a frightening cynical edge that was making her head pound. She didn't dare ask for another partner. The reputation would develop quickly—weaker sex, PMS, can't get along with men—all of that.

Alex's apartment was in an older section close to the business district, where Victorian dwellings were gradually bought and remodeled. She lived alone except for Marvin. The cat was large, lazy, and spoiled, spent the nights in, hid when it was time to go out. Marvin preferred the litter box and the spacious comfort of his home with tall windows and twelve-foot ceilings. He had his favorite places, window ledges or spots of warm sunlight until the sun moved. Marvin was the ideal pet but for his habit of answering the telephone. The ring was more astonishing to him than his owner or else he was quicker than she was. By the time she reached the phone, Marvin usually had the hand piece dislodged from the cradle and sat listening to whatever the caller might say.

It was dusk when Alex entered. She hung up the bed-side phone and remembered the cat had been in. "Marvin, you idiot," she murmured. Marvin sat in the window and returned the remark with a look of placid, supercilious elegance that only a cat can muster. The handsome black coat with white chest and paws was as attractive for her to view as for him to wear. He was certain of it. She admired the fat, impassive face. Her roommate never smiled; her partner never smiled.

Alex pulled off her jacket and dropped the shoulder holster onto the bed. She flipped the kitchen light, reflecting yellow cabinets in tall windows and making the room appear twice as wide. Marvin looked on expectantly as she broke a gourmet dinner from the frozen stack and tossed it into the microwave without looking at the picture. Life needed some surprise. She swallowed three aspirins and stared into the sink, held in a momentary daze by the steady hum. The sound of the *ding* brought her back.

Marvin waited with that endless patience of his breed until Alex scraped the last bit of food from a can. He examined the fishy glob with disdain but eventually began to eat.

They dined together in the bright, silent kitchen, the cat's thoughts forever private, while Alex considered with vague unease such matters as she might ponder. She would gladly have taken counsel from the cat, never able to talk about her work with friends. Discussing police business was unethical and dangerous. Her sister, Margo, was her sounding board, but the long-distance rates were prohibitive. Besides, she knew what Margo thought: Alex's desire to be a cop came from anger over their parents' death, caused by a driver going the wrong way on a ramp. Alex was not persuaded. She was simply an adherent of law and order, utopia through smooth police operation, as she visualized it.

Marvin sat tall at her feet and licked his chest. She tried to catch his eye. "My partner is a maniac," she said, not to be denied companionship and dialogue. The cat twitched an ear but didn't bother to look up.

3

Tuesday. Two P.M.

The estate could have been mistaken for eighteenth-century French countryside. The house was two stories in the front with wings on either side of the main structure. Warm yellow stucco reflected midday sun. Four tall chimneys maintained the symmetry. Front and center, a circular fountain plumed its spray into the clear air.

The mansion was set among ancient hardwoods. Lush green sloped off toward the rear, exposing a fragment of stone wall before it disappeared into the woods. It was tasteful and elegant. It looked like money.

Alex and Lid had waited across the road for thirty minutes. The air was still pleasant; the real Georgia heat had not yet arrived. Lid raised his head to look in the rearview mirror.

"There it is."

They watched as the familiar white postal delivery van worked its way up the street, the driver hiking his accustomed path to each front door.

Lid spoke into the mike. "Wake up, Freddie, he's

here. Be ready but don't move until I tell you. And call another black and white. Let 'em wait in the drive."

Presnell and Colish were also listening and waiting, but Lid didn't bother addressing them. The fibbies would get the message.

At last the mail truck reached the Prather mansion and turned through the tall brick entrance. They watched it move down the curved driveway and circle the fountain. From their position, Lid and Alex couldn't see the carrier walk to the front door, but waited for the vehicle to drive out and turn again onto Jackson Springs Road.

Alex was fidgety. "Why don't we go?"

Lid sat in stoic silence for another sixty seconds before picking up the mike. "Freddie, go."

Willard Prather was heavy like his brother, Obie. His hair was dark, oily, and combed stiffly into place. Willard was tall but not a handsome man. His eyes were weak, his nose a long, unremarkable mass, and his chin nonexistent. He sat at a massive mahogany desk in shirtsleeves and tie. Willard was proud of this room, the polished paneling, marble fireplace, built-in shelves with books no one read, a nine-foot Steinway never played. Normally, he enjoyed trifling with business matters at the heavy, lustrous desk, but this was not a normal day. He sat with loosened collar and wore a haggard, worried face and looked to his Uncle Heinrich, who stood across the spacious library. He had always depended on his uncle to handle any situation, but the older man was aloof. Prather himself was not so concerned that his brother was missing, only that something had gone wrong.

Heinrich Wexler turned a large globe thoughtfully with soft, manicured fingers and appeared composed as he always did. Wexler was a small, delicate man with an Old World look, a fastidious dresser whose clothing emitted a faint, unfamiliar odor. The long-sleeve silk shirt was buttoned to the neck, although it was warm enough for short sleeves. The imported shoes made imprints in the thick carpet. He stood with his back to the heavily draped and shuttered window.

"It's been three days," Willard said for the third time. "What do you think happened to him?"

Wexler looked up. "How should I know? If Obie doesn't know how to make pickups, it's not my problem."

"He's my brother!" Willard snapped. "He's your nephew."

Wexler continued to study the globe and made only a trifling moan.

Willard's care for his brother was largely pretense, but he tried to conceal that smug redneck irresponsibility. He was content to wallow in his own security whenever misfortune lighted someplace other than on himself. "If his body turns up, I'll kill that bastard Braddock."

"You're sure Braddock had something to do with it," Wexler said.

"That's where Asa and Wally said he disappeared."

Wexler moaned again. He didn't consider Willard and Obie the most dependable of nephews—an opinion he tried to keep to himself—and had an even lower regard for Wally Noles and Asa Condon. "I want to check some records before I go," he said at last. "Call me if Obie shows up."

Wexler moved with an elegance and grace that Prather admired without realizing it, a certain Germanic composure and bearing. In Willard Prather, a generation later, such presence was outbred, diluted.

He watched his uncle cross the library. Wexler would spend an hour in the drawing room that housed the walk-in safe.

The Prather mansion was paid for. The import business had seen to that; as well it had provided cover for their more lucrative family enterprise—extortion. Willard had gotten the house, Obie the stock and other intangibles. Neither one had sense enough for honest work. Neither needed it, but they didn't have sense enough to know that either. Both had always worked for their uncle Heinrich in the import business, and were now, supposedly, retired. Willard was especially awkward in the aristocratic setting, a churl rattling about in French provincial pomposity. He had inherited the butler, Max, along with the house.

Max entered carrying the heavy parcel, the other mail resting atop the package. He placed it all on the edge of Prather's desk.

Max was tall and lean but virile. His Eurasian color and manner fitted the quiet dignity of his work. Most of the servants were gone, but Max kept the house and grounds in order. He had the ability to see that such mundane tasks as cooking and cleaning were always accomplished, yet his worldly experience made him believe that he was as deserving of substance as those born to money and education. Murder was an acceptable part of life's struggle.

Willard tossed the other mail aside, took a small pocketknife, and began to cut through the mailing tape binding the heavy box. It might have been a bomb, but he was certain none of the victims knew his identity. He pulled open the carton, and his voice erupted into a freakish animal noise that echoed through the house.

Heinrich Wexler was two rooms away. He dropped the record book, something he would later regret, and hurried to the library. For an instant the vocal quality was mirthful, Wexler thought, yet Willard stood fish-eyed, his back to the bookcase and wanting farther retreat. Styrofoam bits were scattered about the desk. Wexler advanced a few more paces and saw the face, the wide eyes and the baseball. It took a moment to recognize his older nephew, the jaw stretched into torturous posture.

As Willard's feral noises degenerated into sobs, Wexler closed the library doors against Max and a cleaning woman who peered in from the hallway.

"Shut up, Willard! Obie made a stupid mistake."

"I'll kill that bastard Braddock!" Prather said wetly.

At that moment came the sound of voices from the vestibule and hallway. The library doors flung open again. Martin Li Dao led the way, holding a search warrant. The uniforms were right behind.

Max bobbed his head in the rear. "I'm sorry sir, I couldn't stop them. He has a warrant."

"Close the door," Wexler said. He turned to Lid. "I'd like to see that."

Lid stuck out the paper without speaking while Alex, Presnell, Colish, and one of the uniforms spread around the room, prepared for anything, even in this elegant setting. Lid was not surprised to see Prather's uncle. He knew Wexler on sight, a member of the chamber of commerce, supporter of the arts. Wexler had never been arrested, yet he remained a shadowy figure whose business reputation was one of quiet brutality.

Wexler looked at the paper. Reliable sources had identified the owner of this residence as being involved in extortion. At the moment, who that source might be was beyond him. He handed back the warrant.

Lid spied the cardboard carton, exactly what he was

looking for, yet amazing, thrilling for an instant. "My God!" he said.

Alex turned and saw the dead face, the open eyes, then tried to remember that she was a hard-nosed cop. It was she who had made the suggestion about the head in the first place, but the reality was absolute and sobering.

Lid steeled himself and walked to the desk. "Do you usually get heads in your mail, Mr. Prather?"

Willard slumped into the desk chair but stayed well away from the ghastly visage. He wiped his eyes on his sleeves and tried manfully to control himself. "That's my brother, Obie."

Lid looked again. The image of the face and the baseball evoked a vague spasm in his throat, almost humor, which the gravity of death fortunately balanced. "Yeah, so it is," he cracked. "I just never saw him with a baseball in his mouth." Lid felt nothing close to pity.

Wexler poured a half glass of whiskey at the wet bar and set it in front of Willard.

"I'd like you and Mr. Wexler to stay here," Lid said. He turned to his own people. "You know what to look for."

Alex and the uniformed officer left the room. Alex had no idea what to look for, but they had the warrant, so they would look.

The FBI agents waited and watched, two solemn pallbearers. They were trained to be serious and intimidating. Both fit the pattern. Presnell was a big man, tall and heavy. Colish was shorter but muscular, the way the bureau liked its agents. Lid didn't like either one, but privately felt some security in their presence. He also knew they wanted his case.

The uniforms had walkie-talkies, but Lid hated

trying to understand and be heard through the crackle. He picked up the desk phone instead and called the lab. He turned again to Willard.

"Now, Mr. Prather, you mentioned a bastard you'd like to kill. You got any particular bastard in mind?"

Prather glanced at him, looked away, and gulped the whiskey.

Lid kept a straight face. "The lab guys are coming to get your mail, but I know you were just about to call us yourself. Do you have any idea where the rest of him is?"

Willard drank the balance of the whiskey and said nothing.

"Murder is against the law," Lid said. "Whoever the bastard is, you want us to catch him, don't you?" He paused, not expecting a reply, then shrugged. "Well, he was your brother."

The other uniform entered the room and stared wide-eyed toward the desk. "Nobody else is here, Li Dao, just three servants," he said without moving his gaze from the dead face.

Lid nodded.

Colish and Presnell talked quietly together and left the room.

Heinrich Wexler approached Li Dao. "What's with the warrant? That's not necessary."

Lid shrugged. "Standard procedure."

"What the hell are the feds doing here anyway?"

Lid shook his head. He never joked with the enemy.

Freddie appeared at the door and caught Lid's eye. "Alex wants to see you, Lid."

"Stay here. Don't let anybody touch anything." Lid gestured toward the desk, then crossed the hall and found Alex sitting on a stool in the safe. "You guessed right," he said. "You win the head."

Alex ignored the remark.

A heavy wooden table was already piled with papers and folders she had set aside. "That's interesting," she said, indicating a large rectangular book.

Lid pulled it open and stared at the wide yellow page.

Alex glanced up. "Read a line or two."

Lid sighed and read aloud: "Apple bed oaken father wine ace lens chair mustard." He rubbed his beard stubble and muttered something filthy under his breath.

"Lid, have you noticed this place has no electronic security system around the doors and windows?"

"They don't need it. A couple of punks tried to burglarize this mansion a few years ago, at least that was the rumor. Anyway, they disappeared. Nobody called the cops and nobody ever saw them again."

Alex shoved a stack of papers at him. "Are you going to help or just stand around?"

He started to flip through the material. "I should have been a criminal."

The records were what he expected—old invoices and receipts. He tossed anything aside that appeared promising. Lid hated the work but admired Alex's persistence. After thirty minutes, he backed out of the small area, rescued by sounds from the vestibule.

The two-man lab crew entered, first Tony Romano, a heavy, swarthy Italian who appeared to barge, followed by a younger man who moved with even, respectful steps. Romano twisted out a cigarette on the polished brick and came into the hallway blowing the last of the smoke. The partner was slender and blond, years away from middle-age spread. Lid had not seen him before.

Lid liked Romano but deemed it fitting he was named for a cheese. Tony Romano was crude in speech and behavior. He was not a M.D. but thought he knew as much as they did from his years of experience. He said he was married, although Lid had never seen his wife.

Romano was blunt as always. "Where's the stiff?"

Lid pointed at the library and waited.

Romano walked into the room and immediately out again. "Good God, Lid! I thought you were kidding."

Lid's cynical expression deepened. "I told you I'd give you some head, Tony. I never kid about head."

The assistant smiled in appreciation, then gawked at the opulent hallway.

Lid had finally shocked the stoic Tony Romano, to whom life was a gig. Romano played guitar. He had music gigs and stiff gigs. This was a stiff gig.

Romano made a face. "That thing came in the mail?"

"That's right."

"Don't the post office have laws against that?"

"Probably. We got laws against murder too."

"Yeah, I thought we did. How can the doc do an autopsy without the rest of the guy?"

"What's the matter, Tony? You worried about the cause of death?"

Again the assistant grinned.

"You local dicks'll never solve this. It's outta town." Tony shrugged and went back to his job.

Li Dao said nothing. He didn't want it to be out of town. He wanted the extortionists to be in Macon, Georgia. Bibb County. Close at hand. The Prathers were obviously involved, and Wexler was probably in charge. Outta town, he smirked. How the hell would Romano know?

Lid strolled about admiring the polished brick floor of the entrance, the patina of inlaid wood pattern and the lack of dust motes. The hallway was floored with wide strips of dark, polished wood, interior doors stained to match. Soft indirect lighting reflected pale yellow walls and cream ceiling. A lowboy stood against one wall and supported an ancient urn. Lid stood in the center of an antique rug and wondered what it had cost. The hallway was half the size of his house. He would make an exceptional criminal.

Lid glanced into the dining room—and even larger antique rug, gilded mirrors, fresh flowers, chandelier. Sunlight streamed through windows that looked like they had just been washed. He counted the chairs around the large polished table. Fourteen.

Tony Romano sent his assistant out to the van, then looked into the dining room and started up again. "This is outta town, Lid. I'm tellin' ya. Nobody in Macon does this."

"What? Some Jamaican voodoo or something?"

"Hell, no! Nobody does that shit either except on TV. I'm talking New York, the Bronx, Denver. You know, organized stuff. Nobody in this fuckin' town does that shit!" Romano gestured toward the library.

Lid pulled his lips to one side with a serious face and a slight nod, the look he always gave to agree with Romano, whether he did or not.

The assistant returned. "This is nothin', is it, Lid?" Romano continued, now for the younger man's benefit. "We see a lot worse than this. Tell him, Lid! Tell him how I usually break in these new assistants."

The younger man clutched a satchel to his chest and waited.

He sucks them off, Lid almost said, but held the thought for the sake of the round, guileless face and the friendship with Romano. "This is the worst thing I've ever seen," was what he actually said.

An ambulance finally arrived, even though Lid had told them it wasn't needed. He understood—the attendants wanted to see the head. Eventually, Freddie had to spell the two uniforms waiting in front. The lab technician had told them about the package, and they wanted to see for themselves too.

By the time Romano and the new kid and the gruesome parcel were gone, Prather was on his fourth drink.

Lid stood in the doorway to the library and waited to make eye contact. He had it in mind to offer a kind word, but suddenly thought of Bruce Murray and remembered who he was dealing with. Lid gave his phoniest smile and saluted with his left hand. "Don't eat any baseballs."

The front door finally closed behind the police. Wexler walked across the hall and into the safe and found that the record book was gone. He checked the receipt to make certain the police had taken the book. They had. He returned to the library and stood in the center of the room, watching his nephew with disgust.

Willard had removed his tie and now was slouching in the swivel chair. Alcohol had governed his rage into a modest dopey inertia. "We know who killed Obie," he said. "Why didn't we tell the damn cop?"

"What the hell was Obie doing there, getting his fucking teeth cleaned? I'm sure Li Dao would love to hear about it."

Willard thought about that. "I'm gonna have one more drink an' get my gun an' go kill that bastard Braddock. I'll do it myself."

"Brilliant. You do that."

He looked up. His uncle never agreed with him that easily. "Well, what would you do?"

"I would sober up and think."

Willard stared at him in numbed awareness but made no reply.

"Braddock killed Obie; we can be certain of that." Wexler spoke more to himself than to Willard. "The question is, what do we do about it? We won't get any help from Li Dao. He knew to come here and he knew when. It's not likely Braddock told him anything, but we don't move against that tooth fairy until we know what the police know and where they heard it from. Sometimes you meet a man like Braddock who doesn't know how to bend. So we break him. We kill Braddock and his whole goddamn family, but not until we know how the locals and feds are involved."

Wexler walked to the window and stood for a while watching the fountain. It never occurred to him to forget Braddock, to cut his losses. Vengeance was a casual habit, too long inculcated. It had nothing to do with the murder of his nephew. Wexler's disdain for the Prathers was deep and pitiless. He was clever and devious but not perceptive enough to know that he enjoyed little in life, the lust of his soul suppressed, almost extinguished by hardness of heart and denial of intrinsic value in the best of things. No one would guess the ruthless, unforgiving existence he had led, least of all himself. Everybody broke the law. Life was a gamble—a little risk, a little gain. Wexler preferred big risks. Obie's killer was an ordinary dentist working alone, or with the aid of some fiendish accomplice. Wexler didn't know the man, but he knew the name— Dr. Simon Braddock.

He looked around, but Willard was asleep in the chair, his head resting on the leather back, his mouth wide open. He had the same expression his brother had last shown, except his eyes were closed and there was no baseball.

Wexler went to the phone and dialed. He watched Prather and spoke quietly. "The police have the file but not the key. I'll talk to you later, not this phone or my phone. They'll both be dirty before the day's over. Obie's dead," he said without expression. "The bastard mailed his head to Willard, stuffed a baseball in his mouth, and Condon and his buddy were right. The guy on Second is the problem." He hung up and walked out of the room.

"Max!"

The butler came down the hall.

"Willard's sleeping it off. Don't let him leave the house with a gun."

"I can't always stop him."

"You've murdered old men and children; you can stop a drunk!" Wexler said and left.

The Wexler and Prather residences sat on a fifteen-acre compound and shared the driveway as it opened into the street. Formal brickwork and a gate marked the entrance. The rest of the area was surrounded by high wire fencing invisible in the dense woods.

Heinrich Wexler started slowly down the wooded path and mused as he went. The police had been alerted, somehow, to the mail delivery. Next, they would wiretap the telephones. He and Willard could meet at the gazebo until the operation was over. The weather was pleasant and the gazebo was halfway between the two houses. Wexler knew he was breaking his own rule—he had bled the Macon physicians for over a year. He prided himself on keeping an operation deadly but quick—six months at the most—then out. Two or three reliable people was all he needed. The Prathers had been a risk, but he tolerated his half-sister's children because they were family and cheap.

Wexler thought of Simon Braddock and began to squeeze his hands, then his lips. Visualizing the act of murder was akin to sexual arousal, a lethal, malignant voyeurism. It was time to kill another rabbit. Nobody knew that he kept the rabbits for that quiet, bloody rehearsal. Holding the thick fold of skin at the nape allowed the animal's own weight to stretch the white fur and make the knife's slit convenient. The rabbit usually kicked once, sometimes twice; then the blood would flow. It was a very private addiction.

Wexler's residence came into view, another copy of French Renaissance style, perfect in symmetry. The pale yellow manor stood on a flat knoll even deeper in the woods than the Prather mansion and out of sight from the road. He circled the house and came in the front. The wide entryway was a gallery of wall hangings, footed vases, and large potted plants that stood on the floor. He liked owning the paintings, mirrors, and the antique Celtic cross, but never actually stopped to admire them. Landscaping and interior decoration were things to be bought. The parquet floor was a work of art itself, but Wexler only bothered to check that it was spotless. Mrs. Warwick was a good housekeeper.

He found her in the dining room, adding yet more polish to the gleaming furniture. Clara Warwick was part of the estate, only slightly younger than he but young enough to be attractive to him. She served tea or provided sex the same way Max delivered the mail or committed murder. Wexler was not consciously thinking of sex but watched the pendant breasts swing in rhythm with the polishing motion. Their relationship was far beyond any pretense of seduction.

"Clara," he nodded.

She stopped, an unholy votary, and obediently wiped her hands on a clean, dry cloth. "Where?"

"Right here, on the floor."

She removed only minimal clothing and lay on the Persian rug, completely at his disposal. After a minute she felt the familiar pulsing but held her position until he indicated he was ready to get up.

Wexler moaned a few times as he squeezed her shoulders, then struggled to his feet and left the room.

She retreated to the nearest bathroom to clean herself up and put on her lower garments for the second time that day. It was a way of life, a vile, unspoken arrangement that offered peaceful security, and she accepted it. In less than two minutes, Clara Warwick was rubbing the curved backs of the antique chairs again.

4

Wednesday. Two P.M.

Dr. Rachael Brucker's office was in an old building on the sixth floor. Lid had never been there. He rode up in an ancient elevator and found it by the number stenciled on the opaque glass of the heavy wooden door.

It was a cubbyhole waiting room with tired old furniture, not a fancy address and not expensively furnished, a Norman Rockwell original. Her office was a mess like her hair. Like her life, he almost thought, but that wasn't true. Brucker had respect in the field, even though the office didn't look it. She disliked role playing.

"Is that you, Lid?" she yelled.

"Yeah!"

"Come on back."

He followed the sound of her voice through two large rooms. The first was orderly and pleasant with desk, lamps, upholstered chairs; the second contained file cabinets, tables, stacks of records and boxes. Like her hair. Lid dead-ended at another cubbyhole even smaller than the waiting room. Rachael sat at a shallow upright desk with her back to the wall. A tall, open window on her right filled the entire space on that side.

The cubicle was walled with service board littered with memos and letters. A large ashtray sat on the cluttered desktop.

"Your office is a closet, **Brucker**."

She blew smoke that drafted into the outside air. "Bring in a chair, Lid. This is where I live."

"You think there's room for both of us in there?" He dragged up a chair and sat in the doorway.

"This is my place," she said through a smile. "I do my best thinking here away from the phone."

"Your office is a damn closet," he repeated.

"You're the first guy I ever brought into my closet. It may look cramped to you, but I know where everything is and I can reach it without getting up." She brushed an errant strand of hair with the back of her hand and blew more smoke. The dark voice and sultry eyes were unintentionally seductive, but the effect was not wasted on Lid.

"You think we'll need the couch?"

"I'll tell you when," she said, to his surprise. "Now, what about the case?"

He laid copies of Romano's work on her desk. "We're finally getting some action on the extortion case. We got a penis in the mail, white guy, along with this note."

He waited for her to read, impressed that nothing seemed to faze Brucker. She was the complete psychiatrist; she would make a good cop. At last she picked up the top photo.

"Is this the other body part?" she asked.

"Yeah, it was mailed to Willard Prather, all right."

She blew smoke. "You have to watch those high, tight pitches." She flipped through the other pictures. "What do you need to know?"

"Psychological profile on a guy who would do this.

I'm trying to understand why he sent the head. Why not dump the whole body in his front yard? This was a lot more trouble."

She studied the note again as Lid rambled on. "It says he's an old buddy of Prather's. I understand why he sent us the prick—so we'd take the note seriously, investigate. But why mail a damn head? He must have been wondrously pissed off."

She blew more smoke out the window. "He's not an old buddy of Prather's. He's one of your doctors." She looked at him. "Got any idea which one?"

"Why do you think that?"

"Lid, you haven't been a cop all your life. Didn't you play baseball when you were a kid?"

"We were stealing hubcaps that year. What's your point?"

"This is more than pissed off. In the first place, if he wanted you to know who he was, he'd sign his name. The remark about being an old friend is to throw you off. This guy is sending a message, Lid. Look at the picture, the baseball. He's playing hardball. He's playing in their league. That's the message. There's an incredible anger here. He's telling Willard Prather he can be just as violent, just as cruel, as the bad guys."

"Sort of a challenge?"

"Exactly, and a damn good challenge. If I got my brother's head in the mail, it would give me pause. Do you think Prather knows who the doctor is?"

"No way for us to know, but we'd better find him before they do. What is this guy, a macho type, a hunter?"

"Not necessarily, but I don't have enough information to make a guess. Whoever he is, he's dangerous and crazy."

Lid held her gaze with hard, unsmiling eyes. "Go ahead, make a guess."

She took a drag and blew smoke. "He might be emotionally immature, like a child who can't have his way, only this character doesn't cry about it, he kills people. Maybe the dead man was a collector for the mob, and the doc decided to do a little surgery rather than paying off."

"You're sure he's one of the doctors?"

She shrugged. "I'm never sure of anything, but I'd bet on this."

He chuckled. "A crazy doctor with a knife, huh?"

"Exactly, and crazy people are the most dangerous, unpredictable. It could be a woman, you know."

Lid had already thought of that.

Now he could only look at the dark eyes and full mouth, the upper lip curving out the way it did. Brucker slouched there in her pale linen suit, no jewelry, no blouse. She didn't need any. Did she know how delicious the bare neck and throat looked under the jacket?

"Why didn't you ever get married, Brucker?"

"I was married, three years. He thought I was smarter than he was, and it pissed him off."

"You probably were."

"No, I really wasn't, but he thought I was and it's the same thing. I made more money than he did." She flipped her cigarette out the open window.

"What's down there?"

"Just an alley." She lit another cigarette.

"You smoke too much."

She gave her most fetching smile, then took it away. "Go catch the bad guys."

Lid stood obediently, but he wanted her. It had taken time for her allure to seep into his consciousness, but there was no question of it now. He stared unabashedly at the delicate depression at her throat, the slope of her breasts under the coarse linen. It finally became obvious that he was gaping. "How old are you, Brucker?"

Her maturity was beyond coyness. "Thirty-six. How old are you?"

"Fifty-four. Would you like me if I were thirty-six?"

She gazed up into his eyes and spoke the words plainly. "I like you fifty-four, Li Dao."

"Thanks for your help." Lid smiled and tried to look young, then left before he looked foolish. He passed again through the junk room and the neat room, looked at the couch and wondered for an instant if she'd ever had sex on it. She didn't mind that he was fifty-four. She had been married for three years. Not a lesbian. Lid's hormones were flowing.

He left the building and forced his mind back to Brucker's suggestion—the head chopper was one of the doctors. He should've thought of it himself. Doctors liked to cut. A hit man wouldn't have had the stomach for it. The thought worked pleasingly in his mind—the anger, the outrage the killer must have felt. Murder among thieves was vulgar and predictable. This was elegant, a man of position and substance risking everything to protect his family.

Lid considered the irony of his latest case assignment: Pursue the maniac who had butchered Bruce Murray's murderer. Let the doc have at it! he thought, save the taxpayers' money—Li Dao policy again.

Six P.M.

Simon banged the van across multiple sets of railroad tracks on the way to Skip's shop. For two days he had searched the *Macon Telegraph* and the *Atlanta*

Constitution. There was no mention of an extortion ring. He had watched state and local news. Nothing. The head should've reached Prather by now. The cops couldn't ignore a dick in the mail. There was only one certainty: Prather and his hoods knew he had killed Obie and taken the money, a thought that hadn't lost any of its frightening implications.

Simon parked the van and climbed out but waited in the late afternoon sun as he saw the flash of a welding arc. He leaned against the flatbed truck, carefully, not to dirty his suit. It appeared Skip had brushed on another coat of gray. The truck had always been gray— battleship gray—probably navy issue. He kept his eyes averted until Skip finished what he was doing.

The older man looked up and beamed. It was a tired, dark face with two days' beard, wrinkled, used and abused, but it was a good face. Some of the lines of daily grime appeared to have become permanent. His hands and arms were leathery from the sun and the welding arc. Skip wore the only outfit Simon had ever seen him wear, overalls over long johns. Only in the hottest part of the summer would the long johns give way to a shortsleeve shirt.

There was nothing indirect about Skip. He was a bull of a man with voice to match. "Come on in, *Sigh-mon*." He tossed his face shield and gloves onto the workbench and lit a cigarette from the metal, which still glowed red.

Simon had long since accepted Skip's pronunciation of his name, the open, flat southern drawl that made it a longer word to say. Simon put a cold six-pack of Budweiser on the bench and watched the heavy, rough hands pop two tops.

Skip handed him a can, then took a long swig. "Your

phone call sounded serious again, Simon. What'n the hell are you into?"

Simon handed him an envelope. "These are pictures of me. I need two fake ID's—driver's licenses and Social Security cards. The names I need are in there too."

Skip's smile was large like his voice. "Man, you into some big-time spy stuff! What makes you think I can get fake ID's? You not jerking around the IRS, are you?"

Simon rolled his eyes. "You know me better than that, and you know I'm safe. If I get in trouble, it's no skin off your ass. I can pay whatever you want."

"Aye, and that's true. I saw what's in the bag. You rob a bank?"

"No, I didn't rob a bank." Simon climbed the steep wooden steps to the upper room where Skip had a cot, a toilet, and a lavatory. It was hot, a hundred degrees with the closed window and the low roof. He stood on the toilet seat and reached up into the rafters to retrieve an old navy duffel bag.

Skip spoke loudly from below. "What are you doing leaving all that money down here, Simon? What makes you think I won't just take the whole thing and skip town?"

"Because I know you." He climbed back down the ladder steps. "Here. Here's five thousand dollars. That ought to cover it. No questions asked."

Skip took the thick wad of bills. "Where'd all that money come from, Simon?"

"Part of a business deal. I'll give you a cut when I'm done."

"Looks to me like it's mine now." Skip smiled as he stuffed the money into the large overall pocket. "You sure you're not in trouble with the IRS, 'cause if you are, you can take that money and git. If not," he shrugged, "I don't know it's up there."

Simon shook his head. "I don't play with the IRS."

Skip set down the beer can and tossed his cigarette onto the heavy workbench. He opened the envelope and held the small photos at arm's length, then put on his bifocals and looked at the slip of paper. The big callused hands were wet from the beer can; the fingernails were black. "Wallace Noles and Asa Condon. Who are these guys?"

"A couple of good old boys," Simon replied.

"You want their names on the ID's but with your picture, is that right?"

"That's right."

"This don't look like you."

"It's not supposed to. I was made up for a play."

Skip sighed and picked at the stubble on his chin. "I'll see what I can do, Simon."

"I need these yesterday, Skip, the sooner the better." He looked at his old friend without smiling to emphasize the point.

"It'll take me at least a day. I'll call you."

They both took a deep swig of Budweiser, and Skip picked up the cigarette. He sat on a box and, as always, left Simon the most comfortable place, a tractor seat welded to a tripod. It was also the cleanest place. The polished metal was smooth and familiar.

"Wish I had a nickel for every time I sat my ass on this thing."

"Yeah, when I made that it still had some paint on it."

Simon's suit and tie appeared inappropriate in the ancient garage, yet he felt at home in this place, the brown dirt floor, hard packed from so many years of use, encrusted with metal like a beach where shells appear on the surface or at any level beneath the surface. The wooden garage faced the late afternoon sun. Simon squinted into the light and enjoyed the breeze that blew through the opening. Behind the shop and to the right the pile of junk metal stretched away and became higher, at last making a horizon with only the sky showing above. He finished his beer and stood up to leave.

Skip was already on his second. "I'll call you, Simon."

Seven P.M.

The squad room was reflected in the windows by the night sky. Only the maintenance crew was at work. From his cubicle Lid could hear the drone of a floor waxer and smell the polish. His tie was off and his shirt sleeves rolled.

Romano had given a useless report—the dick was circumcised, blood type A, same as the head. Family members might identify the dick, but he doubted it. This bit of wisdom he had delivered with open, innocent eyes.

Dick jokes had been circulating for three days. The body hadn't turned up, but they didn't really need it. They had the head and knew who it was.

The D.A. had come by to point out Mayor Grayson's distress. Grayson had called the chief to urge the utmost cooperation with the D.A. and to demand secrecy from the newspaper. Heads in the mail might cause a panic. The chief imparted Mr. Mayor's wishes to Lieutenant Mimbs, who passed them on to Lid. Mimbs's parting remark was that the fibbies were breathing down his neck, the third time he had mentioned that.

Lid saw his partner enter the large room and waited for her to reach the cubicle. "I thought you'd left," he said.

"I was at the telephone exchange. The district manager wanted to make sure we were getting what we wanted."

"Are we?"

"Yeah, I made a copy of the first call from Prather's house. It's very revealing, may be the old man." She handed him the page.

Lid looked at it silently. "This could be Wexler," he finally said. "Heinrich Wexler. I'll have to hear the recording to be sure. If this is local, he's in charge. Wexler wouldn't be working for his nephew. I thought he was retired."

"Retired from what?"

Lid stared, his eyes unfocused. "These are the bastards who got to Bruce and those children."

"Retired from what?" she repeated.

"Import business. Mostly legitimate." He waggled his hand. "What did the other person say?"

"Nothing. She just answered and the rest of the recording is all Wexler."

"She?"

"It was a woman. Sounded like an old woman. She just said hello. We didn't get the tap a minute too soon. He knows it's there, we won't hear anything else."

"We'll leave it anyway, and let's tap Wexler's phone. You never know." Lid stared at the paper. "He and Willard both called somebody a bastard, but you can't tell from this if he's speaking generally or if he knows who the bastard is. '. . . stuffed a baseball in his mouth and Condon and his buddy were right. The guy on second is the problem.' What does he mean, the guy on second? Is he talking second base?"

"That's what I thought at first, but suppose he means Second Street or Second Avenue?"

"You could be right. Brucker thinks the psycho butcher is one of our doctors."

"What about the search?"

He gestured to a carton piled with documents and paper. "All we got out of that trip was the head. No point in bustin' him for anything there."

"The record book with the funny words!" She nodded toward the telephone message. "He spoke of it on the phone, the *file* and the *key*. It's some sort of code."

"If that's what he was talking about." Lid looked again at the phone message.

He tilted his head and made a sound. "That book could be anything, maybe sentimental value. The FBI can take a look at it."

Alex grimaced. "Prather doesn't strike me as the sentimental type. Besides, it was too neat, like a code. What else did we take that could pass for a file? I'd like to check it out."

He waved a hand. "Check it out."

She sifted through the box and pulled out the heavy book. "Why don't we bring Prather in and ask him what it is?"

Lid squinted one eye. "I don't know, not yet. I don't want to look silly if the book is nothing, have him know that's all we've got. If it is anything, let him sweat about it, wonder what we're doing. He'd say it was something his mother kept, he made it when he was a kid. That's what he'd say to a grand jury."

"Don't tell Mimbs I've got this thing." She started out. "Call me. I want to know what you find."

"What for? The damn cat answers the phone."

She smiled to herself but kept walking.

Lid returned to the well-worn doctor files that were piled against the wall of his cubicle. He lugged the first stack to the top of his desk and began the search. Second Avenue was residential, Second Street more likely, but he didn't remember a medical office on either. The file folders and pages were bent and dirty from his own sweat. He had pored over the files for a year. One more time through.

It took an hour to check them all. Nothing. The investigation had been limited to physicians because they had reported the extortion, but they were not the only people with money. Bankers and lawyers had money. There was a laundry owner who made more than any doctor in town. He'd had to draw the line somewhere. Lid turned to the yellow pages and looked at the sub listings—chiropractors, dentists, optometrists, physicians and surgeons, psychologists, veterinarians.

Suddenly, a word caught his eye—Second Street. Simon Braddock, D.D.S. 2816 Second Street.

Exhaustion suddenly weighed against his concentration. Hunger was causing a headache. Tomorrow. He dialed Alex and waited to hear the click and the silence, drummed his fingers, and waited again.

"Alex Sinclair!" came the breathless voice.

"Why don't you teach that cat to say something?"

"He talks to me. What did you find?"

"Only a dentist, Simon Braddock, 2816 Second Street, must be near the north end where it dead-ends into Riverside Drive." He paused. "Didn't Prather say something about killing Braddock just before we walked in over there?"

"I'm not sure, I didn't catch it. Lid, if that's the man—'the guy on second'—it means Prather and Wexler know who he is."

"Yeah. We'll check him first thing in the morning if he's still alive." He paused. "I'll see you tomorrow, kid."

They both hung up.

* * *

Alex flushed at his final word, a term of endearment, she hoped. Lid had never called her anything but Alex. Thirty years of police work, apparently, had contributed to his abrupt, unpolished manner, the jaded, distrustful view of life. Alex suddenly felt compassion for her partner, a warm, caring sensation, the last thing she had expected.

Marvin walked across the bed and tested her thigh with one paw, then curled up in her lap, pious and deserving. Alex kneaded and massaged until the cat purred in response. She finally whispered her one confidence: "My partner is a maniac." Marvin pushed his head up against her hand and directed the resonant vibration toward her ear. It's all right, he was saying, everything will work out.

Eleven P.M.

Simon half reclined into the soft sofa, his bare feet resting on the coffee table. The only light was the TV flashing late news. He was consumed with private consternation. Five days had passed, and he had kept Marie and Esther as close as possible. But the ID's were ready—tomorrow another plan. He finished his drink and pulled Marie closer.

She turned completely around, pulled her knees under her body, and laid her head against his chest. "You seem stressed lately."

"The office," he shrugged.

Marie patted his arm and snuggled closer.

Simon was ashamed that she was near enough to hear his heartbeats but could never know his thoughts.

Marie was extravagantly loving and beautiful, in ways that made Simon know her life had been easy. Her face opened doors; her smile gained special privi-

leges and bypassed the natural abrasions of everyday
affairs. He had dated her and married her, always with
a certain incredulity that she wanted him, and her
sexual appetite was never disappointing.

Simon ran the back of his hand down between her
breasts and onto her hip. He pulled up the end of the
shorty nightgown, caressed the smooth buttocks, and
realized she was wearing nothing underneath. His heart
rate increased with the familiar surge of blood, and he
hoped he would last long enough to give satisfaction.
He peeled the gown over her head. The sofa was large,
the pillows thick and filled with eiderdown, one of
their favorite places. Thoughts of extortion and danger
vanished as he fell into the moist, warm euphoria of
that other world.

5

Thursday. Nine A.M.

Simon parked the van behind the building and entered his private office. He never bothered to announce his arrival. Roberta would hear the key. She had been with him from the beginning and knew all the sounds the building made.

She came to the office door and waited for him to look up, the perfect bow mouth pouting under her turned-up nose. Her hair was pulled tightly back and tied with a ribbon. The white starched blouse and large rimless glasses gave a neat, efficient appearance.

"There're two cops here to see you!" she whispered, eyes wide.

"What?"

"Two detectives," she said in a natural voice. "They were waiting when I got here." She handed him a piece of paper with the name: Sergeant Martin Li Dao. "He wants to know if he could see you for just a few minutes. I knew he was a cop—he was wearing the suit."

Simon understood. If the suit was wearing *him*, the guy was a dental salesman. They saw at least one a week, three-piece suits with sharp creases in the coat and slacks. It was a standing joke. Anybody wearing a wrinkled suit without a vest wasn't selling anything.

"Are they collecting for Boys' Camp or something?"

"I don't know," she mouthed, wide-eyed again.

"Send them in." He mocked her large eyes and whisper, but felt a jolt of fear. Simon didn't like suspense. He would rather face a matter quickly and learn the news, even bad news. He hung his coat and put on a fresh clinic jacket.

Roberta brought Lid and Alex back to the office.

The large, unfamiliar frame filled the doorway. "Dr. Braddock? I'm Sergeant Li Dao with the Macon police. This is Detective Sinclair." He showed his badge.

Simon stood as they shook hands. Roberta was right. The gal in the pants and jacket could be anybody, but the cold eyes and crew cut belonged to a cop.

"May we speak privately?"

Simon nodded and gestured.

Lid closed the door, and all three sat. "I'll be blunt, Dr. Braddock. There's an extortion attempt being made here in Macon, and we have reason to believe it has been directed mostly against the local doctors. Maybe you've heard about it." He waited. "Has anybody contacted you?"

That was blunt enough, Simon thought as he shook his head. "No. You mean like *pay this money so we can keep the neighborhood clean?*"

"It's a little more serious than that. Some people have died, and we believe there's a connection."

"Who died?"

"A child died in a traffic accident, another disappeared. Then Dr. Bruce Murray was killed when his car ran down an embankment, all within the last year."

"You think extortionists did that?"

"We're not certain. They contacted the victims by mail and demanded money and made threats."

"Why didn't the doctors go to the police?"

"The fathers of the two children did. That's the only reason we know about it, but we have no proof extortionists are responsible, nor do we know who they are. After the initial contact the doctors clammed up, said nothing more came of it. We need some outside help."

Simon had listened with a deliberate expression of repugnance. "If anybody contacts me, I'll call you. That's all I can do."

"One of the extortionists was murdered recently. I'm glad the guy's dead. I'm being candid. If you quote me, I'll deny I said that. You may know something you're afraid to say, but I want you to trust me." Lid paused and glanced around as if to make certain he was not overheard. "Even if I knew who killed this guy, I'd keep it to myself."

It was a corny gesture, Simon thought, a finesse approach that was not this cop's style. Even the female partner looked uncomfortable, staring toward the floor, resting her chin on her thumb.

Lid spoke again. "Any information you give is between us."

"I don't know anything that would help."

"Dr. Braddock, you and your family could be in danger."

There was an awkward silence. Simon's eyes were open and innocent. "I . . . have no suggestions," he said. "What do you think I should do?"

"We think we know who killed Obie Prather."

Simon didn't flinch. "Why are you telling me this?"

Lid shook his head slightly. "Condon and his pal could be right behind us."

"Condon?" Simon repeated with an odd smile. "You've lost me."

"Maybe you haven't met him." Lid paused again. "Right now anything you say to my partner and me is off the record, but that could change. I want these perpetrators eliminated, and I don't care how it gets done."

Alex began to fidget.

Lid leaned forward. "We intercepted an incriminating phone call which mentioned the murder and made a vague reference to revenge. You wouldn't know anything about that? We can't help unless you think you need to be helped."

The cop's advantage was slipping away, Simon could tell. "I don't see why they would bother me," he said, deliberately awkward and embarrassed. "You said 'doctors.' Is that doctors and dentists, or just physicians?"

"We're not that certain," Lid said.

"Maybe I don't make enough money for them, but I'll be glad to call you if anybody contacts me."

Simon could hear the front door open and close as the reception room filled with patients, and he knew the cop had run out of openings.

They stood and shook hands again. The detectives left.

Simon closed his office door and sat again at the desk, disappointed and frightened. The extortion ring remained intact. The police had done nothing but come directly at him. How the hell had they found him? It was a question he had wanted very much to ask but couldn't. Now, too late, he realized that an innocent man would have demanded to know why they were probing with such pointed insinuations.

Martin Li Dao had not been fooled. The cop had talked as if he knew everything, but how could he have known? He knew about Prather, which meant the police had found the head—a relief but no surprise. Why hadn't they arrested anybody, and where had Li Dao heard of Condon? Most important, how had he gotten the name *Braddock*? Willard Prather would have been enraged, but he couldn't have told Li Dao without conceding the extortion itself.

Simon's mental energy seemed to dissipate in mulling over the questions, but answers were not available. What to do next depended on what had happened so far. He began to sympathize with Marie's insatiable curiosity. This would drive her crazy, to work in the dark, patiently, to wait for the deadly pieces to fall into place.

It occurred to him, suddenly, that the police visit would require explanation, and Roberta was nosy. She loved a savory bit of gossip. He would tell her enough to satisfy—better than that, make her an ally in protecting Marie, who would be very upset if she even heard the word *extortion*.

Alex started in as soon as the car door closed: "How the hell could you say that to him? We're cops, not vigilantes. He's the vigilante, and you encouraged him. You can't tell Braddock we don't care if he's a murderer! What if he calls the chief?"

Lid chuckled. "If Braddock killed Prather, he won't call the chief; if not, I think he has sense enough to know we're trying to protect him."

"Don't say *we*. Speak for yourself. If we do our jobs like criminals, we're criminals too."

He grunted. "Tell that to the parents of that Bissett kid, the hit-and-run."

Alex sulked and tried to think of a rebuttal. Conviction and resentment struggled against her usual compliant manner. She finally blurted another objection. "At least we shouldn't tell a civilian that the police don't care who killed somebody!"

"I don't give a goddamn who killed him. I'm glad he's dead. If you want another partner, say so."

The final remark would have been less hurtful if Lid had been angry, but it was casual, only a statement of his true feelings. Alex was crushed and rode back to the station in silence.

Later, Lid sat at his desk and mulled over his impressions of Simon Braddock. The dentist wasn't what he had expected, not oily innocent but not aggressive either. Braddock had good looks; he was a family man with a profession, but none of that was persuasive. There was something vulnerable and open about the face, an almost frightened look that said Braddock was not the type to gift-wrap somebody's head. It was difficult to feel for a man whose income was a multiple of his own, yet Lid's sympathetic image persisted. He tried to picture the dentist committing that grisly act, but couldn't quite make it happen. Experience, however, told him not to read people—a job for lawyers and trial juries—rather to live by the postulate that had served him for years: anybody could do anything.

At one o'clock Lid entered Rachael Brucker's tiny office. Soft lights reflected the warm golden wallpaper and carpet, a more appealing ambience than he remembered. Three upholstered chairs faced the large desk, where Rachel sat in navy blue. A brown leather couch occupied one corner of the room. Lid sensed the tranquility and comfort that seemed to derive from the decor. "This is where you shrink the crazies?"

"Some are unshrinkable. Have a seat."

Brucker's low-pitched voice suited her profession, Lid thought. "I didn't know you head doctors really used couches."

"I don't use it much. It's a universal symbol. Patients expect to see one."

"Can I try it? I've never been in a psychiatrist's office before."

Rachael shrugged with her eyes.

Lid sprawled onto the heavy couch and crossed his arms over his chest. It was more comfortable than it looked.

She watched him without speaking, then punched a button. "No calls, Lil." She lit a cigarette. "What's on your mind?"

"We got some information from a phone tap which led to a dentist who might be the guy who hacked up Prather. Alex and I went by his office this morning, but I was disappointed. He's either a great actor or the wrong guy. He didn't admit anything, like he was genuinely in the dark. I just wanted to see if you had any thoughts."

"What makes you think he's the wrong guy?"

"He doesn't seem the type. Almost a wimp, not aggressive enough."

"What else did you sense about him?"

"Just that. The kind of man who doesn't stick up for his rights, who dislikes confrontations." Lid sat up and swung his feet to the floor. "The kind who blushes too easily. You know what I mean?"

"Yes, but so far you haven't said anything to convince me."

"I was hoping he would be rude and pushy and mean as hell."

"What would that tell you?"

"Seems more like the type to whack somebody and mail his body around."

"Not necessarily. Repressed types can be murderers too. Some of the best psychos are. The world dumps on them for years, and they accept it like lambs. Then one day they walk into a convenience store with a machine gun and start shooting up the place. It happens, Lid. The newspapers quote the neighbors, who say what a quiet, modest guy he was. And a Boy Scout," she added. "He was always a Boy Scout."

"It's hard to imagine a dentist who feels dumped on. They got plenty of money."

"Anybody can feel dumped on. It doesn't matter what he is, it's what he thinks he is that counts. Poor people can be well adjusted; rich people can be paranoid."

"You know what he reminded me of? Those old photos of emigrants on Ellis Island, the modest farmer from Wales who just endured six weeks in steerage. Braddock had that look. Decent." Lid blew air through his teeth. "I was hoping this guy was guilty," he said.

"Why?"

"I don't care if Braddock killed Prather. I just want a lead, I want the extortionists."

"Is that his name, Braddock?"

"Yeah, Dr. Simon Braddock. You know him?"

"I don't think so. Are you after the extortionists or Prather's murderer?"

"Officially both. Unofficially, I'm after the extortionists. I don't give a damn who killed Prather."

"Be careful what conclusions you draw. Braddock may be a surprise. Patients can hide a world of treachery behind an innocent face, sometimes a look that goes beyond simplicity, too pure. Nobody is virginal, Lid."

Rachel Brucker looked sultry and utterly composed behind the thin column of smoke that rose in the still air and appeared blue in the golden room. She took a long drag in silence. Lid studied the luscious mouth as she inhaled and blew a thin stream through puckered lips. Brucker wore clothes well, he thought, with practiced indifference. The navy and white dress looked expensive, only the uniform of the day. She made it appear comfortable and casual, and had the same detachment about her work. Brucker probably had no biases, was not a gossip. Lid liked her. He wanted her.

"What are you thinking?" she finally asked.

He looked at her with a probing squint and gave a measured reply. "I was thinking about Braddock," he lied, "what to do next. We're at another dead end."

"Give it some time. That's not your only case. Work on something else for a while."

The statement jolted Lid and made him realize abruptly that he had not come there to seek advice. He wanted to be with Rachael Brucker, to impress her, but she obviously wasn't participating in his erotic fantasy.

"Thanks, Brucker, wonderful advice. I gotta go."

Lid stalked out of the room and hoped he had hurt her feelings but doubted it. Rachael Brucker had mental toughness not easily pierced. She lingered in his thoughts: her scent, her cigarette smoke, her sultry look, and—worst of all—her maturity, which made him feel juvenile by comparison.

Two-thirty P.M.

"Here they are, Sigh-mon. You can be Wallace Noles or Asa Condon, whichever you choose."

Simon sat on the tractor seat and studied the fake ID's. "Even worn and bent. How do they do that?"

"That's a trade secret. You gonna rob a bank now?"

He shook his head. "I plan to make deposits." Simon got up and mounted the steps to the hot, airless room above Skip's shop. The dirty mirror over the lavatory was the only one available. He arranged the hairpiece and mustache before breaking a sweat.

"How much you putting in the bank, Simon?"

"I'm leaving you most of it." He climbed back down into the cooler air.

"Damn! Is that you?"

"Do you like it?"

"You don't look like yourself."

"It's a rug, to make me look like the ID photo."

Skip hung his thumbs in the overall straps. He was still grinning. "Damn if you ain't somethin'. You can act. You can do anything!"

Simon smiled lamely. This was not the time for a beer and a chat. He climbed into the van. "Thanks for the ID's, buddy."

The grizzled old head nodded.

Simon started off, thinking he should have been a welder himself, something simple and honest. Instead, he had gone for the big bucks and now was in big trouble. Skip was happy; nobody wanted to kill him.

Roberta would reschedule the afternoon patients. He was at the nursing home—a safe excuse if Marie should call. Simon started to go the old familiar highway but opted for I-16 because he wasn't sure how long the business would take. Dublin first, across to Perry, back up I-75. Any bank would do—Nations, First Federal—it didn't matter. The first plan had been a failure. He had risked everything on a single action, but the police, for whatever reason, hadn't touched the extortion ring. The money was suddenly very useful. He left the hairpiece and mustache in place and turned on the A.C. for the first time that season. It was still three days before Palm Sunday but hot for that time of year. The miles passed quickly.

Simon took the Dublin exit and drove the five miles

indicated by the sign, past junky garages and businesses on the outskirts into the quiet little town. Interstates were now the major arteries, isolating small towns back to a slower pace as in the time of their founding.

From the main street he spotted a First Federal sign and pulled into a space. Simon gave his makeup a check and went in.

He hadn't realized how warm it was until he felt the cool interior of the bank. The comfortable room would keep sweat from running under the wig. Simon had expected something old and quaint, but the First Federal had the same decor as every other bank—dark woodwork, wall-to-wall carpet, gaudy brass chandeliers.

He spotted the CUSTOMER SERVICE sign and walked to the desk. The woman who waited to serve him was elderly. Her cheeks and jowls sagged, and Simon recognized the dentures at a glance.

"Can I help you?"

"Thank you." He sat in the chair and faced the wooden name plate: LEILA THOMPKINS. "I want to open a savings account."

"Well, aw' right," Leila drawled warmly. "I need you to sign this, and I need some identification."

Simon laid the Condon ID's on the desk and tried to imitate the signature shown on the driver's license.

"Now, Mr. Condon, how much would you like to deposit?"

"One hundred thousand cash." The moment Simon dreaded. How nosy would she be?

"We have CD's that pay a higher interest rate," she said.

"No, a savings account is fine. I may need to draw the money out in a hurry."

"Then you want a regular account." She went back to her paperwork. "Do you have the money with you?"

He handed over the attaché case.

"It will take a few minutes to count this. Would you like to come with me?"

"No." He shook his head and watched the floral print dress disappear behind the teller counter. She should be baby-sitting her great-grandchildren, but she obviously knew the job. Simon was not concerned about the money but would feel easier when she was done looking at the fake ID.

He sat and listened idly to snatches of conversation in the slow, friendly manner and caring tone. There had been a fire on Ike Wheeler's pulpwood land, but the county fire department had responded well. Daisy Edenfield was quitting down at Cy's hardware. Daisy had been there for twenty-three years, and some were saying Cy had tried to cut her wages. The Methodists were having a surprise reception for the Yankee revival preacher. Southern hospitality in Dublin, Georgia.

The money counting took longer than expected, but as he started to become concerned, the flowery dress returned. "You were five dollars over." She smiled. "Would you like it back?"

"No, put it in the account."

Simon was relieved. Nothing seemed amiss. There were more forms to be signed and another trip behind the teller counter. He said little but felt guilty for deceiving this honest woman. At last Leila Thompkins handed over the ID's, the passbook, and the attaché case. Simon reflected each smile and nod, thanked her for the help, and exited the bank with deliberate composure.

The deception had been successful. Simon sneered at his own lack of sophistication. Bankers were accustomed to dealing with big money. Leila hadn't even been impressed. He climbed into the van and pulled off the hot wig. One more stop, one more bank. He circled the block and headed west out of Dublin.

Three hours later Simon and Marie sat on the patio as the sun settled onto the tops of the pine trees. Simon sprawled in his beloved outfit—shortsleeve shirt, cotton pants, no shoes. Toby leaned against the recliner and raised his head as Simon dug his fingers into the thick coat. Marie still wore her pink biking outfit, tight-fitting Spandex and special shoes. She was not a power cyclist who covered fifty miles at a time, but she did look good in the clothes.

They watched Esther work on the trampoline, her long arms and legs turning gracefully in the cool dusk. *A tall, skinny kid with blond hair*, Obie Prather had called her.

Esther would have her mother's looks, the thought that always came to mind when he saw the profile of chin and parted lips, the delicate fingers and narrow feet. His eyes were drawn to her flawless pale skin and fine hair, nature's gift to the young. He glanced at Marie as she broke the silence.

"Mom called."

"Oh?"

"She wants us to come stay a few days."

It was an old sore spot but suddenly propitious. "Would you like to go?" he asked.

She looked at him. "You haven't taken a lover, have you?"

"I know I'm selfish, I'm sorry. This is as good a time as any. Go visit," he said with private relief.

She patted his shoulder. "You're a good man, Charlie Brown Braddock."

Marie was a beautiful woman, Simon thought,

without a care that she knew of. He should give in more often, easier than the protracted discussions that usually preceded her solo visits. Charleston was a long way for Marie to drive alone, and he missed her body and her cooking. He was, he knew, a selfish bastard. But this trip would hide them safely out of town, giving his private connivance time to abscess. Simon suddenly felt guilt from the deception—ironic to kill almost lightheartedly, then suffer over a white lie.

He gazed at the smooth-shaven limbs, the delicious four inches above the knee that separated ordinary from outstanding. Legs to die for—a trite saying but one he had long understood. A sudden appalling image of bloody punctures into the healthy muscular tissue flushed through his body like a drug. Marie's exquisite physique expanded the outrage at the thought of a deliberate attack. Simon breathed deeply and tried to relax.

Four-thirty P.M.

Alex hadn't been on the Mercer campus for years, and the one-way signs were giving her trouble. She finally gave up the search and parked in a faculty slot. To hell with it—a cop could handle a ticket.

It was a pleasant walk under old trees and beside ivied walls—halcyon days. Thirty-two was not old, but the coeds made it seem so. She cradled the heavy ledger in one arm and tried to blend with the students who ambled in knots across the quadrangle, oblivious to the concrete walkways. The accustomed weight of the small automatic under her arm felt out of place, but the jacket concealed the strap.

She found the right building and hiked the long flight of stone steps that led to the tall entrance. It was one of the original structures, beautiful and sacrosanct.

All universities had such a place, an artist's rendering used as a logo on university stationery.

The ancient edifice contained as much wasted space as office space, with high ceilings and wide stairs on either side. She stopped for a moment to glance at the bulletin board fliers, the offer of a literary tour of England. It was the look and smell of a classroom building, a combination of cologne, body aromas, and young adult lust that almost had an odor of its own. The hallway was infested with noisy students ranging toward the front. Alex wove her way to the last door on the right. She knocked gently and entered.

"Harrison Hall?"

"Alexandra Sinclair!" Harry beamed. He leaned back in his swivel chair with fingers laced behind his head, unabashed by the worn shirt and ill-matched tie. A college professor's outdated attire was always stylish, even an enhancement of style.

"Alex," she reminded him.

"Okay, Alex, you can call me Harry. I haven't heard Harrison since the eighth grade. Besides, it makes me sound like a college dorm—Harrison Hall."

"It's been a long time." Alex smiled.

"So you're a cop."

"Yeah, I'm a cop." She unbuttoned the jacket and pulled it open with both hands to expose the leather holster, an image that she knew was appealing—heavy leather straps cradling soft breasts, the mixture of vulnerability and power.

"Sit down. What can I do for you?"

She took the seat. "As I said on the phone, it looks like a code, and you were recommended."

Alex watched Harry take the ledger and study the first page. He was a small man. His hair and skin were dark. He had a pretty mouth, she thought, but his face was ordinary and he needed a haircut.

Papers and books littered his desktop. Shelves behind him overflowed. Magazines and other materials filled the spaces between the tops of books and the shelves above. A single window was open and unscreened, but the tiny office held a strong odor of mildew.

"This could be a code," he said. "Can you leave it with me?"

"How long? I'm not supposed to let it get away."

"Three or four days."

She gestured assent. "How do you happen to be into codes? I thought you taught English."

"It's just a hobby. I was making up codes and ciphers in high school."

"What's the difference?"

He shrugged. "Most people say *code* when they mean *cipher*. A real code is sort of old-fashioned, probably what this is."

"I remember you in high school, but you were a terrific snob." She smiled. "You never spoke."

"I sort of remember you. A few years make a big difference at that age. Seniors don't talk to freshmen." He looked at her soberly. "Did you ever get married?"

Alex shook her head, feeling that he was still the senior and she the freshman. "Did you?"

"Not yet. How did you come to be a cop?"

It was the resonant voice and half smile that made her feel inferior. *Cop* carried none of the cerebral flavor and prestige of *professor*. "It's a long story you don't want to hear," Alex said, "but I like to think I'm making a difference in the world, in this town anyway. I really need to get back." She stood. "When can I talk to you again?"

"What about Saturday over dinner?"

Alex felt herself grin. Harry had his answer. The invitation was a surprise, but she owed him.

"I'll call you, Alex."

He watched the purse strap swing over her shoulder, exposing the weapon for an instant. A quick wave and a smile. "Thanks, Harry," and she was gone.

A campus policeman was just sticking a ticket under the wiper blade as Alex reached her car. She flipped the one button, allowing the jacket fall open as she reached for the ticket. What was the point in having authority if you didn't flaunt it once in a while.

Eight P.M.

Alex checked in at the office, weary and disheartened but drawn back to her partner by corporeal resolve, either to fight or reconcile. She stood in the cubicle door and stared at him. The night sky reflected her mood. Lid's coat and tie were gone, as usual. She didn't speak, but her expression was clear: did he want anything before she left?

Lid looked even wearier than she felt. He pointed at the chair. "You want a drink?"

She took the seat but shook her head.

He poured a finger of scotch and drank it off. "I listened to the tape, and that's Wexler, all right—the only frigging thing I accomplished today. I'm sorry I'm a bastard, Alex." Not that he would change, just that he was sorry.

"Yeah, I'm sorry too," she replied.

"It's been a crummy day. I pissed you off, and Brucker pissed me off."

She gave him a real smile. "You tried to get her onto the couch and she turned you down?"

"No, not that. I'm too old to have hurt feelings, but

that shrink can get inside my head and make me feel twelve years old. I've been in a piss-ass mood all day."

"Nobody's too old to have hurt feelings."

Lid took a good look at her. "You're really a person, aren't you?"

Suddenly they were friends, Alex thought, due to an alcohol-induced softening of his mood. "Yes, I am."

"And you're really my partner."

"That's right, Lid." She waited, expecting confession or philosophy, but apparently his mind wouldn't change any more thoughts into sentences.

Lid pulled on his coat but didn't bother with the tie. They left the building together. A fine mist of rain smothered the early darkness.

Across the concrete parking lot, a white face appeared in the cheerless night air. "Sergeant Li Dao!"

They both started and clutched with unnatural alarm.

Dr. Guy Bissett stood in the rain, a wretched, desperate creature without hat or umbrella.

To Lid, at least, the pathetic face was familiar. He looked at Alex and gave a reassuring nod. "I'll see you in the morning."

"Are you sure?"

He repeated the nod.

Alex got into her maroon Toyota and drove off.

Lid hadn't eaten since breakfast. He was physically and mentally spent but would do the job a little longer for the sake of the frightened face. "You wanna come in?"

"I need a drink," Bissett said.

Not a bad idea, Lid thought.

They took both cars. Lid followed the Cadillac to a bar on Broadway. At this time of day the place would be empty and quiet.

The room had an old-fashioned pinball machine.

There was a single pool table in the back, but nobody was there. Country music played softly from a radio behind the bar. Most of the lights were hidden in the walls and reflected dimly from the ceiling. Each table had a small lamp with a shade.

They slouched into a booth. Even in the muted light Lid could see the expensive suit and silk tie. Dr. Guy Bissett was still in his forties, trim and fit. The short, dark hair was speckled with gray, but he had the look of an athlete, a jogger. Bissett wiped his hair and scalp with a napkin to remove some of the water, then pulled down his tie and loosened the collar.

The waitress came over and stood.

Lid managed a weak smile. "Scotch, rocks."

Bissett nodded.

She walked away, and they waited a silent moment.

Bissett's eyes were moist and utterly sad. His dark cheeks sagged under the eyes in a way that looked unnatural. He was too drunk to be driving, but Lid guessed that it was not his usual condition.

Bissett spoke, almost a whisper. "I want you to kill those bastards, Li Dao." He touched Lid's shoulder.

Lid cut his eyes to the hand and said nothing. He was sober, a cop again.

Bissett released the coat and glanced around the room. "I want you to kill those bastards," he repeated. "I want them all dead. The investigation, are you still in charge?"

They waited for the drinks to be served before Lid nodded once and stared at the haggard face.

"If you don't kill them, I will," Bissett said.

Lid didn't doubt it. He knew better than to reveal Prather's name, but it crossed his mind. "How long has it been?"

"Last April. They murdered Kyle last April, ran him over like a possum. They killed my wife too."

"He was your only child, wasn't he?"

Bissett nodded. "I might be able to live with Kyle gone, but they killed my wife too. She died, Li Dao. She died that day. They may as well have buried her along with him."

Guy Bissett started to cry, wiped his eyes with a napkin and gulped the scotch.

Lid wanted to commiserate but felt a lump in his chest and had nothing brilliant to say anyway. He drank the scotch instead and watched the other man tremble silently, the napkin pressed against his eyes.

Bissett eventually controlled himself, but his voice faltered through the congestion. "I would understand if she had started to drink or take drugs, but she just died. She's gone to bed. She eats very little, seldom takes a shower. Some days she doesn't even get up except to go to the bathroom. I haven't seen her dressed with makeup in almost a year." He wiped his eyes again.

Lid asked the obvious. "Have you tried professional counseling?"

"She won't go. My best friend is a psychiatrist. She won't even let him in the room."

Lid thought of Rachael Brucker but said nothing. He caught the waitress's eye and raised two fingers. Say something! he told himself. Talk about police procedure, the justice system, something! It was all inappropriate, insulting. He wanted them dead too. Lid was tired. He emptied the glass and knew he was rapidly losing the ability to say anything useful, let alone consoling. Bissett needed responsible counsel. Alcohol was a cheap escape, draining what little energy he had left and pandering to poor judgment. "I'll do it," he said at last.

"What?"

"If I find the guy who ran down your son, I'll kill him. Don't quote me on this. We're just a couple of guys having a drink."

The second drinks arrived. They both took a swig.

"It will depend on a few things."

"What things?"

"I have to know who the guy is and be alone with him. There can't be any witnesses. But if I'm sure he's the right man, I'll kill him," he stated simply, looking into the red, bleary eyes.

Bissett was half drunk but finally relaxed. "You promise?"

Lid nodded.

"You swear to God?"

"Goddammit! I said I'd kill the son of a bitch," he whispered.

They finished the drinks in silence.

"Sunday is the anniversary of Kyle's death," Bissett said at last.

"What about your wife?"

"I don't know. I don't know from one day to the next."

Lid felt again the empty desire to offer consolation. He slurped the ice cubes and ordered another.

Bissett sighed with deep resignation and pushed himself out of the booth. "I appreciate you meeting with me, Li Dao. I need to check on Anne." He wavered for a moment but held the back of the seat. "Remember your promise." The loud nasal tone had no life, only great despair.

Lid watched him pay the tab and weave to the front door, then disappear out onto the sidewalk, a man of superlative ability and stature reduced to a staggering drunk.

Bissett's behavior was unsettling. Lid might have

expected it of a woman, not a man. "I'll kill the son of a bitch," he whispered to the scotch, an absurd promise, he knew, but alcohol had that effect. Maybe neither one would remember it.

Simon Braddock might do the job if he stayed alive long enough. Lid raised his glass. Here's to Braddock. He sipped the scotch. A guy goes out to collect money, and his head comes back with a baseball in his mouth. Braddock had style.

The waitress came back to the booth. He looked up through the warm glow and shook his head. She smiled and left the tab. Lid laid money on the table, then struggled to his feet and knew immediately he was not able to drive. Alcohol worked quickly on an empty stomach. He made it to the phone booth and slumped onto the seat.

Lucille had been out of touch for months, and he didn't need a lecture from his almost ex-wife anyway. That left only Alex. He pondered the choice and dialed his partner. As he listened to the ring, it occurred to him to call a cab. He started to hang up, but the slow motion of alcohol gave the cat time to answer, then came the familiar voice.

"Alex Sinclair."

"I need you."

"What's the matter?"

"I'm drunk and I can't get home."

She smiled, but he didn't see it. "Where are you?"

"I'm at a bar on Broadway. I'm sorry, Alex. I was talking to that doctor."

"Never mind. Tell me where it is," she said, pleased to be needed.

He gave the location and hung up.

The bar was beginning to be crowded, and his booth was occupied by a young couple. He could hear the

ping of the pinball machine and the familiar clack of
billiard balls. Lid hadn't noticed the mirror behind the
bar until he glimpsed his astonished face among the
rows of bottles. It looked older than it should have, and
sadder. He had thought he was a happier person. He
paid the tab and stood at the front window to give Alex
time to get there. Two streams of water zigzagged
down the heavy plate glass and reflected the neon light.
He drifted in the pleasant haze and hoped it wouldn't
occur to Alex that he could have taken a cab.

6

Friday. One P.M.

Prather sat at his mahogany desk and glared at the envelope, cheap letterhead stationery, the kind used to make night deposits. The First Federal logo and the postmark agreed: Perry, Georgia. The printed address was drawn through, his own name and address written above with a ballpoint pen. He looked into the envelope again—two deposit receipts, different banks, different towns. For the third time he checked the names and figures, but the delicate printing would not disappear: Wallace Noles, $94,000; Asa Condon, $100,005. Condon and Noles had never seen that kind of money except on pickups. Wexler had always detested them. Maybe he was right. They had gone into business for themselves. Obie was murdered, the money gone. They had dumped the car. The shadowy specter of Dr. Simon Braddock slowly dissolved into the familiar and more likely images of his own men. The slimy little bastards had butchered his brother.

He slammed the intercom with his fist. "Max, get in here!"

The library door opened quietly; the black tails and white gloves waited dutifully before the desk.

He gave the butler a look. "Put on your work clothes."

Max was unfazed. "Yes, sir. Anyone I know?"

"Condon and Noles. I do the hit, you dump the garbage." There was no change of expression, a slight nod. Max was still his man. "The gazebo," Prather added.

The butler nodded again and left the room.

Nobody was using the telephones, but there was no need to summon Condon and Noles. They checked in once a day without being called. Willard removed a tome from one of the shelves and found the weapon he wanted, an unregistered piece, good for one use. Max would toss it. The revolver was large and bulky but, unlike automatics, it wouldn't jam—six reliable shots instead of fifteen maybes. He flipped out the cylinder and gave it a spin, then went to the bar.

It was three hours later when the chime in the hallway sounded. Max pulled open the heavy door and nodded to the familiar faces.

Condon and Noles entered, obsequious since the recent disaster, wearing jackets and ties to emphasize the fact. They stood side by side like bookends, hands clasped in front of their bodies, awaiting a command.

Prather emerged from the library wearing a bulky hunting jacket without the liner. He was drunker than he had meant to get, but sober enough. "Let's take a walk. We'll be at the gazebo," he announced.

Max gave another silent nod.

Prather, Condon, and Noles went out the front and strolled the path that led into the woods, beside a wide row of day lilies budding out. Blue sky was cluttered with tall, heavy clouds, the first humidity of summer in the air.

The jacket would soon be uncomfortably warm, but

Prather kept it zipped partway. The revolver was not cocked; the muzzle with its long silencer pointed straight toward his crotch. He had an urge to confront them with the deposit receipts, but judgment overruled the alcoholic notion. It was too great a risk. They would deny it and be on their guard. He would kill them quickly from behind.

The quiet, shaded gazebo was out of view from either house, the entrance at ground level, the far side high as the land sloped away. Prather felt a surge of supreme alertness as they stepped up onto the platform. "The gardener's landscaping the back side," he said, gesturing casually.

Noles and Condon walked across to peer over the rail.

Prather was moving with them, his eye fixed on the back of Condon's neck. His blood and adrenaline pumped. A sickening instant of uncertainty inclined against his mental preparation. He fired the weapon quickly, point-blank range.

Condon was dead. Noles had time only to start as he was hit in the side, then the chest. It was done. The ultimate insult.

The muted sound of the revolver echoed in Prather's brain. The outrage of life denied flitted for only a moment. Momentum had borne the deed. Killing was easier than he remembered. He removed his jacket, then the tie. Prather was certain now: they had killed Obie, butchered him, tortured him. He paled. Why would they have *tortured* Obie? Too late to ask.

He sat on the bench and watched flickering shades of pale and darker green as sunlight filtered through the highest tree branches. Thick clematis spiraling the gazebo posts was still beaded with rainwater. The sulfurous bite of gunpowder slowly dissipated.

Prather looked at the bodies. Asa was a hideous

corpse; Wally looked as he always did but thinner
sprawled onto the wooden floor. He studied Asa's hands,
hands that had decapitated Obie. Dead hands. The bodies
were silent, prostrate—an affirmation of guilt. Why
hadn't they dumped Obie's whole body? Using the mail
was risky and pointless, not something he would have
done himself. The cleverness of misdirection.

The gutty sound of a small engine reached him
before the tractor came into view. Max steered around
the curve and down the middle of the path, staying
clear of bulbs and azaleas on either side. He switched
off the engine.

In the abrupt silence Prather could still hear the
revolver's pop. He handed over the gun. "Get rid of
this too."

Max took the weapon and glanced at the cylinder to
see how many shots had been fired, amused perhaps
that Willard had needed three slugs to kill only two
men. Without comment, Max went about his work.
Condon was easy to drag to the trailer cart. Then came
the heavier Noles, whom Max pulled by the ankles,
bouncing the fat head from the platform to the hard-
packed ground. Max was a thoroughly profane human
being, able to traffic in murder and its attendant ills
with ease.

"Do you want them where they can't be found?" he
asked.

Prather shrugged. "Toss them in the river."

Three P.M.
Lid had deliberately come without Alex. He stood at
the counter and waited in the bright, sterile atmosphere. Soft, trifling music was the only sound except
for a distant mechanical pulse. The dental office had a
peculiar medicinal odor, not offensive but distinct. Lid

glanced at a large green and white poster: CROCODILES LIKE TO FLOSS! The cartoon creature's smile revealed an enviable set of teeth, more than a human being or the ancient reptile possessed.

Roberta walked back into view. "May I help you? Oh, you're the detective!"

"Yeah," Lid said with a phony smile. "I wondered if I could talk to the doc again."

"Have a seat. He may be on a break."

Roberta walked to her boss's office, tapped gently, and stuck her head in the door.

Simon slumped at his desk and hoped his familiar look would speak for him—*Do I look like I'm not doing anything? What?*

"The cop is back, the detective."

He rolled his eyes. "Send him in."

Roberta knew something was going on, and was enjoying it. "I could say you're fatigued."

"Fatigued?" The weary expression deepened. "Bring the guy back here, Roberta." Simon thought about her choice of words. He had been fatigued since nine o'clock that morning. Perhaps Roberta knew him better than he thought.

She returned and left Lid in the doorway.

"I'm Martin Li Dao. Did I catch you at a bad moment?"

Simon looked up. "Come in, Sergeant. It is sergeant, isn't it?"

"Yeah, but call me Lid. Everybody does." He took a seat. "Just thought I'd touch base. Anybody contact you yet?"

"No."

Li Dao ignored the room, the books, the certificates and other wall hangings, but kept his eyes on Simon. "Do you know Guy Bissett?"

"I don't think so."

Lid forged ahead. "He's a local doctor. His son, Kyle, was killed by a car about a year ago. I thought maybe you knew each other."

"I remember the incident, but I don't know the guy. Are you making any progress on the case?"

He nodded. "I could still use some outside help."

"Do you have any idea who the extortionists are?"

Lid looked hard at Simon. "Yes, we do."

"Well, who are they?"

"That's extremely confidential, Dr. Braddock."

Simon leaned back in the chair. "I understand that, but you keep coming to me for help and I don't know who we're talking about."

"You are one of the potential victims. I don't know how they missed you."

Simon spread his hands.

"What I tell you may not be repeated. If they know we're on to them, we lose everything. I don't want these murderers to walk." Lid held the eye contact and waited for Simon to nod. "One of the key figures is Willard Prather. He and his brother are gangsters—high-class hoods. He lives over on Jackson Springs Road. The brother was murdered last week. I told you about it."

Simon couldn't resist. "Who killed him?"

"I don't know. You could have killed him for all I care. Prather's uncle may be the man in charge, Heinrich Wexler, old guy who lives next door. They're all killers, and there's some woman involved. We heard Wexler talk on the phone to her. They're the leaders. We take them out, the whole thing falls apart."

Roberta tapped the door again and made another appearance. He had a phone call. Simon waved her off.

"You have his phone tapped?" Simon asked.

"Yeah, his phone and Prather's. We searched Prather's house and found a record book, but it's in a code. My partner's working on it."

"How do you know it's a code?"

"He mentioned it on the phone and mentioned a key. Kind of a silly-ass code, but we're taking it seriously. It might reveal everything if we could find the key."

Simon was falling into an old habit—trusting and naive. Marie nagged him about it, yet he knew instinctively that his immaturity and innocence served him well, as now. It became the heart of his act. He understood what Li Dao was doing. The verbal maneuvering was only play. His opponent was miles ahead, not a man to give anything away accidentally. Li Dao had come there intent on revealing information. The cop knew he had killed Obie Prather, and didn't seem to care. They could use each other as long as both maintained the facade of ignorance. This was a solo act, without sanction from higher police echelons.

Lid abruptly stood. "That's about all I know. If you get any information or theories even, pass them directly to me."

"Are you the only person working on the case?"

"Sometimes the best way to work is on your own. That's why private detectives can be effective. They don't have a chain of command."

The answer sounded evasive, and the question Simon most wanted to ask was the one thing he could never mention: how had Li Dao got on to him? He needed more information but couldn't afford to appear eager. He maneuvered the cop out the door. "What will you do if you find out who killed the Prather guy?"

Lid smiled broadly and looked him in the eye, then stared away down the street. "I won't ever find out, Dr. Braddock."

"I think you can call me Simon."

"Take care of yourself, Simon. Don't talk to any cops except me."

Simon went back inside and pulled the door closed. *Li Dao knows I'm a murderer!* The thought was exhilarating. Lid had given him everything but Prather's Social Security number. The transparent pretense was necessary, one feigning ignorance while the other leaked information in a casual but deliberate charade. They had forged an unspoken agreement Simon could only hope Li Dao would not violate.

Lid drove slowly and mused. For the second time he had virtually accused the dentist of being involved in murder. An innocent man would have reacted with violent denial, but Braddock could not be roused, a stance that evoked annoyance but no small amount of admiration. Surely Braddock understood that he was trying to help; nobody could be that naive. *You could have killed him for all I care,* Lid had stated deliberately. He had searched Braddock's eyes for that knowing glimmer, but it had never come.

Four P.M.

The cottage was only a few blocks from Heinrich Wexler's house. He tooled the Mercedes through the wrought iron entrance, down the long brick driveway under hickories and oaks that stood about the swept lawn. Tinted stucco and tile roof were pale in the late afternoon sun. They had always referred to the house as a cottage though it was large and elegant, two stories, Spanish style. Only the gardener knew the pink flamingos were the usual trappings of less pretentious homes. But these were expensive, and the effect was not as unbecoming as he had first thought, gaudy appointments made acceptable by people accustomed to having their way without challenge.

Wexler parked outside the carriage house.

His mother's personal driver stood in shirtsleeves and blew the last bits of dried polish from the Rolls-Royce with a hair dryer. The monthly wax came with the job. He was a tall black man. His name was Luther Steele, though Ilsa Wexler scarcely remembered it. She called him a nigger whether or not he was in earshot, but Luther was a modest man who accepted the affront for the sake of the job.

Wexler ignored him as he entered by the side door and moved carefully down the narrow hallway, tripping in spite of his care and cursing the clutter.

The cottage was a warehouse of boxes containing clothing, hats, shoes, jewelry, purses, and other items, most with price tags still attached. Wexler hated the house but didn't complain to his mother. The eccentricity of the ancient matriarch was never mentioned. If the servants thought it odd, they dared not say so. After so many years, even Heinrich Wexler consciously or unconsciously considered his mother's behavior normal.

His best defense had always been not to think about it. Years earlier, he had warned her of the fire hazard, but she ignored him. Since then the accumulation of things had steadily grown. He remembered when the upstairs rooms were still accessible, now occluded with storage of clothing and accessories that would never be worn. The wide stairway allowed only narrow passage to the second floor, to ghostly rooms covered almost to the ceiling with old sheets and bedspreads. Wexler had not been on the second floor in years. The living area was restricted to the ground level.

Wexler stopped in the living room and pulled back a

sheet that covered boxes behind the sofa. He wrestled a cardboard box from the row of other packages and slid it to the floor. It was not so dusty, protected over the years by the cloth cover. There was no legible marking, though he remembered the word *memorabilia* written in crayon. Wexler opened the carton and laid the books aside one at a time. Yearbooks, textbooks, ledgers. Eventually, he took up a small blue volume and brushed the cover, but the lettering was gone. He opened to the title page: U.S.N. Codes and Signals. SEAMAN HEINRICH WEXLER was written in ink.

He turned the worn pages. Memory of the assignment came into his mind, the day he had been issued the book. He had gotten his request—the signal corps. It was a thing very appealing, the secrecy, the privacy of sending messages indecipherable to all but one only, and the power of controlling others by appraisal.

The navy had not bred him to criminal conduct; rather, his own tendencies made the work enticing, almost embarrassing in his youth as the mysteries of the craft were unveiled. Radio, flags, or lights, the fascination of concealment was always there, an attraction that corrupted unaware into clandestine, underhand nature. He followed naturally into the family tradition of threats and extortion.

Wexler perused the code book for several minutes, then returned the carton to its place.

He walked silently to a den, converted into a bedroom, and peered into the warm, stale darkness. It was a small room that the extra furniture made even smaller. There were two chests of drawers, one completely inaccessible, blocked by a table and a sewing machine. A dusty sheet covered another large object. Wexler had forgotten what it was. The only other furniture was the bed and a Victrola.

The closet overflowed, the door sagging under the weight of coats and dresses that hung on the outside, but none of it could be reached. Cardboard cartons and bags filled the floor space to the corner of the room and under the bed. Access to the small bed was now from one side only. Potted plants lined the heater cover under the windows, but the faded yellow shades were drawn.

"*Mein Engel?*" came the weak query. "I always know your footsteps, Heinrich."

He approached the bed. "How are you feeling, *Mueni*?"

"I am here," replied the slow, childlike voice. "I want to shop today, but you do not come."

He held the bedpost and gazed down toward his mother, his eyes not yet accustomed to the light. She lay propped up on pillows, a long silk gown showing above the covers.

"*Mueni,* what do you need? You have everything here."

"I have no dress for Easter. Luther will take me."

"You have hundreds of dresses you've never worn," he said, though he knew it a futile objection.

"There may be one upstairs in the bedroom." A pause. "But no, the color is not right."

"Luther can take you tomorrow."

"You are *mein* only *Sohn.* Luther is a nigger." She said it with a pleasant smile. "How does it go with the Braddock child?"

"We must be careful with Braddock. My main concern is how the police knew to come after us."

"Remember what your father taught, *mein Engel*—injury as well as death to compel the herd. Injure the child. Mutilate her in some way. That will end the defiance."

"Yes, *Mueni.*"

"The dentist must be destroyed, *mein Engel*. You will see to it?"

Wexler stared at his mother and nodded. The authority behind the family business passed from one generation to the next and still resided in her frail body. He was in command, but she was the source of his will. Heinrich Wexler was aware of that bond.

"Leave the key with me, Heinrich. It serves no purpose at Willard's now that the file is out of our hands. We don't want the police to discover that also. The file is useless without the key."

"Yes, *Mueni*. That is a good thought."

"Sing to me a happy song, *mein Engel*."

Wexler turned to the Victrola and fumbled in the weak light. The wood was smooth and familiar. He gave the crank a few turns, opened the top, and placed the needle at the beginning of the 78 rpm disc. The background hiss lasted for several seconds before French horns and strings blended quietly under the tenor voice: *"Was meine Frau mir befehle, treulich sei's erfuellt!"* Wexler sang along in his pathetic tenor/soprano croon.

Ilsa Wexler superimposed her own gray harpy chant. *"O Engel, mein Engel, Luther will go with me; Luther will go . . .* Sing to me, Heinrich," she repeated.

Wexler's voice cracked again into the pitiable imitation as the recorded voice declaimed loudly: *"Ich ruf's: du sag's, und grollten mir tausend Frau Isolden!"*

The air in the room was hot and still. Dust motes floated in the late afternoon rays of sunlight. She was almost asleep when the music ended and the heavy needle repeated its noisy slide through the last groove. She cleared her throat with a gargling sound. "Disfigure the child, Heinrich."

"I will."

"And take the ferns to the outside. They get not enough sun here."

He grunted.

"Rub my chest. I still have the pain."

Wexler hesitated.

"I want it now, Heinrich!" Her voice was suddenly sharp.

Without reply Wexler took a step, sat on the edge of the bed, and placed his fingertips against the fragile sternum. He massaged up and down, slowly, gently, following the curve of ribs, careful to avoid mammary tissue. It was in these moments that he truly hated his mother. The massages were proper enough, yet he feared lest the male housekeeper suddenly enter the room. What would a hefty, virile man like Carruth think?

At that moment, Willis Carruth was watering the potted geraniums along the carriage house wall. Sunlight filtered through the old trees on the west side. He held a two-gallon can with one hand and admired the muscular bulges in his arm. Carruth was short but massive. This job he didn't mind; cooking and cleaning he detested. He also hated his title—housekeeper—but he liked the money.

Luther Steele whistled to get Carruth's attention.

The housekeeper looked around. "Are you gone, Steele?"

The black chauffeur nodded and walked over. His was a quiet, dignified presence, well suited to the post and traditional outfit. Black cap and bow tie. Steele had little desire to talk. Engaging Carruth in pleasant conversation was a daily effort. Carruth's opinions bored him, and the tight little ponytail was repulsive, an affectation he had never understood. Carruth could usually find fault or get into a scrap, but Steele had noticed that he challenged white men as well as black.

"What's he doing?" Steele asked.

"Rubbing her down."

"Is he singing to her?"

"I'm afraid so."

"You think they get in bed together sometime?"

"How the hell should I know, Steele? Crazy old Nazis! They probably march around the room together."

Steele made a final clumsy attempt. "Why don't you give her a thrill, Willis? She might like to have a man like you."

The look of revulsion was tinged with pride. "My masculinity would kill that old woman. I've hurt girls before."

Steele winced with irritation that Carruth thought the suggestion was serious. Steele watched the huge shoulders and thick neck, the tightly bound wad of hair curving back toward the nape. But he wouldn't be overly critical; black men were body builders too.

"I'll be goin' on. See you tomorrow," he offered lamely.

Carruth said nothing.

Steele got into his own car and started out, then disappeared down the brick driveway under the hardwood trees.

The sun had set when Wexler finally emerged from the kitchen side entrance and spotted Prather's car turning into the drive. The customized yellow Cadillac convertible was an antique and the only one in town. Wexler knew it was important. The nephew disliked older people in general, Ilsa Wexler in particular. She was his only living grandparent, his mother's step-mother at that. He never paid a visit.

Wexler met the younger man on the drive. They needed to talk, Prather said. The gazebo.

Wexler followed the Cadillac back down the hill into the Prather-Wexler compound and parked where the drive was closest to the gazebo. They walked through the woods without speaking, Prather impatient, Wexler deliberate. The sky was white, the air beginning to cool.

Prather waited until they were seated on the circular bench. "I had to pop Condon and Noles," he said. "They killed Obie." He handed the deposit receipts to his uncle.

Wexler squinted and groaned as he examined the slips of paper. He had no care that two men were dead, especially those two, but he abhorred needless killing. "I can't imagine Noles and Condon having the stomach for that job. How do you know they killed him?"

Prather was casual and self-assured. "Those are valid bank vouchers."

Wexler stared at the slips of paper and was silent for a time. "Where did you get these?"

"They came in the mail. Here's the envelope."

Wexler looked at it. "Where're the bodies?"

"The river."

"Max?"

Prather nodded.

"He should have buried them!" he snapped. "The cops'll be back. Are you ready for that?"

"So what are they gonna prove? They got no gun. They got nothing."

A lifetime of cynicism and hatred welled up into Wexler's delicate features. "We say that all our lives. Then one day they do prove something!" he shouted. "Then what? The risk was unnecessary. It was stupid, Willard! Stupid!"

Prather suddenly stood. "It had to be done. The bastards killed Obie. Anybody touches a hair on his head is a dead man! Obie was family. Nobody pushes me like this."

Wexler was still in a rage but didn't want it to show. "They did not kill him," he stated with cool authority.

Prather looked at his uncle.

"If they're skimming you, they don't send you the damn bank records."

"So?"

"This bank never heard of you." He tossed the receipts into the air with deliberate disdain. "They got no reason to mail you anything."

"Those deposits are real," Prather said. "Somebody set up Noles and Condon. I don't give a damn who it was."

Wexler's hatred and disgust held him in silence. He might have felt pity, but it was not his nature. His head began to throb. Eventually he spoke again. "Nobody set them up. Somebody set *you* up. The same person who made the deposits sent the receipts. Braddock set you up, Willard. Braddock used your money to get you to kill your own men. *Our* money. Nobody spends $200,000 of his own money to knock over two guys. A hell of a lot cheaper to hire it done! Condon said they had a million, and that son of a bitch dentist holds the balance of it!"

Prather stared at the wooden floor, still beaded with water from Max's recent hosing. "What should we do?"

Wexler was hoarse from yelling. "We hit the guy."

"You said we should wait."

"I don't mean Max. We smack him from out of town, no connections. I'll handle it. Braddock's begging for it. It's a goddamned entreaty." He breathed audibly and moaned and wiped his face.

"Who do you have in mind?"

"None of our gentleman friends from the city." Wexler stared blankly and nodded his head. "A man who lives in the swamp. I'll have the rest of that money," he said with conviction.

The white head continued to nod as he stood to leave. "Braddock is a dead man. The swamp rat loves to kill people. He'll kill the child and the wife too."

7

Saturday. 6:30 A.M.

Simon slept lightly between dreams and often woke to consider his actions with fear and amazement. Through the half awareness of slumber, the horror of who and what he was rose up to invade his mind. A week had passed, incredibly. Nothing had happened. This was Saturday, two days since Marie had mentioned going to Charleston and he had encouraged her to do so. When would she leave? A weekend was not long enough to make the trip worthwhile unless she kept Esther out of school for a day or two. Spring holidays were coming up, but that was another week.

He sighed aloud, then looked at Marie and hoped she hadn't heard the sound. Asking about the trip should have been an easy thing, yet he knew it would cause suspicion. She would read something into the simplest query.

Simon suddenly had the urge to wake Marie and admit the whole deadly business, to get them out of town immediately. He touched her shoulder and looked at her face, the disheveled hair draping across her cheek. At his touch she turned slightly and brushed her fingertips over her mouth to remove the blond strand.

He withdrew, poised on the edge of confession. All confidence waned as he realized how ludicrous, how utterly painful and grievous such a confession would be. He settled back into his pillow.

6:45 A.M.

Alex felt a handful of soft fur as she groped for the telephone. "I've got it, Marvin . . . Yeah?"

"Alex, there're a couple of stiffs at the morgue we need to check out."

Silence.

She squinted at the clock and waited for her mind to catch up to her heart. "Hello, Lid. Yes, I'm fine."

"I'm sorry. Did I wake you again?"

She made a loud groan and stretched gloriously against the cotton gown. Lid could wait while she moaned her blood and muscles back into action. "People shouldn't die on Saturday morning."

"They died yesterday, but they had some help."

"Why us?"

"The fibbies have already ID'd them from prints. One guy is named Condon."

She was suddenly awake. "Condon? Okay, give me a few minutes."

Alex hung up with Marvin's assistance. The cat continued to spar with the telephone as she headed for the bathroom.

Twenty-seven minutes later, Alex entered the city morgue, wearing her Saturday attire—faded jeans and stretchy shirt, a white jacket slung over one shoulder. Her hair bounced in its usual perky manner, but her face was still puffy around the eyes.

Lid was waiting.

"Have you seen them?" she asked.

"No, the odor of that place closes my sinuses."

They passed through the last set of double doors into the bright, cold room. Country music blared from a radio. The lone technician looked up as Lid flashed his badge.

"Morning! I'm Li Dao, this is Sinclair," he shouted over the din. "Could we see the stiffs who were brought in last night?"

The young man turned down the music. "A couple of feds have already been by."

"Yeah, I'll bet."

The lab coat walked to the row of stainless steel tables and pulled back the plastic covers. "They look pretty good. Couldn't have been in the water long. A fisherman found them."

Good was a relative term, Alex thought, especially coming from a keeper of the morgue. She had seen dead bodies before and tried to remain expressionless as she stared at the faces. It was not necessary to touch the corpses to know that the tissue was cold, heavy, and dense. Her gaze was drawn to the fixed stare and the jagged, gaping hole between eyebrows and hairline.

"Where were they?" Lid asked.

"South of town, just off I-16 near Swift Creek."

Lid took a long look at each face. "Which one is Condon?"

"That one. The one with the bullet hole coming out his forehead. Shot at point-blank range from behind. Through and through. No slugs, no weapon. Large-caliber. The other guy took two to the body." He flipped the cover back to the knees so the tourists could appreciate the bloated torso and bullet wounds. Alex had seen enough.

Lid looked at his partner. "You know him?"

She shook her head. "Neither one."

"What are their names?" Lid asked.

The technician had to look at the tags again. "Asa

Condon and Wallace Noles. The feds have files on both of them."

"Condon and Noles," Lid mused. He raised his eyebrows, but Alex shook her head again. The names didn't mean anything to her either.

Lid looked at the man in the white lab coat. "When were the bodies found?"

"Eight o'clock last night. They were shot middle of the afternoon."

"Okay, thanks. How do you stand this odor?"

"You get used to it." He smirked.

"It's freezing in here."

"You get used to that too." He covered the bodies again and went back to the radio. "The doc'll rip 'em open this afternoon," he yelled. "Come by any time. It's a real mess."

Lid gave a lame smile as they retreated to escape the odor and the loud music.

Lieutenant Pratt Mimbs was waiting as they entered the squad room, deserted on Saturday morning. Lid's superior was younger than he, but one of few men in the department for whom he had unqualified respect. Mimbs was small and sinewy, pound for pound the strongest man on the force. His features were sharp and his clothes were sharp. He always wore the same outfit, tight suits and narrow ties.

Lid knew what he was there for. "You working today?"

Mimbs ignored the question. "You been to the morgue?"

"Yeah."

"You or Alex know those guys?"

"I'm afraid not."

Mimbs stuffed out a cigarette and sighed through the

last of the smoke. "It belongs to the fibbies, Lid, and they don't want any help."

He waited, but Lid showed no reaction.

"I know it's been your case for a year and Dr. Murray was a friend, but that's the way it is." Another pause. "Goddammit, Lid. Don't get your ass in a sling and expect me to bail you out."

"What did I say? It belongs to the fibbies. Fine."

"Yeah, I hear you, but I don't believe you. All those files belong to Colish and Presnell as of Monday morning. You got that?"

"Got it."

"Alex?" Mimbs demanded as he lit another cigarette. She shrugged.

"And all that material you got on the search. You'll have to turn that over too."

Lid squinted one eye and made a sound.

"Look, Lid, I know it's been a dead end. Bodies and dicks start turning up, the fibbies are interested again. Big case makes them look good in Washington."

From the first time Alex had seen Mimbs, she thought he belonged in a zoot suit—dark, slick hair, tiny pointed mustache. His small, muscular physique would look right in the thigh-length jacket with wide, padded shoulders, baggy trousers tapering to narrow cuffs. She wanted to tell him so but wasn't sure how he would take it. Alex enjoyed the verbal sparring, the image of Lid's six-foot-plus physique towering over the lieutenant.

"Alex, you're responsible for him," Mimbs said, jabbing a finger as he turned to leave.

Lid sat at his desk and waited until Mimbs was gone. "What about that code book?"

"Harry Hall has it. I'm having dinner with him tonight. I'll get it back."

"Find out everything he knows."

She raised her eyebrows. "I thought we were off the case."

"What I do on my time is my business."

Alex recognized the tone. "I'll help if I can, but I don't want Mimbs on my neck. He likes you, but he doesn't even know me. He could get me kicked off the force for interference."

He flicked at her concern. "I'll handle Mimbs's wiry little ass."

"Have you known him long?"

"Five or six years. He does his job and avoids red tape. He likes short reports, so everybody likes him."

"He seems pretty straight to me."

"Just the company line. He'll back us up if we need it."

Alex was pleased, yet apprehensive, to hear her partner say *we* for the first time. The one word projected a plethora of images, a entire future of time and events endured together, creating an unstated but shared reliance, powerful, invisible, like something between husband and wife. Partners should have that.

Eleven-thirty A.M.

Tubby Milken pulled the rattlesnake back with his hand each time it attempted to crawl away. Finally, the animal assumed the traditional deadly coil and vibrated its tail. Tubby smiled and extended the machete until the snake flung its body in a blur, making a dull thud as the fangs struck the flat metal.

"Hoo, I bet that hurt." He placed the heavy boot atop the reptile's head and chopped it off with a single blow. The six-foot body continued to writhe. Diamondback for supper. He leaned against the pickup truck and watched the snake.

The sun was high, but Okefenokee heat and

humidity would not be oppressive for another six weeks. Tubby wore nothing but overalls and high boots. The single garment stretched over his short three-hundred-pound frame, exposing fat shoulders and upper arms. His face was pudgy, his eyes vacant. He spat a stream of tobacco juice toward the snake's head and wiped his mouth.

The affable warmth and solitude were hypnotic. Tubby lay on the warm sand in the shadow of his truck, shading his eyes with his arm. Sleep unexpectedly prevailed. After a time he woke but dozed again unconcerned and didn't hear the car approach or the door close.

The stranger looked at the fat body and hoped this was the right man. He noted the rise and fall of his chest and knew the man had killed the snake, not the other way around. Tubby was not a pretty sight, a beached whale with tobacco juice running down his cheek onto the sandy earth. One testicle bulged through a hole worn in the overalls. The stranger picked up a slender pine twig and gently probed the testicle until Tubby roused and grabbed his crotch.

"You're about to lose something, aren't you?"

Tubby squinted at the light and sat up.

"Are you Tubby Milken?"

"I might be." He got up and sat on the tailgate but didn't brush himself off. "Do you work for the gub'-ment?"

"Not likely. I got a job for you."

Tubby looked at the other man, the clean, neat appearance, the shortsleeve shirt and dark glasses. "You from town, ain't you?"

"It doesn't matter where I'm from. I've got a job for you. Ten thousand dollars. Half now, half when it's done."

"What's the job?"

"There's a guy in Macon who needs to get dead."

"Does he work for the government?"

"No. What difference does it make?"

"I don't kill no feds. I ain't saying I ever killed anybody, but I don't kill no fed."

The stranger noticed the dull expression. "He's not a fed."

"Who you work for?"

"You know better than that. You don't know me or who hired me or who hired him."

"And I'm supposed to trust you? I trust that snake, but I don't even know who you are."

"This is who I am." He extended a white envelope. Tubby stared at it for a moment and licked his lips, then took the packet, tore it open, and looked at the thick stack of bills.

"I give you a name, an address, and a map. You kill this guy or his wife or kid, or all three. I meet you here a week from today and you get the other half, but at least one of these people has to die."

"You said the guy needed to get dead."

"Not necessarily. Kill any one of them and you get paid."

Tubby spat and wiped his chin. "Ten thousand dollars ain't much. Fifteen would be more like it."

The stranger hesitated for only a moment, then nodded in agreement. "Fifteen.

Tubby looked into the envelope, gave a scowl and wiped his chin again. "That means you owe me seb'm and a half today."

"That's all I've got. Five now, ten next week. Here's a city map with the name and address. It's all marked."

Tubby took the map but didn't look at it. "All I

need's the address. I always know where I am. I bet you don't know where you are right now."

"I think I do."

"This here's Florida." He grinned and spat tobacco juice. "See that big water oak? You git on the other side of that, you're back in Georgy!" Tubby was extravagantly pleased with himself. "I knew you didn't know where you were."

"I guess you're right," the other man said, forcing a smile. "I'll meet you here one week from today, same time, same place." He looked at his watch.

"Ten thousand dollars," Tubby reminded him.

"Ten thousand dollars. Don't play with us, Tubby. Do the job or you'll be next on their list."

He got back into the car, closed the door, and clicked the seat belt into its slot, all with a deliberation Tubby found comical.

"Don't you play with *me*, Mr. Georgy tag, or I'll know where to find you!"

Tubby watched the sedan move away through shaded black water until the sandy trail disappeared among moss-laden cypress trees.

As far as Alex was concerned, the relationship with Harry Hall was strictly business. She hadn't thought about him in a physical way. He called Saturday at lunchtime. She should dress casually. They would spend the evening at his apartment. He would prepare the dinner. It sounded like a tired line, but she was a cop and had a gun. She could handle Harry.

He picked her up at seven.

Alex immediately noted the clothes again. Harry was wearing beige cotton pants that had never felt an iron and a shirt that could only be described as faded tan. He held the car door, which didn't surprise her. He would be unaware of women's lib. The old Pontiac looked a wreck but ran well, and he was a deliberate driver. She made mental notes: Harry was not impressed by clothes or cars.

He drove northwest on Mulberry Street beside the white profusion of Yoshino cherries in the median, up the long slope of Georgia Avenue to College Street. College ran along a high ridge of land, at one time the finest residential area of Macon. The huge old houses were no longer single-family dwellings. The yards were deep and ivy-covered, the front walks excessively wide. They passed the Massee Apartments at the crest of the ridge, a tall, ancient landmark among stately mansions.

Alex commented with surprise when he finally pulled to the curb. It was a more fashionable neighborhood than where she lived. He had only a couple of rooms, he told her.

They climbed brick steps to the yard level, then strolled the long front walk and mounted marble steps to the porch. Tall columns supported a high roof on three sides over the polished marble porch, all part of the antebellum style. The stone floor extended into the vestibule and under the molded pediment and double doors of his apartment entryway. Two rounded marble steps led down into the main room, an elegant dwelling in its day, now rental property.

Under a high ceiling hung unframed oils, watercolors, and posters in pleasant disorder. The carpet was peach-colored—a hippie pad, Alex thought. She noted the table set with china and crystal. Harry was gay. She was having dinner with a gay hippie. Not that it mattered; now he wouldn't make passes.

"May I take your gun?" He laughed. "I've never said that to a girl before."

She dropped her jacket and the leather harness on a chair.

Harry punched at his stereo and walked toward the kitchen. "Would you like some wine?"

Alex smiled and made a sound, then settled onto a couch as unfamiliar vocal music suddenly cascaded from the speakers. She gazed about. The wall on either side of the entrance was concealed by tall shelves. Books and LP's covered the length of the room. A heavy oak table butted against one of metal and Formica, both supporting lamps and covered with books and maps. In the center of the room stood two telescopes and another instrument she couldn't identify.

He returned with the wine.

"Are you redecorating?" she asked.

"No, this is the way it looks."

Alex didn't hide her smile. "What's the weird music?"

"Fifteenth-century French. Would you rather hear something else?"

She shrugged.

Harry punched other buttons, calling up Tijuana Brass.

At least he was up to the sixties. "Who's your favorite composer?" she asked to make conversation.

He grinned. "Mozart's first, Schubert's a distant second, and everybody else is way back in third."

Alex didn't know enough to argue. She hadn't requested a discourse, but he rambled on about musical style. She enjoyed watching him. Harry's face brightened when he spoke, in a way that told her he was in love with life and couldn't be insulted by her opinions. She guessed that he was earthy, one of those characters who hiked and canoed and got excited looking at rocks.

He would be at home in any company, a thing she envied without understanding.

Harry removed the top from an ottoman and took up Willard Prather's ledger. "I haven't had as much time as I need with the code. I kept it there so I wouldn't lose it." He set a wet beer can on the coffee table and slouched beside her. "This is definitely a code, but it will take time to break with such a small sample."

"You've got a whole book of it."

"Yes, but it's not conversation. I think this is record keeping. Each page may be a different account indicated by the first word. The other words are probably numbers and dates."

"You mentioned a cipher."

"A cipher uses substitution. *A* could be *B*, *B* could be *X*. A code uses words and symbols to represent other words or phrases. *Sky* could mean *chair*, *Monday* could mean *kangaroo*. It's a primitive technique but difficult to crack. A single short message in a code would be impossible to break."

"It seems rather childish. What ever happened to computers?"

"Computers can be accessed. A homemade code might be safer. This one is tough. I like to experiment with position codes. Eric Greindl and I have a running dialogue going about the English department." Harry rolled up a magazine to demonstrate. "The Spartan army generals used them. They wrote the message on a long, narrow strip of parchment wrapped around a cylinder. The person at the other end needed a cylinder of the same diameter to understand the message."

Alex was suddenly attracted, charmed by the deep, clear voice. Harry was articulate and had compelling interests. He sounded like a teacher, fascinated by the physical world but above man-made vogues superimposed on that world. It was easy for her to imagine that he endeared himself to college students, especially those with any artistic sensibility.

"Will you be able to break the code?"

Harry got up and walked back to the kitchen. "Perhaps. Shall I keep working at it?"

"Keep it as long as you like," she said, to her own surprise. The book belonged to the fibbies as of Monday morning. Lid's insolent attitude was rubbing off.

She sipped the white wine and looked about his apartment with admiration and amusement. A computer sat atop a workbench along with seedlings under fluorescent light. A box kite dangled and turned slowly in the window, a delicate mobile at the end of its fragile line. At one end of the dinner table was an antique wooden bowl heaped with potatoes and onions.

She watched him over the countertop. Harry's skin and hair were dark. He was small in frame but of average height. He still needed a haircut. Preparing dinner appeared to please him, a simple act that his hands remembered and esteemed.

She had drunk three glasses of wine by the time he brought in the plates of food. Alex didn't recognize anything except the roll. She wouldn't ask but savored each mouthful and continued to sip the wine. Her own knowledge of culinary art extended only as far as frozen food and microwave. Harry was a chef—good husband material. Maybe he wasn't gay.

He finished ahead of her and walked back to the kitchen.

Alex felt euphoric and pleasantly useless. "Now what?"

"Dessert on the roof."

She smiled but said nothing. Harry was fun. She

enjoyed being entertained without the old facade of dating.

He came in again holding two plastic glasses with tops. She would carry the desserts; he would get the chairs. She followed him into the marble hallway, upstairs, out onto a flat roof through wide French windows. Harry positioned the chaise longues to his satisfaction and took one of the desserts.

"Lie on that," he said.

"Flat?"

"Yes, flat."

Alex smiled in the cool darkness and did as she was told, keeping the glass upright.

"Just sip the straw once in a while." He settled onto the other chair.

"What are we doing?"

"We're looking at stars."

It seemed a silly thing, something she and Margo might have done. She looked into the sky and fumbled to find the corner of her mouth with the straw. "What is this stuff?"

"It's called *strawberry thing*. I invented it one night when I was really drunk, out of everything except strawberries and rum."

"This is more than strawberries and rum."

"Whatever is on hand—sugar, vodka, ice cream, vanilla."

"You're trying to ply me with liquor."

His words were open and flowed without any disjoining of thought. "Yes, I probably am. I like to look into space to keep a perspective. The Earth is a very small place."

Alex could hear his voice but saw only the starry night. She sipped the cold, sweet liquid and gazed into the magic sky, which brightened as the silence stretched into minutes. Somewhere a dog barked, far below and out of sight. She was still tipsy, giddy. The old *strawberry thing and stargazing* trick.

Harry finally spoke again. "See the big star low in the west? That's a red giant. If that star were where our sun is, its outer surface would reach beyond Mars."

"A fat star," she said and immediately regretted the trifling remark. The truth was, she had never looked at the sky like this.

Harry began to point out stars and have her repeat the names: Sirius. Betelgeuse. Rigel. Aldebaran. Alcor. Could she see Alcor? She could. They lay together in the vast blackness, finding new stars each moment as their eyes grew accustomed to the night. The galaxy was a miracle, the Earth, a speck of cosmic dust. How many galaxies were there? Billions. The resonant voice told of sailors and sextants and myths—mysterious ancient lost art.

Time slipped away in the private lecture. Harry was a rare individual, captivated by the infinite, unrestricted by the petty. His manner exuded a sweetness she could sense, joyful and unrestrained. Harry would be great in bed.

The dessert was finished long before she felt a chill and commented on it. It was a struggle to gain their feet, weak and unsteady from the sudden exertion and the alcohol. Eventually they made it inside to the bright hallway, then grappled with the chairs and stumbled and giggled down the massive stairway. Alex saw a figure in the corner of her eye.

"Good evening, Mrs. Morris!" Harry boomed, deliberately effusive.

"Mr. Hall," came the curt reply.

Alex detected the disapproval. Mrs. Morris had witnessed other women and other whiskey on the roof.

They closed themselves safely behind the apartment door. The room still held the warm, pleasing aroma of baked bread. Alex excused herself to the bathroom.

As she returned, Harry stood in the large, darkened space and focused a projector. "Sit here and relax and drink this." He settled her onto the sofa with a hot, heavy mug and sat beside her on the carpet.

"What are we drinking now?"

"I don't know. It's warm and creamy and chocolate, Irish whiskey."

"You're trying to get me drunk and fat."

"We're already drunk. Just watch this. You'll enjoy it." He clicked the first slide.

Alex recognized Allen Marker High School, no longer there, burned to the ground by one of their upstanding classmates. "The old alma mater. Where did you get that?"

"I made it. I've shot thousands of pictures all over the world." He clicked and paused.

"That's me! How did you get that?" Alex was startled but agreeably surprised at the oversize image, brightly colored against the white wall. "I used to sit on that bench and read."

Harry studied the slide. "Pretty good composition. It made a nice picture because you didn't look up. I didn't know who you were then."

The clicker continued to sound through the fan's steady whir—football games, parades, dances. Alex slurped the hot, creamy whiskey and watched the images click past, increasingly aware that she was enjoying his company. Harry was educated but unpolished, a happy combination. She glanced at him furtively in the projector light and tried to justify her thoughts. Harry needed a shave and a haircut, but thick, dark hair always grew rapidly. He had no interest

in clothes. At least they were clean clothes. She
became drowsy and lustful. Harry was better-looking
than she had first thought. His nose turned up slightly
at the tip, not a classic profile, and his skin possessed a
dusky, Mediterranean cast to which she had an instinc-
tive aversion. Still, there was the beautiful mouth, that
mouth which spoke of other worlds with such elo-
quence. Alex suddenly wanted to kiss his mouth, to
feel the full lips around her tongue, to satisfy his desire
to savor the universe.

It was hours later when she moaned slightly and
turned her body, then felt the afghan over her shoulders. Alex panicked and strained to see in the darkness.
She breathed heavily but finally remembered where
she was. The silence was deadly, still, a house asleep.
How much time had elapsed?

Harry pulled himself up out of his chair and knelt
beside the sofa.

"Harry?"

"Yes, you went to sleep on me." His voice was still
clear and even.

"What time is it?" she garbled.

"About one o'clock. I was afraid to go to bed. You
might have waked up and not known where you were."

"I knew you were trying to get me drunk."

Harry gazed into the clear blue eyes now black in the
shadowy stillness. "I do want you, Alex, but only if you
want me back," he whispered. He waited through a long
moment of silence, then leaned over and gently kissed her
cheeks and mouth. There was still an instant of uncertainty before she took his face in her hands and Harry felt
the ancient joy of acceptance. The delicious ritual began.

It was late Sunday afternoon when Alex returned to
her apartment. Marvin needed to be fed. The weather

was warm and clear. She opened the tall windows and back door to let in outside air. The phone rang, but the cat was eating and wouldn't be bothered.

"Alex Sinclair."

"I've never had a cop before," came the opening words.

She smiled. "I've never been had by an English teacher."

There was a pause as they both gave a moment of respect to the comic remarks.

"I love you, Alex."

"I love you too!" she heard herself say. "At least I think I do. Give me time to breathe, Harry!"

"I'll give you time. Can I see you tonight?"

"No! Call me tomorrow."

Harry wouldn't push it. "Okay, I'll see you tomorrow." He made a kiss sound and hung up.

Alex looked at her companion. "I got nailed by a hippie English teacher." Marvin appeared to consider the remark, then began licking himself. "Something like that," she said.

Alex thought about her statement, suddenly ashamed even in front of the cat. It was nothing like that. Harry was wonderful, magnificent—hackneyed words, but words that would have to do. She was in love. Saying the word aloud to him for the first time seemed to awaken, so gently, some deep, tender place. Alex had already tried to persuade herself that Harry was a lusty, joyful interlude, and timely at this low point of her life. But it was too late to call it anything but love, that exuberant, obsessive piling up of feeling for another human being, and measuring all things freshly and with devotion through the eyes and spirit of that person. If it was not love, the feeling itself would be an embarrassment. She wouldn't even consider their life together, not yet, but savored the thoughts for the moment, to hold in some private place. Harry had happened so quickly. Margo would be surprised and pleased. Her baby sister had snared a man, a wonderful, warm, intelligent man, a college professor.

The telephone rang again. "Harry, you horny devil," she said, then picked up the phone from the wall. "Alex Sinclair."

"Alex! Where the hell have you been? I've been calling all day."

"This is Sunday, Lid. Didn't you go to church?"

"Well, I called a couple of times, then after a while I wanted to make sure you were okay. Where were you?"

"I was on a date."

"All day?"

"It started last night."

"A twenty-four-hour date?"

"Almost."

"With the code guy?"

"Yes, with the code guy."

"You're dedicated. Did you get the book?"

"Not yet."

"You didn't get the damn book? What were y'all doing?"

"I was *with* the guy, Lid. Okay?"

He chuckled. "I'm glad one of us is with somebody."

"What did you want?"

"I had to make an unpleasant trip, and I wanted you along because I never know how to act and women are usually good at it."

"What?"

"You remember the doctor, Guy Bissett?"

"Yeah . . ."

"His wife committed suicide this morning."

Alex tried to speak, but her eyes welled with tears and her throat tightened. She wanted to be a hard-nosed cop, but it didn't work. "How?"

"Some kind of pills."

"I'm sorry, Lid. I'm sorry I wasn't with you. I know how awkward that is; anything you say sounds stupid. Did you go over there by yourself?"

"Yeah. I didn't have to go at all, but I went. Anyway, that's all I wanted."

"How's Bissett doing?" she asked.

"How do you think?"

There was a pause. "Are you okay?"

"Sure."

"Have you been drinking?"

"Nope."

Alex paused again. She ached for Guy Bissett, a man she had never met, but no words of comfort would come to mind. "Thanks, Lid," she said warmly. "Thank you for checking on me. I'll see you in the morning."

Lid grunted something and hung up.

Alex got up to hang the phone and sat again at the kitchen table, suddenly very tired. The white curtain blew gently against her shoulder, a consoling gesture from God or the breeze or whomever. The sound and feel were pleasant, but she was not the one who needed it. She pictured Guy Bissett alone with Martin Li Dao, all the engines of his compassion producing only clumsy condolence. *I'm sorry we couldn't find your son's murderer sooner, or maybe your wife would still be alive.* Judge Gaston was right: Lid was a good man. At least he tried. She had probably been having her third orgasm that beautiful Palm Sunday morning as Anne Bissett drugged herself into death. She had not met Dr. Bissett or his wife. Maybe she should've called, tried to make friends, maybe introduced Anne

Bissett to Dr. Brucker on some pretext. Maybe there wasn't a damn thing she could have done. Alex was overwhelmed. Life was too much. She couldn't defend and protect each pitiful creature involved, in whatever way, with the Macon Police Department. She wondered, not for the first time, why she had become a cop, then made the same silent admission: girls who married doctors and lawyers were debutantes straight out of high school. Her family hadn't had the money or position, and, she thought with honesty, she had lacked the interest. Her friends who worked in banks hated it, and her days of waiting tables were years in the past. The matter settled in her mind again. She liked her job but deserved some time of her own. She had the right to fall in love.

Marvin wrapped his tail around her leg and made a clear chirruping request. Alex got up and let him out the door.

8

Monday. Two-thirty P.M.

Lid could see that the FBI taking over the extortion case had advantages. Neither the mayor nor the D.A. had called him, and Romano wasn't ragging on him about what a sorry cop he was. It was a relief to put Bruce Murray out of his thoughts for the moment and concentrate on other cases, to see things fall into place, and to remind himself that he was a good cop after all.

Mimbs would have his head if he knew his sergeant was keeping silent about a vigilante, but Lid was relaxed. Nobody else had discovered Braddock. Now it was the fibbies' case, no longer his responsibility. Alex was the only problem. Give her time, he thought. She'd be jaded and cynical soon enough.

He had expected the fibbies to be waiting at his office first thing, but it was the middle of the afternoon when Presnell and Colish arrived. Presnell nodded with deliberate civility.

"Li Dao, we need everything you've collected on the extortion case."

Lid's relationship with the FBI was a pretense of amity at best. He pointed at the files on the floor and sat at his desk as Colish and Presnell toted off the stacks of folders.

Presnell reentered the office mopping his brow. He had finally removed his coat.

"I thought you guys didn't sweat," Lid said.

Presnell ignored the crack. "Mimbs said you didn't know the two dead men. Is that correct?"

"That's right. Alex hadn't seen them either. The feds know anything?"

"We know they died rich. The day before they bought it, somebody made cash deposits for both of them, two different banks, around $100,000 each."

"How do you know that?"

Presnell's smile was contemptuous. "We knew immediately. Bank down in Perry, one over in Dublin. Banks have to inform the IRS of large cash transactions. Drug dealers."

Lid could live with the insult. "Who made the deposits?"

"Not the two dead guys."

"Who?"

"The same man made both deposits. He was tall and blond, had a mustache, used false ID's."

"Lots of luck."

"It's not luck; it's hard work." Presnell left the cubicle.

Lid stifled a smile. Braddock had used the bagman's take to sow destruction in the extortionists' ranks.

Alex came in, animated and bright, glowing, Lid thought. She took the seat and tipped her chin into her shoulder, admiring the short, unpolished nails. "I think I'm in love!"

Lid stared through the statement. "Have you heard about the deposits of money for Condon and Noles?"

She was offended, not surprised. "Colish told me. Did you hear what I just said?"

"You may be in love? Crap." He turned to the window and sighed. "That's all I need to hear on Monday."

"Don't be a grouch just because I had a better weekend than you did."

She was right and Lid knew it. He looked at her with a pained expression. "Everybody likes to get laid, Alex, but when you fall in love, you get married. Then you quit your job."

He was a small boy railing against the inequities of life, and he had just given himself away. "You like me, don't you?" she asked.

"Maybe I do."

"Don't worry. He doesn't make enough for me to quit working."

"Who is the guy?"

"Harry Hall," she said.

The name didn't register. "Did he tell you anything about the code?"

"Not really."

"That's right, you were in the sack the whole time."

She grinned. "He needs more time to work on it. He did say it contained bookkeeping like you thought, dates and amounts."

"Let him keep the thing until Presnell screams. He won't miss it for a while. What do you think about the bank deposits for the dead guys?"

"They were set up."

"Who did it?"

"Braddock," she said.

Lid waited but Alex said nothing more. "How do you figure that?"

"The same as you do. The same way the fibbies will."

He looked doubtful. "We only made the connection with Braddock from the one phone call—'the guy on second.'"

"Lid, I know you don't like the feds, but they're not stupid. They'll figure it out just like we did. And they won't hold back. They'll be over there tomorrow with a search warrant, maybe an arrest warrant. I think your buddy Braddock is in trouble."

"Why is he my buddy?"

"I can tell you like him. Braddock may have Wexler believing Condon and Noles killed Obie Prather, which would mean Wexler killed both of them. Braddock may take the heat off himself from Wexler, but he won't fool the feds."

"Hard for me to believe he could fool Wexler."

She frowned. "We've got an elaborate scenario based on flimsy evidence, and we could be wrong. Braddock may have nothing to do with this."

Lid frowned back. "Look, I talked to the guy again Friday. We might be wrong, but I don't think we are, and I'll tell you something else. If Wexler was fooled, he won't stay fooled for long. He'll put it together before the fibbies do. You may be right. Braddock could be in way over his head."

Lid got up and grabbed his coat.

"Where are you going?"

"To see that crazy damned dentist."

"You want me to come?"

He shook his head on the way out. "Let me do this alone."

"Don't get in trouble!" she called. Don't get *us* in trouble was what she meant. Alex smiled to herself. Her partner liked her. Lid would never admit it, even to himself, but he liked her. She would take her compliments any way she could get them.

Roberta recognized Lid immediately. "Have a seat," she said. "I'll let him know you're here."

The smell of the office was becoming familiar. Lid sat in the reception room along with an old man and a kid with a swollen face who sat close to his mother. She kept her arm around him. The kid clutched his mother's skirt with a subdued look of pain and fear. The old man was empathetic, but the child kept his eyes averted.

After a few minutes, Roberta came in and escorted Lid back to Dr. Braddock's private office to wait. He took his usual seat.

The paneled walls displayed the doctor's various degrees and licenses in small black frames. Latin to confuse the enemy. Pictures of his wife and daughter sat on a shelf along with medical textbooks and catalogs.

Simon suddenly entered in surgical garb, peeling off rubber gloves. "Lid? What do you need?"

Lid was equally abrupt. "There've been some developments. I'm off the case; the FBI has taken it over. Two men were found murdered, shot. One had worked for Prather. We got his name from the phone tap—Condon, Asa Condon. The other guy was Wallace Noles. Anyhow, they were probably killed by their own people. Their bank accounts were too fat to suit Wexler and Prather, but it won't take them long to figure out what's going on with the money."

Lid paused but didn't bother to ask if anything sounded familiar. He knew the answer—the innocent look, the head shake.

Simon maintained his poise but wondered if he had failed again. "Lid, slow down. You're off the case?"

"Right."

"Two men were murdered?"

"Right. And whatever I've figured out, the feds will figure out." He looked hard at Braddock. "They play by the book, Simon. You know what I mean?"

Simon nodded.

"I was hoping we would break the code by now," Lid added.

"What about the key? You mentioned a key."

"Yeah, there's a key, but we don't know where it is."

"Where did you find the book with the code?"

"Prather's house. Look, Simon, you and I can be direct, right?"

"Right."

Lid nodded at the pictures. "Is that your wife and daughter?"

"Yes."

"Take a trip," he said quietly. "Get your family and get out of town for a week or two. Take a vacation. Give the feds a chance to crack this case."

"You've worked on it a year, and you haven't cracked it."

"They've got more manpower, more funds. I don't always like the feds, but they get things done."

The meeting was awkward for Simon, conversation that itself amounted to a confession.

A tap came at the door. Roberta. "There're some men here." She made a face. "FBI."

Simon was composed. "Put them in the waiting room."

Roberta's frightened brown eyes widened as she shook her head. "They don't want to go to the waiting room; they want to see you. One has a search warrant and no sense of humor. They seem awfully serious."

Lid moaned. "They'll say I'm interfering."

"You can leave by the back door," Simon said.

"They've already seen my car."

"You can be a patient. We'll be in surgery."

"What?"

"Roberta, go tell them I'm in surgery. Bring a blank chart and fill it out on Li Dao. Get him to sign it and write up some past appointments, prophy and stuff. Send Julie back."

Roberta left.

"Come on, Lid. Let's get you in the chair."

Lid didn't like what was happening but followed Simon into a treatment room and lay back on the heavy rounded seat. The fibbies were acting sooner than he had expected. "Are you sure this will work?"

"Shut up and open your mouth."

He could only obey as Simon unceremoniously entered his mouth with a long silver instrument. He felt the needle prick, then pressure from the lidocaine.

Julie entered, identical to Roberta in the peach skirt and white blouse.

"Get his coat and put a bib on him," Simon said.

Julie did as she was told, working silently, efficiently. She snapped gloves over her doctor's hands.

Roberta came into the cubicle and held a form in front of Lid's face. "Sign at the bottom."

Lid scribbled his name and immediately heard the electric motor powering the chair back into position. The overhead light came on. His jaw and tongue were beginning to numb. He felt a cloth cover being laid over his chest, and hoped Simon knew what he was doing.

Simon rolled his stool up under the dental chair and looked around at Roberta. "Are the feds happy?"

"No, they're not! They didn't seem to believe me. I

told them they'd have to stay there, but I don't know if they will."

Simon pulled up his mask and went back to the patient. "Lid, do you feel that?"

"No."

Lid watched fingers move in and out of his mouth but felt only pressure and heard the constant suction. Then he heard Roberta speak behind him.

"I told you not to come in here! Dr. Braddock is in surgery."

"Nice try, sugar. I know Li Dao, even the top of his flat head." Presnell's loud voice and large frame dominated the room as he walked around the side of the chair to get a head-on view. His suit and tie were out of place beside the dentist and assistant, who were gowned and gloved, and the patient, who was draped.

The flap procedure was only minor surgery, but it didn't appear so to Presnell: two vertical incisions through the buccal mucosa, gingiva pushed deeply into the vestibule, exposing a section of mandibular bone, the white plastic tip dipping adroitly to suction blood.

Braddock spoke through the mask. "I hope you're sterile, you son of a bitch! Roberta. Call the police and call my lawyer."

Presnell turned pale and backed against the wall.

"Never mind. Get him out of here. I can't stop what I'm doing to deal with a fainter."

Roberta and Colish helped Presnell out of the small room.

Lid was wide-eyed. "'hat did you do to 'e?"

Simon was smiling behind the mask. "Not a damn thing. I cut you open, and now I'm gonna sew you back up."

Lid felt the convenience of being indisposed; explanation to the fibbies was unnecessary and impossible. He and Braddock were not breaking the law, not exactly. Lid recalled his words to Rachael Brucker: the dentist was *either a great actor or the wrong guy*. Braddock's act remained impressive.

Julie flipped the overhead light switch as the chair automatically resumed its upright position. Simon ripped off his gloves and pulled down the mask. "That'll be a hundred bucks."

Lid had a cheek full of gauze. He tested the numb chin with his fingertips and waited for Julie to leave the room. "Simon, I can only guess at what the feds are looking for, but I hope you've got nothing to hide—like a brown paper sack full of money."

"They can have anything they find."

Totally innocent, Lid thought. Never for a moment did Braddock slip out of character. "The feds will check your house too. Other agents are probably there right now. They'll look anyplace they like—the attic, the garage. They can look into your bank accounts too."

"They're welcome to look," Simon said.

Roberta appeared in the doorway. "Dr. Braddock, your wife is on two."

Simon walked to his office with Roberta tagging along. "Did you take care of the FBI agent?" he asked.

"TLC. He's sitting with his head on his knees. I put a wet cloth on the back of his neck. What do you want me to write on Detective Li Dao's chart?"

Simon shrugged. "Mandibular left quadrant. Call it *osseous contouring and root planing*."

"Do you want me to charge him?"

"Damn right, on paper anyway. The FBI might keep his chart, so make it look normal. And don't let him get out of the chair. I need to talk to Marie privately."

Roberta walked out and closed the door.

Simon punched line two and picked up the phone. "Hi!"

"Simon, the FBI is here."

Simon instantly heard the frightened edge in her tone and felt his anger surge and fall again. "I know, they're here too. Just cooperate with them. I'll explain it all later."

"Explain it now!" Her voice had a quality Simon knew well—just before she was about to cry.

"Honey, it would take too long to explain over the phone. Look, the FBI is not the problem. I've been trying to help a police detective with a case. There's an extortion ring operating in Macon, and we might be in some danger until this is over. I want to get you and Esther out of there."

"Extortion! Are you being extorted?" Her voice rose in pitch and volume.

"Well, I was contacted, but it's important you don't repeat that to anybody, especially not to the FBI."

"I hope you didn't pay them anything!" The fear had changed to indignation.

"No, I certainly did not. Marie, listen to me and stop talking. Wait until the FBI leaves, then pack enough clothes to spend the night away. I'm sending Skip to pick you both up."

"Simon, I don't even know Skip."

"You know Skip."

"I met him once and that was years ago. I wouldn't recognize him if I saw him. Why can't you come get us?"

"I want you out of there as quickly as possible. The FBI people are here too, and my detective friend. Please just do what I tell you. I'll meet you later. Skip will know where."

"Esther's not even here. She's down at Molly Kitner's house."

Simon cringed. He had endured the weekend in a silent panic each time Esther was out of his sight. "Well, go get her back!"

There was a long pause. "Okay," she answered softly.

"Bye."

"Simon . . . !"

"Yes?"

"I love you."

"I love you too. Bye-bye." He hung up the phone, then dialed again and held his breath until he heard Skip's voice.

"Skip, this is Simon. I need you, life or death this time."

"Aw, Simon, what're you into now?" came the unhurried drawl.

"Just listen carefully. I don't have much time. I need you to pick up Marie and Esther and take them to your place. Can you do that?"

"I guess that's legal."

"I owe you big for this one, buddy. The FBI is there. Wait until they leave, then go to the front door. She's expecting you."

"The feds are after you?"

"Skip, please just listen! The bad guys may be after us. Get her out of there fast, and beware of anybody who doesn't look like a fed. I'll be at your shop as soon as I can get away."

He hung up as the door opened abruptly. The three-piece suit said *salesman,* but a salesman always waited to be shown in.

"Dr. Braddock, I'm Special Agent Colish. This is Agent Guthrie." He flipped the badge case. "We have a search warrant for these premises, also for your bank accounts and safe-deposit box. We will appreciate your cooperation."

Colish presented the paper, but Simon only gestured in acquiescence.

"May I have the key to your safe-deposit box?"

"What are you looking for?" Simon removed the key from a ring and tossed it onto the desk.

"Our investigation is in connection with an alleged extortion."

"These file cabinets will have to be opened," said Guthrie.

Simon found the right key, handed over the ring, and walked out.

Lid was still sitting in the big chair awaiting dismissal.

Simon entered and pulled the gauze out of his mouth. "Roberta will set you up to come back and get the stitches out. I'm taking a vacation. You're right, there's too much going on around here. Marie and I will be spending a few days at the beach as soon as the feds get out of our hair."

Lid looked at him with deadly soberness. "Will they find anything?"

"No, they won't," Simon said. "Look, if you get any other information about the case, call Roberta. I keep check with her when we're out of town."

Lid stood up and got his coat. "You'll never talk to me, will you? Sometimes you have to let other people help, Simon."

"You're right. That's true."

Lid pulled on the coat and handed Simon a card. "That's my home number. Call if you need me. Do I get something for the pain?"

Simon scribbled on a pad. "I thought cops were tough."

"Nobody's as tough as he thinks he is."

"We do what we have to do." Simon ripped off the small piece of paper and handed it over without expression.

Lid moaned and walked off down the hallway. The understanding between them remained unspoken. He reached the parking lot and ignored Presnell sitting in his car with the door open, still embarrassed over the syncopal episode.

"The FBI has left," Roberta said. "You didn't really mean for me to call the police or your lawyer, did you?"

Simon gave her a look. "Did they take his chart?"

"Yes, they did, sort of an afterthought, but they took it."

"You gave him a copy?"

"Yes, I gave him a copy. What's going on?"

"He's supposed to be a patient. I want him to know when his appointments were in case the feds question him."

"Aren't they all on the same side, the police and the FBI?"

"Theoretically. I've been trying to help Lid on the extortion investigation, but he doesn't get along too well with the feds. They would have called him on the mat for interfering in their case. It was a harmless deception."

"Seems like an awful lot of trouble."

Simon shrugged.

"Did the extortion people ever contact you?"

"I told you I'm not rich enough."

Roberta gazed at the ceiling to remind him that she knew what he made.

"Marie and I are going to the beach for a few days. It's not fair to put her under this kind of stress. Cancel eight working days. We'll aim for Friday week. I'll check with you. Li Dao may call here, and I want to know exactly what he says."

Roberta saluted. "I'll take notes."

Four P.M.

Tubby Milken rode by the Braddock house for the fourth time. It was still quiet, no activity, one car visible toward the rear. By now he had hoped to be on I-75 almost to Tifton, then over to Waycross and home, but the driveway on Marcus Lane South had only now cleared of the black cars with black tires, the kind that struck terror in his heart. Local or federal, he knew they were law enforcement.

The feds were his personal anathema. Tubby had heard frightening stories of their resourcefulness and persistency. He had once killed a bystander and might even shoot a cop if necessary, but not a fed. Tubby never hated his victims, never killed in anger or even from avarice, but only to provide himself with the basic necessities. It was a simple code made easier by his habit of utter turpitude.

The late afternoon air was warm and pleasant. Two doors away, children played in the front yard and street, but there was no activity at the Braddock home, no reason for further delay. Tubby turned into the driveway and stopped behind the BMW. With toolbox and overalls, he would easily pass for a plumber or other tradesman long enough to fulfill his contract. He had always worked quickly, not out of fear lest the gruesome task go amiss, but for the sake of the money never far from his thoughts. He waddled into the shade of the three-car garage and noted that it was bigger and nicer than the shack that was his home.

Marie answered Tubby's knock at the carport door.

"Hi!" she said with an ingratiating tone and smile. "Let me gather my things and lock up."

Tubby was momentarily perplexed. He hadn't spoken a word. In the same instant came the sound of the front door chime.

"Wait just a minute," Marie said and walked away.

A lustful urge came over Tubby completely by surprise, but such things took time: do the job and take the money. He opened the tool kit. The 9mm automatic with silencer attached was already cocked, filling the length of the large metal box. He fingered the weapon, his most expensive and useful possession. Then he hesitated. He wouldn't kill outside. Let her see to the door. The caller would leave or he would kill them both inside the house.

Marie assumed it was the FBI. She saw through the front window the grizzled head and work clothes. Simon's warning of danger gave only a moment of panic before the face became familiar. Skip. She pulled open the heavy door. "You *are* Skip, aren't you?"

"Yes, ma'am, Miz Braddock. Simon told me to pick y'all up."

The fear suddenly returned. "Then who's the man at the back?"

"I don't know. I didn't see any FBI, so I rang the bell."

"He's not FBI. He's dressed like you and has a toolbox."

They looked at each other in indecision.

"You better stay here, Miz Braddock. Let me see who he is."

Skip walked across the thick front lawn and around the side, aware, for the first time, that he had let himself be dragged into a perilous situation. He stayed well out in the open as he approached the carport. A fat stranger cradling a metal box came into his view. It was wrong. A man wouldn't stand next to a bench holding a heavy toolbox; he would set it down.

Skip looked toward the front yard and spoke loudly. "Y'all bring it on in the carport! At least it'll be out of the rain." He walked toward the other man, who was squinting into the bright sunshine, then focused on his nose and delivered a quick lift jab from the shoulder.

The blow was unexpected. Tubby's head snapped back as he stumbled and sprawled onto the concrete floor. Blood spurted from his flattened nose.

Skip had seized the open toolbox and fumbled in midair for its contents, astonished to find himself holding the long weapon. He entered the house quickly and closed the door behind himself.

"Miz Braddock, let's go in a hurry!" he yelled.

Marie and Esther were waiting in the living room. Marie saw the gun and shoved her daughter toward the door. "Esther! Run! Run!"

She raced over the lawn, holding Esther by the hand, and climbed as quickly as possible up into the grimy truck.

Skip was already in the driver's seat.

The engine cranked easily, but Marie agonized at the slow, painful acceleration. The old flatbed was not designed for speed. She rested her feet on a pile of heavy, rusted chain and said nothing, but kept her eyes to the front. Marie was panicked, longing to look out the back window but pretending nonchalance for Esther's sake. She squeezed the child's hand, too tightly.

Skip held to the speed limit but kept an eye on the rearview mirror.

After twenty minutes, he parked the truck out of sight behind his shop. They entered by the back door, and he turned on the lights. "This is my place. Simon told me to meet him here."

Skip immediately rinsed his knuckles. There were no cuts.

"Will we stay very long?" Esther asked.

"I hope not,'' her mother said. Marie's oversize T-shirt and denim skirt were casual but clean. She looked about the grim establishment but didn't find a place she was willing to sit.

"Your daddy should be here soon," said Skip. "Why don't you try out the tractor stool? That's your daddy's favorite spot."

"Mom, I need to go to the bathroom.''

"The top deck, matey. Just climb right up that ladder," he said.

Esther started up the ladder, inverted stringers with twelve-inch step, seven-inch riser depth. She held the rail and maneuvered the climb.

Marie watched and waited for the bathroom door to close. "Skip, do you know who that man was?"

"No, ma'am. I never saw him before," Skip replied in a voice less accommodating than the tone he had used with Esther.

He was angry, Marie could tell, an ancient warrior past his physical prime. His arms were dark and hairy, still creased between muscle groups.

"You don't think he followed us?" she asked.

"I doubt if he did anything for a couple of minutes."

"I hope you didn't kill him," she said.

"Nobody dies from a punch in the nose." Skip took up the automatic, removed the magazine, and jacked the last round from the chamber. "You see this thing? This is a silencer. Only one reason a man ever uses one of these: to kill somebody! They're not even legal. That guy came over there to get one of y'all. Be glad I punched him." He tossed the gun onto the bench and unloaded the magazine one slug at a time with his thumb.

Marie looked at the gun, the smooth, heavy curves and clean angles, the round silencer designed to snuff out life with elegant discretion. She had seen them on TV, but this was cruel reality. Marie hated the gun. "Please keep that out of her sight," she said.

Esther climbed carefully down the steps. "It's hot in there."

"Yeah, there's a window, but it's closed. If you were on a navy ship, you'd come down a ladder frontwards, fast as regular steps, but your legs aren't long enough for that."

"Were you on a ship?" Marie asked.

"Yes, ma'am, thirty years! Had one of them sunk out from under me."

"What did you do?"

"I held real still and hoped the sharks wouldn't find me. But I couldn't stand shore duty, retired when they tried to reassign me."

A car horn sounded.

Skip walked to the huge barn doors and peered through the crack. "There's your daddy." He pulled the doors wide so the van could move through the opening. The vehicle appeared larger inside the welding shop and seemed to fill the whole space.

Simon got out and hugged Marie.

Skip closed the doors and pointed at the gun with his eyes. "We had company out at your place, Simon."

Simon looked at him. "Are you all right?"

"Just barely," Skip said.

Simon tried to maintain an appearance of calm for Marie's sake. "We'll be here for a little while, honey."

"How long?"

"Till morning."

Marie's eyes widened, but she was careful in front of Esther. "I don't think there're any beds here, darling."

"I know. We'll sleep in the van. We can make out some way. Look, I've got a plan, but it will take time to explain."

Esther was clawing her legs. "Mom, something's making me itch."

Marie took a close look. "My gosh, you're covered with mosquito bites! Simon, look at her ankles."

"They're bad this time of day," said Skip. "They don't usually bother me, but it don't help none to close this place up. They come through the walls."

"They're not this bad at home."

"They're not this bad anywhere. This is a junkyard, Miz Braddock. There're a million things out there that collect water. You live near a junkyard, you're gonna have mosquitoes."

Simon took a bill from his wallet. "I need you to do one more thing, buddy. Get us some hamburgers and fries and Cokes, and get some insect repellent. Get three bottles, one apiece."

Skip took the fifty. "Am I feedin' myself out of this too?"

Simon nodded.

"Come on, Esther," Skip said. "You wanna ride and get away from the mosquitoes?"

Marie spoke before Simon could object. "Yes, go with him, honey. Skip will take good care of you."

Esther got up and walked after the old man.

"I figured y'all had some talking you needed to do," Skip said without smiling.

The door closed. Simon realized with embarrassment how out of place they were in the dusty garage. Neither one would sit anywhere other than the van. He pulled off his coat and tie and laid them on the front seat.

Marie only waited and listened until the truck started off. "What in the hell is going on?" she demanded but didn't wait for a reply. "That old man saved our lives today! Literally!" She picked up the heavy gun and held it out. "Some fat son of a bitch came to our house today with this! He would have killed us both, Simon!"

He searched his thoughts for an opening statement.

"He would have killed Esther." She barely got the words out, with tears in the voice.

Simon held her and said nothing, but she didn't expect it. He always cried when she cried.

Simon tried to visualize Esther in mortal danger but couldn't hold the image. He thought of Guy Bissett, his son murdered, his wife a suicide. Easy habitude steeled him into unearthly resolve.

"You're hurting me," she said.

Simon released her shoulders, then held her at arm's length. "I'm sorry, I didn't realize . . . let me explain it all. There's an extortion ring operating in Macon. They send letters to doctors and demand money and make threats. I got the letter two months ago."

"I want to see it!" she said.

"I threw it away because I didn't want it to upset you."

"Upset me?" She flashed her wide eyes toward the rafters.

"Some of the doctors got the letter over a year ago. Two of them went to the police, and apparently the threat was carried out. Two children died, or at least one died and one disappeared. They still haven't arrested anybody."

Marie looked at him in horror. "I remember a doctor's son involved in a traffic accident."

"Yes, that was one of them."

"And the child who disappeared last fall?"

He nodded. "I've been in contact with Sergeant Martin Li Dao of the Macon police. The other doctors have clammed up."

"I can see why. So you showed him the extortion letter?"

"Yes." It was his first open lie to Marie. Simon hated the feeling, but he was not ready for the horror of confession.

"So now they've come after us."

He took her shoulders more gently now. "The police know who the main culprits are. They're getting close to the proof. The extortionists are fighting among themselves. They killed two of their own people recently. Li Dao thinks the end of it is near. When the leaders go down, that will end it."

"So what do we do—hide in a hole until it's over?"

"Something like that."

"What about the FBI?"

"Their investigation is separate."

"But they acted like we were the criminals. You should have seen them! I know they thought we were hiding something, but they wouldn't say what it was."

"They're hard men because they deal with scum most of the time. Innocent people have died, and they are trying to sort it out."

"I thought they were rude! I've never felt so insulted." Fear mixed with anger in her expression. "Well, maybe they were only doing their jobs."

Simon desperately wanted to give assurance that everything would come right in the end, but his words would have lacked conviction. "I want you to go to your mother's for a few days."

"What about you?"

"I have to stay here and work with the police."

"It's their job. Why do the police need you?"

It was a very good question for which he had not a very good answer. Again he wanted to tell the truth, but courage betrayed him. Marie was not stupid. Only another deplorable lie would suffice.

"They need me for bait."

"No!" she yelled. "Let them get their own bait! You're not paid to take that risk."

"It's not like you think. They only want me here to answer the phone." He paused and sighed, avoiding his next statement. "If the bad guys come after you, they usually call first to see if you're there. The police are setting it up now. The house and office will be completely protected."

"I don't like it."

"I don't either, but we're already in it. We can't go home or by the office until the security is in place. I want you and Esther out of town." He paused, but Marie was silent. The counterfeit explanation would not hold up long. "Tell me about the man who came to the house today."

Her words came in short, angry bursts. "He was fat. Skip punched him. We barely got away with our lives, Simon!"

Marie had other questions, but fatigue and depression were wearing her down. She was angry that they were in the situation, more angry that there was nothing to do about it. Fear held her resigned and silent. She sat in the van and fought the mosquitoes.

Skip returned with the fast food and insect repellent. Simon and Marie immediately rubbed the sticks over their arms and wrists, covering the oval welts already there and already itching.

The van was the only comfortable place to sit and

eat. Marie nibbled; the others ate heartily. Skip eventually broke the silence.

"What's the plan, Simon? Y'all gonna live down here?"

Simon was not able to joke. "Esther and Marie are leaving first thing in the morning."

Marie looked at him but said nothing.

"Well, I've got to get home," Skip said. "Vashti will think I've run off." He tossed his paper and plastic in the direction of a fifty-five-gallon drum. "Y'all better cut off these lights if you're trying to hide out. You don't want this place lit up like a Christmas tree. Bye-bye, honey."

"Bye," Esther responded.

"Y'all have a good night now, y' hear? Best you can, anyway." Skip was large and lumbering. He closed the door with a bang like he did everything.

The sound of the truck eventually faded, leaving the Braddock family in pathetic, dignified silence.

The welding shop was in an area of heavy industry and railroad tracks and would be deserted until morning. It was possible not a single vehicle would pass during the night. They had camped in the van the summer before, but this was hardly camping. Neither tried to put a good face on the situation, mentally and physically spent from frustration and terror.

Marie took Esther up into the bathroom for whatever ablutions were possible with liquid soap and paper towels. She settled herself and Esther in the van.

Simon sat on the tractor stool. It had not been a hot day, but as darkness came he felt the humidity for the first time and resigned himself to his wet, gummy condition.

At last he turned off the lights, making a sad, gloomy darkness, even after his eyes became accustomed. Only the slender, scanty stripe between the tall doors severed the murk but not the mood. The streetlight was a block away.

"Does Toby know where we are?" Esther asked.

"Toby's fine," Marie assured her, but she was having similar apprehensions. Was the front door locked? Were any lights on? Marie mused longingly and lavished maternal protective thoughts on their comfortable home as she rubbed Esther's back until the child went to sleep.

Eventually, she and Simon lay in the silent blackness. The odor of bug repellant hung in the stale air. There was much to be said, but they hadn't the strength or the words to begin.

9

Tuesday.

"What time is it?" she whispered.

Simon climbed over the seat to keep from waking Esther, banged his head against the roof of the van, and struggled up to the front. His heart was pounding. He flipped the map light and looked at his watch. "It's almost seven."

"Esther's legs and feet are cold."

"You'll have the heater once the engine warms."

Marie crawled stiffly out of the vehicle and climbed the steps, one riser at a time.

Simon had never used the toilet in the tiny upstairs bathroom. He relieved himself outside onto the scrap metal as always. The sky was bright before sunrise, but the air was still cool. He returned and sat at the back door, away from the van, where Esther was still asleep.

Marie descended the ladder with even greater care, then pulled up a wooden box and straddled it, past being concerned about the dirt.

He held out a thick wad of bills. "Stuff this into your purse. It's around twenty thousand dollars."

"Where did you get that much cash?"

"I got it yesterday. Just don't lose it and don't let anybody see it. Here's the plan. Everything has to look normal when you arrive at your mom's. There's no point in explaining all this to her. Drive to Atlanta. Buy some new luggage and new clothes for both of you, anything you like. Stay overnight in a hotel if you need to."

"Why can't we go by the house to get clothes? You said the police would be there."

"No! Somebody might be watching the house and follow you. I want you out of town now."

"I'm not really in the mood to shop."

"You'll get in the mood. Please just do it this way."

"What will Mom think when I arrive in the van?"

"Tell her the BMW's in the shop."

"What about Esther? She'll tell Nana everything."

"I don't know. Make up something. Tell her it's police work and we don't want to worry Nana with it."

Marie didn't like the plan, but the new, frightening realities were persuasive. "Be sure to check Toby's food and water," she said.

"I will, and don't call me; let me call you," he said. "I'm not sure where I'll be."

"Will you call me every day?"

"Every day."

Marie was finally silent but disheartened, and yielded to the plan in spite of fear and uncertainty. She went back to the van and held the child, then helped her climb the steep wooden ladder.

Simon propped open the garage doors and backed the van out into the white morning light.

With no food and no proper bathroom, little preparation was needed before the departure. Esther returned and accepted his hug, then crawled sleepily into the passenger seat.

Marie squeezed him and pushed her face against his neck. "Will you take care of you?"

Simon nodded. "Don't worry about that. You just do the same for you and Esther." He held the blond head and kissed her mouth before releasing her to get in on the driver's side. "Don't stop to eat until you're well out of town, Forsyth maybe."

She fastened the seat belt and looked through the open window. "I love you." Her words was painfully sincere.

"I love you, Babe!" Simon replied with more light-hearted voice but with a lump in his throat.

He watched the van out of sight with a heavy heart. She had the easier part of the separation. At least there were new sights and decisions to occupy the mind. He could only worry for the safety of the trip.

He reentered the garage and closed the tall doors behind himself, completely alone in the quiet semi-darkness. Less than sixteen hours had passed since he and Lid had done their surgery act. It seemed much longer ago. This was the life of a gangster, running, hiding out in dark, grim places. He would call Ollie. Somebody had to feed Toby.

Simon picked up the gun, examined it and felt the weight, then cocked it and pulled the trigger. The son of a bitch would have killed Marie and Esther with this, he thought. Simon's only experience with guns was firing an M-16 on a rifle range. The whole business had been play, target practice, remote from actual combat in spite of the constant admonition that the black circle was the enemy. This gun was more dangerous, secret and illegal. He would hide it with the money.

A careful search of the workbench and ground produced fifteen bullets. The small projectiles were cool, heavy, and smooth in his hand. He reloaded the magazine and shoved it into the handle. Simon had never owned a gun but thought to fire it once out of curiosity. He cocked it, pointed carefully at a large, undressed beam forming a corner post of the garage, and squeezed the trigger. The gun unexpectedly jerked in his hand. He heard the muted pop and simultaneous thud as the slug struck the heavy wood. The corner of the shop was jarred from the impact. Dust sifted down through shadowy light. The weapon had a surprising appeal. A feeling of power but great danger.

With the doors closed, Simon could feel the temperature in the shop already starting to rise. He was *at the beach,* he remembered. Roberta would be neat and cool and efficient as she answered the telephone. *I don't have an opening on my schedule for about two weeks.* Then she would think about her boss and his family lying in the dazzling sun, listening to the surf.

Grim realities pushed back into his thoughts. He had killed, yet the extortion ring was intact. Condon and Noles undoubtedly had deserved what they got, but the effort to throw Willard Prather off the track hadn't worked either. The fat man with the big gun was proof of that. Lid had said the code book would expose everything including the female accomplice, but the police didn't have the key. They had been on the case for a year. How long could he live in a welding shop, a fugitive from outlaw justice? His wife and daughter were exiles. Total strangers were waiting to put them to death. That was the problem—the gangsters only had to wait; he owned a house and a business and couldn't hide out forever.

At last he heard the truck. Skip came through the doorway smiling. "Sorry I'm late! I brought you some eggs and stuff."

Skip's overalls and long johns appeared to be fresh. He had shaved. Simon thought it was the first time

Skip had ever looked cleaner than he did. "Thanks, buddy," he said, ripping into the plastic containers. The aroma itself was a comfort.

"Marie and Esther are gone?"

"Yeah, they're on the way to Charleston, her mother's place."

"What the hell are you into, Simon?"

"Extortion," Simon said. "Somebody's trying to shake money out of the local doctors. I'm working with a police detective, but I need to stay out of sight for a while."

"Hoowee! You're gonna get your ass killed." Skip stared at Simon. "Let the police handle it."

Simon swallowed a mouthful of grits and bacon as he pulled more cash from his pocket. "I need you to get me a few other things: toothbrush, shirts, shorts, socks, and a bug."

"You better write all that down. What was that last thing?"

"A bug," he repeated, dumping two sugar packets into a styrofoam cup.

"A bug? What's a bug? If you want a roach, we got plenty of them around here."

"You know what I mean, a listening device, a bug."

"Oh, them metal bugs. The police can get you one of those."

Simon tried to let his facial expressions argue while he ate at the same time. "This ain't exactly legal. Don't hassle me, Skip. Can you get one?"

Skip hesitated and maintained the dubious smile.

"Go upstairs and take whatever money you like."

Skip finally nodded. "I'll see what I can do, Simon."

"You can get the other stuff at Kmart or Wal-Mart, or it might be less trouble to go by the house."

Skip's eyes widened. "I'll go to Wal-Mart. That fat boy could still be around."

"I'm sorry to keep imposing on you." Simon waited for reassurance, but it didn't come. Skip apparently was sorry too.

Simon looked at him. "I'll always owe you for what you did yesterday. There's no way to pay that back."

"He was a bad chap. Yes, sir, that round man meant to do some damage."

"What did you do to him?"

"I just popped him one in the nose and got out of there before he could recover. If you ever want to stop a man, hit him in the nose. It hurts like a son of a bitch, and he can't see for the blood. I learned that in the navy."

"How so?"

"A guy hit me in the nose once. I never forgot it either. Takes forever to stop bleeding and hurts for a week."

"Here're the things I need," Simon said.

Skip took the list and looked at it. "I'll be back directly, Simon. Keep the place locked and I'll put the *closed* sign out on the front. When I open those doors, you'll have to stay up in the head if you don't wanna be seen. You don't never know when somebody'll come driving up."

Skip left out the back way and slammed the door again.

Nine A.M.

Alex admired the vase of red roses and counted the blooms with her eyes—two dozen. She knew what they had cost. The note was unsigned: *Some cops just can't hold their liquor!* She smiled at the ease with which the strawberry thing had charmed her out of her pants. She had already called to thank him. *Who is this?* Harry had replied.

She wished the roses had been delivered to the apartment rather than work. The squad room was filling up, and the flowers had already elicited comments. To top that, she had worn a new suit, pale lavender, wondering all along if it was too feminine for the job. But she looked good and felt good. Somebody needed to dress up the place.

Colish stopped at her desk. "Looks like you have an admirer, Alex."

She feinted a blow at his shoulder. "My partner gave me these. Doesn't Presnell ever send you flowers?"

"Funny. Look, I need the book. The warrant lists some sort of code book, and we don't find it."

"I'll pick it up tonight. You'll have it first thing in the morning."

"Presnell wants it now."

"I don't have it now. It's not at my place."

"Can you go get it now?"

"No!"

"You know I don't care, Alex, but Presnell will call this *failure to cooperate with the FBI*."

"Harvey, don't give me this legal baloney. You'll have the damn book in the morning, and you won't make heads or tails of it anyway."

"You might be surprised what we can do."

"Oh, yeah? How'd you do with Braddock?"

"Zilch. The guy is clean." He gave her a look and walked off.

Lid was right, Alex thought. She borrowed her partner's language and spoke to the roses. "Fucking fibbies!"

Eleven A.M.

Lid attended the funeral alone. The cemetery was

old and beautiful—a waste of good real estate, he thought. It was the right time of year for a graveside service if you had to go to one, not too warm or cold. The clear sky showed only high, thin cloudy wisps that would deliver no rain. Lid had already signed the book but decided to see the business through to the end. He stood with his back to one of the fat, spade-shaped cedars and watched the final rite unfold.

Guy Bissett sat in the middle of the front row under the tent, but Lid didn't know the other adults and teenagers who sat beside him. The doctor looked at nothing and showed no emotion. Everything that could be taken away from him was already gone. Lid hoped Bissett didn't remember the promise made that rainy night in the bar.

He had never met Anne Bissett, now closed forever inside the metal container beneath the heavy cloth pall with embroidered cross. He doubted Guy Bissett took consolation from any of it—the prayers, the incense, the holy water. Somewhere nearby, a mocking bird offered cheerful condolence against the sound of the priest droning through the traditional liturgy. Lid was almost out of earshot behind the large circular crowd. He listened to the bird instead.

His old friend Bruce Murray lay buried only a few hundred feet from where he stood. Lid hated the memory. Perhaps if he had gone to Willard Prather's house and shot a few holes in him, Bruce Murray and Anne Bissett would still be alive—a pleasant thought, but absurd and too late. Besides, he had known nothing of Prather's involvement until Braddock had given him the lead.

Lid watched the ancient ceremony and realized that his theory about Braddock had shifted strongly from conjecture to hope. The dentist appeared quiet and malleable, but Lid didn't believe it. Beneath the surface Braddock was irascible and savage, one who made his own chances and took them.

The priest's voice became uplifted in adoration and interfered with the sound of the bird. Lid was ready to leave. He wanted to see Brucker anyway.

It was one P.M. when he stood in the tiny waiting room and called her name. She walked into view.

"Li Dao! Come on in. Lil's off and I'm taking the afternoon to clean up." She blew smoke and stubbed out the cigarette.

Lid had never seen her in sweatpants and pullover top, which emphasized her shape. The auburn hair was pulled back and tied behind her head. She was barefoot.

"My junk room is beginning to look like a real room. All this stuff needs to go into the hall so maintenance will pick it up."

Lid groaned and made a face but pulled off his coat to help with the boxes and stacks of paper. He liked his hard, dangerous appearance, the brown leather straps creasing his starched white shirt. The gun was part of his body.

"Is this a social call?" she asked.

"I guess so. Anytime I see you, it's social, Brucker."

"Why is that?"

"One day I may get lucky."

Rachael ignored the comment.

"Well, I need to check with you on something," he said. "The FBI has taken over the extortion case. Bodies and pricks were beginning to pile up, and they can't have the locals beating them out of network coverage. I want to be certain our stories match in case they ask."

"I'll tell them whatever you like, Lid."

"What about your written records?"

She pulled up the front of the sweatshirt to mop her brow, exposing her middle from navel to bra, then collapsed into the desk chair and lit another cigarette. "I never allow anyone to see my medical records without a warrant or subpoena. What are you worried about?"

"Braddock. I have a pretty good idea he's become a vigilante."

"And you didn't mention that to Mimbs?"

"That's right."

She was amused. "Forget it. I never made any notes about our conversations, only a charge sheet for my hours with the department and a few sparse comments about the lecture and discussion."

"Good," he nodded.

"You're still brooding about that case, aren't you? If the feds want it, let them have it."

"Don't you ever become personally involved?"

"Watch it, Lid, you're breaking the first rule of therapy."

"Yeah, I know. Bruce Murray was an old pal, and then there's Bissett . . ."

"What about Bissett?"

"His wife committed suicide. I just came from the funeral."

"Oh, God. I hadn't heard that. They lost their son only a few months ago."

"It's been a year. She killed herself on the anniversary of his death—took a bunch of pills. Bissett came by the department last week. We sat in a bar and had drinks, a few too many. The man was really worried about his wife, reaching out for help. Obviously I didn't help the poor bastard."

Lid sighed noisily. "The guy started crying. We sat there in a booth, and he actually started crying."

The memory was a trigger mechanism, unexpected and untypical. Lid's eyes were suddenly full, his chest tight. He fell mute and wished Brucker would say something, but she sat in silent evaluation. If she noticed anything, she didn't say so. He waited until his voice was reliable. "I'll never tell anybody about Braddock. He can kill the whole goddamn bunch."

There was no eye contact, but he saw her move behind him and felt the arms close over his chest. Her face pressed against his cheek. The cologne had a fragrance he hadn't noticed before. He realized, oddly, that they had never touched until now, never shaken hands or jostled elbows. Lid treasured the moment, which was all the more arousing because it was not an overture, only a consoling gesture.

Two P.M.

The welding shop had gotten three phone calls, but Simon hadn't bothered to answer. His clothes and body odor were well past offensive, but he couldn't clean up until Skip returned with soap, razor, and other wherewithal. Blue-collar types had little concept of time or appointments.

Simon sat on the tractor stool staring into the hot, still air. He had paced and sweated for hours in the semidarkness of the closed garage, brandishing the cool, heavy automatic until its shape and weight were familiar. The weapon had drawn him back with almost sensual, alien appeal, corrupt and seductive, a thing he wanted to hold again.

Simon was in the cave but hardly aware of it. Conscious appraisal was pointless. The cave was always there with easy, unwanted access, to cope with, to endure, now suddenly essential. Obie would not be the end of it.

At last he heard the truck door close. Skip came in noisily and flipped the light switch. He tossed his packages aside and smiled broadly. "Why are you sitting in the dark, Simon? Nobody'll notice the lights in the daytime."

"The lights make it hotter in here."

Skip held a small round object up to view. "How do you like it?"

"Is that what I think it is?"

"That's a bug, Simon!" he announced in a voice that could be heard down the block. "It's flat and easy to keep out of sight. Stick it anyplace you like and tune it in on this box, just like listening to a radio."

"How does it work?"

"It's got a tiny transmitter in there and a battery that ought to run it for months."

"What's the range?"

"You can hear it easy for five or six hundred feet." Skip was still beaming. "Put it anywhere, then get within range and you can hear a pin drop wherever that thing is."

Simon looked at the device and slipped it into his pocket, then picked up the automatic and gave the silencer a tightening twist. "I need you to take me somewhere."

"I got you some clothes too."

"Later."

Simon walked out the back and squinted in the sunlight but relished the fresh air. He had been in hiding for almost twenty-four hours. His suit was dirty and wrinkled, more noticeable in the natural light.

Skip followed reluctantly, locked the garage, and climbed up into the truck.

"Go across Spring Street bridge," Simon said.

Skip started out but felt obliged to speak. "Simon, you're on your own if you get in a jam."

Simon barely groaned. The warning was unnecessary.

Skip headed toward East Macon, down Walnut Street, Spring Street, over the muddy water of the Ocmulgee. He was still concerned. "What are you up to?"

"I'm only planting the bug."

Skip drove in silence.

They started up Jackson Springs Road. Simon watched the house numbers on the small reflective markers. "Stop here. Drive around and come back in fifteen minutes. If I'm not here, go on." He was already out, the door closed.

Skip shoved into low gear and started off.

No other cars approached as Simon crossed the road and entered the Prather estate in the quiet afternoon sunlight. He had the gun stuck under his belt, concealed by the coat. He squinted at the mansion and walked deliberately along the edge of the driveway. The circular fountain was silent from a distance but noisy as he passed it. A polished stone floor surrounded the portico. The house was classic and imposing, more impressive close up.

His attack was utterly foolish, the act of a desperate man, but Simon didn't know he was desperate. Outrageous plans worked precisely because they were outrageous.

He mounted the front steps, which curved up from either side of the porch, then paused at the massive front door. The huge knob turned with solid, smooth action under his touch. Simon closed the door behind him and stood in the vestibule, looking into the cool, elegant hallway with a hand-woven rug, listening for any sound. The memory of this moment would be more frightening than the moment itself. Now it was nothing, the acting out of a drama that could end however it did.

Simon walked to the nearest door and entered, closing that one behind him. The library was semi-dark, the shuttered windows providing the only light. As good a place as any. He stood on tiptoes and slid the bug atop the books on the highest shelf, then gazed around and thought of the key. The room held myriad good hiding places. It was lavish in a way that made him pause to remember why he was there.

In that moment he heard a footstep and the action of the door latch. No time to react. In the next instant he was face to face with a tall stranger in handsome black and white attire. Simon pointed the gun with both hands and waited, unaware that the butler knew the weapon better than he but had never looked at one from that end.

Max stood perfectly still inside the doorway, maintaining the dignity of his office.

"Close it." Simon pointed with his eyes.

Max calmly closed the door, fatally misreading the intruder.

Simon waited only for the other man to face him again before squeezing the trigger. The sound was much louder than he wanted or expected as the body hit the floor and the slug struck the wall.

"What a machine!" he whispered. He walked over and took a close look at the red hole in the center of the forehead.

Simon heard other footsteps and saw the doorknob turning again. He waited, then pushed the door closed behind the second stranger. This man wore a sports shirt and slacks. He was no servant.

"What's your name?" Simon said.

"Willard Prather." Prather had turned quickly and

paled at the sight of the weapon pointing straight into his face. He steadied himself with a chair back. "Is that Max?" The words came out as a husky whisper.

"I didn't ask his name. He's dead. Have a look."

Prather saw well enough from where he stood. "How did you get in here?"

"Shut up. If you speak again, I'll kill you." Simon's tone was pleasant, his mouth and eyes balanced on the edge of a smile. He looked about. "Somewhere in this room is the key to the code book. Produce it or you're dead. You have fifteen seconds."

Prather glanced at Max, then stared at the enemy— rumpled, unshaven, a man on the run.

Simon shrugged. "It's all the same to me."

Prather was persuaded. "Right over here," he said, stepping across the room. He pulled down a small soft-cover volume and handed it to his strange assailant, who was still dangling the weapon like a toy.

Simon didn't know what he was looking for, but flipped it open in his left hand and noted two columns of words. "Good," he said.

He paused to savor Prather's astonishment, then spoke quietly. "My name is Simon Braddock. I killed your brother, Obie, and I'm going to kill you too, but not today."

Prather staggered awkwardly, but Simon held the automatic with both hands and pointed it straight into his face. "I promised Obie I'd kill you, but that was before I cut his head off. This key is all I want for the moment."

Prather was shaking.

Simon walked to the door, then turned and looked at the other man again. "Of course, you could always kill me first." His smile finally emerged as he stepped into the hallway and closed the door.

Prather slumped into the nearest chair and tried to assemble his thoughts. It was several minutes later before he went to the bar and poured whiskey into a glass, holding the bottle with both hands. He walked to the body for a closer look. One shot, right through the head. There was blood on the carpet and the wall. Prather drank the whiskey, walked back to the bar, and poured with a steadier hand. At last he picked up the phone and dialed.

"I need Uncle Heinrich. . . . Mrs. Warwick, this is important! I need him here as soon as possible. . . . No, not the gazebo, the library." He banged the phone into its place.

Five P.M.

Alex sat on a granite grave marker and gazed into the ancient trees overlooking the Ocmulgee River. Lush greenery draped into the water, high from spring rain. Late afternoon sun still reflected in the distance from I-16 traffic on the river's opposite side, but the mechanical whine was faint.

Harry leaned into the trunk of the old Pontiac and filled another balloon from the helium tank. His frayed blue Dockers contrasted with a white dress shirt that appeared brand-new. He wore a tie but no belt. The button-down collar was unbuttoned.

She waited dutifully and amused, red balloons in one hand, green in the other. The stone was cold against the back of her legs, but Alex didn't have a free hand to pull down the skirt. "I don't believe I've ever sat on a tombstone and held helium-filled balloons."

"Your education was neglected, Alex."

"Are you sure this is legal? It seems disrespectful, sitting on a grave."

"Certainly it's legal. This is the Hall plot. Uncle Hal

would be delighted to have such sweet ass sitting on his face."

She smiled.

He straightened and looked at her. "Okay, it's six o'clock. Let the green ones go."

"All at once?"

"No, a few seconds apart so each can be wafted by its own private air."

She opened her thumb and forefinger. "Go, balloon. Be wafted by your own private air."

They watched until the green ball became a black spot high in the northeast sky. She released the second. Harry followed it with shaded eyes. " 'I wandered lonely as a cloud.' "

She looked at him.

"Wordsworth."

"Harry, what the hell are we doing?"

"We're freeing balloons, to go where they will, to seek their fortune in that vast ocean, to enjoy the serenity of space or descend again and risk the joys and pitfalls of this fragile place."

She released another balloon and chuckled in spite of herself. "This is fun. I've never done this before. Why are we doing it?"

"Children would never ask such a question. Balloons are quiet and peaceful and wonderful. Balloons are our friends." He smiled and looked at Alex. "This is probably the most important thing you've done today."

"That may well be true."

"Besides, it's a high spot and it's beautiful. Riverside Cemetery is the best-kept secret in town. Some of these stones date back to the mid-nineteenth century." Harry turned and pointed. "There's a horse buried over next to the Confederate soldiers' plot. Beyond that, a whole section entirely Jewish. It's a history lesson to stroll through here."

She released the fourth balloon and watched again as the green globe floated high above the water.

"That one wants to go with the river," he said, "to see where it joins the Oconee and has baby rivers."

"Is that what they do?"

"Maybe the Ocmulgee just wants to hear the news—what's been happening up in north Georgia around Lake Rabun."

"And the Oconee hears the news from Macon?"

"Right. Someday I'd like to take a trip from New Orleans up the Mississippi to its source. Each time we come to a fork, we'll take the larger side until the canoe scrapes bottom in a little creek."

"Am I in this canoe with you?"

"Certainly. You're always with me."

"What do we do when we get there?"

"Plant a flag and say *this is where the Mississippi begins.*" He pointed down the slope. "See that big oak? We'll come over when it's raining and stand there above the water with an umbrella. You can hear the rain and watch it fall into the river."

"You've done that before?"

He nodded. "It's peaceful and quiet and nobody bothers you."

"I don't doubt that."

"You can see the railroad tracks from there. The line runs along the edge of the river at the bottom of the ravine. I used to bring my nephew to that spot when he was little to watch the train go by. You can look right down on top of it."

"You probably enjoyed it more than your nephew did."

"Trains are our friends, Alex."

She grinned at him again. "When do we release the other balloons?"

"First the green balloons, then the red ones. You're not experienced at this, are you?"

"Apparently not. What's the point?"

"For one thing, it tells what the wind patterns are at different times."

"Wind is our friend?"

"Exactly. I put notes in the balloons with my address and phone number and ask the finder to let me know where it landed and what color it was."

"Does anybody ever contact you?"

"Sure. It appeals to something in human nature. Most of them land over in North Highlands or East Macon, but one made it to Warner Robins and another went upriver to Juliette."

Alex sat clown-like with the red balloons. She was drawn to Harry. Many people might think such thoughts, but few would carry them out. "Harry, why do you want to know about wind patterns?"

He held his arm above his eyes and squinted after the last balloon. "I want to know all things."

"All things?"

He turned toward her with the look she had come to cherish, the dark eyes that smiled even before the mouth stretched out tiny dimples from his muscular cheeks. "Well, I'd like to understand a few things— weather patterns, Mozart, stars."

"Would you marry me, Harry?"

"Yes, I will, but not until we finish with the balloons."

She spread her fingers, allowing the red globes to ascend quickly. Her face said *I love you* better than words could have.

He gave a mock supercilious stare. "This bodes ill,

Alexandra. You have released them at once, to be wafted by communal air."

She stood and brushed off the lavender skirt. "Quite so, sire. Let us return to the castle."

"To what end?"

"I wish to have my body fondled."

"A wondrous thing!" He gave her the smile again.

Eight P.M.

Marie immersed herself under jets of bubbly water as two days' worth of dirt, sweat, and stress slowly dissipated. The room with the hot tub had cost extra, but it was worth it.

Esther stood staring through the sliding glass doors, her golden head and slender brown body wrapped in separate towels. Lights from cars and buildings were showing in the early dusk.

The day had been tiring for Marie but fun for Esther. They had shopped the endless caverns of Lennox Square, then eaten lunch in a large, crowded Fuddrucker's and spent an hour in a raucous video arcade.

The beds and floor were covered with varicolored plastic sacks, each displaying the logo of its store. Every item they had brought into the hotel was new. Marie had eventually enjoyed shopping just as Simon predicted. Easter sales were beginning, and she was a bargain hunter.

She watched the child in the mirror mounted on the bathroom door. "Esther, please don't go out on that patio; we're on the twelfth floor. Besides, you're still wet."

"I'm just looking at the cars, Mom."

Marie closed her eyes and imagined that the last traces of the welding garage grime were melting away. She slid down and submerged her head in the hot, soapy water. Simon had handled the situation with prudence, she thought. His family came first. Spending a night in hiding was only a small inconvenience. His dealing with the police detective was especially amazing. How many weeks had he known about the extortion ring and said nothing? He had worried and feared all that time, yet kept it to himself. Still, she was proud of him. It had taken courage for Simon to go to the police, although they might've planned together. Why had he not consulted her?

At last she pulled herself from the soothing water, a reluctant fetus giving up the amniotic fluid. Esther's hair needed to be dried and the pajamas located; labels had to be snipped off and suitcases packed. Marie dried herself and pulled on the new robe, then emptied the other packages until she found the pink and white pajamas. Eventually, she settled Esther into bed. Watching television later than usual would induce sleep in the strange surroundings.

When the eleven o'clock news came on, she turned off the TV and other lights, crawled into bed, and started the nightly rub with her fingertips. Her eyes and ears became accustomed to the limpid, pulsing stillness that was a hotel room. She felt Esther's inhalations through the smooth back and heard sweet, shallow baby breaths in the silence, high above traffic and other earthly sounds.

Esther was almost asleep but turned her head and mumbled. "Mommy, will that man ever come back?"

Marie kissed the back of her neck and spoke quietly. "No, honey, Daddy and the police won't ever let him come to our house again." She snuggled deeper into the covers and cradled the soft, warm body.

Esther curled into her mother's embrace. "It was fun."

"Why was it fun?"

"We got all new stuff."

Marie smiled as an enormous weight of concern and guilt dropped away into the darkness. Whatever Providence had dulled the childish awareness of reality received her prayer of thanksgiving.

Sleeping in the van had been intermittent and fitful, but they could all make up for it tonight. She suddenly missed Simon. When Esther was smaller, they had held her at the same time, together, one on each side. It had been a long time. She yearned to be with him in their big bed with Esther in the middle. The hotel room was clean and pleasant, but it was not home. At least Simon was there, warm and snug, taking care of Toby and the house.

Eleven P.M.

Wexler knocked repeatedly. "Clara, wake up! I found your note."

Mrs. Warwick finally opened the bedroom door and tried to appear half asleep. A faded hairnet covered the plastic curlers and salon-dyed auburn hair. She wore her most bedraggled robe, a deliberate attempt to appear dowdy and avoid sexual arousal.

Wexler was still wearing a suit with a silk shirt buttoned to the neck. "What did he say exactly?"

She clutched the robe at her throat. Her face was pale without makeup, her eyes dark, eyelids nonexistent. "He wanted to see you immediately. He made it sound urgent."

"Was he drunk?"

"I don't think so. His voice was high and tense. I can tell when he's upset, Heinrich. You'd better go."

It didn't work. Wexler pulled the loose end of the bow knot, allowing the robe to fall open. The feel of her breasts under soft cotton had always been irresistible. He caressed her body through the gown until he was ready, then pulled it off over her head. Clara was long accustomed to the cavalier approach and serviced him in a routine manner.

Wexler hadn't bothered to take off all of his clothes. He dressed again quickly and looked at his watch. "I'd better see what he wants. Leave the outside lights on.'

"Yes, sir," she said, resuming her domestic station.

Wexler went out the back and walked the familiar, sparsely lighted path. A rabbit stirred as he passed the cages. Azaleas and other blooms were colorless, and the gazebo appeared a heavy shadow. He felt the damp, cool air and wondered if he should have brought an umbrella.

The front of the Prather mansion was bright from lights under the eaves and porch. Wexler climbed the steps, rang the chime, and waited. He watched the lights from downtown, distant and silent.

Prather himself finally opened the door. He was dressed, but the shirt and pants were wrinkled and stained. His face was haggard.

Wexler knew he had been drinking. "Has Max gone to bed?"

"He's dead!" Prather's voice was high and incredulous.

Wexler hesitated but showed no change of expression. Condon and Noles had been expendable, but the butler was adroit. Wexler crossed the vestibule and walked into the main hall, awaiting Willard's explanation.

"Braddock was here; he killed him!" Prather blurted. "What?"

"The dentist—the guy you were gonna take care of—he was here. He had a nine millimeter automatic with silencer. The guy's a psycho!"

Willard opened the library door and allowed his uncle to enter. Max's body lay where it had fallen.

Wexler felt a moment of weakness but held on, unwilling to show any debility in front of his nephew. "Are you telling me Braddock just walked in here brandishing a gun?"

"I don't know how he got in. What happened to your swamp man?"

"Who answered the door?" Wexler demanded.

"How the hell should I know? I never heard the chime."

"Well, you lock the goddamn thing, don't you?"

"Max is keeper of the door, Heinrich. Why don't you ask him?"

Wexler ignored the sarcasm. "When was he here?"

"This afternoon. What happened to your swamp man?" Prather repeated.

Wexler walked to the center of the room and faced Prather again. He tried to appear relaxed as he reasoned. What *had* happened to Tubby?

"Did you see Braddock?" Wexler asked.

"Yes! He stood right where you are and pointed the gun in my face. I'm telling you he's crazy."

"Why didn't he shoot you?"

"I don't know. He said he would kill me later. I don't know what the son of a bitch meant by that."

"How do you know it was Braddock? Have you ever seen him?"

"No, Obie and Asa have seen him."

"Well, they're not a helluva lot of help, are they?"

"He said he was Braddock."

"What, he introduced himself? He left his fucking business card?"

"Not exactly. He said he was Braddock. Said he had

killed Obie and cut his head off. How would he know that if he didn't do it?"

Wexler was getting a familiar headache. He sat in a comfortable chair to begin anew. "Willard, I'm very tired. Nobody walks into a room and shoots somebody, then gives you his name. Explain that. Start from the beginning."

Prather sat at the heavy desk, slurped his ice cubes, and poured more whiskey into the glass. "I walk into the room. He's behind the door with the gun. Max is already dead. And this is the worst part—he knew about the key. I don't know how, but he knew about it. He said I could join Max or give him the key."

"You didn't give it to him, I hope."

"I had to. This guy is a lunatic; he'll do anything."

"Jesus! Why didn't you say you knew nothing about it?"

"You didn't see it, Heinrich, Max lying there with an extra hole in his skull, Braddock calm as a judge. He meant precisely what he said. There was no anger, no emotion, nothing. The man is out of his mind. He's crazy, and you can't deal with crazy people! Besides, if your shooter was worth a damn, Braddock would already be dead."

"We don't know for sure that it was Braddock. Jesus, I don't believe this! So the police have the code book, and now somebody has the key." Wexler was up and pacing.

"What does he do, give it to the police?"

Wexler disregarded the question. "If we don't get one of them back, we're out of business. We have to assume it's Braddock. We may not be able to deal with crazy people, but we can damn well kill them. We hit Braddock tonight and retrieve that key."

Prather gestured, spilling the drink. "I can't find the son of a bitch. He hasn't been to his home or his office in twenty-four hours. Your man botched the job and scared him off."

"He didn't scare him very far," Wexler said, giving Max a nod. "I can't believe he simply walked in and out of your house. What happened when he left? Why didn't you follow him?"

"I don't know. I was in a state of shock, thinking about Obie."

"You're in a state of being a chicken-livered jerkoff! What was he driving?"

"I didn't see it."

"Superlative work, Willard. He was driving something unless he dropped in here from a damned helicopter."

Wexler's anger and frustration choked his thoughts momentarily. He sat again. He needed Prather. Further reprimand would not serve his purpose. "It may be cop-killing time," he said finally. "If we can't recover the key, we recover the book. Do a search on Li Dao and the woman cop."

Prather scowled. "I don't wanna search a cop."

"You don't want jail either."

Wexler felt the panic rise. His head began to pound. He and his mother had always managed to stay in the background. Their lives were open and casual, without guards or security systems that only suggested illegal activity. Braddock couldn't know that they existed, yet he had gotten to Condon and Noles and to the Prathers. Braddock knew of the key too. How could he know of the key?

"Keep looking for Braddock," Wexler said as he walked to the door. "And lock the gate." He looked at Prather. "Search the damn cops, Willard, and dump Max before he gets ripe."

10

Wednesday. Five A.M.

Harry's apartment was a nest, secure and quiet, away from the phone, away from the world. Alex savored his touch. The night had been interrupted by soft, wet exertion too many times. It was a delightful new feeling to want to be held at this early hour, at any hour. Their lovemaking was artless and mutually fulfilling. He murmured soothing words of reassurance and kissed her mouth throughout the moment of unspeakable comfort and exhilaration. Her heart was gladdened at the sound of his voice. They sighed and moaned between drowsy fragments of conversation, but eventually slept again.

It was hours later when Alex finally waked and felt slept out. Her internal clock and the color of the daylight told her it was late. "Harry, what time is it?"

He groaned and tried to focus his eyes. "Nine-thirty."

She panicked for only an instant, then relaxed and resigned herself. "I've never been two hours late for work."

"Will Lid be upset?"

She stretched and moaned. "He'll think it's hilarious. Mimbs will be upset."

"Who's Mimbs?"

"Lieutenant Pratt Mimbs. I'll say it was forcible rape. I'll take him a balloon. What time is your first class?"

"Eleven. I don't recall using force." Harry dragged out of bed, still nude, and headed for the bathroom. "Would you like to shower together?"

She watched him walk away and smiled. "Yeah, I would, but I'd also like to get to work before lunch."

"Shower with me tomorrow?"

"Unless I get a better offer."

It was ten-thirty when Alex reached her desk. She tried to hide in the turmoil and concentrate on work, but Mimbs's angular features and sharp mustache were in the tail of her eye.

He finally came over to the desk and fondled a rose.

Alex continued to write. She eyed him at belt-buckle level and thought of the zoot suit, then raised her head to meet his gaze. "Lieutenant?"

"Nice flowers," he said.

"Thank you."

Her phone rang. Alex waited through an awkward moment.

"Shit," Mimbs muttered. He looked at the wall clock and walked away.

Alex picked up the phone and smiled as several fingers wagged in her direction. Mimbs had delivered the message: don't let it happen again.

Lid hustled out of his cubicle but not to joke. He was still struggling to get his arm into the coat sleeve. "Let's go!"

Alex transferred the call and hung up, grabbed her purse and ran after him. "What?"

"One of my neighbors just called, said my front door is open."

With the siren, the ride would take only a few minutes. They sped through the parted traffic under a gloomy sky, out Vineville Avenue and Forysth Road. Lid drove without speaking; Alex radioed for help. She hated the siren and was glad when he flipped it off at the last turn.

The black-and-white was already there as Lid pulled in. An elderly couple, the Othmars, stood in the yard across the street and watched. Lid knew they had cornered the uniforms the minute they arrived and repeated all that was said over the phone. He gave them a wave of appreciation. The Othmars were good neighbors.

Two officers waited on the stoop. Lid recognized them but couldn't think of their names. It didn't matter.

"We've checked it out, Sergeant. Nobody's here, but the place is really torn up. No sign of forced entry."

Lid only groaned. "You wanna question the other neighbors?"

The uniformed officers nodded and walked away.

Alex followed Lid into the small living room, scattered with books and papers. She saw her image in a mirror over the mantel. Brass candleholders of various sizes flanked the mirror, undisturbed. A gas heater sat in front of the closed fireplace. There were plants, photographs, and other knickknacks that showed a woman's touch.

Drawers and cabinets hung open throughout the house, their contents dumped onto the floor. Alex was appalled. The invasion was repugnant, a personal attack. It was not even her house, yet she could imagine the helplessness Lid must have felt.

"What a mess!" she whispered. "Do you find anything missing?"

"How could I tell? I don't know what they were looking for. Not the TV. Damned if I know."

Lid stood in the middle of his bedroom and looked about. The closet door was open. Everything on the shelf had been dragged out onto the floor. The dresser drawers were emptied, the one bookshelf upended. "I never make the bed. Now it matches the rest of the place."

Alex couldn't joke. She was angered at the offense and felt sorry for him. He was hiding his true feelings. She picked up a paperback—*The Bloody Corral*—then noticed that all of the books were westerns and mysteries. Alex was charmed to find that he owned such a collection. It made him more appealing.

They went out the front door again.

Alex looked out from the stoop of the small brick house. The neighborhood was old, developed in a time when sidewalks were made, paved even before the streets were paved. A row of elms lined both sides. All the houses had screened porches with awnings, black driveways and metal carports, in addition to older, free-standing garages. Directly across, a basketball hoop and net hung on the front of a garage, awaiting the neighborhood pros who were in school. A dog and cat lay sprawled together on the asphalt court. The backyard fences would enclose gardens and swings, Alex thought. It was a quiet, appealing view. She and Harry would live on such a street.

"I like your house," she said.

Lid rolled his eyes. "It doesn't take much savvy to get through these locks. They keep out dogs and children, I guess."

"You know what I mean. I like the neighborhood too."

"It's been here awhile. I remember when the road was dirt. In dry weather we'd keep the front windows closed because of the dust."

He pointed. "I used to have a tree house in that mimosa."

Alex looked up into the pink blur and tried to imagine little Martin Li Dao nailing planks of wood onto the old tree. She glanced at him when he wasn't watching. Lid was the essence of cop-ness, yet he had been a little boy like any other, happy and full of play. Her feeling was warm and sympathetic. "Did you play cops and robbers when you were little?"

He squinted his eyes with steely pride. "Cowboys and Indians."

The Othmars had gone back inside, but two other neighbors had come out to sweep front steps and see what the activity was. The two uniforms returned. "Nobody else saw anything, Sergeant, just your neighbor across the street. You find anything missing?"

"No, but it was thorough. They got what they wanted or they didn't. Don't bother to keep an eye on the place."

"Whatever you think, Sarge," the uniformed officer said, turning away.

"Thanks! Thanks a lot, guys," Lid called after them. He stood and gazed down the street even after the black-and-white was gone.

A diesel engine sounded in the distance where the tracks ran between steep clay banks. Lid's happy memories of playing there seemed to have lost something over the years. The smooth pistons of modern locomotives lacked the appeal of steam power, with its insistent, detached chugs.

"What are you thinking?" Alex asked.

He came out of his trance. "I don't know. I'll figure it out when I clean up. Didn't look like vandalism, not enough damage. Let's check your place."

The idea hadn't occurred to her. "Do you think this is police related?"

"You're my partner. We won't know unless we look."

They got into the car but rode without the siren. The drive back to town would take longer than the trip out. Heavy clouds had finally started to layer a fine mist. Lid switched on the wipers. Alex rode in silence but entertained horrible visions of what they might find at her apartment. She finally groaned.

"Ohhh, I don't want to clean up my place in the rain."

"Is it less trouble when it's sunny?"

"It seems like it. If my apartment is trashed, I'll move in with Harry. It'll be a sign from God."

He chuckled. "Be careful what you say. What if it's not trashed?"

"Then it won't be a sign."

"You'd make a good Christian, Alex. Manipulation of God is one of the oldest tenets. Are you gonna marry the guy?"

The smile was more girlish than she intended. "Yes, I think I am."

"Alexandra Hall. How does it sound?"

"It sounds perfect!" she said.

Lid smiled to himself as he remembered the previous afternoon with Rachael Brucker, a delicate touch, no words spoken, but it had been a beginning. He wouldn't share the incident with his partner, didn't want to sound like a teenager swapping lies with his friends.

They fell into silence. The wipers banged back and forth, leaving the windshield clear for only an instant before it misted over again. Lid had never been to her apartment. He followed directions: down Pine, right on First. She pointed out the house. Two story. White. Tall windows. Which apartment was hers? First floor, right.

Lid stopped in front and looked at the house, one of those he had passed a thousand times but never noticed—typical gingerbread trim, open front porch with windows to the floor.

They got out and moved up onto the porch quickly because of the rain and the circumstances. He drew his revolver and waited as she peered through the living room window.

"Nothing is out of place," she said.

They entered the hallway.

Alex unlocked her door and gave it a shove. "Nobody's been here," she whispered.

"Let's look anyway," he said.

She followed as Lid checked each room and opened every door before holstering the weapon.

"That's all of it," she said aloud. "I only have three rooms and a bath."

Lid stood in the doorway to the bathroom. "A stained glass window in the john?"

"It's a classy place." She was suddenly pleased. The room was cool and fresh. Clean white curtains puffed gently, but the wide eaves kept rain from blowing in. The canopy bed was made; her slippers were positioned evenly on the edge of a braided rug; all of her clothes were put away. She hadn't planned for a visitor, but he had come on the right day.

Marvin sat tall and proud on a chest at the foot of the bed, awaiting human approval. Alex picked up the phone from the floor and dropped it into its place. "There's your favorite cat."

"Yeah, what's that cat's name?"

"Marvin, Lid! I've told you, Marvin."

"Hello, Marvin, you furry beast."

"Be nice. Someday I may not be here when you call. You'll have to talk to him."

"You're never here when I call, and I always talk to him. The damn cat doesn't say anything back."

"You must be polite."

Lid nodded with exaggeration. "Farewell, Marvin." The cat stared with cold, unblinking eyes, the customary serene countenance of its kind.

They walked out onto the porch again and watched the warm rain beat the nandina hedge. Heavy wisteria vines quivered at the far corner of the rail.

"At least I don't have to clean up my apartment."

"And you don't have to move in with Harry," Lid replied.

Eleven A.M.

Simon lay on the cot in the tiny room and listened to the rain. He had finally shaved and washed as best he could, but missed his shower. Skip's taste in clothes was what he expected—matching gray cotton pants and shirts. White socks.

Simon was weary and bored, but the shop was safe, he kept reminding himself. He needed the solitude to come down from that strange mental place and think ordinary human thoughts again.

Over twelve hours had passed since the violent, bizarre visit to Prather's house, frightening now in retrospect. Simon wondered for the first time what he would have done if the front door had not been open. It didn't matter. It was open. He had been very lucky. Numerous blunders might have occurred but hadn't. If he had missed the pickup with Skip, some acquaintance would've stopped and offered a ride, and he was supposed to be out of town.

He had finally met Willard Prather himself, the brother Obie ID'd under such exquisite duress, undoubtedly the man who'd sent the killer against him and his family. Simon had wanted to dispatch him while he had the chance, but then the bug would yield nothing. Li Dao had mentioned a woman. Prather and Wexler had asylum until the woman could be found. The threat to Prather had been a bluff, but the bluff had worked and the key was an unexpected find. He would mail it to Lid.

The rain began to dwindle as Simon heard the truck. He met Skip in the doorway and pushed him outward. He would eat on the way.

Skip locked the garage door from the outside and climbed back into his seat. "You don't have that gun with you, I hope."

"Nope, just the radio receiver," Simon said.

"I don't like being a part of breaking and entering."

"I didn't break in; I walked in. Besides, you're just giving me a ride."

"They're gonna put your ass in jail for trespassing," Skip warned, then drove in silence while Simon ate from a styrofoam container.

Twenty minutes later, Skip halted the truck at the same spot he had paused the day before. "Stay far away from the house, Simon," he yelled as he pulled away.

Simon had only the receiver, the weight and appearance of an ordinary transistor radio. The gate was closed, but he squeezed between the wrought iron and brick, then started down to the driveway as if he belonged. The land sloped away to the left, making a ridge between him and the house. In a few seconds he was even with the side of the mansion and stooped several times on the chance someone might peer from a window.

Then he spotted the gazebo, high at the back, offering both cover and concealment. Simon stepped over pink and white hyacinths and pushed between wet holly bushes and clematis vines. He crawled well under the wooden structure and lay on his back. The ground was sandy and dry. Rough joists and flooring planks were only three feet above his face. He could see the underside of the gazebo roof through cracks in the floor.

Skip had set the receiver's frequency and shown him how to fine-tune. Simon put the earphones over his head and turned on the device. Nothing. Rotating the volume knob did not affect the silence. Perhaps he was too far from the transmitter. It might be a long wait.

For over two hours, Simon lay in the cool, shady hiding place. The soft rubber earphones imposed an intolerable deafness. He pulled them away from his ears occasionally to hear the reassuring sound of water dripping onto the roof from the tall green canopy.

The rain increased and made a pleasant sound against the wooden shingles but was muffled with the earphones in place. The air became chilly as the wind picked up and blew water across the gazebo deck. Simon sat up and hunched over the receiver to keep it dry.

At last he heard something through the earphones— a door closed, a drawer opened and closed. He adjusted the volume control. Then came the sound of rustling paper, and a voice: *Heinrich, it's me . . . Yeah, we've taken a couple of swings . . . Yes . . . Later.* He heard the telephone hang up; silence; a door open and close; silence. The telephone conversation was worthless, but Simon was satisfied. The bug worked.

It stopped raining, but Simon's head and shoulders were already wet and cold. He lay back again and looked at his watch. Two o'clock. Another two hours to wait. Simon drifted into a painfully rational moment: he was a doctor, a professional man, hiding out like a youngster at play. It was pathetic, disgusting. He considered the odds that there was another dentist in Macon trespassing on private property, planning a murder. Not likely.

Simon focused deliberately on the cave. Suddenly he was beside himself, watching from the outside, a stranger strangely possessed, piteous and grave. He felt a tenderness for that sad alien who lay where he was. The sensation faded, leaving an eerie calm. Simon rubbed his face in his hands. "You're crazy, Braddock!" he whispered. "I know," he replied as he always did.

Time passed slowly. Sunlight eventually streaked through the tall trees and wafted shadows over the wet ground. The wait was comfortable enough, hidden and supine on the soft earth. He spotted an occasional mosquito, an intrepid forager who had followed him from the welding shop.

At long last he heard a door close, the sound of voices again: *The carpet's okay. You'll have to repair the wall . . . Yeah, I will. We tossed Li Dao's place, but the book wasn't there . . . What about his partner? . . . The rest of it will be done before dark. I don't want to kill a cop unless I have to . . . This is vital, Willard. Kill anybody you please, but get that damn book! What about Braddock? . . . Still no sign of him . . . Once we have the book, we kill him. Meantime, we burn his house . . . What? . . . Sunday morning at eleven, we*

*torch his house. I'll kill him soon enough . . . Heinrich,
in broad daylight? . . . It's Easter. Everybody's in
church . . . Somebody from out of town? . . . Somebody
from way out of town . . . What if we don't find Braddock or the book? . . . You find him! I'll check back
later. Don't disappoint me.*

Simon heard a door close, then silence.

They had used the name *Willard.* Simon couldn't
recall Willard Prather's frightened voice from the one
meeting, but that had to be him. The other voice was
Wexler. The words rang in his ears: *Once we have the
book, we kill him . . . Sunday morning at eleven, we
torch his house.* Marie would have been staggered at
the thought. Simon knew they wanted him dead, yet it
was shocking to hear the words spoken aloud. He
understood the reference to the *book.* They were desperate because he had the key. Li Dao was right—the
code book was incriminating.

Simon resigned himself again to the cool afternoon
air: the drudgery and boredom of a cop on stake-out. At
last the door opened and closed again. There were
other indeterminate sounds, nothing of value. Simon
smiled at the familiar rattle of ice cubes, a drink being
poured. He wished he could taste it. Skip would buy
him a bottle.

At ten minutes to four, he switched off the receiver,
knelt in the soft dirt, and urinated, then crawled stiffly
out of his nest and trespassed his way back to the road.

Four-thirty P.M.

Harvey Colish stood at the desk without speaking
until Alex looked up.

"Oh, I'm sorry, Harvey, I forgot the thing. I'll get it.
I'll get it right now; I was just on my way out."

"I'll only be here about thirty minutes," he said.

"I'm back in twenty." She tossed the purse strap over her shoulder and started out, then stopped abruptly and turned. Colish was out of sight. She walked back to the phone and dialed, then waited; redialed and waited again.

Lid looked out from his cubicle and gave a wave that said *see you tomorrow*.

Alex walked over and opened his door. "Are you ready to go?"

"Anytime."

"Would you come with me?"

"What do you need?"

"Just come with me to Harry's. I want to make sure he's all right."

She was pale and her voice was timorous, Lid thought. He grabbed his coat and followed without question. "Do you want the lights?" he asked as he slid under the steering wheel.

"Just drive."

Lid thought it an unfamiliar demeanor, as if some unseen power had enjoined her to meekness. The perky manner was gone. "You think something's wrong with the guy?"

Alex didn't reply.

He made a sidelong stare, then gave it up.

"I've been thinking," she said finally. "What if somebody's looking for the code book? They'd call before breaking and entering. The book wasn't at your house, so they called my apartment and Marvin knocked over the phone. They didn't come by because they thought I was there. Harry has the book, Lid." She wiped her eyes.

"Don't talk yourself into a good cry, Alex. Those guys don't know Harry Hall."

"We're not sure of that!" she said, crying audibly.

"They could have followed me. I just called and he didn't answer. He should be there now."

"He's in the john," Lid groaned. "Besides, it's been a week. Why would they come after the book now?"

He parked on the street.

They climbed the two flights of steps, crossed under the huge columns, and entered the once elegant residence. She tapped the door lightly and tried the handle. When it turned, they drew their guns in unison. Lid stepped in front of her and pushed the door with his toe.

They knew in an instant the apartment had been searched, but followed procedure as they entered quickly and paused back to back, listening for any sound. Most of the lights in the room were on. Lid didn't move until he saw a man's feet and legs on the kitchen floor, extending from behind the counter.

"Don't come over here, Alex." He knelt beside the body.

"Should I call an ambulance?"

Lid could tell she was trying desperately to maintain the professional stance. At last he looked up and shook his head. "He's dead." He said it without thinking yet deliberately in order to get it said.

Alex dropped the automatic and cried aloud, a childlike animal wail without preparation that stabbed him with anguish.

Lid walked over and held her for several minutes while she cried. It was the same hopelessness he had felt with his former partner's wife and with Lois Murray, but those experiences had taught him nothing. There was no consolation.

At last he settled her onto the sofa and looked around for Kleenex but there wasn't any. He ripped off two sheets from the paper roller over the sink. All the blunders of his career weighed and focused upon this moment of utter failure. His partner's lover had been murdered, and the best he could do was to hand her a paper towel.

Alex took the ludicrous offering and buried her face in her hands.

He sat on the sofa and waited for several more minutes while she cried and moaned and tried to suppress the sound with her hands.

Suddenly she was still and silent. She wiped her face and sat up, then caressed the top of the sofa cushion with her hand. "We made love right here, Lid, the first time."

"Don't think about it, Alex. I'll make the call."

She immediately cried again.

Lid walked back to the kitchen and hoped she wouldn't listen to the call, the familiar jargon, the standard operating procedure. The ambulance and lab crew would arrive in minutes. There would be an air of great urgency but all too late.

Lid covered the torso with his coat. "Alex, I never met Harry," he said gently. "He was hit in the chest." He hesitated. "It can wait if you like."

Alex stood and walked into the kitchen. She took one look, then nodded her head and went back into the large room.

Lid got up from his squatting position and looked at the room, a worse mess than his own house had been but there was more in Harry's apartment to scatter about. "I wonder if they found what they were looking for."

"They found it," Alex said. "He kept the book inside that stool, and the top is off."

"I'll take you home as soon as the lab gets here." Lid thought of her clean, cool apartment. Only hours before, they had checked it out, played with the cat, and joked about her moving in with Harry Hall. She would need somebody to stay with her, but he couldn't very well do it himself.

Alex picked up her gun with trembling hands and stuck it into her shoulder holster.

Lid watched her gaze over the room. Alex would know better than to straighten Harry's books and recordings so thoughtlessly ripped from the shelves. Tony Romano would be aghast if she touched anything.

"You want a drink?" Lid asked.

"I'd like a strawberry thing," she mumbled.

"What?"

"Nothing. Never mind."

Five-thirty P.M.

Simon sat on the tractor stool and dialed the number. Marie was out. Her mother would deliver the message: no news, everything is fine. He was secretly glad to miss her, to be spared the agony of fabricating more lies and contriving imaginary activity. The phone call itself was all that mattered. He dialed again.

"Good afternoon, Dr. Braddock's office."

"Hi, kid."

"Well, hi!" Roberta said. "You really did call. I thought you were kidding."

"I just thought I'd check with you, see if we got any good mail."

"Lots of good mail, I made the deposit. You just missed your cop buddy. This is getting so wild."

"He came by?"

"No, he called and he had bad news. He said you wanted to know anything happening with the case."

"What happened?"

"A man named Harry Hall was murdered. He was helping the police with some kind of code. Anyway, they found him dead in his apartment, and the bad guys found whatever they were looking for. Detective Li Dao told me not to tell anybody but you, said it was confidential and all that."

"Look, do what Li Dao says. Don't repeat anything he tells you except to me."

"Are you sure you're safe?"

"Sure I'm sure, unless the tide floats me away."

"Where are y'all?"

"On vacation."

"I know that. I mean which beach?"

"If you knew how to reach me, it wouldn't be a vacation."

"Hmm! How do Mrs. Braddock and Esther like it?"

"They're having a ball, Roberta. I'll check with you again in a couple of days."

"Don't get burned."

"Oh, no. Don't get bored." Simon hung up.

They had killed to retrieve the code book only one day after he had taken the key from Prather's library. Not a coincidence. His first attempt to aid the police had availed nothing. Now one of the cops was dead, or somebody working for them. Simon moaned in indecision. Better to rely on the listening device and work alone. He would hold off mailing Lid the key; it might come in handy.

Skip banged in the back door and interrupted the thought. "Suppertime, Simon, and I stopped by the liquor store like you said. At the rate it's going, we'll spend the money in a week."

"No, we won't spend it all. You'll get a cut." He made eye contact with the older man. "I'm serious. I owe you."

"Well, for God sakes, be careful, Simon! I don't wanna have to explain to Marie how you did something stupid and got in trouble. You look awful, you know. Them new clothes are already dirty."

"I'm living in a welding shop."

"Yeah, well, I know this ain't the Waldorf-Astoria. I brought you some chicken, thought you might be tired of hamburgers."

"I'm sure it's fine, whatever. This is what I'm looking for—sippin' whiskey." Simon pulled open the rectangular box and slid out the cloth sack.

"Damn if that ain't the cutest bottle of liquor I ever saw! You know what that thing costs?"

"Yes, I know what it costs. You want a shot before you go?"

"No, thanks. Vashti'd smelled that fancy whiskey on me and kick my ass." He was out the door.

The sound of the truck was the only sound, and Simon listened until it faded away. He opened the styrofoam container: chicken, mashed potatoes, slaw, and a roll. Later.

He drained the plastic cup Skip had left and poured the tawny liquid over the ice, then added a little water in deference to his stomach. Simon took a long swig, using the straw to keep ice out of his mouth. He needed the drink. His nightly dream of the decapitation had given way to vague images of the library murder. Mr. Rabbit and Mr. Squirrel were always close by, capricious and fanciful, yet never out of place. Alcohol would deaden his mind to the point of banishing all dreams.

There was no doubt Wexler and Prather would carry out the threat to burn his house. He could always call the police and say, *Gangsters plan to burn my house!* and they would say, *How do you know?* and then what?

Let it burn. It was insured. He was murdering their people—an equitable trade. The problem was the FBI. They already suspected him of killing Obie. An arson attempt, successful or not, would provide an obvious connection and bring him back under suspicion.

Simon felt a powerful urge to foil the plan, to preserve personal belongings, things money would not replace. Arson was not murder, yet it was a form of murder. He finished the drink in a swig, then found the number Lid had given him, dialed, and waited.

"Yeah?" Lid answered.

Simon replied in falsetto. "Li Dao, shut up and listen! Somebody is planning to burn the house at 208 Marcus Lane South on Sunday, eleven A.M. That's Easter Sunday."

"How do you know that?"

"Eleven A.M.," he repeated in the high, silly tone.

"Where did you hear that?"

Simon hung up. He knew he wouldn't have made the call without the whiskey, that ancient inducement to ridiculous behavior. No matter. Lid could think what he pleased.

Simon continued to mix the bourbon and water until the ice was gone, then drank the warm brown liquid without the straw. He had people to kill, he mused with a shudder, and needed an alibi. Simon probed his thoughts. There had to be a plan, something simple, foolproof. Gradually, he edged into the cave, a controlled maneuver, a borrowing of that vicious mentality in order to formulate a vicious scheme. He sipped at the plastic cup and mulled over his options. The bottle was almost empty by the time he went to sleep on the ground in the new Wal-Mart ensemble.

11

Maundy Thursday.

Simon waked in the brilliant shaft of light even before he heard the horn. He struggled with difficulty to his feet. His heart raced. His first thought was the police, but he peered through a crack in the wall and recognized his own van. Marie. His head pounded. He didn't try to imagine why she was there but opened the large doors and stood back, allowing her to drive into the shop. He closed up as the van lights disappeared, plunging his eyes and head into the relief of darkness.

She got out and hugged him without speaking. Simon relished the feel and smell of her warm body. He couldn't see what she was wearing, but the material was soft and light.

"Simon, what's going on?"

He hesitated.

"Wait, I have got to go to the bathroom."

Simon still had not spoken, too dumbfounded at her unexpected arrival, and only watched as she flipped the map light and struggled up the ladder. He could feel and smell the heat from the van's engine.

The shaft of pale light steadied on his watch as he focused his eyes: 3:30 A.M. He had slept about six hours and knew he wouldn't sleep again. Wednesday had been a long day. This was Thursday. He walked quietly out the back door and urinated on the ground. The night was cool, damp, and still. He reentered the garage, sat on the familiar tractor stool, and stared into the darkness. His last thoughts before passing out had been of Marie, what to tell her, how to tell her. He had told half-truths because she was under such stress and he couldn't bring himself to tell the whole truth. Now was the time. The plan he had come up with required that Marie know everything. Simon was amazed and terrified at the enormous risk. What if she divorced him? He rubbed the smooth metal, his favorite seat for beer and companionship, ironic now to think these thoughts and make such ghastly confession from this venue.

She climbed back down the ladder, and he held her again.

"Why are you here?" he asked.

"Simon, you smell awful!"

"Yeah, I guess I do. It's been a tough two days."

She backed up and looked at him in the meager light. "Where did you get those clothes?"

"Skip got them for me."

She didn't understand but would let it go for the moment. "I called the office. You told me not to call, but I thought it would be all right to chat with Roberta."

"You talked to Roberta today?"

"Well, about eight or ten hours ago. I caught her just as she was leaving. She thought we were on vacation! The police haven't been there or the FBI—nobody. I want to know what's happening."

"My God! You drove all that distance alone at this time of night?"

"Yes."

"Where's Esther?"

"She's at Mom's. I went by the house first, but it was all dark and there were no cars, so I came here. You said there would be police protection."

"I lied." It was the first honest statement he had made, but he had to begin somewhere. "We need to talk. I have to tell you the whole truth."

They found in the darkness the same two boxes that had served as chairs once before.

"I've told you part of it," he began. "There is a Detective Li Dao. We've talked several times, and he's given me a lot of information. I haven't admitted anything to him, but he knows. We understand each other."

"He knows what?"

There was a long pause.

"Do you remember the man who came to our house Monday?" Simon asked. "You remember what he looked like?"

"I'm surprised I haven't had nightmares."

"You showed me the gun, big and heavy, large-caliber." He looked at her in the darkness. "He wanted to point that thing at Esther and pull the trigger. That slug would have gone through her little body without even slowing down and carried her blood and bone and life through the wall on the other side."

She wiped her eyes. "Why are you saying this to me?"

"You need to be fully aware of the kind of people we're dealing with."

"I'm aware of it!" she snapped.

He paused again. "Okay. I met with one of the extortionists, a man like him who had killed before and would again if it suited him. They prey on the innocent and unsuspecting. They got Guy Bissett's son and the Lanier girl who was kidnaped. I've tried to imagine how terrified that child was, how she must have begged for her mother before they put her to death. You know that's what happened."

Marie was fighting tears. "Simon, why are you doing this to me?"

"Because I'm not innocent and I'm not unsuspecting."

"What are you telling me?"

"I'm telling you I killed the guy," he said quietly. "Then I cut his head off and mailed it to his brother."

Marie was faint and would have collapsed, but she was already seated and leaning against the wall. There was no comprehension, no response.

Simon waited, then spoke again. "Marie?"

"I'm here."

"That's not the end of it. I got two other hoods killed. I didn't actually do it, but I set them up. Now there're only two left: Wexler and Prather—the brother who got the head in the mail. When they die, the extortion ends." Simon wouldn't bother to mention the mystery woman or the servant in livery.

"Simon, you can't do this." Her voice was quiet, pale and incredulous.

"It's already done."

"What do you mean?"

"In my mind, it's done." Simon said the words but feared revealing this unfamiliar part of himself, far deeper than the obsessive-compulsive nature Marie had long accepted.

"Simon?"

"Yes?"

She paused. "Are you making this up?"

"No."

Marie yearned for denial, contrition at least, but this

was confession only. She waited again. "So Esther's daddy is a murderer?"

Now it would come: anger, tears, hysteria, threats—the entire repertoire of female emotion—not that he didn't deserve it or expect it. "Well, there's murder and then there's murder."

"What does that mean?"

"You know what I mean. I didn't come into Prather's life; he came into mine, to take what he wanted or damage our bodies in some way."

She thought it an odd expression. "That's why we have the police."

"I have no quarrel with the police. They do certain things well. They make arrests if they have evidence, but they can't kill people. I can . . . and I do."

"What happens when you get caught?"

"Don't ask me that or I'll say something you don't want to hear."

"I am asking you!"

"It doesn't matter. I *will* put Wexler and Prather to death. Nothing anybody says or does can change that."

"It's your destiny?" she asked with sarcasm.

"I don't wallow in philosophical horse shit. Wexler and Prather have made themselves my enemy. They're a threat to you and Esther. I had two months to decide what to do, Marie. You've only known about it for a few minutes. In two months you'd do the same thing I did." He paused. "How are you taking this?"

"How am I taking this? Simon, I'm numb! I'm horrified!" Her voice broke. "I'm in the depths of despair. Our marriage is over. Your life is probably over. You casually announce you're a goddamn maniac, and you want to know how I'm taking it? I'm taking Esther and moving to Idaho." Marie blotted her eyes again.

"That's about what I thought you'd say."

"That whole story about police protection was a lie? You've been working on your own?"

Simon didn't answer.

Marie started to cry aloud. "Simon, I can't believe this! I just can't believe it. You're the sweetest man I know; you're gentle; you know nothing about guns or self-defense. It's not too late for therapy."

He chuckled sardonically. "Yes, it is. What would I say—*Stop me before I kill again*? You're missing my point. The police have gotten nowhere, and this has been going on over a year."

"The professionals can't find their dicks in the dark but the super-dentist will solve the case? Simon, this is not TV!"

"I have no interest in solving the case, but I will put an end to it. When the criminals are dead, it's over."

Simon could mark the gauge of her mental anguish by the language. Marie rarely used four-letter words, and he had never heard her say *goddamn*.

"You're a vigilante. That's the word they use for it—vigilante—a guy who gets pissed off and takes the law into his own hands."

"It will all be done in a few days."

Her nose was stopped up. He could hear the tears in every painful statement. "Simon, I don't want you hurt. Maybe you've been lucky so far, but you're in no-man's land. You could be shot by the criminals or the police. I can't bear the thought of your sweet, beautiful face bashed up."

Bashed *in,* he thought. Simon held her and wished for some supernatural balm to pour over her wounds.

She finally separated herself from him. "Why on earth did you cut the man's head off?"

"I had to. Anything less would not have been appropriate."

"Appropriate?"

Simon would not defend the word. The strange hour, the fatigue, and the darkness would speak in his favor.

"What about your detective friend?"

"Martin Li Dao. They call him Lid. He's a good man, and he knows what I'm doing, more or less. He also knows it's the only way it will get done."

"My God!" she whispered. "A detective on the police force knows what you're doing?"

"He won't turn me in."

"How do you know that?"

"He told me and I believe him."

"And he can't change his mind?"

"No. I don't question Lid's integrity and morality."

"What in hell does this have to do with morals?" she asked.

"Everything. Murdering children is immoral."

Marie obviously had no argument with that, and she found herself drawn, unaccustomed, into the power and conviction of his mind, a willing disciple in deadly, alien accomplishment. It was brief but sublime admiration.

Dusty shapes of the welder's craft were discernible in the first light. The fearful, astonishing conversation would take on new life in the daylight, a separate entity requiring fresh examination and assessment. They went out the back door to stretch sore muscles, enjoy the cool air, and look at the eastern sky.

Marie had always held a warm, agreeable image of herself and Simon as one being. Now he was a different creature in a different place, pulling her into that place with him. It had a strange new language, painful to utter. "Simon . . . how exactly do you kill people?"

"I'll tell you when it's over."

She bristled. "Any lawyer would call this *mental cruelty*. I really should divorce you."

"And move to Idaho?"

"Yes, most wives would do that. You expect me to stay married to you, never knowing when you might go crazy again?"

"The chances are slim that something like this will ever happen again."

"Who's taking care of Toby?" she asked, after a moment.

"Ollie," was all he said.

Simon felt enormous relief that the conversation was over, not only because she knew, but because he had survived the self-doubt her brutal maturity always imposed. He didn't need to be reminded of his own puerile behavior. "I need your help," he said at last. "There're some things only you can do, but I want you to go back to your mother's. I need Don's help too."

She heard him but made no reply, her mind already surfeited with frightful thoughts and images.

Seven A.M.

A wooden boat floated on still black water as the sun's rays splintered across the low horizon, reclaiming the swamp from fog and the quietude of night. Two hoary companions sat in silence for the joy that silence was, though they always said it was not to scare the fish. Dragonflies rested on cypress knees, old friends because they preyed on gnats and mosquitoes.

One looked at the other and pointed, then rowed without haste or speech toward the submerged object. The boat drifted alongside and nudged the dead body into gentle bobbing motion. The fat man in overalls floated facedown in the warm water, his back displaying numerous marks of injury. They debated the cause of death—gator or gunshots—then deliberated over what they should do. Somebody had to go for the sheriff. If they left the body, it would drift. Maybe they should push it to shore. It didn't really matter. The discovery had ruined the fishing.

Marie shifted uncomfortably on the van seat and finally resigned herself that sleep was over. Her clothes were wrinkled and stale. The ghastly business struck into her consciousness again like an electrical shock, even before she sat up and pushed back the tousled mane of hair. "What time is it?"

"Eleven-thirty," he said from his position in the driver's seat.

Simon got out first and took her hand as she stepped down out of the vehicle. He held her in a long embrace. Her body was warm from the sleep.

"Bathroom," she whispered at last.

Simon let her go and watched the long, slender legs climb the ladder.

He had spent all morning in the musty darkness, moping impatiently while Marie caught up on sleep, thinking this was time that should be spent under the gazebo. He had even placed the earphones over his head and turned on the receiver but he knew the transmitter was miles away.

She climbed back down and embraced him again. "You smell better," she said.

"I tried to clean up and I shaved."

She rubbed his cheek with the back of her hand and kissed his mouth.

Simon was almost aroused, but it was not the time. "What did you tell Nana about driving back in the middle of the night?"

"I told her we were having trouble," said Marie.

"Marital trouble?"

"What other kind of trouble is there?"

"I hate the thought of her worrying about us."

"What about me worrying about you? Besides, it had to be a pretty good excuse; I'd only been there twenty-four hours. I couldn't say there was a leak in the plumbing. She knew something was bothering me, so it worked out. I asked her to keep Esther for a day or two while we talked."

"How is Esther?"

"She's fine. She likes being at Mom's."

"What about Don? Will he go along with the plan?"

"You know Don, he'll love it."

She hugged him again. "What about us when this is over? Will we be happy? Will we still have a marriage?"

"We'll always be married and we'll be happy, but things will never be exactly the same. Don't expect it. We cope with life as it comes to us and do the best we can." He let her go and walked to the back door to stare at the junk pile in midday light. "I remember on the phone when I first mentioned extortion, your response was indignant. You were worried that I had paid them something. That was the choice: pay for the rest of your life or resist. Well, anybody who leans on me is dead."

He turned and walked back to her. "I know what I'm doing because I have inside information, and I'm good at it."

"What if you get killed?"

"You would probably remarry in a few years."

His bluntness matched her own, and Marie fell silent.

"Do you want me to go over the plan again?" Simon asked.

"No, I get the idea. Don and Esther will love it. Simon, I can't believe we're doing this." She paused. "I guess there's no choice at this point. At least there won't be any pretense in front of Mom."

"How do you mean?"

"Don't you think I have ample motive for distress?"

Simon didn't respond to the question. "You need to get on the road. I've got work to do."

To his surprise, she climbed into the driver's seat, closed the door, and looked at him through the open window. "Let's get it done."

He leaned in and kissed her lips. "Do you remember everything?"

"Yes."

"Have you got everything?"

"Yes!"

He pushed his fingers into the thick mat of hair and caressed the back of her neck, then kissed her mouth again.

"Drive fast. Take chances."

She smiled at the old paraphrase of *break a leg*.

Simon opened the heavy wooden doors and waited for her to back out.

They squinted in the midday sun and smiled and waved, but both knew the banter was a great pretense and felt this parting no less painfully than the last.

Simon closed himself up again and loitered impatiently until Skip arrived with lunch. Barbecue. He ate in silence and watched Skip through the open back door, tattered overalls leaning over the gray fender, head and shoulders out of sight under the hood. Simon had never even looked at his van's engine. It started and stopped. That was all that mattered.

They left as soon as he had eaten. The few minutes of breeze and sunlight had come to be the greatest joy of Simon's day after escaping the garage. The sky was mostly clear; there would be no rain.

Skip finally spoke. "You ain't got that gun, do you?"

"No," Simon said. "Skip, I need a sun lamp, the kind you can lie under and get a tan. Where do you find that?"

"Lighting store or Georgia Power Company. I can get you one, I reckon. What do you want that for?"

"I have to look like I've been to the beach."

"Why don't you just go to the beach?"

"Get me the lamp, will you?"

"I'll get it, but you'd better take it easy and don't burn yourself up. You tend to overdo things, y' know? You drank twenty-five dollars' worth of liquor last night."

"Yeah, I guess I did."

"How do you feel?"

"I feel fine," Simon lied. He felt slightly better than awful, and it had taken six aspirins to get to that point. He hoped the barbecue would stay down.

Skip grinned and shook his head. "You would've made a good seaman."

Skip knew where to rein the truck without being told. He paused for only a moment, then ground through the lower gears and disappeared over the hill.

Simon entered the estate for the third time and followed the low areas, keeping an eye on the mansion. The shrubbery and rocks and dry rills of matted grass were more familiar.

He reached the gazebo without incident. The natural aviary was alive with the twitter of birds. Leafy shadows in mid-afternoon sun played against the wooden floor. Dogwoods and azaleas were in bloom, but the aroma was fresh earth and hyacinth. He crawled under the structure and took up his position for the wait.

Simon was asleep when a sound startled him back to consciousness. He looked at the watch. Almost four hours had elapsed. His head was better. He concentrated on the earphones. A door closed; silence; then a woman's voice, answered by a man's: *You ever read any of these books? . . . I've read some of them . . . Thanks. Same time next week? . . . I'd like you again tomorrow, twenty-four hours, noon until noon Saturday . . . Why don't you get married, Willard? It would be cheaper . . . You got any better plans? . . . It's your money . . . The maid won't be here. We'll have the house to ourselves . . . Will you behave? . . . Don't I always?* Simon heard several notes from the piano and remembered where it was in the room. Then came the woman's voice: *Where's Max? . . . He quit last week, just walked off.* A pause, more piano. *Why don't you marry me? . . . I'm not the type . . . Let's go upstairs.* He heard the sounds of giggling and soft scuffling before the door closed him into silence.

Prather and a paid companion, Simon guessed, but not the woman he was looking for. Tomorrow they would be alone in the mansion for twenty-four hours, an ideal time to get to Prather if he could discover the identity of the female accomplice first. *Max* must have been the guy in the tuxedo. Simon looked again at his watch. Five P.M. Another hour to wait.

Simon pushed up on his elbows and slipped the headset down around his neck for a moment of rest. Then came the last thing he expected—voices, not from the bug but close by in the immediate area. He needed to turn on one side and stretch out his cramped muscles but could only lie flat again and wait. The voices grew louder, then came the sudden, startling sound of footsteps on the wooden floor above him.

"Flowers are God's gifts and they harm no one," uttered a childlike voice. "A pale green canopy. Beautiful! Just beautiful, Heinrich. A delicate little love nest. And you deserve to be surrounded by beautiful things, Heinrich. There is so much evil in the world. You deserve it, *mein Engel*."

Simon couldn't see the bright eyes as they darted about, the ancient head with scant hair and deeply lined face.

"This beauty is for you, Heinrich," she said, "not for the rabble. You treasure the finer things."

Simon remembered for a terrifying moment that he had not brought the gun. He was a rabbit, that helpless prey of more vicious creatures, his only defense absolute stillness and silence. He dared not turn his head, only his eyes. Two figures moved slowly about in the gazebo. The footsteps were loud, so close was his head to the underside of the flooring.

"He still does not please me, Heinrich. The housekeeper could work better for what he is paid. He thinks to be insolent because he does more for us, yes?"

"Willis does kill for us, *Mueni*. That is worth something. He recovered the code book."

"The driver gives me more respect."

"Luther does his job, but he is only a chauffeur. He knows nothing of the business. Willis would kill to protect you. He is a powerful man."

"Willis?"

"Willis Carruth, *Mueni*. He might be more respectful if you remembered his name."

"I pay him for respect. I pay him to clean and to kill and do anything I ask. He is a servant, Heinrich. Luther knows better his place."

Simon could see Heinrich Wexler's face clearly, the delicate features, the silk shirt. *His uncle, old guy who lives next door,* Lid had said. Simon knew that Wexler could see him as well if only he focused his eyes at the right spot.

"The driver knows his place, *mein Engel.* He is only a nigger, but he has regard for our station."

"Luther Steele does what I hired him to do, *Mueni.*"

There was a pause. Simon watched the movement of the dress as she slowly took a seat on the circular bench. He glimpsed the face, old and drawn, an ancient tortoise. She fumbled for her necklace and fingered the cameo, the seed pearls.

"If you had brought the key when I asked . . . remember the family, Heinrich."

"Please, *Mueni,* we got it back. You are the source."

"Yes," she said with softer tone, "and you are *mein Engel.*"

"Where did you put the book?"

"Guess, *mein Engel.*"

There was a long exhalation. "I don't know, *Mueni.*"

"Hee hmp hmmm," she cackled. "My footlocker. Under my bed. I know you use the book each week. Tell me, *mein Engel.* Did you talk to him about it?"

"Who?"

"The housekeeper. When he killed the teacher, did he tell you about it?"

"Willis doesn't talk much, *Mueni.*"

It struck Simon, stupidly, that this frail crone was the woman he was looking for. He longed for the weapon, even thought to finish the job with his bare hands—Wexler was old; she was decrepit—but he hadn't the skill. It would be clumsy, difficult work. Wexler might have a gun, preponderately superior to youth and strength. Simon forced himself to remain motionless.

"Sing to me, *mein Engel*."

"Mueni, O Mueni, Du bist der Lenz nach dem ich verlangte . . ." came the weak tenor croon.

"Give me your hand, Heinrich. I want it now. Yes, closer . . . closer." The voice became slower and quieter.

The words and groping were strangely familiar. Sexual play. Simon assumed the elderly woman was Wexler's mother, though he wouldn't have guessed she was still alive. He wondered what they were doing but dared not move his head.

"It is better in bed, Heinrich. Sunday is good when the servants are not at the cottage. Your fingertips relieve the pain. Sing to me, *mein Engel*."

"Frisch weht der Wind der Heimath zu: mein Irisch Kind, wo weilest du? . . ."

"Heinrich, you and the housekeeper can have the dentist, but I want the child. Take them quickly while the weather is pleasant, not sticky and hot with summer."

The words rang in Simon's ears. He fell again into the deadly conviction of that savage place, and closed his eyes, ostrich fashion, as if his very glance might draw Wexler's gaze.

"We are watching his home and office, *Mueni*. When they return, the child is yours."

Simon heard the rhythmic patter of her feet in gleeful anticipation. Marie had called him a maniac; this old woman was the anti-Christ. He wished again that he had brought the gun.

Ilsa Wexler rocked gently and smoothed the silk dress over her lap, then rose from the seat without assistance. "Help me, Heinrich," she said.

Simon scarcely breathed as the careful footsteps moved above him. The silence was abrupt as they stepped from the wooden platform to the ground. The voices faded.

Simon understood everything except the reference to the *cottage,* presumably her home. He would find it. Wexler and his mother would be there without servants on Easter Sunday. This was Maundy Thursday—Good Friday in a few hours. The significance did not escape his thoughts, but theological meandering was for purer minds. Simon only knew Wexler and his mother would die on Sunday.

Heinrich and Ilsa Wexler walked slowly up the path between azaleas and hibiscus to where Luther Steele was waiting at the Rolls-Royce and holding the door. Wexler helped his mother into the car, then got in on the opposite side.

"Take me home, driver," she said.

Luther started off.

"The housekeeper, Heinrich. He cleans only the floor, not under the furniture."

"There are boxes under everything, *Mueni.* Cleaning is difficult."

"He will move the boxes and move the furniture. Carruth is only a servant, and he is strong enough. Speak to him, Heinrich."

"Yes, *Mueni.*"

She ran a finger along the edge of the window. "You clean the limousine well, driver."

Luther Steele maintained the dignified expression that he was paid for. "Yes, ma'am, thank you, ma'am."

"The car is cleaner than my house. You know that, don't you?"

"I don't git inside the house very often, Miz Wexler, but I try to keep the Rolls clean."

"You see, *mein Engel*? This driver is also a varlet, but respectful. He knows his place."

Luther wasn't sure what a varlet was, but it sounded better than nigger. He stopped at the side entrance to the cottage, then hopped out and opened the rear door but knew better than to offer his hand. Mrs. Wexler didn't touch the help—not the nigger anyway.

He waited until they were clear before driving the Rolls-Royce into the carriage house.

Willis Carruth was emerging from the storeroom. "What are you smiling at, Steele?"

"She ain't happy over yo' housecleaning."

"She said that?" he snapped.

"You ain't been getting under the furniture."

Carruth unconsciously assumed a bodybuilding pose before he caught himself. After a moment he seemed to forget that anyone else was present, but only tightened his shoulder and admired the biceps through the tight-fitting short sleeves. Eventually he walked away toward the house, muttering to himself.

Ilsa Wexler had already changed into a powder blue robe and slippers. She and Heinrich perched upright on a sofa amid the crowded disorder of the cottage living room. A crystal globe weighed heavily in her lap, her fingertips resting on the glass.

"Touch it, Heinrich," she whispered. "Touch it with me."

He placed his hands over hers and waited as she peered into the colorless quartz. The tactile sensation was arousing. He would have Clara Warwick service him immediately on his return.

"Yes," she whispered, "Sunday is the day. It is a good day to burn out this man who attacks our family."

For Heinrich Wexler, it was an all-persuasive voice. Only her words could impel him to accept any counsel, wise or foolish. Her dwelling was a warehouse, her faith astrology, yet he could not go behind the power and security he felt in her being. She had suckled him into allegiance neither age nor frailty would diminish.

Carruth stopped in the doorway, his wide frame filling the space.

Heinrich Wexler straightened up.

"Schnapps!" Ilsa cackled.

Carruth nodded and walked back to the kitchen.

Wexler sat reluctantly, his heel butting against packages of unknown contents. The sofa had a homemade flounce as if the covering made the storage acceptable.

She patted his hand. "The cards and the charts agree, *mein Engel.* Sunday is good for the arson. The arrangement has been made?"

"Yes, *Mueni.*"

"And when they return, I have the child?"

"Yes."

"Is she fair, the child?"

"I haven't seen her, but the mother is fair. You will like her, *Mueni.*"

The old woman rocked gently and fondled her throat.

Wexler remembered the act of murder and worked the muscles of his lips and tongue. He squeezed his thighs together and released them. The swamp rat had been too far away for him to make the drive comfortably, but there was always Braddock. In the meantime he would kill another rabbit, but it was not the same.

Carruth came in and left the whiskey.

Heinrich Wexler sat in late afternoon light and quietly sipped his drink, holding the glass for want of a place to set it. He worked well on his own, he thought, without his mother waiting for a report. It was her impatience and nagging that had made the dentist so elusive. Max and Obie were gone, Asa and Wally and Tubby Milken—five men lost to one recalcitrant customer. But none of that mattered. Braddock would have to show up sooner or later.

"Sing to me, *mein Engel*."

Without hesitation he began the eerie, soft chant. *"Mueni, O Mueni, Begehrt, Herrin, was ihr wuenscht. O Mueni."*

Carruth stood in the kitchen and listened. From the beginning, he had never understood the Wexlers. Now, after a year and a half, he cordially detested them, but the salary and covert bonuses were all that mattered.

"O Mueni, O diese Sonne! Ha! dieser Tag! O Mueni . . ."

Carruth shook his head and moved quietly away.

Five-thirty P.M.

"How's it hanging, Li Dao?"

Lid waited for Romano to slouch into one of the seats opposite his desk. "It's hanging just fine, Tony. What's new in the chop shop?"

"Same old stuff. What about that teacher who got iced? You report it to the feds yet?"

Lid knew what Romano had stopped by for—to see how badly the locals were screwing up the fibbies' case. He and Alex had lost the file that should have been delivered to the federal bureau. "I made the report," Lid said.

"Yeah, I'll bet the feds are pissed." Romano was enjoying himself. "Presnell was pissed, whataya think, Li Dao?"

"Special Agent Presnell was pissed," Lid agreed.

"That was a shame too, that Hall guy. Did you see his place? I mean, there was a man who appreciated the finer things! Did you see all that stuff?"

"I saw it," Lid said.

"I mean, he had CD's, LP's, out the wazoo. All the great ones. Caruso!" Romano made an ambiguous gesture and sang the first words of *"O Sole Mio."*

Lid guessed that Caruso was the only name that had come to mind. Romano didn't know *mio* from *bambino,* but he could have his Italian moment in the sun.

"That guy even looked like he's from the old country," Romano said. "Shame to kill a guy like that."

Now they're brothers, Lid thought. He doubted that Harry Hall or Tony Romano either one had ever seen the old country. "Yeah, I'm sure if they'd known he was Italian, they would've left him alone," Lid said.

"Funny, Hall don't sound Italian."

"Maybe he changed it. Maybe it used to be *Hallo*."

"Maybe so," Tony replied seriously. He got up and opened the door. "Shame to get a guy like that killed. I know the feds were pissed, Li Dao." He waggled a finger and walked away.

Lid hadn't considered himself personally responsible for Hall's death, but Romano was always there to assign blame, to keep him straight.

Mimbs entered across the large room.

Lid followed him to his office, but the lieutenant was already on the phone. He waited.

Mimbs had been with the mayor in Atlanta and appeared spiffier than usual—stiff white button-down, narrow tie with a small, tight knot. His face even had the mayor's cosmetic glow, Lid thought, touched over by the same salon. Something about bodyguard duty in the big city gave the added blush. The word was that Mimbs himself aspired to be mayor someday. Lid thought privately that he would be good at it. At least Mimbs was on the right track—to get into politics, hang around with the people who're already there.

The lieutenant finished his conversation and looked up.

"I got a call last night," Lid said. "Ten P.M. A guy says somebody will burn Braddock's house on Easter morning."

Mimbs took off his glasses and rubbed his eyes. "Whatever happened to Easter egg hunts?"

Lid gave a lopsided smile.

"Did the caller leave his name?"

"Sure—and his phone number. He just said 208 Marcus Lane South would be torched Sunday morning. He mentioned eleven A.M. specifically. I looked it up; it's Braddock's house."

Mimbs twisted the ends of his mustache. "Was he angry or threatening?"

Lid shook his head. "Didn't sound like he gave a damn. I tried to keep him on the line, but he had his say and hung down."

"Did you get it on tape?"

"Nope."

"You got any idea who or why?"

"Nope. I think we'd better stake it out."

Mimbs sighed and leaned back in the chair. "We'll stake it out. The feds will want in."

"Yeah, I know, because it's Braddock. You tell the bastards."

Lid left for the day and headed toward Alex's apartment. He did have an idea *who* but wouldn't share the thought with Mimbs.

For the second time in two days, he parked in front of the huge white structure with steep roof and tall chimneys. A grandmother house. The railing and porch had been painted every summer since 1895. He mounted the steps. The screen was unlatched, the heavy front door already open. Lid stood in the cool hallway and tapped at Alex's door. "Alex, It's me."

"Come on in," she said with a quiet voice.

"It's locked."

Alex opened the door and walked away, still blotting her bloodshot eyes. She slouched into a chair and pulled her legs up under the edge of the robe.

Alex appeared small and sad, a whipped puppy, a pathetic contrast to her bright, chipper manner of a day earlier when they had checked out the apartment. Lid felt again that empty desire to console, yet he had no words to comfort his young partner.

"You aren't getting dressed today?"

"Why bother now?" She shrugged. "I called Mimbs and told him I wouldn't be there."

"It's okay. I'm sure he understood. I started to bring you a pizza for supper. Have you eaten anything?"

"No."

"Did you have lunch?"

"Coffee."

"Would you like me to get something for you?"

She finally gave him a wan smile. "Not yet, thanks." Alex paused. "Harry's funeral is tomorrow. His parents will be there and God knows who else. I've never even met them."

"Did they know you were seeing each other?"

"I doubt it. I hope not; they'll hold me responsible. I guess I *am* responsible."

"You know better than that," he said without conviction.

"I won't even be able to sit under that canopy thing. I might have spent the rest of my life with Harry and had children, but I can't even sit with his family." Alex pulled Kleenex from a box and spoke with it pressed against her eyes. "I'll stand around and look like the rest of the crowd, people who went only because it was polite and they had to go, people who wished it was over."

She looked at him. "You know what's funny, Lid? I thought Harry was gay. I swear, the first time I was with him, I thought he was gay. He's such a great cook and has so many varied interests . . . had so many interests."

"If I knew anything wonderful to say, I'd say it. I remember what you told me. When people go to visit, whatever they say sounds stupid."

There was a long silence.

The cat walked across the floor and hopped up onto a window ledge, but Alex ignored him. "Nobody knew about Harry, not my friends, not even my parents."

"Why don't you tell them?" Lid asked.

"No. You know and that's enough. If I need to talk, I'll talk to you."

He gave a single nod. Alex would combat in her mind the excessive unfairness, that ageless battle forever coped with but never won.

"I'm sure Mercer is agog," she said. "They have a special service planned, and the students will all be teary-eyed or at least they'll have gossip to last for a while."

"Did he get along well with his students?"

"I don't know, I guess so. Harry was interested in so much besides English literature. The universe. Music. He was funny too. He must have been a good teacher." Alex looked at him and blotted her eyes. "How can I feel like this about somebody I barely knew?"

Lid said nothing.

"He was murdered by scum who never read a book or look at stars, people who have only one interest—money. That's true, isn't it, Lid?"

"That's true."

She had half expected some mollifying rationale, but he offered nothing. Lid was a cop who had toughness that went beyond the physical, asking for no favors and giving none. Alex admired her partner for the first time. She gave a wan smile. "Maybe I see why you like Braddock. Our suspicions are correct, aren't they? He *is* a vigilante."

"Yes, he is." Lid paused, but knew he was supposed to continue. "I'm opposed to vigilantes the same as you but for different reasons, I imagine. You probably object on principle. I only care because they're clumsy and innocent people are likely to get hurt. I've watched scum walk free out of the courts longer than you have, Alex. I like Braddock because he's good. He has a terrifying deep anger, but it's controlled by intelligence. Brucker says a person can be intelligent and immature at the same time. Braddock probably finds it intolerable not to be in control of his own destiny, and he'll do anything to maintain control."

"Even murder?"

"Anything."

"And you plan to help him?"

"I *have* helped him." He shrugged. "He's my dentist. I just have conversations with the guy."

"Will you feel guilty if he gets himself killed?"

"Braddock will do what he's doing with or without help."

Alex stared at him. Lid looked like a cop—the hard face, the hard eyes, the crew cut. Everything he did was for the job. He had lost his wife and son for the sake of the job. He could always find another dentist.

"You know what Harry said?"

Lid waited.

"He said when he looked at a starry sky, he knew that nothing we do on Earth is very important."

"I know nothing I've ever done is important, and I don't even have to look at the sky."

She finally smiled. "Go home."

They stood at the door. Lid turned and put his arms around his partner and patted her back.

"Thanks for coming by," she said.

He got to the outside door.

"Lid."

"Yeah?"

"Let me know if there's any way I can help Braddock."

Seven P.M.

The Howard residence was in an old Charleston neighborhood, but the view from the back was exceptional. Grassy, brackish water and palmettos stretched away toward the Ashley River. The sun was an orange ball perched atop the distant horizon, making golden fluff of the western clouds.

Marie and Don sat on the wooden steps, halfway up from the lower deck to the tree house deck, overlooking a lagoon. They were both barefoot, clad in shorts and shirts. Don was Marie's masculine equivalent with perfect skin and long, shaggy hair. He had a natural athletic physique that he did little to maintain. She was older than her brother, but they might have been mistaken for a couple. Only the eyes and thick blond manes revealed them as siblings.

"Don, you've got to promise you'll help me."

"You haven't told me what it is. Reminds me of the time Turk made me promise to suck the blood out of a snakebite, then told me it was on the head of his dick."

Marie smiled. Don was the family comic. She liked his humor and used it now to temporize and avoid the issue. The direful subject could wait another few minutes.

"What about you and Simon?" he asked.

"Everything's fine between us. I made that up."

"What for?"

She paused. "Well, listen and don't interrupt. We've got big problems but not marital problems." She suddenly yearned for him to interrupt, to suggest some familiar diversion—clamming or wind surfing—but reality would not disappear. "Promise you won't tell any of this to Mom."

"I promise."

Marie gazed into the western light and said nothing.

"The longer you wait, the more gruesome my fantasies are becoming."

"That's the right word for it. Okay . . . the doctors in Macon are being extorted by some group of hoods." She waited, but Don made no response. "Apparently they're paying off, except for your brother-in-law."

"Did he go to the cops?"

"Nothing so ordinary." Marie paused again, unable to speak the words. She lost her composure and stopped to wipe her eyes.

"Ree!" Don took his sister by the shoulders as he saw her distress. "What did he do?"

Long seconds passed before she could say it aloud: "He's murdering the criminals one by one."

"Jesus!" For an instant Don was genuinely amused, but his laughter was an awkward, embarrassed reaction, unintentional and unpredictable on hearing the ghastly news. "Simon? Simon is the biggest wimp I know!" He stared at Marie, but she didn't smile. "Tell me you're making this up."

"That's exactly what I said when he told me."

"Simon is not a killer," he said almost in a whisper.

"Not ordinarily. This extortion thing got to him, Don. They threaten families and they've murdered a doctor and they've murdered children."

"Why the hell didn't the doctors go to the police?"

"Some of them did. Those are the ones whose children were killed. Like I said, Simon is the last person you'd expect . . . anyway, he's doing it."

Don's expression changed to repugnance. "How does he kill people?"

"I don't know. He said he'd tell me later."

"How do you know he's even doing it?"

"Oh, I believe him. The last four days have been a nightmare. A guy came to our house and tried to kill us; we spent a night hiding in a welding shop. Esther and I spent the next night in Atlanta. We can't even go home. The FBI searched our house, and the extortionists are probably watching it now. Simon has two more people to kill, and then he says it will be over." She paused and shook her head. "I can't believe I'm even saying this."

"Why did the FBI search the house?"

"They suspected Simon of killing one of the hoods." Marie stopped again and took deep breaths. "He did kill the man; they just can't prove it. He seems to cover himself well. They searched the office too. He has this cop friend, a detective, who gives him information and tries to help."

"A private detective?"

"No, he's on the police force. I know what you're thinking: why would a detective help somebody kill people? Well, I don't know exactly. He seems to admire Simon. He's a cop and he hates gangsters."

Don wondered for a moment if the outlandish tale was payback for a lifetime of one-liners. "Ree, you'd better not be making this up."

Marie looked at him unsmilingly and shook her head.

"So what does he do now?"

"He kills the last two members of the extortion ring."

"What if they kill him first?"

She shook her head again but said nothing.

"What if he gets caught?"

Marie only tightened her lips and wiped her eyes.

"How does he know who they are and where they are?" Don asked.

"There's a lot more to it that I don't know. His cop buddy is very knowledgeable."

"Why the devil didn't the police handle this thing in the first place?"

She shrugged. "It doesn't matter now. The point is, Simon has started down a path and there's no turning back. We kill them or they kill us."

Don hated her choice of pronouns. "Where is he staying?"

"I don't know that either, probably the welding shop."

"About a hundred years ago you said there was something you wanted me to do."

She managed a weak smile. "I need you to pretend to be my husband."

"Ree, I am not going to bed with you."

Her smile broadened. "I want you to take three days and go to the beach with us—you, me, and Esther."

"What's the plan?"

"Can you get away from the pizza shop for the weekend?"

"Ree, I own the franchise; I do any damn thing I like. Turk can run the store."

"Simon wants us to go to Hilton Head and stay at the Patterson, eat out, charge everything on plastic. I've got his credit cards and driver's license."

"To give him an alibi?"

She nodded. "You both have light hair and you're about the same size."

"No, I'm a lot bigger. I've seen him in the locker room."

"Will you be serious?"

"Relax, Ree. Nobody looks at driver's license pictures. They copy the Social Security number and hand it back."

"Do you think it will work? I'm a year and a half older than you."

Don beamed. "A weekend of sand and chicks. Simon picks up the tab. Sure."

"Remember, you're my husband and you'll have to act like it."

There was a long silence.

"You know I've always liked Simon okay. He's weird, but if he makes you happy, he makes me happy. Still, if the idiot gets himself killed, it leaves you and Esther alone."

"That's why we've got to do this right. I told Esther not to say anything to Nana because we don't want her to be bothered and all that."

"What does Esther think?"

"She's seen so much TV she doesn't know it's real. She thinks there was one bad guy and the police caught him. Esther's okay, just don't mention it to her."

"What can we tell Mom? She'll go crazy if she hears the truth."

"Here's the story. Simon and I are working out our problems. We're spending a few days together away from home and the office, but don't want Esther to miss the beach. You're coming as a baby-sitter. Will she buy that?"

"She'll buy that. What if she wants to come too?"

"She's not invited. We've got marital problems. I don't want my mother along."

"Yeah, I think that'll float," Don said.

They sat together in the cool twilight and said nothing more. The orange sky was gone, the thousand sounds of a spring night beginning, each tiny creature of air and water coping with its own need to survive. The one fact that precluded all other options went unspoken: Simon had already killed; there was no turning back.

12

Good Friday. Ten-thirty A.M.

Alex sat apart in the dimly lit sanctuary. She wanted to be alone and had not looked for a familiar face. It was the oldest Episcopal church in Macon, seldom filled except on Easter Sunday and Christmas Eve, never for a funeral in spite of the large number of Mercer students and faculty, who were mostly Baptists. The chancel and nave were darker than most churches she had seen—holier or gloomier according to one's view.

The two-piece dress was new. She had not bought it with a funeral in mind, but the blue and gray were appropriate. Alex had attended Episcopal services before and had watched the others to know when to stand and sit and kneel. Now she didn't care, her heart heavy with despondence and anger. She would do nothing to impress the Episcopal church with her knowledge of its ritual; let the church impress her.

Some of those in attendance would die themselves within the year, here now to befriend the god of death before that unveiled confrontation. Those who were younger bravely viewed for another and from a distance what they would only abhor for themselves. The chancel was Spartan in preparation for the three-hour Good Friday service, purple Lenten hangings removed and the altar stripped bare except for the cross draped in black, coincidental but appropriate.

The organ began to sound and gave her a point of focus. It was not a balm but solid and unyielding, deliberately stating reality and truth: Harry was dead.

Alex was aware of the procession, the crucifer, the rector reading aloud, and the pall. Then nothing more, lost in her own thoughts. The red giant Harry had shown her was in its appointed place. The fact that she was earth-bound didn't make the star less existent. The galaxy was dangerous and beautiful and real. Alex took joy in the thought.

She got up or sat, along with the others.

At last the rector stood at the bier and made the sign of the cross. For the first time she listened to his words: "The Lord bless you and keep you; the Lord make His face to shine upon you and be gracious unto you; the Lord lift up the light of His countenance upon you and give you peace, both now and evermore. Amen."

Tears streamed down her face as reality struck her unexpectedly and with full force: the benediction was not for the congregation but for Harry alone. He was gone.

Alex followed the crowd back out into the mid-morning sunlight and thought of the red giant, invisible now in the refulgent splendor of our own star. At some point during the service, she had understood Harry's perspective. The galaxy was substantial and we were part of it. His death was a tragedy, but more important, it was reality. She would die too. The rector would die, the crucifer. The church had made no apology for death. She was impressed.

The procession to the cemetery was long and slow.

Memory of that previous Tuesday afternoon was still fresh as she passed again under the heavy brick entrance. She recalled the gentle tug of the red and green helium-filled balloons and wondered if the Oconee had received news of the Ocmulgee. Harry had touched and tasted the earth with gladness. Alex felt a peace, unexpected and potent, which flooded over her pain and offered infinite hope.

The graveside service was brief but colorful, almost medieval, she thought. The rector wore a long cape of embroidered brocade, cream, gold, and green. The crucifer, in black and white, had carried the heavy golden cross from the chancel all the way to the open grave, and stood in stolid reverence as the leader of a crusade might have looked. A younger boy waited to one side in a red cassock and white surplice, holding the church flag with stark dignity. The picture was a comfort. This was Harry's church. Alex felt strongly that she should be an Episcopalian.

It was noon when she returned to the department. She walked straight into Lid's cubicle without speaking and stared out the window as if her garb were an emblem of sacrifice, earning a certain reverence.

Lid thought she was unusually attractive in the tunic jacket and pleated skirt, more feminine in the church attire, which contrasted with his own rumpled appearance. "How was the funeral?"

Alex turned back from the window, wary of putting forth her thoughts for his sanction. "It was nice. I guess that's not the way to describe a funeral."

"How was it nice?"

"I was just remembering the things Harry said about the universe, what a speck the Earth is. Instead of chasing around after extortionists, I should be reading poetry or smelling flowers, appreciating something."

The phone light blinked, but Lid ignored it. He gave a gentle smile. "We can't all be poets. Some of us have to make shoes and bake bread."

"And arrest the bad guys?"

"You're good at the work."

Alex looked out the window again. Maybe she was good at it, maybe not. She had been an honest cop—until recently. She wanted to think of Lid as an honest cop. They both knew what Simon Braddock was doing; neither of them cared. Alex felt another pang of guilt and indecision. She and Lid didn't admit it, but they would both have regrets if anything happened to Braddock. Still, it was a little late to express their theory to Mimbs. If they were wrong, no harm done. If they were correct, Braddock was already a murderer, past help. Let him take his chances.

Walter Presnell stuck his head in the door. "Excuse me, Alex. Li Dao, do you know where Dr. Braddock is? His receptionist says they're at the beach . . . she didn't know which beach."

Lid pictured the receptionist supporting Presnell's huge body while he had the fainting spell. He smiled easily. "I thought he came up clean."

"He did, but he's still our best suspect. Don't you think he'd like to know somebody's threatening to burn his house?"

"I don't know where he is," Lid answered honestly.

Presnell made a face and walked away.

"Who do you think made the anonymous phone call?" Alex asked.

"Anonymous," Lid said.

"Do you really not know where Braddock is?"

"No. He said they were going on vacation. Maybe he went and maybe he didn't."

"Where else would he be?"

Lid looked after Presnell and chuckled. "I don't know. If Prather turns up dead, we'll know Braddock's not at the beach."

One P.M.

Army camouflage would have served him better than the gray outfit. Simon had laid hidden in a clump of azalea shrubs near the gazebo for almost an hour before a cab came into view on the circular driveway and deposited the girl, too far away for him to tell much about her. He waited several minutes after the cab was gone before making a move, hoping they were in a bedroom far from the downstairs windows. Breaking and entering was simple enough if time and stealth were no matter. Skip had shown him how to use a glass cutter, but Simon still worried that Prather would hear a sound and arm himself. Another calculated risk.

He passed behind the gazebo, circled the mansion, and approached the west side, where the windows were close to the ground. Pale spring foliage hid the Wexler house beyond the next ridge. Simon crouched between the shrubbery and the foundation and peered into the library. The sheer transparent curtain and drapery partially obstructed the view, but the room appeared silent and motionless. Prather's whereabouts was unknown.

Simon pushed a large rubber cup against the pane and felt the suction, then used the glass cutter to draw a square. A couple of yanks served to show that there was good suction, but the glass remained intact. He popped it inward with the heel of his hand and cringed at the sound of breaking glass. A rock would have done as well. He pulled on rubber gloves and waited, but nothing was happening. At last he unlatched the window and shoved it open enough to slide it into the carpet.

Simon remembered the beauty and spaciousness of the room from his first visit. As then, he was not inclined to stop and admire. He recovered the bug. The possibility that it would be discovered and traced back to Skip was remote, yet it was a simple precaution.

There was no evidence of Max's recent murder. Even in the semidarkness Simon could see that the wall had been repaired and the carpet cleaned. Perhaps now when Mr. Squirrel entered the room in his dream, the blood and bullet hole would be gone from that too.

Simon waited at the door and listened. Eventually he peered out, then stood in the bright entrance hall. His memory was jogged by the decor, the wide, polished floorboards and dark paneling, antique furnishings and tasteful color tones. He hadn't thought of the hallway since his first visit, yet everything was familiar. The image had been there like a snapshot, stored in a few brain cells. The appreciation was brief; Simon was in the cave.

At last he heard the sounds of distant voices. Simon started up the carpeted stairway and discovered gratefully that there were no squeaky floorboards in this splendid dwelling.

The voices led him easily down the wide, carpeted hall to an open door. He stood against the wall and listened as the dialogue of indifferent substance turned bitter.

"Why don't you tell your uncle to kiss off? Are you afraid of the guy?"

"I ain't afraid of anything. It's a matter of integrity. I like to be treated with respect."

"You're a little boy, Willard. You never have grown up."

"What? I'm walking the street and you're living in a mansion?"

"That's exactly what I mean. I know how to earn a living. You got nothing to do but live in this rich-bitch place, and you're not man enough to handle that."

Simon heard a stinging slap.

"You bastard! Let go of me!"

"I'll show you a man, slut!"

Sounds indicated wrestling on the bed. At that point Simon entered the room, the long automatic and silencer held with both hands.

Prather and the girl were nude, she on her back, he astride his companion on his knees, both hands about her throat. The girl could see the intruder, but Willard had his back turned.

Simon stood quietly and watched as she struggled and gestured violently to point out the danger and to protect her own life. Her eyes were wide and her face crimson as the full weight of Prather's body bore down upon her for several minutes.

Simon was sublimely indifferent to the outcome. He waited until Prather was satisfied the hired companion was dead, then placed the muzzle close to the nape of his neck and pulled the trigger. The weapon jumped in his hands; the slug penetrated the headboard and wall with a loud thud.

Prather jerked forward and collapsed heavily onto the king-size mattress.

The exact thought struck Simon as when he had killed Max: *What a machine!* Even in this moment Simon knew his action would later be a ghastly, terrifying memory. For now it was releasing him from the cave.

He examined the girl with watchful attention, listened for breathing, and felt carefully for a carotid pulse, but there was none. It was hardly necessary to inspect Prather to make certain the deed was accomplished. Simon looked at the fat, bloody face and remembered his promise to Obie: *I'm going to kill your brother too.* He mused with satisfaction that he was a man of his word.

He retraced his steps, left by the back door, and skulked again to a position near the road, to return to the sun lamp, the mosquitoes, and the boredom of the shop.

Two-thirty P.M.

Marie and Don were dressed like beach bums, but Mrs. Howard wore a stylish summer dress, color-coordinated, accessorized. Her wrists dangled with an excessive number of bracelets as she lathered pimento cheese onto whole wheat bread and lectured at the same time. "You've got to accept each other as you are. Marriage is always a compromise."

Marie made a face. "Mom, Simon and I are not getting a divorce. We just need to bitch now and then. Stop worrying about it. And stop fussing over lunch. We'll eat something when we get there."

"Esther likes pimento cheese."

"Yeah, I like the compromise you and Pop made," Don said. "He lives in Vidalia and you live here." Don laughed at his own statement.

His mother tilted her head. "Our divorce is very civilized." She set the package of foil-wrapped sandwiches on the table. "It's supposed to be a hot, sunny weekend. You're sure you don't want me to come along?"

"Thanks, Mom. I'd rather you didn't. Don can entertain Esther while we spend some time alone."

"They're working to save their marriage, Mom, not end it. You get it?" He tickled his mother from behind.

"I get it!" she shrieked. "Y'all have a good time."

They said their good-byes from the driveway and started out, Esther buckled in the back of the van with her thoughts and whatever play she could find on her own.

The trip would take only an hour, but Marie relished the stint. Her life had come down to small increments of time, compartments that insulated her from decision making. For an hour she could vegetate, releasing her mental grip, allowing wild, chaotic thoughts to soar unheeded.

But the weight of reality would not be so easily ignored. "Did you practice signing his name like the driver's license?"

"Ree, will you relax? Someday you'll look back and remember this as fun."

"I don't want it to be fun; I want it to be over."

Don didn't argue but drove in silence through the city streets and intersections, back out to the bright, open highway.

After passing through Beaufort, the landscape began to appear swampy. Flat, low bridges spanned miles of open marsh where egrets perched safely away from the road. Exposed black soil glistened around grassy islets. Low tide. The black ribbon of highway led cave-like through scrubby oaks and Spanish moss. Every bridge and curve on the state highway was familiar. Hilton Head was a second home.

At last they mounted the high bridge from the mainland to the island. The marina lighthouse was discernible, visible only on a clear day. "I'm home!" Don said. "I love the hot, sticky air and the sand. I was a jellyfish in a previous lifetime."

She looked around and finally spoke. "And now you've been reborn to chase chicks in bikinis?"

"Hey, I don't have but one chick at a time."

"You're not a slut puppy like Turk?"

"Turk's not so bad. He has standards."

"As long as she's willing, white, and had a bath sometime in the last month?"

"She doesn't have to be white."

Marie moaned but smiled.

"It seems a waste to get a hotel room when we could stay free with Aaron and Ellie," he said, "or at Charlie's or at Turk's place."

She made a face. "Turk's place is a fishing shack, notorious for sexual excesses and substance abuse. I would never allow myself to go to sleep in that dump."

"Why not?"

"I'd probably wake up with some guy I'd never seen before, or some guy and some babe." Marie looked back at the road. "This is not a regular trip. We need a receipted hotel bill. Simon suggested the Patterson because it's huge and expensive, a tourist trap. We need to avoid people we know, and that could be hard on Easter weekend. This is spring holidays."

They fell back into silence.

Marie knew Simon was right. The Patterson had a golf course, tennis courts, a driving range, hiking paths, and lagoons—places to hide.

The traffic became thicker, the stops more frequent. Finally, Don turned from U.S. 278 into the quiet, mani-cured grounds of Palmetto Dunes and followed the signs, watching out for the bikers and roller blades. The speed limit was 20 mph. Sunlight spattered through scrubby oaks and Spanish moss onto the sandy grass and macadam. The asphalt road curved gently among slopes and lagoons, splitting and rejoining as the ancient trees appeared in the center of the roadbed. It all looked to be organic, the directional markers, the sprinkler system, as if the man-made structures had grown there along with carefully planned shrubbery and flowers.

He stopped at the very front of the hotel to allow the Patterson staff to carry the luggage and park the van. *Dr. and Mrs. Braddock and daughter* climbed out and accepted the unrestricted, fawning attention. Even on the landward side of the tall building the ocean breeze could be felt. The bellhops were trained to be alert and accommodating. They wore brightly colored shirts and shorts for livery and had matching Jamaican accents, authentic or shammed.

The hotel itself was a cavernous labyrinth of shops, restaurants, bars, and convention rooms. Potted trees surrounded an indoor fountain in the center of the lobby. An expanse of glass overlooked the deck and pool with the ocean beyond. None of their friends were likely to stay at the Patterson or shop there, but he and Marie would avoid the bars and restaurants.

Don followed the bellhop to the front desk while she diverted Esther to avoid any question of the falsification.

They went straight to their room and changed into beach wear. Esther would be satisfied with nothing less than getting to the ocean immediately. They followed her down the escalator, out onto the breezy deck.

Everything about the Patterson was elegant, spacious, and inviting. There were dozens of chairs for sunbathers, two lifeguards, pool bar, sandwich shop, apparel shop—no convenience lacking for Patterson guests. Steps from the deck to the dunes were wide and shallow; the walkway was lighted from hotel to beach for those who strolled at night.

They hiked the long, polished boards stretching across soft white powder. The tide was out, leaving a wet and miraculous width of sand. Pelicans hovered against the wind or skimmed the wave tops looking for food. Sunglasses were still needed against the late afternoon light and the sting of dry sand that drifted in the stiff breeze.

They lay on their stomachs and watched Esther paddle in the shallow surf.

Marie spoke loudly to be heard. "Mom thinks Simon is with us; Esther thinks her daddy's working; the hotel thinks you're Dr. Braddock. We'll have to keep Esther away from the desk. That man who checked us in called you by name twice. They teach them to memorize everybody's names."

"Only the doctors." Don pointed with one finger. "Hey! A little breast action, ten o'clock."

"Will you stop looking at girls and act like a husband?"

"That's the way husbands act."

She ignored him and closed her eyes and tried to relax, then smiled in spite of herself. Don was her twin in appearance and temperament, an invigorating tonic that prevented her from dwelling morbidly on Simon. Marie needed that silliness, diversion against more grim considerations.

Marie held herself against the dry sand with heightened awareness and forced the minutes to elapse. The roar of the surf was a familiar sound, but never with such deliberate focus as now.

Don nudged her. "Another string, two o'clock."

Marie opened one eye and peered at the passing bikini, the rounded cheeks wobbled in casual allurement. "That is disgusting."

"You have to have the right ass for it. You'd look good in one of those, Ree."

She ignored him again.

Don was accustomed to numerous and diverse female companions, especially at the beach—another sandy, wind-blown chick, possibly even *Miss Right, Miss Forever*. She was out there somewhere. But the timing was wrong. Marie's marriage, even her life, was at risk. It went strongly against his natural tendency, yet he would behave and play the husband role, ignoring the landscape of luscious, skimpily clad physiques.

"I'm afraid Esther may be getting too much sun. Come on, honey! We're going in," Marie called.

Esther ran ahead through the white powder, past the sea oats, and onto the wooden walkway. She waited under the outdoor shower as the warm water washed away sand and salt.

Don and Marie stopped long enough to spray their feet, then followed again, watching Esther's callused summer feet knock against wooden planks, her footprints fading with each step.

Esther waited on the lobby level, her wet nose pressed against a glass storefront. She wanted a shirt.

Don glanced at his sister. "Will you relax?" he said as they entered the shop. "If we run into anybody, we say Simon had business and will join us later. I'm your brother, for chrissake."

"I know, but we've told the hotel management something else. It would just be simpler to avoid meeting anybody."

Marie took the Patterson-Hilton shirt from a rack. "Try this one."

Esther pushed her head and arms through the holes

and pulled the shirt over her wet suit. She found a mirror and gazed at herself.

Marie turned suddenly to Don. "Kiss my mouth."

"What?"

"Do it now."

He leaned forward in the shadowy light of a small overhead spot and kissed her gently on the lips. "Would you like some tongue?"

"Very funny. Pay for the shirt."

Marie and Esther waited in the lobby. Esther pulled on her mother's sleeve. "Mommy, why did you kiss Uncle Don?"

"Because he's a sweet boy and sometimes he deserves a sweet kiss." She held her daughter by the shoulders and nuzzled her noisily about cheeks and neck until she giggled.

Esther ran ahead of them to the elevator.

"What was that all about?" Don asked.

"The desk clerk was ogling me through the window. I thought it was a nice touch."

"Yeah, he's been watching you. He admires your ass."

"How do you know?"

Don made a face. "I know what men like. Besides, you have a celebrated ass, Ree. You really should wear one of those string suits."

"Who celebrates my ass?"

"All my buddies used to talk about your ass. I sold pictures in high school."

Marie rolled her eyes for his benefit but enjoyed the thought. She half hoped he was serious.

The reality of what they were doing suddenly struck into her mind. Deceitful behavior was trashy. Maybe she belonged in a string bikini, the kind worn by coarse types, a signal not missed by young studs on the make.

She and Don were aiding a murderer. What was it called? *Abetting?* Maybe they were only *racketeers*. Or *felons*. Lawyers undoubtedly had some name for it. Marie fought the sickening anxiety and hoped she wouldn't have occasion to learn the proper legal terminology.

13

Saturday. Eight-thirty A.M.

Simon turned slowly in front of the hot light, basted with a combination of sunscreen and bug repellent. Even lathered in the gel, he saw mosquitoes coursing about, seeking an unprotected area.

At precisely nine he made the call to Marie.

"Just thought I'd check on you and Esther," he said.

"We're having a fine time. Especially Esther. How are you?"

"Same as always. I worked yesterday at noon, again tomorrow morning at eleven."

Simon kept it brief and hung up quickly, no need to prolong the painful conversation, which only made him ache to be with her and Esther. He had given the message—the times for which he needed an alibi.

Don and Esther were sprawled across the bed while the TV squawked and bleeped cartoons. Sunlight pierced the louvered windows and made bright shadows across the rumpled sheets and spreads.

Marie sat on the other bed and thought another prayer for Simon. Then she realized that Don was looking at her, waiting and expectant. "Yesterday at noon, tomorrow at noon," she said.

"We need an accomplice," he said.

Marie was startled. "We can't take anybody into our confidence. How do you mean?"

"Someone who would look at a photograph of a stranger and say, *Oh, yeah, that's you-know-who.*"

She looked bewildered.

Their conversation needed only a thin disguise in front of Esther. "We have evidence enough that we were here, but it won't fool anybody," Don said. "The militia is brighter than that. They'll bring a photo and ask the manager if he can identify the guy. Let me handle it."

"Who would do such a thing?"

"Anybody with sufficient monetary incentive. I was thinking of your buddy."

"The man who checked us in?"

"Why not? We see him every day, and he's taken special notice of us—you anyway. I tell him we've got personal problems and need a little help."

"And he would prevaricate?"

"Ree, you are so pure. For a thousand clams he wouldn't think twice."

"What if he wants to know what the problems are?"

"That's why we pay him. If this were some legitimate activity, he'd do a favor for free. Look, Simon is familiar with the Patterson. You fill in the details. If he needs an alibi, he'll have a fistful of charge receipts. The feds will most likely bring pictures of both of you. We have our man here prepped to make the ID."

"What if they don't happen to ask him?"

"They will. He was on duty when we checked in."

"Why is he supposed to remember us?"

"I'll coach him. Maybe we played cards together. I'll get a story straight with him."

"What if some other employee says the picture is not Simon?"

Don made a face. "Nobody else has even noticed us. One ID will do the job. Relax!"

Eleven A.M.

Alex was jealous of her Saturday mornings and liked to sleep late undisturbed, but the ringing sound bore relentlessly into her brain. She shoved Marvin to the floor and grappled for the phone. "Alex Sinclair," she mumbled.

"Alex? You sound like you're still in bed. I didn't wake you, did I?"

There was a long pause. Alex was glad he couldn't see her puffy eyes or smell her breath. She spoke slowly through a groan. "I was just lying here thinking about lying here."

"Well, you might be interested to know—Prather was found murdered."

She cleared her throat and answered with a cutting tone. "Good for him. I can't think of anybody who deserves it more."

He laughed. "You know these phone lines are routinely taped, don't you?"

"So? It's not our case. I'm only expressing a personal opinion. You're downtown?" She cleared her throat again.

"Yeah, I know it's Saturday. Look, I'm going over there. You wanna come?"

Her words were hard and bitter. "No, thanks. I've lost interest in seeing the rest of Prather's house. Let the fibbies have it. How was it done?"

"Shot in the back of the head, just like Condon."

"Who found the guy?"

"The old man, his uncle."

"Well, that's wonderful. I like to see families get together."

Lid smiled. "Go back to sleep."

Alex dropped the phone into its cradle, gave Marvin a passing caress, and rolled over onto her other side.

Rachael Brucker had waited until he hung up before entering.

Lid admired again the exposed throat and V shape of bare skin under her jacket. It was a planned effect. Nothing that luscious happened by accident.

As he stood, she placed a hand against his cheek and kissed his mouth noisily, unmindful of other people in the outer office. "Good morning!" she said.

His steely resolve melted. "Good morning yourself. What are you doing here?"

"Looking for you. What are you doing here?."

Lid hoped his flush didn't show. "I'm going to see a dead guy. You wanna come?"

Rachael lit a cigarette. "You're fun to be with, Li Dao. Who is he?"

"Willard Prather, the extortion case."

"The guy who got his brother's head in the mail?"

Lid nodded.

She chuckled and blew smoke. "Was this one chopped up?"

"No, he was all there."

"Have you found a body to go with the head?"

"Naw, it's supposed to belong to the same guy as the dick. Romano says the lab could make a match if the department would buy the right equipment. I think he wants an electron microscope to play with."

She laughed through the stream of smoke, making

small, detached puffs. "Does Romano know what he's talking about?"

"How the hell should I know?"

"How did this one die?"

Lid grabbed his coat. "Somebody shot him through the head."

"That would do it."

She linked arms with him as they walked out of the cubicle.

Lid was pleased but embarrassed by the stares they were getting. He was a married man, older than Rachael. But this was police work—a convenient excuse.

They rode toward the river in the warm morning air.

Lid was filled with a unique, blissful alertness of one in love, yet he felt sure he was not in love. He was ardently old-fashioned, mature enough not to fall into that fatuous habit of divorce and remarriage, yet devoured with guilt at the thought of adultery. He glanced at Rachael and felt his resolve dissipate in the warmth and fullness of her company.

She lit another cigarette and blew a smooth, steady stream, completing the embodiment of Rachael Brucker. Lid wanted to taste her tongue even though the surgeon general had warned that it would kill you.

They passed through the police block at the entrance to the Prather property and stopped beside the noisy fountain. Three black-and-whites and two other cars were parked the front of the mansion.

Two uniforms waited on the porch. They gave Lid and Rachael a nod and opened the door.

The inside of the house was bright and quiet. Lid took her arm. "Look in here. I want you to see this dining room."

She stood in the doorway, then walked to the table and rubbed her fingers over the smooth surface.

Lid looked around to see a familiar face descending the stairs. "What are doing here, Tony?"

Romano sucked his teeth and scratched his crotch. "The feds are working my ass until they get their own crew in here. Somebody don't like these Prather boys. At least they left all of this one." He beamed. "How come you fucking cops don't ever catch anybody?"

"Don't ask me, ask the fibbies."

"If you ever caught anybody, the federal boys wouldn't have to take over."

"Why don't you lab guys make something out of the evidence?"

"You gave me a dick. What am I supposed to make outta that?" Romano walked back into the library.

Lid followed and saw the open window. "Breaking and entering?" he asked.

"Maybe." Tony smiled. "What's Brucker doing wit' you? You drilling that, Li Dao?"

Lid hunched his shoulders in a noncommittal gesture. "What have you got?"

"We're looking for prints, blood, the usual."

Lid reflected with relief that Braddock bought rubber gloves by the case. "Where're the bodies?"

"They were upstairs, fucking and dying, but they're already in the morgue."

Lid gave him a look that showed his disapproval.

Romano shifted smoothly into a professional bearing. "Prather was shot at close range in the back of the head. I think the girl was strangled."

"Any sign of a struggle?"

"Yeah, Prather's arms were clawed up. He probably did it to her, then shot himself in the back of the head." Tony smiled again.

"Get anything for ballistics?"

"One slug but it's pretty flat."

"Do you have any theories?"

"Zilch. Don't worry. The fibbies will save your ass. Nobody in Macon pulls this. These Prather boys are nothing. Messengers. I'm telling ya, it's from outta town."

Lid nodded. Romano might be right. If he *was* right, killing the local scum wouldn't be the end of it. Where would that leave Braddock?

The unanswered questions were no longer so troubling. Lid was a bystander, watching the deadly, entertaining game with only a casual interest in the outcome. He would report the latest murders to Roberta, as per their agreement, but doubted it was necessary.

Rachael was still giving herself a private tour.

Lid mounted the stairs and found the murder scene. He stood beside the bloody, rumpled bed and wondered if Simon Braddock had been there. Lid tried to recall the smell of the dental office and sniffed the air as if the distinct odor might have clung to Braddock's clothes. There was nothing revealing, no aftershave, no telltale cigarette butt. What would a dentist leave behind? Maybe one of those round cotton things they liked to stick in your mouth. It was a silly thought, yet he was relieved that Romano had mentioned no such evidence.

Rachael came up from behind and put her arms around his waist. "Let's buy this place, Lid."

"It's probably for sale," he replied cynically. Lid looked down at her tobacco-stained fingers and gazed at the king-size mattress with lustful contemplation. He cherished her touch and the reassurance it gave. His hardness and savvy provided no haven from romantic rejection.

He heard footsteps in the hall and felt awkward. "Do you want some lunch?" he asked.

"We can eat anytime. Let's go to the couch."

"What?"

"I told you I'd say *when*. When."

"Oh," came the dull-witted response. Lid said nothing more for fear she'd change her mind.

They left the Prather estate and drove back toward the bridge and downtown. He turned onto Walnut Street and headed to the old building.

What the hell, Lid thought. Lucille had left him; he needed to be loved and companioned; Brucker was only a roll in the hay. The rationale worked quickly as his passion overruled his intellect.

They came into the building from the rear parking lot, rode the pokey elevator to the sixth floor, and entered her suite of rooms.

Rachael led him to the couch and began to disrobe, watching his eyes soften into abject lechery.

Lid was an innocent lover, accustomed to the modest diffidence of his generation. Her exhibition seemed a mild taint but hardly dissuasive. Far past was the point of reason, the point of no return.

He finally tasted that luscious mouth, his tongue probing the full upper lip as it curved back into the corner of her cheek.

Rachael submitted to his every advance, and enjoyed it in a routine way, unaware of the ecstasy she was providing Li Dao.

The blissful encounter took an hour. The time seemed much shorter to him.

They were barely dressed again when a loud

knocking sounded from the hallway. Lid struggled up
reluctantly and went to the door.

The young man who greeted him was handsome and
muscular. He was looking for Rachael.

She recognized his voice from the other room.
"Andy!" she shrieked and met him in the doorway.
"Oooh, where have you been?" She took his face with
both hands and kissed him squarely on the mouth.
"Lid, this is Andy Campbell; Andy, Martin Li Dao."

They shook hands.

"Andy is an old flame. Actually, he's my cousin."

"About fifth cousin," Andy agreed.

Andy Campbell wore his hair long and dressed casually in faded Levi's and shirt. His skin and muscle tone
had the appealing look of youth. The trim waistline
was an entitlement, a thing older men maintained only
through rigid diet and exercise.

Lid smiled and nodded and struggled with jealousy.
It was exactly the way she had kissed him. He sat and
watched the animated exchange. Andy was in his twen-
ties. He and Rachael were old friends. Why should he
be envious? He was a married man; Rachael was a roll
in the hay.

Andy suggested they have drinks and dinner together.
Rachael echoed the proposal, but Lid declined. Her persuasive words were annoying and made him think how
little she really understood him. She finally gave it up,
kissed him again on the mouth, and told him to behave
himself until she saw him again. Lid made the appropriate response and took his leave, abruptly ousted by a
younger, stronger bull.

The sun was still above the horizon, but the late Saturday afternoon streets were quiet. Lid drove toward
his office in lewd contemplation. The kiss had lost

much of its meaning, a gesture, part of her outgoing nature. Rachael was tough. She had taken control and initiated everything, but it was simply her manner. Never had he experienced more rampant lust and fulfillment only to come away with such defeated spirit. He would get over it. Teenagers fell in love, not old men.

Even before he parked, Lid recognized Guy Bissett standing in the same place he had waited that other night in the misty rain. His wife's funeral had been a week ago today. Lid groaned. At least it wasn't raining. He left the keys in the ignition as he got out.

"Are you looking for me, Dr. Bissett?"

The younger man walked over. "Can we talk?"

"Not here, the bar."

"I don't want a drink," Bissett said.

"I do," Lid replied.

He followed the Cadillac to the same bar, and they took the same seats. The other booths were empty, but the pool table was in use and the pinball machine pinged away in the background. The bar was sleazier in daylight and without the scotch fortification. The plastic seats and bar stools were badly worn. Pale sunlight revealed cracks in the tile floor and splits in the ancient wallpaper.

Lid noted the doctor's costly suit and silk tie. Bissett had not been drinking, but his face was drawn and he seemed on the edge. Lid ordered a scotch.

"How is the case coming?" Bissett asked.

"It belongs to the FBI."

"I know that, but are they doing anything?"

Lid waited for the drink to be served and took a sip. "They don't tell me."

Bissett scowled, obviously irritated. "We spoke very openly the last time we were here."

Lid nodded.

"Do you know anything off the record? Anything that would help me?"

"Help you what?"

"Li Dao, we're being candid, right? Just two guys having a drink, like you said."

Lid nodded again.

"I've got a gun."

"So?"

Bissett was annoyed at having to explain it. He leaned forward and spoke quietly. "Look! I buried my son a year ago and my wife last week. Nothing in the world matters a damn to me. Can you understand that?"

"I do."

"You said you'd kill my son's murderer if you could to it with impunity. I'll do it with or without risk. All I need from you is a name." His voice was rising in intensity. "Nobody will know where I got it."

Lid was surprised at Bissett's memory from the scotch-hazy night. "You are a person of value," he said simply. "Someday you will consider yourself that again."

"If I need a homily, I'll go to church, Li Dao. Give me what I need! I know you know something."

Li Dao's look and voice were harsh. "Yeah, I know something. I'll give you some information but not what you're asking for."

Bissett waited.

"My ass would be in a sling if the department knew the things I know and haven't reported. Like I said before, you repeat any of this, I deny the hell out of it. The only reason I'm telling you is because of your family." He took a swig. "You want the names of the extortionists, to hunt them down one at a time and blow their brains out, right?"

Bissett smiled and nodded.

Lid looked hard into his eyes. "It's already being done," he said quietly. "A hood was killed several weeks ago, then five days later two others were gunned down. Only yesterday one of the leaders was shot at point-blank range in the back of the head. They're still picking bone splinters out of his bedroom wall."

Bissett's smile widened. "Do you know who's doing this?"

"Yes, I think I do, but don't ask."

"Is it you, Li Dao?"

"No."

"Is it a cop?"

"I told you not to ask. Look, you don't want the guy who's killing those bastards to be caught, do you?"

"Hell, no!"

"The best way to help him is not to mention this to anybody, ever."

Bissett nodded. "Can you thank him for me?"

"I'll do that."

"Have they matched the bullets? Did they all come from the same gun?"

"The feds have retrieved only one slug. The first guy was decapitated." Lid glanced around. "By God, don't repeat this," he said quietly. "The killer cut his head off and mailed it to the leader of the extortion ring. A mean son of a bitch, wouldn't you say?"

Bissett's face was poised between revulsion and delight. "Yeah, I'd say so."

"There're only two gang members left. The feds know who they are, but they don't have enough evidence to bust anybody."

"That pisses me. Do you know who they are?"

"Yes."

"Does the exterminator know?"

"Yes."

"Do you think he'll get them?"

"I know he will, and that will be the end of it."

Bissett was relieved. "I want to know when he does it."

"I'll call you when it's finished." His voice had an abruptness that said the conversation was over.

"Thanks, Li Dao." Bissett made eye contact and nodded, then got up and walked out of the bar.

Lid sat alone and finished his drink. He was not certain the last two criminals would be destroyed as promised, but he had felt obliged to comfort the doctor. It was police work in a way. Calm the man and steer him away from a foolish act. Besides, he doubted Guy Bissett actually possessed Simon Braddock's violent, destructive nature.

Lid mulled over his meetings with Braddock and wished for a second opinion, input from another cop, but that was not to be. He and Alex had weighed the meager evidence and relied heavily on instinct. An innocent man would never remain so passive under questions that were clearly accusations, yet Braddock had been remote and indifferent. Lid resigned himself. Traces of doubt remained, but it didn't matter. Proper police procedure hadn't been a concern for a long time. Now his partner was also angry and bitter. Whoever the vigilante was, he had nothing to fear from Li Dao and Sinclair.

Eight P.M.

Parallel rays of sunlight streamed through the Patterson lobby. The desk clerk was slight, dark, and neat.

Don waited until he appeared to be leaving for the day, then accosted him in the stairwell. "Excuse me. I wondered if you could do a favor for me."

The quick eyes snapped around with habitual eagerness. "Yes, sir. You're Dr. Braddock, aren't you?"

"Yes. You checked us in yesterday."

"I remember. I'm Sammy Self."

They shook hands.

"Could we get out of here? There's an echo," Don said.

They walked through the outer door into the pale sky and the warm, humid odor of the sea. The desk clerk's short hair stood stiff, but Don's tangled blond mat was buffeted by the sticky breeze.

Don smiled. "The lady and I are not what we appear."

Sammy's eyes lit up.

"Here's the problem. At some time in the near future, somebody might show up here with photographs for you to identify. I know they'll get around to you because you checked us in. I need you to say, *Yes, that's Dr. and Mrs. Braddock.* I'll pay a hundred dollars for your trouble."

Sammy returned the smile. "This will be a private investigator, right?"

"Maybe."

"I never thought you were married."

Don was startled. "What do you mean, you never thought we were?"

"Married couples don't cuddle in public; lovers do that. What'd y'all do, borrow the kid? Her husband hired a detective to follow her, didn't he?" Sammy was clearly pleased with himself.

"Look, you don't need to understand it, just identify the man as Dr. Braddock."

"Why would he have a picture of Dr. Braddock if he's looking for you? Didn't Dr. Braddock hire the detective?"

"I didn't say it was a detective. You said that."

"Who else would it be?"

Don shrugged. "The police, the FBI, anybody. It doesn't matter."

"It matters to me! I'm not getting involved with the real police for a hundred bucks."

"Sammy, it's an easy thing. Anybody who comes in here and shows you a picture, you simply identify the man as Dr. Braddock."

"Not for a hundred bucks! . . . I'll do it for five," he said after consideration.

Don paused for effect. "Okay, five."

"What does Dr. Braddock look like?"

"A lot like me. About my build and hair color, but his hair is shorter."

Sammy looked at the shaggy honey-blond mane and athletic build. "Let me get this straight. Any picture they show me, I just say, *Yeah, that's Dr. Braddock*?"

"That's right. You don't really need to know what he looks like."

"Okay, I can do that. What about the money?"

"I don't have it with me. You'll get it tomorrow."

Sammy smirked. "How do you know I won't take your money and say nothing to the cops?"

"Because I'll come back and kick your skinny ass."

Don stared at the smaller man without smiling.

"One other thing, and this is very important. We all three played cards for an hour or so yesterday right after lunch."

"I got off at one. I could say that. Why did we play cards?"

"It would give them reason to believe you might remember Dr. Braddock's face. Anyway, we played poker for an hour."

"I don't know how to play poker."

"What the hell, Sammy? Do you play Hearts?"

"Yeah, I can play Hearts."

"Okay, we played Hearts for an hour."

Sammy shrugged in agreement.

Don smiled warmly to erase the threat. "Good. You'll get the money tomorrow."

Sammy nodded and walked away.

Don watched him out of sight and smiled that Self thought he was bedding down a girl he had never touched, his sister at that. Marie had overdone it.

14

Easter Sunday. Ten-thirty A.M.

The weather was ideal for traditional Christian rites, indoor or outdoor, but the dogwood blooms were past their prime. There was little traffic except in the vicinities of churches. The Macon streets were washed and steamy after a rain. Simon reveled in the clear morning air, and took delight in escape from the welding shop. He had gotten as clean as a spit bath would allow but still smelled the sunscreen lotion. His clothes were thoroughly stale.

Skip wore his Easter best—long johns and overalls. "How long do you want, Simon?"

"Fifteen minutes."

"I don't know nothing about this, I'm just giving you a ride."

"This is the last time."

Skip looked at him. "Yeah, I know you. Once you get your mind set on something, there ain't no more talking about it."

They rode in silence. The trip was quicker than usual through the deserted streets. Simon looked up with interest as they approached the cottage.

"That's the one, Simon . . . Hoowee! What is all that?"

They cruised by slowly and gawked at a line of cars down the drive and beside the carriage house.

"Don't stop," Simon said. His spirit sank in the devastating moment. Days of planning and inconvenience were suddenly trumped. "Go back to the shop."

"What are all those folks doin' there? They havin' a Easter Mass?"

Simon sighed noisily. "Yes, that's what it is."

"I don't know what's happening, but I feel better with you not gettin' out back there."

The conversation reached a lull as Simon tried to plan anew. Prather's body had been discovered sooner than he expected, but getting him was not enough. Wexler and the old lady had to die before Marie and Esther were safe. They could return to Charleston for the week. He would have only himself to consider, running his practice part-time and living somewhere—not the welding shop, he thought with distaste. He would stay armed at all times and have the office door monitored, possibly a bodyguard. Lid might have a suggestion, but that was a last resort. His main care was for Marie and Esther. They would have to stay out of town.

Alibi was another problem. The beach deception would serve for Prather, but now there was no plan for Wexler and his mother, the killings or the alibi. Were they always alone on Sundays or did the servants have off because it was Easter?

The more Simon pondered, the more he saw what splendid occasion and masterly planning had slipped away, destroyed by random chance. At the bottom of his thoughts lay the conviction that he would dispatch the Wexlers even without an alibi in order to protect Marie and Esther.

Eleven A.M.

Lid, Alex, and three federal agents lay on their stomachs in the pine straw and watched the rear of the Braddock residence. The back of the BMW was visible in the open carport. They wore one-piece outfits. Olive drab. There was no conversation, no movement. The arson threat was police business, but the FBI had come along by choice. It was a difficult stake-out, Easter morning with church attendance the only activity, no unusual vehicles likely to be parked along a residential street. Any commercial van or truck would alert the arsonist, not a problem on weekdays. Mimbs had placed only one van on the street, and that two blocks away. Lid and the others had approached from behind and waited in the woods, unusual manpower for one threatening phone call, but the Macon Police and the Federal Bureau were frustrated and determined.

Alex still felt anger and grief over her loss. It was pleasant to lie in the woods on Easter morning, their own private sunrise service a few hours late, an occasional bird call to sound through the silence—musings she was not likely to share with her peers.

Colish was wearing the headset. "Somebody's coming," he said quietly.

A dark sedan drove into view and stopped behind the BMW. The driver stood out on the concrete and took a case from the backseat. He wore a suit and tie.

The stake-out crew turned to Lid, who knew Simon best. Braddock?

Lid shook his head.

The stranger seemed to belong. He made no furtive glances but disappeared into the carport.

"Go!" Colish spoke softly into the microphone.

They waited again until the undercover van turned into the drive and blocked the sedan. Then all five were racing across the deep open yard between house and woods, Lid trailing the younger, swifter men. Suddenly and unexpectedly, the sound of gunshots cracked in the quiet air. The driver of the van was hit. The stranger was down. It was over.

"That son of a bitch shot me!" The driver squeezed his arm below the shoulder.

"It's just a scratch, Bagley. Somebody get me the first-aid kit."

"What about the other guy?"

"He's dead."

The freshly pressed suit with starched white shirt lay sprawled and bloody on the concrete floor, an implausible sight on Easter morning.

The FBI agents were into the suitcase quickly— potassium chlorate, sulfuric acid, igniters—standard tools of the trade.

Lid carried a singular enmity for people who plundered or destroyed property. He looked at the face, but it was unfamiliar. As usual, his feelings didn't follow the company line—he was glad the arsonist was dead. But he also knew Mimbs. The lieutenant would be pissed even though they had played by the rules: when fired upon, return the fire; if you shoot, shoot to kill. The arsonist was nobody. Mimbs would want to know who had hired him. *Seven of you!* he would yell. *All you had to do was cuff the guy! Why didn't we let him burn the damn house? At least it might raise some public indignation.* Yeah, Mimbs would be pissed.

Even before the ambulance arrived, neighbors in church attire were gawking at the scene with horror and fascination. Mothers held their children back away from the carport, where the body and blood could be seen. The reverent attention and Sunday clothes were fitting.

"Anybody here know where Dr. Braddock and his family are?"

Presnell's question elicited only head shakes.

"We think they may be at a beach," he added. His smirk was intended as a smile.

"They might be at a South Carolina beach," somebody offered. "His wife is from around there, maybe Charleston."

"Nobody knows an address or a phone number?" Presnell waited but got no response.

Lid was privately amused. Braddock didn't give away the time, let alone his address and phone number.

Presnell spoke aside to Colish. "We keep the stakeout. I want Braddock brought in the minute he sets foot back on this property."

"What's the charge?"

"Probable cause. Nobody else's house is being torched."

"We leaned on Braddock before, and he came up clean," said Colish.

"We lean on him again," Presnell said. "I got pressure from Atlanta and Washington, and I'm sure the locals are enjoying this, especially Li Dao."

The ambulance arrived and took away the body. The crowd of onlookers drifted away immediately, predictably. The show was over.

Noon.

Simon stood under the sun lamp with eyes closed. He had heard the news on the radio. Somebody had tried to burn his house. The announcer hadn't given a name, only the address.

Simon's anger was drawn out by the hot light.
Wexler had tried to destroy what he and Marie had
built together through years of planning and labor. It
was very much like murder. He cared not for himself
but held images of Marie measuring rooms and poring
over drawings. They had made uncounted trips to the
new house during the months of construction. On one
occasion she had snagged the back of her hand on a
nail while carrying a stack of wallpaper books. It had
been nothing at the time, but now the accident leaped
to Simon's mind with poignant, savage import. Marie
had drawn blood for the house. The memory was a
searing pain out of all proportion to the importance of
the incident. He was still in the cave.

Three P.M.

Lid sat at his desk and wrote the report. Mimbs had
already heard the story but would want to see the
written account first thing Monday morning. The large
room was empty and quiet on Sunday afternoon, more
so on Easter. It didn't feel like Easter. He could have
had dinner with Lucille and Marty but hadn't made the
effort to arrange anything. It was hypocritical to
impose on special occasions when he wasn't there on
ordinary occasions. He talked to Marty once a week,
and the boy seemed happy enough.

Lid's self-pity led him to think of his partner. Alex
was also alone, now more than ever. He had neglected
to ask her plans for the day. She had a sister, he
remembered, maybe they were together.

Visions of Rachael and the visitor interrupted Lid's
concentration. It was indecent for her to see someone
ten years younger, not so a man eighteen years older.
The rationalization rested uneasily in his mind, the fear
of crossing that line between a good lay and foolish

emotional attachment. Lid would err on the side of celibacy if necessary.

The smell of her cologne was still in his clothes or else it was in his memory. He wanted to call her but wouldn't risk rejection, a foolish thought yet the doubt was there. Her affection was real but not directed to him alone. The young man had given witness to that.

Lid finished up, resentful that he had spent Easter afternoon alone. He left and drove unconsciously toward Rachael's building, not from habit but desire, and because the drive didn't need courage, which a telephone call did.

The parking lot was nearly empty, but her car was there. Lid parked, entered the deserted building, and took the elevator, which groaned slowly to the sixth floor. He tapped on the door and waited, tapped again, finally banged noisily. Nothing.

Suddenly, he heard the elevator descending, a sharp drone in the stillness as the ancient equipment creaked toward the ground floor. It stopped and started again. Then he heard her voice, loud and floating up through the silence, the sultry laugh trailing off into a giggle.

With a surge of adrenaline, Lid mounted the open stairway, leaping two steps at a time to the seventh-floor hallway. He stood to keep her office entrance in view. The voices were louder as the elevator opened. They reached the door and he saw them, Rachael and the young man. She looked desirable as always, but Lid watched the boy. His hair was dark and shaggy. He probably hadn't shaved since the day before. He slouched casually with one hand in his hip pocket and looked older than Lid had remembered. The limp shirt hung appealingly over his hard, straight physique.

Rachael giggled, struggling to find the key as her companion embraced her from behind and sniffed the back of her neck. They looked good together, Lid admitted. Then they were inside and the door closed.

Lid leaned against the rail and peered down into the stairway. Suddenly there was movement in the corner of his eye. He turned.

"Can I help you?" asked a stranger.

Lid placed a finger over his closed lips and flipped out his badge.

The other man stopped abruptly, held up his hands, and retreated.

Lid felt foolish, but it was habit. He took the elevator and gained the ground floor, relieved that he had not confronted Rachael and her companion.

The refracted light was thickening in the sunset. He drove through the alley and back out onto Second Street, still lustful but glad to have gotten away unseen. For reasons of her own, she had made love with him, but Lid knew he would not bear comparison with the younger man. Memories from his teenage years: the pubescent desire for a kiss only, the greatest expectation but seldom gratified. Now even the ultimate gift seemed a thing of little matter. The generation gap was real.

Seven-thirty P.M.

Don and Esther lay on the bed and watched TV.

Marie was working on her makeup and sipping a glass of wine. She looked at them in the mirror, bare legs side by side, Esther imitating her uncle's slouch. She was almost as long as he was, growing up too fast, Marie thought. She caught Don's eye in the mirror. "Have you paid him?"

Don looked at his watch. "He doesn't get off until eight. Let me see the end of this game."

"You're not going to dinner like that, are you?"

He squinted.

She finished what she was doing and stood. The white sheath accentuated her bronze skin and leggy physique. "How do I look?"

"You look terrific," he said without looking.

"You look good, Mommy."

Marie wished Simon was there, somebody who truly appreciated the result of her makeup skills, the honing of her delicate feminine wiles. "Let me take it to him," she said, attaching the second pearl earring.

"What for?"

She posed and smiled. "It might give him a thrill."

"I'm sure you do that." He handed her an envelope without taking his eyes from the game. "His name's Sammy but don't say anything to the little twit, just give it to him. I rehearsed him twice. It's all set."

Marie walked out and closed the door. The wine was an abatement to fear and inhibition. For the first time she was intrigued by their deception and bribery.

The lobby was quiet on Sunday evening except for the ubiquitous piped-in music—*dental office music*, Simon called it.

Sammy saw her from across the way. He avoided recognition but left his post and fell into stride as they followed the arcade away from the front desk. She held up the envelope for his taking, but Sammy ignored it. They eventually stopped and faced each other.

He smiled. "That's not gonna do it."

"What do you mean?"

He ogled her unashamedly. "It will cost you a little more than that. I can cooperate with you or not," he added, maintaining the smile. "I always knew you weren't married."

Marie was suddenly sober and terrified. She paled at the stupid mistake, so easily avoided had Don made the payment. She would have joyfully doubled the amount to maintain the cash agreement, but it was too late for that. Take the counter offer or lose the alibi. She found her voice. "What do you mean, you knew we weren't married?"

"I knew the guy was your boyfriend."

She understood his thinking: what was one more lover to an adulteress? Sammy was not unattractive, but Marie was appalled by the consideration, until this moment utterly remote and unthinkable. Yet Simon had murdered for his family's protection, such a shocking, brutal affront as to make adultery pale by measure.

"Once!" she stated sharply, stabbing the air with one finger.

Sammy took the envelope and nodded slightly through his smile.

"No kissing!" she emphasized.

He shrugged.

Marie followed silently down the wide hallway. She was faint. Her panic soared. At least she was on the pill. No. This was not happening. She would never go through with it. She almost turned and fled. Don would beat the *little twit* to death with his bare hands. The thought faded. She followed like a hireling. Tears slid down her cheeks.

Eight P.M.

Willis Carruth leaned against the kitchen table with the chipped porcelain top, the only clean work surface in the room. It had been a long, tiring Sunday. The funeral arrangements for Willard Prather had been made. The day had seen an unaccustomed flow of traffic to the cottage, an excessive number of telephone calls. The police had been there, and other visitors who were strangers to Carruth, older people, somber in appearance and demeanor. The Wexlers were finally alone.

He waited and listened. They were on their second drinks, well past the old lady's dinnertime. Carruth felt unfamiliar anger and desire for revenge. Concern for his employers was a novel sensation, but an assault against the Wexlers seemed an attack upon himself, and overbalanced his dislike for them and for Willard Prather, whom he had liked even less.

"Schnapps!" came the weak, harried voice.

Willis carried in the ice and whiskey for the third time, holding the heavy tray with one hand, his arm bulging through the tight sleeve.

The Wexlers sat together on the small sofa, looking very uncomfortable amid the clutter. Heinrich appeared older than usual, his face pasty and lined, jowls losing elastic integrity. His eyes drooped in their sockets. Ilsa Wexler's face no longer sagged. The flesh was dried out from the inside, leaving a shell of skin that held the body together.

Carruth was aware of the social gap between his employers and himself. He and Wexler were not friends. He straightened up to leave and cleared his throat. "Mr. Wexler, I didn't know your nephew very well, but I want you to know your enemies are my enemies. If it's the dentist you want, say the word and he's dead, quiet and clean like the schoolteacher."

"The child, Heinrich," Ilsa said.

Wexler despised his mother when she made that sound. He smoothed over his white hair with soft fingers and appeared to consider. It was he who had discovered Prather's body with the girl and had spent twenty-four hours in careful reflection, not to embark on a course without planning. The most recent murder had stunned him more than the others, but now he was in control and able to recognize Prather's utter baseness without conceding the slightest personal taint. He posed with his lips and his eyebrows.

"Perhaps my mother is correct, Willis. We forget the dentist and his wife. We take the child—alive. The usual bonus. You are at your own risk." He look at Carruth with a savage eye, curiously inappropriate for a man so frail.

"Quiet and clean," Carruth repeated. "Think no more about it."

Wexler looked up as Carruth hesitated.

"I was thinking about security again, Mr. Wexler. I'm not always around, and your mother is in danger without electronic surveillance. Mr. Prather needed that."

"No!" Ilsa said. "Next you'll have dogs and fences, Heinrich. The police notice that. Our neighborhood has always been quiet. No, Heinrich."

Wexler glanced at Carruth and gave a nod.

Carruth left the room.

15

Monday. Six A.M.

Bright sky showed through the edge of the blind. Marie lay in bed and looked at the clock. She wanted it to be later. Esther breathed easily beside her, her pale face partially draped in a blond veil. Don lay sprawled across the other bed. She would let them sleep.

In a few brief moments the Hilton Head assignment had become an odious task. She wanted to leave as quickly as possible. To her own surprise, she felt a modicum of satisfaction along with anger and shame. It was not the supreme sacrifice but something related. In war there was always a price to pay, but the mental destruction was yet to be assessed.

For another hour Marie waited for Don and Esther to rouse. Her feat of noble betrayal had been the only option. Without the alibi Simon would spend his life in prison, with lawyers and psychiatrists for consort, rather than a soft, caring wife. Her flesh would no longer minister to his need, except perhaps as a very old man when neither was interested. Marie pushed her face into the pillow and thought with whimsical distaste that all of the Patterson beds felt the same. Her arena of combat.

Don finally began to stir. Esther scrambled up without speaking and turned on the TV. Don sat on the edge of the other bed and moaned, then staggered into the bathroom.

It was another thirty minutes before everybody was dressed and civil. Acting did not come naturally to Marie as it did to Simon. She feared lest Don read her mood and inveigle the truth. His reaction would be rash, unlike Simon's passionless, calculated responses.

Through the early morning as they ate breakfast and packed to leave, Marie forced the event from her mind so as not to reveal anything in voice or expression. At last Don took Esther to the beach for a final view. Marie begged off and waited in the lobby.

She sat beside the fountain and watched the stream of water break into a million crystals with appealingly hypnotic sound. Sammy Self walked by without seeing her and took the down escalator. Marie cringed and watched his blurred image through a watery fold. She had a loathing desire to look at him, to see his hands and the way he walked. She followed out into the parking area and watched as he chatted amicably with one of the groundskeepers. She studied his face and especially his hands, deliberately fostering her hatred.

At last Sammy got into a red pickup truck and backed out. Two signs stood in the rear window, one reading JESUS IS LORD, the other AUBURN TIGERS.

Marie suddenly felt sadness more than anger. Sammy was Everyman, noble on occasion yet ruled over by an all-pervasive desire that took release as it could, blunting the name of Godliness.

She was glad when Don paid the bill, the van was brought around, and the bellhops carried out their luggage; glad again to be out on the highway, over the sparkling bridges and onto the mainland. Then she saw the roadblock, state patrol cars with flashing lights on either side. The sudden panic was a new experience, unaccustomed fear at the sight of authority.

"Ree, they're only checking driver's licenses."

"Be sure to show them your license, not Simon's."

"Will you relax? You're making me nervous."

He was right about the purpose for the roadblock. The state trooper held his license while Marie scrambled through the dashboard compartment for the insurance receipt. The routine inspection unnerved her, and she worried even after they were passed. The encounter might eventually serve to show the FBI she was with her brother, not her husband, but there was nothing to be done about it.

They reached the little town of Hardeville and took I-95, crowded with north-south traffic, the Yankee artery to Florida. They crossed the wide Savannah River to the sandy marshes of south Georgia. Marie thought of the previous night and pretended to be asleep to escape conversation, to reason privately in the hypnotic sound and movement of the van. Strangely enough, concealment would be easier from Simon than from Don, who had more experience discerning her moods. Still, the idea of hiding anything from Simon was repugnant, not the basis for a good marriage. Someday she would tell him, when the time was right. Yet the truth might become a source of bitterness, a verbal weapon for him to wield in a moment of jealousy; more likely, a constant reminder of his failure as a man, one who had forced his wife to make such sacrifice. Even in deliberate lustful infidelity, confession assumed forgiveness and was a cowardly act, burdening the innocent spouse with knowledge of the dreadful fact. No, Sammy Self would forever be a skeleton in her own private closet.

Eleven A.M.

Skip sat on the tractor seat and swigged a can of Budweiser. "It's hot as hell in heah, Simon! I'll be glad when I can open up the place."

"You should try it for a week." Simon envied Skip. After Marie arrived and they were gone, Skip would return to his drab, prosaic life, free of chaotic violence and legal entanglements. He had heard Skip speak of Vashti for years, but had never met her. She probably wasn't anyone he would care to meet. They were not wildly in love, but who was at that age? Simon imagined that they had an arrangement, an acceptance of each other that most marriages eventually came down to.

Simon sat leaning against the back wall and read the story in the *Macon Telegraph* for the third time. Prather had been *shot at close range* and *was found nude with a female companion*. The police *knew of no motive for the murders*. Simon gazed at the words—*no motive* instead of *no suspect*, but he assumed it meant the same thing.

He was washed and shaven and had already eaten lunch. The ill-fitting apparel was well past needing to be laundered, not that it mattered. The welding shop stint was only hours short of a full week, a thought that would have pleased him better had the plan been completely successful. Heinrich Wexler and his mother were still out there somewhere.

Skip came across the dirt floor. "There they are, Simon."

He and Skip held back the heavy doors as Don maneuvered the van through the opening. They closed up again.

Esther hopped out and gave her father a hug before scaling the wooden steps.

Marie was in control until she saw him and fell into his arms. Simon was only a murderer; she had opened her body to another man. She cried and shook. "Is it over?"

"Almost. I'll tell you later," Simon whispered, keeping his frustration behind a blank face.

She suppressed her tears and resigned herself for the moment.

Don tried not to notice and turned to Skip. "Hi! I'm Don."

They shook hands. "Yeah, Don, everybody calls me Skip," he announced loudly. "I think your brother will be glad to get out of this place."

"Brother-in-law," Don corrected him.

"Oh, you're Miz Braddock's brother. Simon don't talk much about his kin. All you blonds look alike to me."

Marie separated herself and followed Esther up the ladder.

Don had thought nothing of the reunion, but as the moment arrived, he was unexpectedly embarrassed and awkward. He knew Simon as well as anybody, but shook his hand as a stranger and gave a pathetic smile. "How did it go?"

Simon frowned and shrugged. "Thanks for your help. I'm gonna have to stash you here for a few hours." He indicated the shop.

Don looked about and made a face. "Then what?"

"I don't know, wait until we see the lay of the land. This is not the time for a visit. It might give ideas to the FBI."

"You look like a mill worker," Don said.

Simon scowled to shut him up. "I had Skip pick up some work clothes for me."

Skip spoke up. "Well, I figured Simon didn't need to be wearing no tuxedo if he's hanging around the shop."

"You look fine," Don said. "I'm just not used to seeing you in work clothes."

The girls climbed back down the ladder. They were fetchingly alike in cutoff blouses and shorts, blond heads and brown skin, an angular, wobbly filly and its perfectly formed mother.

Skip handed Simon the key. "Just lock up when you get done."

"Thanks, buddy. We'll be out of your way by morning."

Marie took Skip's large, callused hand with both of hers and looked into his face with unfeigned warmth and gratitude. "I really appreciate everything you've done for us."

"Aw, Miz Braddock, don't go gettin' teary-eyed. Simon and I take care of one another."

The old man needed more expression of appreciation, for what, Marie was uncertain, but she could tell he was uncomfortable with female effusion. Skip was Simon's buddy. Let him handle it.

Skip got out as quickly as he could.

Marie noted again the provincial aura that seemed to vanish along with Skip, a homey, congenial tenderness that she missed. No apology was needed for being unrefined and poor.

Simon made a sound. "That's the first time he ever left out of here without banging the door."

"I hope I didn't hurt his feelings about the clothes."

Simon shook his head. "Skip's fine."

Don was thinking along with Marie. Simon was too

abrupt with his old buddy, but that was Simon. He was, after all, a murderer.

"Did you buy something for me to wear?"

Marie opened a suitcase. Simon stripped out of the filthy gray uniform and changed into beach clothes, shorts, and matching shirt. She straightened his collar and smoothed the sandy hair, fussed and groomed and enjoyed touching him again. "The sandals are Don's. You need a trim. It's hanging over your ears. You got more tan than we did."

Simon turned to Don. "Sorry, buddy. We'll be back as soon as possible. Don't turn on any lights."

Don grimaced. "This is sounding later and later."

"I don't know. It may be an hour. It may be after dark. We won't leave you overnight. The bug repellent is on the bench."

"Will I need that?"

Simon looked at the bare legs and sneakers. "You'll need it."

He climbed into the van and adjusted the seat and the mirror, and waited for Don to pull open the garage door. "Lock up from the inside," Simon yelled as they backed out. "I might call, so answer the phone if it rings."

Don stood in the open doorway, thoroughly forlorn and out of place. He nodded and made a gesture.

Simon was content to be in his driver's seat again with cool air circulating around his arms and legs. It had been a week, but his hands and feet quickly remembered the mechanical routine.

Marie was organized, enjoying the moment with fresh thoughts and attention. She gave him back his wallet and a zipper bag with the receipts from the trip. "We were in Room 631," she said. "We played Hearts with the desk clerk Friday after lunch for about an hour. His name was Sammy. Don paid him to say you were there."

"You played Hearts?"

"Not really. Don just paid him to corroborate our story, to identify you from a photograph if necessary."

"What's his name?"

"Sammy Self."

"How much did he pay him?"

"Five hundred" . . . *and my body*. "What did you mean about it being almost over?"

"Later."

His voice had a coldness that crushed her spirit. Marie wouldn't pursue it in front of Esther, but her bright outlook sank back into frightening speculation and anger. Simon wasn't the only one who had taken risks and scarred his soul with sacrifices.

Simon rehearsed mentally: they had been to her mother's in Charleston, then spent three days at the beach; they were tired from the long drive. He was well into character before turning onto Marcus Lane South and glancing at the rearview mirror.

"Somebody's with us," he said.

Marie turned to Esther with willful calm. "Remember, honey, we're teasing people that Daddy went to the beach, not Uncle Don."

The house came into view. Sunlight sparked silvery flecks from the slate roof. Behind the rich, dark brick and collegiate leaded glass was their private sanctuary, a symbol of former integrity.

Marie hadn't seen the house in a week, not since the frightful afternoon they had fled in the welder's truck and wondered later if the front door was locked. It was a gratifying vision, asylum from fear and stress, from the FBI and Sammy Self.

Simon turned the van into the drive and noted that

Ollie had cut the grass and picked up newspapers. The other car followed as expected. Simon stopped behind the BMW, out in the open so the van could be cleaned and vacuumed.

Esther hopped down and ran toward the trampoline. Toby came to greet her, joyous and quivering.

Simon got out of the van.

The suits and ties approached immediately, not quite uniforms, Simon thought, yet identifying and frightening.

"Dr. Braddock, I'm Special Agent Colish. This is Special Agent Presnell," the younger agent said, leading with his badge as always. "I wondered if you would answer a few more questions."

Colish had a strong, pleasant face and straight features. Every hair was combed into place, silent protest against anybody with hippy tendencies. His eyes were already developing that squinty, exacting look of one whose job it was to be suspicious.

"What do you want now?" Simon asked.

"Are you aware that a man tried to burn your house yesterday?"

"What?" Marie's alarm was genuine. "When did that happen?" she demanded.

"Yesterday morning, ma'am, about eleven. The police got a tip, and we staked out your house. The felon fired his weapon, and we killed him, right there in your garage. None of your neighbors knew where you were."

Marie turned and peered into the carport with searching indignation, but Simon didn't bother to look around. "Who was the guy?" he questioned.

"His name was Rick Grote. The last address we have on him is Newark, New Jersey. This was the way he made a living." Colish was attentive, eager to examine and weigh.

Simon's reactions were scant. "You think it had to do with the extortion ring?"

Presnell spoke for the first time. "We know it had to do with the extortion ring. We keep wondering why they're after you." He stared and waited.

Simon would not be cornered. "All I know about it is what your agents told me. How did you get a tip?"

"Anonymous phone call."

Simon said nothing more.

Marie felt she had been bludgeoned, but started to unload the van with silent resignation. Let Simon answer questions. He was better at lying.

"Why would anybody want to destroy your house?" Presnell asked again.

"I don't know."

"Would you mind telling us where you were Friday?"

"We were at the beach."

"Which beach?"

"Hilton Head, South Carolina."

"Can you prove that?"

"No, I can't prove that! Why the hell should I?"

"Dr. Braddock, you're not being charged. We do have a warrant, but we don't have to use it if you'll cooperate. A man we suspect of being connected with extortion was murdered Friday, and we want to know where you were."

"You think I killed him?"

"It doesn't matter what we think. These questions have to be asked. Do you own a gun?"

"No, I don't. Who got murdered?"

"A man named Willard Prather."

Simon shrugged.

"Were you with a group at the beach?"

"No, we didn't see anybody we knew."

"Did you stay in a cottage?"

"We stayed at the Patterson-Hilton, got there around noon Friday and left this morning."

"Did you charge the room?"

"I charged lots of things."

"Do you have receipts for those charges?"

"Well, yeah, I've got that." He reached into the van and handed Presnell the worn leather pouch.

Presnell zipped it open and fingered through the receipts. "We'll have to keep these, Dr. Braddock."

"I need them back."

"You'll get them back. Was anybody else on the trip besides you and your wife and daughter?"

"No."

"Did you talk to anyone while you were there, friends or relatives?"

"No. We were only there a couple of days. I didn't talk to anybody else. We played cards with a guy, but I don't know who he was."

"When was that?"

"Friday afternoon."

"You don't remember his name?"

"Sammy *something*. I think he worked at the hotel."

Presnell nodded. "If I were you, I'd sleep with one eye open."

Colish handed him a slip of paper, a police receipt that he took without looking at it. "Watch your back," Colish said.

"Yeah, thanks."

Simon stood with pretended calm as they drove away. Marie came up and took his arm. "What about the house?"

He groaned. "I found out about it and tipped off the police."

"*You* called the police?"

"Yes. I disguised my voice."

"How did you find out? Lid told you!"

Simon decided to leave it at that. "Yeah, Lid told me. They're not likely to try again after their man walked into a police trap. I heard how it came out yesterday."

Marie was suddenly shaking again and her eyes were wet. "Why the devil didn't you tell me?"

"I wanted your reaction in front of the feds to be spontaneous. Pretending to be surprised is difficult."

He was right, but the anger was still there. "And wherever you were, you just sat there knowing somebody was about to burn our house?"

"That's not the way it was."

"Well, how was it? Her voice was rising with each question.

He pulled away. "You don't want to know how it was."

She heard the anger and spoke with a quieter tone. "What about the other business?"

"Later," he said again. "I've got to go by the office."

Without another word Simon got into the van, backed around, and started out the drive.

He had reacted badly and he knew it. It was a disappointing reunion. He would kill anybody else who was unkind to Marie, yet he was offering unkindness himself. She smothered him, wanting to know everything, to see everything, but it was her home too, he reminded himself.

Simon stopped the van and turned around. The afternoon was a waste until he apologized.

One P.M.

Lid retreated to his cubicle and answered the phone. It was Romano, reporting that Prather had been killed

with a nine, and reminding him again that he was a
klutz. There was no record that Braddock owned a gun
of any kind. Lid had already checked. He hung up
without arguing the second point.

Mondays were always hectic and this one was
worse. The arson attempt and killing had created quite
a stir. Everybody was back on his case. Mimbs had
twisted hair out of his mustache ranting about the
stake-out, but that was window dressing. Mayor
Grayson had come by personally to express his concern. Mr. Mayor had questioned the use of service
revolvers in a residential area. *Yeah, we'll hang our
cocks out there to give him a target next time,* Lid had
muttered.

And finally Lucille had called; she and Marty
needed money.

Lid stared at his partner through the glass door. Alex
was emotionally mature, more so than he, a thing that
was easy to admit when he was pissed off. They were
good for each other.

The phone light blinked again, and Lid answered it.
Another reporter. Everybody wanted to hear about the
arsonist firsthand. He buzzed Alex. She was charming
over the phone. He watched her as his thoughts became
more serious. They had been together only six weeks,
but she was already injured, a chipper little bird with a
crushed wing. She would never get over the pointless murder of Harry Hall. Lid abhorred the memory
for her sake.

She hung up and he walked out to her desk. "I've
got to go by Braddock's office to get my stitches out,"
he said.

"I'm coming with you."

"What for?"

"I'm your partner; I go where you go. I'd like to see Braddock again."

He shrugged. "I don't think he'll be there."

"You said nobody knew where he was."

"We don't."

Alex followed him down to the car. Braddock had led to Prather, to the code book, and to Harry Hall. The dentist was a strange, shadowy connection to those few gentle, happy days. Alex suddenly realized how much her attitude had changed. *I don't give a goddamn who killed him,* Lid had said of Obie Prather. She didn't give a goddamn either.

It was a short drive. They parked behind the building and walked to the front door.

Roberta lit up when she saw his face. "Detective Li Dao! I think Dr. Braddock will be happy to see you."

"I didn't know he was here."

"Well, I wasn't expecting him either, but he just came in."

They followed the pert orange and white stripes down the hallway to Simon's open door.

Roberta was enjoying the game. Her boss had said they were at the beach; his wife said no. It wasn't her problem. "Dr. Braddock, you have some company," she trilled.

Simon was sitting back in the chair with his bare feet propped on the edge of the desk, tossing pieces of mail toward the trash can. He beamed. "Li Dao! Come on in."

"You remember my partner, Alex Sinclair."

Simon stood and shook her hand. "Sit down."

They took the seats as Roberta closed the door from the outside.

Simon was still wearing the shorts and shirt. "We just got back from the beach."

Lid noted the tan. He and Lucille hadn't been to a beach since before Marty was born, but Simon's dark face and ruffled appearance made the thought appealing. "The beach agrees with you." He paused. "I suppose you've heard about your house?"

"Yeah, the FBI were the last people we saw before we left, and they were waiting on the doorstep when we got back."

"When was that?"

"Couple of hours ago."

"Then you must know about Willard Prather."

"Who?"

"Willard Prather. He was murdered Friday, shot through the back of the head at close range."

"The brother of the guy who had his head cut off?"

"That's right."

"Yeah, the feds told me about it. They think I killed him."

"Did you?"

"We were at the beach."

Lid stared at him, but his sober gray eyes didn't believe. "What about my stitches?"

Simon picked up the phone. "Roberta, would you get his sutures out?"

After a moment Roberta opened the door, and Lid followed her down the hall.

Alex and Simon were alone for the first time. There was a long silence as she watched the junk mail flip toward the corner of the room. She stared at the dentist, evaluating, admiring the tousled blond hair. Braddock was good-looking, she thought, and relaxed.

Simon finally looked up as a heavy catalog banged against the wall. "Li Dao told me you were trying to crack a code. How's it going?"

"Not good. Somebody murdered the cryptographer and stole the code book."

"Did you know the guy?"

"Yes, I was in love with him." She spoke without thinking, then wondered why she had said anything. It was none of Braddock's business.

Simon fell silent in a moment of guilt and tried to fix the picture in his mind. The young woman seated across his desk had been in love with the code expert Roberta had told him about over the phone. He had even remembered the name through his drunken stupor. "Harry Hall?" he asked.

"Yes."

"I'm very sorry." The words sounded foolish in his own ears. Why would he be sorry when he didn't know Hall? Then he realized what his brain had meant—sorry he had gotten the guy killed—but Lid's partner had no way to know that.

A question slowly formed in Alex's mind: where had Braddock heard of Harry? The newspaper called it *burglary* with no mention of the code book. Only the police knew. She looked at the dentist and spoke impulsively. "Dr. Braddock, the one man I ever really loved was taken from me by these thugs, and I want them punished." She didn't smile. "If you ever need an alibi for anything, just ask."

Simon blushed. "What? I should say we were having tea or something?"

"You never know." Alex was suddenly bold again, her tone calculated and hostile. "What if you hadn't been at the beach Friday when Prather was killed? Maybe I sat out on the terrace with your wife for brunch while you puttered in the yard. It might have happened that way."

"How do you know we have a terrace?"

"Lid and I were there yesterday when they shot the arsonist." Alex rested her chin against her thumb and pointed a finger as they made eye contact. "I'm serious. Just say the word."

"I appreciate that," he chuckled. "You think we should make up a signal? If I need you, I'll whistle?"

She shrugged and pointed again. "Why not?"

He returned the gesture. "If I need you, I'll point."

Simon suddenly appeared awkward. Alex couldn't tell if the embarrassment was real or feigned, but it occurred to her that she had used the same approach Lid had taken on their first visit, and to which she had objected so violently. She felt relief when her partner returned.

Simon smiled and nodded through the small talk and continued to toss mail toward the trash pile until they left through the back door.

Roberta came to the doorway as if to receive instructions.

Simon only smiled. Her fondness for gossip was transparent. "I have a *terrace*," he stated.

Roberta looked at the ceiling and walked away.

Alex rode in embarrassed silence and wondered about her offer of an alibi.

Lid finally glanced her way. "Why are you sighing?"

"Lid, did you mention Harry to him?"

"Yeah, I told him about it."

"And the code book?"

"Sure. I think so. Why?"

"Nothing. I thought I saw a chink in his armor but maybe not. You're right about Dr. Braddock. He's very relaxed and speaks freely but doesn't admit anything."

"The bastard's crazy. You won't worm anything out of Braddock."

Alex understood: Lid had kept the dentist apprised of the case; Braddock's mention of Harry Hall didn't necessarily mean he was involved. Perhaps her flippant remarks about an alibi had sounded foolish or even insulting, but it was already done. Alex cringed to think how ridiculous she must have appeared, especially if Braddock was innocent.

Six P.M.

Simon had napped for over an hour, unusual for him but the stress-born fatigue hung like a weight and drugged him into sleep.

Marie was edgy and wouldn't rest until they talked again. She came into the den to open the drapes. Her movement roused him.

Simon took a few deep breaths. "What time is it?"

"Almost six."

The Seth Thomas struck six times in agreement.

She sat on the edge of the sofa, leaned over, and nuzzled his neck. "How do you feel?"

He made a sound.

"The people on the block have been calling and coming by about the arsonist," she said, "and there were messages on the machine. Mrs. Baxter was nosy as usual. She doesn't like anybody 'loitering' in the neighborhood who is not 'our kind.' "

"What did you tell them?"

"I said there was some sort of extortion attempt, but the police had broken it up. I mostly lied and played ignorant."

"That old woman loved it. She needs something to occupy her mind." Simon groaned and sat up. "We've got to get Don. You and Esther have to go back to Charleston with him. Y'all can take the BMW."

She slid her hand under his shirt and rubbed his chest. "Tell me about the extortion ring."

Simon pushed her hand away. "The two leaders are still alive, a man and a woman. It would have been over yesterday, but there were too many people around, funeral home business."

"What funeral home?"

"Nephew of the guy. Parted this world Friday, but the body was found sooner than I thought it would be. Anyway, a lot of people were there, so I had to put it off a week."

"It sounds like you're planning a family outing—if it rains today, we'll go next weekend."

"Marie, you don't know what evil is until you hear these people. I've eavesdropped with a listening device. I've heard them speak and plan. The mother is the worst of the pair."

"The mother? You're killing the whole family?"

He looked at her and spoke with short, clipped sentences and urgent plainness. "Marie, you don't know. I do know. The woman will die. Count on it. Benevolence doesn't accrue with age. That old bitch is Hitler reincarnated, and I will put her out of her misery. Soon." The deadly tranquil anger was rising. "And I'll do it with great joy."

Marie spoke in a whisper. "Simon, you're frightening me."

"I'm sorry. It would frighten you even more to hear her plans for Esther."

"What?"

"I didn't quite get it all. Some kind of sexual abuse, then death. Anyway, those two are dead and there's not a damn thing you can do to stop it."

Death. Marie's mind stuck on the word. She was shocked and stunned but wouldn't give in to tears. She held herself in place so as not to rush into the bedroom and embrace Esther, revealing a certain weakness and fear that she eschewed at that moment. She and Simon would sit together as adults and discuss the matter. "How do you kill them? You said you'd tell me when it was over. I want to know now."

"I have the fat man's gun with a silencer."

"You don't know anything about guns."

"I know how to work that one."

"How many have you done so far?"

"Two. Two bullets—two dead men. Well, three. I slit the first one's throat and let him bleed to death. The second two I shot through the head, one right between the eyes, the other from behind." Simon had always thought to avoid offending her with graphic descriptions and spoke as against his will, releasing anger through hideous language.

Marie wore an expression of utmost revulsion. "From behind? How close were you?"

"About two inches."

"Did he see you coming?"

"No. It's easier that way."

"Easier for whom?"

"For him. It didn't matter to me. He was strangling a hooker when I came in. They were arguing about something."

"What happened to the hooker?"

"He killed her."

"Why didn't you stop him?"

"Marie, I'm only trying to protect my family. If he hadn't killed her, I would have."

Marie was stunned anew, and faint, glad she was not standing. She wiped sweat from her upper lip and spoke quietly through deep breaths. "So what's the plan?"

"You and Esther go to your mother's. It will all be over next Sunday. I'll work part-time at the office and stay in different places at night."

"That's not safe, Simon! If those people know who you are, they only have to follow you."

He shook his head. "They won't make a move for a while. They know the cops are on to them."

"Then why can't we stay here too?"

"I won't be able to concentrate on anything with you and Esther here. I can take care of myself."

She gave him an unmistakable look. "Simon, I am not leaving again. This is our home, and I'm tired of being terrorized out of it. I can shoot a gun as well as you can."

He doubted it but didn't say so. "What about Esther?"

"Let her go with Don," she said. "I'll rest easier if she's over there."

Simon would settle for the compromise. "Let's go. The sooner they leave, the better." He started to pull on his sandals.

Marie walked into the bedroom and waked Esther from her nap, but didn't reveal her feeling of urgency as she packed a suitcase and maneuvered the departure.

She followed Simon in the BMW and made up a story for the child, not remotely akin to the truth but with ample extenuation so as not to frighten her. The elaboration was not needed, Marie knew. Esther had never complained of their recent excursions or the nights spent in unfamiliar places. Marie felt shame at that easy trust and acceptance.

Her thoughts were still racing. Simon was a murderer. He killed people. He took their lives as if those lives were his to take. There was no way to say it that sounded any better. But they deserved killing. They had earned it, like he said.

Then she remembered the FBI. The case was no longer in the hands of the local police. She knew a couple of Macon policemen by name—Fred, who helped at the school crossing, Ernie at the Saturday farmers' market. The Federal Bureau of Investigation was a far more frightening image.

Don stood in the doorway as they stopped behind the garage and got out. He was greasy with the stick repellent and wore a weary face.

"Have you been bored?" Marie asked.

"I'm hungry and I've got a headache," was all he said.

Simon handed him a wad of cash and stood back as Marie made a hasty explanation. They looked alike, Simon thought. Don was appealing, even tired and angry and with a headache.

Marie turned to Esther and brought the precious face to her mouth as she always did, and noised about the soft cheeks and neck. "You and Uncle Don take care of each other." She couldn't stop her tears but tried to hide them. Two of the three people in her universe were leaving again.

She and Simon reluctantly watched the BMW out of sight.

Seven P.M.

The two strangers were in the hotel manager's office for quite some time, but Sammy Self could guess who they were. They had the serious clothes and that look, the expression that said they already knew the answers before they asked the questions. He went about his job with nervous expectancy while his mind repeated the casual lies.

The Patterson manager finally came to the door and motioned him inside. He was a tall man with wavy silver hair and craggy features. His dark suit sharply set off a loose-fitting fuchsia vest matching those worn by the bellhops.

Sammy stood as if at attention: alert expression, dark, neat jacket with identifying badge in the lapel, a faithful minion who could do no other than comply with the wishes of his superior.

His boss got right to the point. "Mr. Self, these gentlemen are with the FBI. They have questions about certain guests who were here recently. You were on duty when they checked in. Do you remember the Braddocks?"

"Please!" The agent wanted to do his own interrogation but raised his hand too late.

The name FBI was still ringing in Sammy's brain, but he tried not to appear startled. "I remember them, a doctor and his wife."

"Do you remember anything in particular about Dr. Braddock?" the stranger continued.

Sammy looked at the men, but they were unfamiliar, nameless faces that went with the badges and suits. "Nothing," he shrugged. "We played cards once."

"When was that?"

Sammy thought for a moment. "It was Friday around lunchtime."

"How did you happen to play cards with him?"

"Both of them. I got off at one and was waiting around for a phone call. We sat right there in the lobby in front of the desk."

"How long were you with them?"

"About an hour."

"So you remember them both."

"Oh, yeah." He smiled. "She's easy to remember."

"But you remember both of them."

"Yes."

"Why do you think they were playing cards right after checking in? Why didn't they go to the pool or the beach?"

"I don't know. Middle of the day, maybe it was too hot."

The agent placed three photos on top of the desk. "Mr. Self, can you identify any of these men?"

Sammy felt a sudden panic. This was not the way it was supposed to go. He looked at the pictures, remembered the blond hair and the statement that Dr. Braddock looked *a lot like me*. He made his choice. "I think that's Dr. Braddock."

"You think?"

"Well, it's hard to tell from one photo. Like I said, show me his wife—I remember her." He looked at his employer with a knowing grin.

The agent gave a sympathetic smile. "Did you notice anything unusual in their behavior? Anything at all?"

"No."

"Did they say anything you thought was odd?"

"No."

"What did Dr. Braddock talk about?"

Sammy thought. "I don't remember. Nothing special. Are they criminals or something?"

"No, nothing like that. Thank you for your help."

The manager smiled at him and nodded. He was excused.

Sammy walked back to the main desk, almost trembling at the thought of the vast authority he had defied, yet his curiosity was piqued more than ever. He had gotten involved with dangerous criminal types, then survived a brush with the FBI. Sammy wiped his brow when nobody was looking, then gradually relaxed,

proud of his performance on both counts. Best poon-
tang I ever had, he thought, and the cheapest.

Don was amused at Esther, who sat in her accustomed
place in the back rather than the passenger seat, properly
buckled in and chauffeured. Don always liked being
with his niece. Esther was beautiful, and the blond head
made strangers mistake them for father and daughter. He
enjoyed the pretense without the responsibility.

For a time Don felt great relief to be out of the
welding shop, tooling along the highway in the BMW.
The novelty wore off as fatigue and darkness settled in.
Monday had been a tiring day, and it wasn't over. They
wouldn't arrive before midnight. There was no easy
way to go—indirectly on interstates or straight across
on two lanes. He opted for the two lanes.

Don had been hungry all afternoon, but waited for a
place he knew where the house specialty was barbecue
and Brunswick stew. He pulled into the sandy parking
area and admired the unpretentious neon proclama-
tion—EATS!

They entered the homey, greasy establishment and
took his usual table. A radio made an indifferent appeal
in the background. Don didn't need a menu. He smiled
at the waitress across the room and held up two fingers.
She would understand—two barbecue specials.

The restaurant walls were littered with mounted fish
and pictures of people holding up fish. There was a
framed picture of Elvis and one of Hershel Walker. A
wooden plaque made the announcement: *Food like
Mamma would've made, if Mamma could've cooked!*
The rest rooms could be identified by wooden cutouts
of a man and a woman nailed to the doors, undoubtedly
the same artist who had designed the plaque. The
lighting was provided by chandeliers made from

wagon wheels. Two large, clamorous refrigeration units stood against one wall of the dining area.

Only two of the other rough wooden tables were occupied, a family of four and a short weight-lifter type who had come in alone.

The waitress brought over the heavy tray.

Don knew the barbecue was good; more important, the service was almost instantaneous. He savored the familiar aroma and taste, and felt his strength restored.

Esther ate without speaking. She was never much of a talker in any case but hummed as she always did when the food was to her liking.

"Love Me Tender" wafted against the blare of the refrigerators. Don looked at the picture of Elvis. Maybe it was a coincidence or else the owner loved the King and had a stereo. The music reminded him of Turk, who was Elvis's greatest fan. Don hoped the pizza shop had been busy. He would sleep late in the morning and drive over by lunchtime, eager to be slinging pies again.

Elvis shivered into a fourth tune; it was a stereo.

Don finished and waited for Esther, who was not able to eat everything on the plate. He eventually offered her the rest room, but she declined.

He paid the check. The waitress didn't flirt the way he remembered from past stops. She had never realized he was married until now.

He and Esther walked out into the cool night air. Esther climbed back into the rear seat, buckled herself up, and allowed him to close the door. She said nothing, but sat with the serene look of a princess enduring the requirements of her station. Marie would enjoy the story.

Don drove again in silence, watching the speedometer, watching the white line. Cruel, troubling

thoughts of Marie kept flashing into his mind, but there
was nothing he could do but wait and hope. Simon was
weird, Don thought. He would hate his guts if Marie
got killed in all of this. Even if it was Simon who got
killed, that would leave her to raise Esther alone. Don's
warmest caring and affection went out to the child,
untouched by the world, unaware how precarious her
little life had become.

The bleak landscape crept by, invisible in the
darkness. Marie's fancy car had lost its appeal. Don
whistled and hummed and struggled to stay alert, but
the long day had taken its toll, and the hot beef barbecue was acting as a nightcap. He wouldn't make it
without coffee.

"Do you want to go to the bathroom?" he asked for
the second time.

"I'll go at Nana's."

It didn't sound like a woman. Wait until she got a
little older. "Well, I need to get some coffee unless you
wanna drive."

"I don't know how to drive yet, Uncle Don."

Something else to tell Marie.

He pulled off into a truck stop and parked next to the
outside rest rooms, away from the glare of the front.
"I'll just be a minute. Don't do anything crazy."

Esther was stoic. Don knew the look and didn't
expect her to say anything.

He walked to the john and pushed the filthy door
well above the MEN sign, reaching as high as possible
to avoid the smudge of burnt motor oil and handprints.
The odor of urine and the pungent chemical used to
suppress the odor of urine both assailed his nostrils. He
stood in front of the urinal in the bright white room and
tried to ignore the smell. His back was to the door, but
he heard it open again. Then he finished and turned to

face a short, massive stranger. As he attempted to pass, the other man grabbed him. In his last conscious moment, Don recognized the man in the diner.

Midnight.

Marie finally understood and shared Simon's passionate lovemaking. The tenuous hold on normalcy, on life itself, pushed the act far beyond the ordinary show of affection and physical relief. They spent themselves and lay in the silence and the darkness. Simon eventually snored.

The times were few when Esther had slept over with her friends, now only the second visit alone to her grandmother's, more disconcerting to mother than daughter. Not in eight years had Marie gotten up in the night without caressing the golden head to check her temperature and breathing.

The FBI agents hadn't spoken to Esther about the trip, to trick the child and obtain a contradicting statement. Perhaps they had over-prepared. Simon could have spared himself the hours in front of a hot light. Nobody had noticed he was working on a tan.

It was only twenty-four hours since the insufferable experience with Sammy Self. Simon, if he knew, might shoot Sammy in the back of the head, Marie thought, given his late behavior and new skills. Perhaps when the ordeal was over, they would make another trip to the Patterson. She could invite Sammy to her room. *Sammy, this is my husband, who kills people when he's not fixing teeth. Honey, this is Sammy I told you so much about. He had a climax inside my vagina. Blow his damn head off.* The inane thought sat forcefully in her mind as she perceived what an immense and monstrous act was murder. Her anger and ill will toward the hotel clerk paled by comparison. But that was

Simon's nature. He knew nothing of boxing or fighting, wouldn't know the way to rough someone up. If enraged, he could only ignore the offense or kill the offender. There was nothing in between.

16

Tuesday. Six-thirty A.M.

Alex had already called in sick. She had been in the tub over an hour, talking long-distance to her sister. Margo was her comfort in distress even at this early hour. There was no shower, but Alex had grown to like the tub baths. The large room reminded her of church because of the stained glass that flickered shadows of tree branches against the tile.

She turned the left faucet again with her toes to keep the water comfortably hot. Marvin sat in a ball on the hamper with lightly closed eyes.

Thoughts of Harry Hall lingered and trickled like an exquisite melodic line, then folded and repeated in exuberant echo. The time they had spent together was brief, yet even his casual conversation stood out in her mind, filling her with a mixture of delight and profound sadness. The memory of his death also persisted. She dwelt upon their lovemaking and tried to dismiss the flashes of that face on the kitchen floor with eyes glazed.

Margo listened with singular patience and restraint, then explained as tenderly as she could that a normal period of grief was not enough. Alex should retire from police work. It was far too dangerous, not suited to her nature.

Alex was undecided. She could feel the beginnings of change, of washing through her days in a deluge of law enforcement legalese, yet untouched by it all. She lay submerged except for her head. An occasional tear slipped into the hot water, but she kept sounds of distress from being heard over the phone.

Eventually they hung up,

Alex would not share her thoughts about Simon Braddock, not even with Margo. Braddock was the second object of her musing, expanding in her imagination as the days passed. She barely knew the man but hoped for his safety. If their theory was correct, the dentist was killing the people who had murdered Harry. The feds had the same thought, but circumstantial evidence often remained just that. Meanwhile, Simon Braddock hovered in her quiet moments of preoccupation, a vicious animal who had her blessing.

Seven A.M.

Marie heard the telephone but waited as usual, since it was on his side of the bed. She looked at the clock as the phone rang again. It would be her mother saying Don and Esther had arrived.

Simon finally roused and pulled the instrument to his ear. "Dr. Braddock speaking."

"Simon . . . this is Don."

"Don? You don't sound like yourself."

"I'm in a hospital. Where's Marie?"

"She's right here. What happened?"

Marie was already sitting up, wide awake.

"They got Esther," Don said.

"They got Esther?" Simon whispered with horror.

Marie raced for the kitchen extension.

"I was in the john at a truck stop." Don spoke slowly through his pain. "It was a big guy, short but very muscular, weight lifter."

"Are you all right?"

"Yeah. Concussion. I'm in a hospital in Aiken."

Simon could hear Marie's intermittent gasps through the kitchen phone. "Are you sure they got her?" he asked.

"Yeah. Nobody else saw her. Truck stop owner is afraid I'll sue him. He thinks I fell."

Marie cried aloud.

"What about the police?" Simon asked.

"No police."

Marie finally spoke with a tearful, quavering voice. "Don, are you all right?"

"Yes. Headache. Doc says I'll be here a few days. He didn't want me to make this call."

"Can you give me your number?" Simon interrupted.

"Wait. Here's the nurse."

Simon got the information and hung up, then walked to the kitchen, where Marie stood staring at the backyard. The phone dangled against the floor at the end of its coil. Simon hung it up. He knew better than to console or rationalize. The situation was far beyond self-delusion.

Marie's weeping was quiet, resigned in her fragile hold on reality, as if the purest essence of consolation would not bring her again into harmony with life. She turned and looked at him. "We've lost her," she said plainly. She stood with astonishing dignity, awaiting his voice and his touch.

Simon offered no condolence but gazed into an imaginary distance. "No. We will win this," he said. "There is a way, but I need your help. Get dressed; wear long pants and your boots."

Marie said nothing as she walked out of the room.

Simon made a phone call, then followed her into the bedroom. He took her by the shoulders and looked into her face. "I need you to take me somewhere, then come straight home. Skip will meet you here. Follow him in the van. Do whatever he says."

Marie listened silently, without speaking the questions in her mind. She continued to dress, too numb and terrified to harass Simon.

They dressed quickly and left together in the van, Marie behind the wheel. Neither of them commented on the clear sky or the early morning chill.

Simon reflected privately: he would kill anyone in his way but take the old lady. If Esther was already dead, the Wexler woman would also die. The idea hovered repulsively, but he was in the cave, that unnatural place where he thought what he had to think and did what he had to do. Taking the old lady would be impossible if Wexler was there. The weird affection between him and his mother was essential to the ransom. Nobody else would care.

There were others, Willis and Luther, names he had heard under the gazebo. Willis was the housekeeper she had reckoned so displeasing, the muscle man, the one who had killed Harry Hall, undoubtedly the cretin who had attacked Don and taken Esther. He would die. Luther was a driver, not part of the clan, but he would die if he got in the way.

Simon held the heavy, alien companion and checked to see that there was a round in the chamber. That deadly authority was always a solace, but now it must be wielded with finesse. He looked straight ahead again. "After you drop me, get back home and wait for Skip. He'll lead you out to the Skinner property from the pulpwood road, not the front. We'll make the swap for Esther there."

Marie concentrated on driving and said nothing.

The Tuesday morning line of traffic was unbroken on Spring Street, but most of it was moving in the opposite direction. Simon looked into the Ocmulgee and longed for his carefree teenage years swimming in the muddy water. Ocmulgee—an Indian word meaning *clear water*—maybe when the Indians were there.

Marie stopped the van at the place Simon indicated.

He turned and kissed her on the lips. "I'll see you later. Just relax."

She waited until he was out, then started off without replying, struck by the absurdity of his remark.

Twenty minutes later, Marie was home again. Toby ambled into the three-car garage and nudged her leg as she climbed out of the van. That honest, scruffy dog language said that everything was okay, but Marie ignored him.

She walked back into the kitchen and stood in the strange, heavy silence. "Yes, I'm relaxed," she whispered, but what else could Simon have said? They were two people against the universe, two unworldly, naive individuals against a mob of insidious and scheming men who did whatever was needed to achieve their will. Even the motives and methods of Sammy Self were suddenly innocuous compared to the enemy they faced. She recalled a remark Simon had made over a baseball game: *They got two chances—slim and none.*

She wanted to wait in Esther's room with the books and toys, to sniff the pillows, but she knew better. A man would take a stiff drink, but she had no wish for that. Marie felt a great need to make a deal with somebody—God, anybody—to have Esther whole and safe again. She searched for a point of reference to measure her indignation and shock, some benchmark, as if the right word would cope with the horror and the anger, but there was no word. She and Esther were the same flesh. Eight years ago the small, wet animal had emerged, part of her body from that moment and forever, something only a mother would understand. Marie was stunned into a round quivering silence that went beyond hysterical weeping.

The flat rays of sunlight shone through the windows and across the kitchen floor. Esther's breakfast time. Marie would go about her normal activities—the dishwasher needed to be unloaded, the sugar bowl refilled. She got as far as setting up the coffee machine, then stood at the window and stared blankly into the backyard. The hollies were covered with tiny spiderwebs sparkling with dew, one of nature's artistic touches. Simon would probably spray them. She gazed at the silver crystalline patches in a deliberate trance to allow her mind a few moments' rest. At some point the black liquid purred into the clear glass pot and brought her back to reality, but neither the quiet, pleasing sound nor the familiar aroma had the usual appeal.

Simon entered the private Wexler property through the ornamental wrought iron of the main gate. The house didn't look like a cottage, more like a fortress. The marbled gray tile roof was a bad match for yellow stucco, which had been painted many times and needed it again. The front entrance had a look that told him it was rarely used. High above the leafy shadows, a squirrel clicked angrily at noisy blue jays.

Simon wore a sports coat, buttoned to conceal the weapon. He walked rapidly over smooth, polished brick, and stepped onto the lawn as the driveway curved toward the carriage house, where the back of a limousine could be seen.

A black man in black attire abruptly came into view and stood behind the Rolls-Royce.

Simon gave a casual wave.

The other man returned the gesture and walked back out of sight.

That would be Luther, Simon thought. The chauffeur *knew nothing of the business,* he remembered.

Simon pulled on rubber gloves and tried the door. It was locked. He shattered one of the glass panes with his elbow and looked toward the garage again. Luther remained out of view.

Simon unlatched the door and let himself into the utility room, entry hardly more difficult than the Prather invasion had been. In lieu of guards and cameras, the extortionists used a deadlier type of security—a casual willingness to kill.

Simon waited and listened, then took the gun with both hands and walked quietly down the dim hallway, checking each room as he passed. The hall opened into a tall, deep room with exposed beams that supported a vaulted ceiling. Windows and fireplaces were at both ends. He searched the stately room with his eyes. The clutter was a surprise.

A fearful thought struck him—the old lady wasn't there—then equally sudden relief as a feeble cackle sounded in the distance.

"Mein Engel?"

Simon walked toward the voice and discovered his withered adversary propped against pillows in the small bed, alone in the darkened room. Simon said nothing, but held the long weapon and waited.

Ilsa Wexler looked anything but dangerous. She

made no cry but only stiffened and spoke with a fragile tone. "What have we to do with you?"

Simon kept his voice firm but polite. "Remain silent and no harm will come to you. Get up. We are going to meet your son."

"I'm not dressed."

"There's no time for that. Put on a robe."

"I want to refuse!"

"Don't make me force you." He smiled. "I mean you no harm."

Simon released the hammer and stuck the automatic back under his belt. He gently maneuvered the frail body out of bed and into the robe and slippers.

All the while the strange little woman chanted. *"Mein Engel, mein Engel, ich komme, ich komm', O Mueni, yes . . ."*

Simon was not startled at the ludicrous vocalization. He had heard it before. "You have a lovely voice," he said.

"Heinrich likes to hear me sing."

Simon helped her through the cluttered hallway, past the kitchen, and out the side door. He held her arm as they crossed the lawn to the garage area. They stepped onto the clean, washed concrete at the front of the garage.

Luther Steele looked up aghast as they entered.

"Driver, do you know this man?" she asked.

Simon stood behind her and looked at Steele. He held the weapon up to view and nodded.

"Yes, ma'am, I know him."

"We're taking a ride," Simon announced.

"This is not good!" she complained. "Heinrich wants me not to leave."

Steele's eyes were wide. "He's got the gun, Miz Wexler. We oughta do what he says."

"Everybody relax. I'm not gonna hurt either one of you."

Luther donned his cap, stood at attention, and opened the rear limousine door.

"No, your car," said Simon, "and lose the hat."

Steele's car was old and small, but they all squeezed into the front seat. He started out.

"Now, Luther . . . it *is* Luther, isn't it?"

"Yes, sir!"

"You will leave Mrs. Wexler and me at a place I will direct you to, then report back to her son, Heinrich. I'm sure I don't need to tell you what will happen if we're stopped by the police."

"No, sir!"

"Good. Now drive toward town. Use the Fifth Street bridge. Memorize the route, it's a long way."

They were an unlikely trio driving slowly through the pleasant morning air, Ilsa Wexler chanting odd bits of lyrics as they crossed her mind and Simon never failing to compliment the singing.

Steele listened for directions and drove in silence. He followed the broken white line far out of town, eventually leaving the old highway for black-topped county roads where traffic was sparse. At last the road was dirt, then a trail. The deer hut came into view.

"Stop here. Do you think you can find your way back?" Simon asked.

"Yes, sir, I know I can."

Simon reached over, switched off the ignition, and took the keys, then led the complaining Ilsa Wexler over uneven ground to the picnic table.

He returned and handed Steele his keys. "Here's the plan. Go back and tell Wexler I have his mother. He has my daughter. We make the swap here as soon as you can get back. Don't drive beyond that last trail where we cut into the woods. I can see the spot from here. Anybody comes past there, the old lady's brains are splattered. Understand?"

"Yes, sir, I understand."

"Any questions?"

"I want you to know I had nothing to do with this."

"Just make it fast. Tell Wexler she's got nothing to eat or drink and no bathroom."

Steele nodded enthusiastically as he backed around and started off.

Simon looked at the bizarre diminutive figure seated at the picnic table. The powder blue robe and matching slippers contrasted curiously with pine branches and brown straw floor. The air was still cool, but it would be warm soon enough. He had been focused on the business at hand, and now considered again the loathsome possibility that Esther was dead. Simon shoved the thought out of his mind. The ancient prune would die in either case, yet the purpose of her kidnapping was defeated if Esther was already gone. He hiked back up the slope and tried to think other thoughts.

The only sounds were occasional bird calls and pleasing air currents that gently moved in the tops of the pines. Shadows played across the top of the rough wooden table, only a few yards from the deer hut where he had butchered Obie Prather. Simon sat opposite the Wexler matriarch and made calculated conversation.

"I'm sorry we have to go through this, but it will be over soon. Heinrich will come for you."

"Heinrich will come. Heinrich will always come for me."

"He is a faithful son," Simon said.

"*Mein Engel* is always a good boy. And he brings the

sweet child. He brings the child back to you. It is only a bad mistake."

Simon gave a phony smile. "Yes, we all have our jobs to do, and we must control the rabble. Your family and mine should lay aside the feud. We are not servants, we're the masters."

"I have told Heinrich this!"

Simon nodded and gazed into the distance. This old lady slipped between cruelty and tenderness, unaware of the incongruity and self-delusion. No surprise Wexler and the Prathers were warped from her influence. Perhaps Ilsa Wexler was not so much evil as she was crazy. It didn't matter; he would kill her anyway.

Eight-fifteen A.M.

Marie heard the truck groan into the driveway. She walked out the back, got into the van without a word, and stoically took up her post, waiting for Skip to move the truck so she could back.

Skip got out and walked to the very spot where he had punched the fat man. "Miz Braddock, I'm not sure that van can get where we're going."

Marie spoke through the open window. "I'll go anywhere you lead."

"I got some cold drinks," he drawled with the loud, raspy tone. "I don't know how long we'll be out there."

"Do you know what Simon is doing?"

"No, ma'am. Some kinda meeting in the woods. I'm afraid Simon is in some serious trouble. I'm keeping outta sight."

She looked at the kind, wrinkled face and callused hands. Skip needed a shave and a haircut, probably a good scrubbing. "Do you think the meeting will be successful?"

"Simon usually knows what he's doing."

* * *

Ten-thirty A.M.

Luther Steele felt the terror rise as he saw Heinrich Wexler standing in front of the garage. Luther drove over the brick surface with a shudder and parked beside the carriage house.

Wexler was waiting as he opened the door. "Where the devil is Mrs. Wexler?" he demanded.

Steele stood out on the concrete and spoke quickly to avoid the volume of Wexler's rage. "She been kidnaped, Mr. Heinrich! But she's safe. The man had a gun! Said he wants to trade fo' his daughter."

"Who?"

"I don't know *who* he is, but I know *where* he is. He told me to bring you and his daughter back out to the place."

"Where are they?"

"Just out in the middle of the woods, sittin' at a table."

Wexler paled. There were times he hated his mother and times like this when he cringed in fear for her safety. He stared into space for a moment, then walked to the garage telephone.

Steele watched the haggard face, the fancy shirt, the shoes that looked different from any shoes he had seen. Mr. Heinrich had everything. Why didn't he just sit back and enjoy life?

Wexler moved in the short distance the telephone wire would allow. "Willis, handle that child with kid gloves! Don't hurt her! Tell her she's going home. We'll be there in a few minutes." His voice was terrified. "You don't need to understand it. Just do as I say!"

He slammed the phone and walked toward the Rolls-Royce. "Get in, Steele. Drive. Tell me what happened."

Luther retrieved his hat. He backed the Rolls-Royce and started out on a second urgent assignment, relating the story as calmly as he was able. "He was a very polite fella and easy with yo' mama." Luther kept shaking his head. "I don't believe he'll hurt her."

Wexler had regained control. "We didn't kidnap the child, Steele. She just came into our hands. We'll make the swap, all right."

It was not an open discussion. Luther knew better than to question the voice from the rear seat.

Their destination was not far, a house set apart, widely separated from other houses. The chauffeur waited as ordered while his employer entered the small dwelling and reemerged with Willis Carruth and the slender blond child.

Dirt streaks on Esther's face revealed dried tears.

"Go wherever you're supposed to go," Wexler said. He closed the sliding partition between the front and the passenger section.

"What happened?" Carruth asked. "I was all set."

"A change of plans," Wexler said.

"You're the boss." Carruth flexed his upper body. "I could snap her neck with one hand."

Esther began to cry.

"Shut up, Carruth! That will not be for you when the time comes. You can handle the end of it. For the moment, I want this to go smoothly. Don't move a muscle unless he does. That's an order. Remember, Mrs. Wexler is there." Wexler tapped the child on the back. "We're taking you to your papa."

Carruth held his tongue.

Esther quieted to an occasional sniff, but they both ignored her.

Wexler watched the scenery and made no comment. The highway changed to narrow black-topped roads, then to dirt roads that led deeper into the county. White dogwoods showed through the woods. Daffodils and clover bloomed on the banks and in the ditches. The limousine was out of place zipping along unpaved roads, leaving a tall, hazy puff from the dry Georgia clay. At last the road was little more than a trail.

Wexler opened the partition as the limousine stopped.

"They right over yonder, Mr. Heinrich." Luther pointed. "He said nobody oughta come past where we are."

"Stay in the car," Wexler said. "Willis, you come with me."

Wexler got out, holding Esther painfully by the arm. He scanned about alertly. It was an isolated spot; he was vulnerable.

Suddenly, the exchange was taking place, without preparation and more quickly than he had expected. Simon Braddock appeared at the top of the ridge with Ilsa Wexler on his arm, walking toward them. Simon placed his hand on her arm to aid in balance and modified his pace to her need. She might have been his own mother, his manner so becoming, but the jacket was unbuttoned deliberately to expose the gun.

Carruth unbuttoned his own coat and fingered the heavy automatic.

"Willis!" Heinrich Wexler snapped. "Don't make any sudden moves." Wexler didn't know Braddock but recognized the baby blue robe. He wanted better advantage in the meeting but could only stand and wait.

Esther attempted to jerk away but felt the grip tighten.

"Is that your father?" Wexler looked down at the

child, who continued to make sobbing noises and was too distraught to answer.

At last they were face to face beside the limousine. It was an awkward, desperate moment but for Simon's affable appearance and decorum. He fixed Carruth with his eyes, Esther in peripheral vision. "Esther, go on up the hill to the picnic table and wait," Simon said.

Wexler released the arm, but nobody watched the slender body start up the slope with long, unsteady strides.

Wexler took his mother by the hand and helped her into the car.

Simon Braddock and Willis Carruth maintained eye contact until Wexler turned back to Simon.

"She's a fine lady," Simon said, still holding Carruth in the corner of his eye. "I tried not to frighten her."

"I appreciate that," Wexler said.

Simon looked at the smooth skin and delicate features, and felt the alarming disparity between Wexler's cordial demeanor and that insidious dialogue he remembered from the gazebo. "You and I should stop harassing each other," Simon said. "I know how to mind my own business."

"I don't tell you how to pull teeth, and you don't teach me the import business?"

"Exactly."

Wexler made a sound and extended his hand.

Simon spread his arms and backed away. "Not with this he-man standing here!"

"What?" Carruth said with a resentful face.

Simon grinned. "Well, I know when I'm outclassed."

"Willis, please wait in the car." Wexler's voice was stern.

The housekeeper waddled over and swung into the limousine.

Simon Braddock and Heinrich Wexler shook hands.

"There is nothing more valuable than honest understanding between men of business," Wexler said.

Simon nodded. "Yes, sir. I agree with that. Truce?"

"Truce."

Simon could read the hatred in his eyes. Wexler was a good actor but not good enough. Simon released his hand. "Have a safe drive."

Wexler got back into the limousine.

Simon waited for the long car to back around over the rough terrain. He watched until it started away before walking slowly, then more quickly back up the hill. Enormous relief flooded his mind, but there was other business to consider.

Skip waited beyond the picnic table.

"Are they gone?" Simon called out.

"Yeah. Miz Braddock tried her best to wait for you, but I told her you'd be pissed if she didn't get herself and Esther on out of here. They were both pretty upset. What the hell's going on?"

"Hurry!" Simon started to jog.

They trotted back to the truck through trackless underbrush and sage grass. Simon got in the passenger side. "Step on it! I led the driver out here by the old road, and he'll go back the same way."

Skip cranked the engine and started out, still puffing from the run. "I thought y'all were friends. I saw you shaking hands with some guy. Didn't it go all right?"

"Academy award."

"You was playactin'?"

"I gave it my best shot."

"You sure you know what you're doing, Simon?"

"Get to the cottage. This will be the last trip."

"Yeah, matey, you're right about that. This is the last time I take you over there."

Skip bounced the truck slowly across an open field and through a shallow ditch, then shifted into higher gears on the dusty clay roadbed.

They rode in silence.

Wexler sat behind the glass partition of the limo with mixed feelings of fear and relief. Carruth was right—the cottage needed security, but they were safe for the moment. Braddock would be seeing to his daughter.

Wexler had measured his adversary quickly, always more fawning to a man he considered a fool than to one he respected. The tall blond stranger had seemed provincial, almost rustic. Braddock had viciously murdered Obie, then Max. Now he wanted to be friends. Wexler sneered at the memory of the trusting eyes and the handshake. "We kill them all, Willis," he said quietly, "but they've got to suffer first. We behead the child while the parents watch, then the wife. Braddock dies last."

"Stupid nerd never heard of a bodybuilder," Carruth muttered. " 'He-man,' " he quoted with disdain. "Why were we worried about that pussy? I'll kill him for free, Mr. Wexler."

"Relax, Willis, you'll get paid."

"Heinrich, I want the child," said Ilsa.

"Shut up, *Mueni*!" The harsh tone was a surprise, perhaps, to all three passengers. They ended their various complaints and rode in grumpy silence.

An hour later, Luther drove through the heavy iron gates and brought the limousine to a gentle stop beside the cottage. He held the door for the Wexlers while Carruth walked ahead.

Wexler led his mother to her bedroom. For the first time the shadowy cottage and the clutter were not such an annoyance to him. He would let her relax for a time before hearing the details of Braddock's attack, then plan his own retaliation.

"Let us have schnapps, *mein Engel*."

It was barely lunchtime, but Wexler didn't object. He walked to the kitchen. "We'll have schnapps now. Have one yourself."

Carruth took that as a compliment. "Can I fuck the Braddock woman before we kill her?" he asked.

Wexler nodded. "We'll need help with this one. Get the nigger we used with Milken. Braddock will enjoy watching his wife get fucked by a nigger."

At that moment Simon stood only a few paces from the kitchen table, inside the walk-in pantry. The door was ajar, but Simon was still, his breathing silent. He held the weapon with both gloved hands and rubbed his finger gently over the trigger. Small pressure to release enormous force—the clitoris of the machine.

Simon was patient, but apparently the housekeeper had no reason to come into the pantry. He listened to the sound of drinks being prepared, then took a cautious step and peeped through the doorway.

The stranger was facing away, the short, powerful body he had watched as the swap was made. Wexler had called him by name—*Willis*—and he fitted the description Don had given over the phone. This was the housekeeper the old woman was complaining about, the man who had taken Esther. Simon was several feet away but had confidence in his ability and would not risk the sound of movement. He kept both eyes open and steadied the weapon with both hands, aimed for the ponytail and squeezed the trigger.

It created a great clamor as Carruth fell across the

table, breaking glasses and dropping the bottle. Boxes and canned goods banged to the floor and rolled about.

"Willis?" Wexler's loud cry contained both question and alarm.

"I dropped it," Simon replied in a monotone. He aimed the gun at the open door and waited as heavy, rapid footsteps approached.

Wexler came into view, stooping in the hall to pick up a can. He straightened in the doorway without an instant to recall Willard Prather's warning: *He's crazy and you can't deal with crazy people!*

Simon's hands were already steadied into the same position he had used with Max (*sight picture,* they called it in the army). He squeezed off the second round.

Wexler in turn jolted backward against the wall, then collapsed awkwardly onto the hallway carpet.

The house was abruptly quiet again.

"I'm glad you're dead, you son of a bitch." Simon paused and allowed the dense rock barrier in his mind to dissipate. Wexler and Carruth were dispatched. The risk was over.

Simon walked to the matriarch's room. The pale figure propped in the small bed would be an easy kill. He stood before her for the second time that day, the same calm posture, the same gun. Simon had decided to say nothing. His experience under the gazebo had alerted him to the danger of listening devices or recordings.

Ilsa Wexler was also silent but assumed a haughty, regal posture as if she thought herself a queen and him a peasant. It was a quaint pose, Simon thought, like the vanity of age pretending youth, obesity hoping for the allusion of petiteness. Perhaps it was only the human spirit holding on to that last vestige of dignity, in any case, the usual poor effect.

As she started to speak, Simon pointed the automatic at the wrinkled forehead and pulled the trigger. The body bounced once and was still.

"What a machine!" he whispered. He gazed at the hole between the eyes and watched the spattered blood seep into the pillow sham. His killing pattern might aid the police—everybody shot once through the head. No matter. They would match the slugs anyway.

He pulled the footlocker out from under the bed and opened it. The record book lay on material scraps and cloth in the quiet musty odor of old fabric. He removed it and glanced at the first page, then closed the footlocker and shoved it back under the bed. Anything out of place might give the police another shred of evidence to pursue.

The murders were over—two weeks of solitary deviant behavior. He had fired the weapon six times and had five bodies for the effort, an enviable efficiency rate. Nine rounds left, nobody else to shoot. Simon wasn't quite disappointed, yet he understood a serial killer's mentality. Eventually it became only a thing to do, like skipping stones across a pond, extraneous to any moral precept.

He took a final look at the other bodies. Wexler appeared small and harmless crumpled on the hallway floor, the smooth white hair spattered with red. The large man lay belly down, perfectly balanced atop the worktable. A pale blue haze hung motionlessly in the kitchen, and Simon could detect the caustic odor. He stuck the weapon under his belt, retrieved a sack from the pantry, and walked out into the bright day.

The carriage house matched the cottage in architectural design and color. A spacious second-floor apartment was unoccupied. Simon stood in the open entrance with the long automatic and waited for Luther to look up from his newspaper.

Steele squinted into the morning light until his eyes rounded with astonishment. He remained seated but raised his hands. "I had nothing to do with it!"

"Shut up, Luther. Put your hands down. We need to talk."

Steele said nothing. He was older than his assailant and possessed physical strength of only tenuous character.

"I just killed Wexler and his mother and the big ugly guy," Simon said deliberately. "Now I can either kill you or give you two hundred thousand dollars. Which would you like?"

Steele tried to clear his dry throat. "I'll take the money," he squeaked.

"Here." Simon tossed him the sack. "Go ahead, have a look."

Luther was bewildered. He held the sack with trembling fingers but slowly unrolled the top as ordered. It was more cash than he had ever seen.

"I need a ride. We can talk on the way. Your car, not the limo."

For the third time that day, Luther assumed his post under duress and started down the driveway.

Simon kept the gun out of sight and rode with the heavy book on his lap. He glanced at the driver and wondered if a black man could turn pale. "Relax! We don't want to wreck the car."

Luther was trembling, too dazed and terrified to respond. He drove out onto the road and started down the hill toward town.

"Go out Broadway. Just drive and listen, Luther. You may not be aware of it, but the people you've been working for were criminals, murderers. They *needed* killing. They murdered two children within the past year, and a doctor . . . and God knows who else. It was a business with them."

Simon paused to collect his thoughts. "I could just as easily kill you too, but it's simpler to pay you off. The money was theirs and it's not marked. You can spend it."

He waited again, but Luther was silent.

"Here's what I want you to do. Give yourself the rest of the day off. Go in to work tomorrow and discover the bodies. Call the police. Tell them what you found. You never saw me; you never heard of me. Got it?"

"Yes, sir!"

Simon took a long look at Luther. "Now, don't be a hero and tell the police what really happened. That money was made by criminal activity, and if I get arrested, I tell the cops about it. They'll want it back," he emphasized. "Do we understand each other?"

"Yes, sir! Sure do!"

"We have an agreement?"

"Yes, sir!"

"Don't be so damned subservient, Luther. Nobody owns you."

"Yes, sir!" he said again, but at least he was smiling.

They rode for a way in silence. Luther was feeling relieved, but his hands were still shaking. "Sir. Er, where are them bodies?" he finally asked.

"Why do you care?"

"I don't like coming up on no bodies. Kinda like steppin' on a snake."

"Wexler's in the hallway, the big guy is in the kitchen, and the old lady is in her bed. Don't worry. They won't say anything to you."

Simon guided Luther through the industrial section

and picked a corner. "This is fine. Let me out right here."

Luther was never so happy to comply.

Simon stood out on the sidewalk. "I'm not really sure of the amount there." He indicated the sack. "It's around two hundred thousand."

"Thank you, sir," Luther said weakly.

"Would you really like to know why I didn't kill you?"

Luther's eyes were small dark circles surrounded by white.

"I needed a ride." Simon smiled and spanked the roof of the car twice. "Have a good life."

Luther burned rubber.

It was over.

Simon walked the two blocks to the welding shop. He took up his place on the familiar tractor stool without a word.

Skip broke away the welding rod and pushed up his face shield. "How did it go?"

Simon nodded. "It's over."

The wrinkled face didn't smile. "Is it really over?"

"Yeah, it's really over. I would've brought you some beer, but I was afraid to stop. My driver was a little edgy."

"You're still packing that big gun. Nobody's after you, are they?"

Simon laid down the gun. "No, but I need to get rid of it."

"Leave it with me." Skip picked up the weapon. "I'll put it where nobody'll ever see it again. What have you got there?"

Simon tossed the account book onto the bench. "That's a code the cops have been looking for."

"You'd better get rid of that too, Simon." Skip went back to his work.

Simon pulled on rubber gloves, then retrieved the small paperback from the attic. He scanned the key and eventually noted familiar names—Carlyle, Lee, Ziegler—local doctors. He ran his finger down several pages before finding his own name: Braddock. The one word opposite was *thimble*. He took up the code book and turned the leaves slowly, watching the top left corner. The record was handwritten. Many of the pages were filled.

At last he saw it: thimble. The encoded page showed no more than a score of words and the key was alphabetical. Simon wrote in each translation, then read the entire page: Braddock S 35 dentist 208 Marcus Lane South office 2816 Second Street Marie 32 Esther 8 Episcopal choir Thursdays four Obie Doraville $2000. The rest of the sheet was blank. The bookkeeping system was crude, almost childlike, Simon thought, as if somebody enjoyed playing a game. The Braddock family was only a page in that book, their lives worth less than that to the extortionists. Simon unlatched the hard cover and pulled the sheets up over the metal studs. The *Braddock* page slid to the dirt floor. "Burn that, will you?"

Skip looked up and laid the acetylene flame to the paper. "Why don't you burn the whole thing, Simon?"

"Maybe I will. I haven't decided." Simon watched the paper turn to ash, then put the book back together.

He searched the key and found Guy Bissett's name. *Lamp* was the corresponding code word. Again he turned the large yellow leaves until he found the Bissett page, but looked up only the last word. The deadly translation was not surprising: *terminate*. Terminate the child or terminate the extortion? Probably both.

They were willing to lose one paying customer to make an example.

"I'd like to leave these books over the john for a while. The feds might search my house again. The rest of that money is yours, buddy."

Skip grinned. "How much do you reckon is up there, Simon?"

"I don't know, three or four hundred thousand."

"Don't you wanna take a handful of it?"

"No, thanks. You deserve it. Just don't spend it all at once."

"*I* know how to pace myself. You're the wild man."

Simon smiled weakly. "How about one more ride home?"

Skip extinguished the torch with a pop. "I'm glad to get that gun away from you, Simon. Now you can go back to filling teeth."

Simon made no reply. He felt a great fatigue and longed for his bed. He wouldn't attempt to describe to Skip the satisfaction of leaving the hard-packed ground and the tired old building. It was over. The worst week of his life. The incredible morning.

One P.M.

Marie gently stroked Esther's smooth back and watched her sleep, safe in the covers of the king-size bed. She would not leave, her eyes and fingers unwilling to give up the image and feel of the warm, precious body.

Since the welding shop confession, Marie had known with odd, tingling pride that she was married to a savage, as primitive and mindless as his ancient ancestors. The thought had been smothered at first by the immediacy of other concerns, yet it was always there, scarcely hidden. The rescue of Esther released in her again that fierce, clannish self-esteem. There were no moral or social principles to stand against the caveman, brutish and uncivilized. Simon was a crocodile brain, who dared whatever had to be dared. Marie could only hope that shrewdness and judgment would somehow control the older instincts.

The images vanished in an instant as she heard the truck in the drive. Marie walked through the kitchen and picked up a dishcloth without thinking why, then went out the back.

They stood on the patio while Simon held her in a long, silent embrace.

Marie's joy was beyond words. He and Esther were safe, however unlikely, however miraculous. There were so many questions she was afraid or unable to speak. She cried and shook and held the cloth against her eyes.

"Where's Esther?" he asked.

Marie sniffed and wiped her face. "She's asleep. I gave her a long, hot bath and she crawled into our bed."

"How is she?"

"Physically fine, but she's very subdued. What happened with you?" she asked.

"It's finished. Wexler and his mother are both dead, and the muscle man who beat up on Don and took Esther. I enjoyed killing that son of a bitch! I enjoyed all of it."

Marie spoke in a whisper. "You killed three people today?"

"I told you yesterday they were dead. Where did you think I was?"

"I don't know. I thought once we got Esther ... I mean, I was so relieved to get Esther back, I thought it was over."

"It *is* over."

"You didn't stay very long."

"It doesn't take long."

Marie was still trembling. "I just didn't expect it so soon. I'm glad they're gone." She started to cry again. "How do you know you weren't seen?"

"Marie, I wasn't standing out in the middle of the street. We were inside the house."

"Somebody could have seen you leaving, or arriving." Her crying became audible.

"Nobody saw me."

"You can't be sure. We went to a lot of trouble to alibi the one Saturday, but you did these in broad daylight."

"Nobody saw me."

"You don't know that! You're so immature sometimes!"

"Who the hell ever said anything about being mature? If you want mature, you should have married . . . who's that smug son of a bitch lawyer?"

"Norman Cary," she said quietly.

"Yeah, Norman. You could still have the bastard if you want him. He runs around on his wife."

Marie became silent and sullen. She sat on the edge of a chaise longue and wiped her eyes. "Are you sure they're dead?"

"Sure I'm sure."

"And nobody saw you?"

"No."

"Tell me about it."

"What?"

"The man who took Esther. I want to know how you killed him. Describe it to me."

"Why?"

"I want to think about it awhile."

Simon didn't argue. "I was about twelve feet away. He had his back to me. I aimed very carefully and blew his head off. The slug went in the back of his head and out the front, taking most of his brains with it."

Marie kept her face impassive. "Good."

It didn't sound like Marie, Simon thought. He looked at her face, beaten down with fear. Her eyes were puffy, her nostrils flared and red. All of the usual poise and self-assurance were gone. It was the first time he had ever thought she was unattractive. He stood with his arms around her shoulders and held her head against his body.

Marie eventually pulled herself up and started inside. "Sit out here and rest. I'll make lunch."

"I'd rather have breakfast," he said.

Simon dropped his coat to the brick floor, kicked off his shoes, and slumped onto a recliner. The sun was high, but a gentle breeze made the patio comfortable. Toby came over and collapsed at his side.

Simon was mentally exhausted. He closed his eyes and started to review. Don's terrifying phone call seemed ages ago. The loathsome killing spree was over. It had taken some nasty turns, but at least the job was done. He hoped it was done—maybe he should have kept the machine. He felt a moment of panic, but Skip had probably disposed of the weapon by now anyway. The moment passed. Simon felt his beard stubble and remembered that he hadn't shaved or showered. His clothes were dirty and wrinkled. He probably had body odor to spare. Killing people was stressful, tiring work.

The problem was an alibi. He didn't have one. The FBI had made it plain they suspected him of something. Suppose the bodies were already discovered; the feds were on their way. He opened his eyes as his thoughts raced ahead: he had been at home all morning puttering in the yard. They had eaten lunch on the patio and could not hear the phone from outside. He should be wearing his puttering clothes, he thought, but was too tired to move.

Lid's partner would give him an alibi. Alex *something*. Was she serious? *Yes, Detective what's-her-name was having brunch with us on the terrace*. It didn't sound very convincing. Besides, such business needed careful planning in advance, and he doubted she would actually go through with it. In any case, he couldn't think of her name.

The last of the pollen blew like smoke from small pines near the back of the lot and covered the trampoline with a golden dust. Simon cringed as he thought of the kidnapping. What was done was done. If Esther needed psychotherapy, they would see that she got it. He wondered if Marie needed an analyst. She always faced situations with a toughness that made it difficult to tell if she was hiding pain. Simon groaned. He knew what she would want. She'd try to get *him* to go to a shrink. He closed his mind to the annoying thoughts and closed his eyes against the bright sky.

Marie came back out with a tray and sat on the other chaise longue, but Simon was asleep. She stirred melting butter into the hot grits and tasted the end of the fork, then nibbled a bacon strip and sipped the coffee. The steam disappeared from the eggs. Eventually she ate it all and hoped he wouldn't wake up.

She went to their bedroom, and watched and listened as Esther made soft clicking sounds, breathing through her open mouth. Marie searched with her eyes and her heart to uncover the injuries, to prepare a flood of perfect balm and healing.

She would have liked a hot tub to soak away the pain and the fear, but opted for the shower in order to be out and dressed when Esther woke.

Simon unexpectedly joined her.

Marie hadn't heard him enter the room or peel off his clothes. She was not in the mood for sex but took it as a good sign. She leaned her soapy body against him. "I'm sorry I said ugly things to you."

Simon put his arms around the narrow shoulders and felt the warm, slippery breasts against his chest. "I'm sorry I'm selfish and immature."

Marie didn't argue. He was selfish and immature, but he wasn't sorry. She patted his back. "I thought you were napping for the afternoon."

"I thought you were fixing me breakfast."

"You ate it, don't you remember? Then you zonked out."

"That's okay, Braddock, I'll eat a burger. I want to go by the office anyway."

Marie rinsed off and left him with the shower. Esther was still asleep. Marie wrapped her wet body in terry cloth and sat with a blow dryer. The sound didn't bother the child.

Simon came into the room wearing a towel and studied Esther's face, then began to dry off. He knew Marie was watching and analyzing, diagnosing him to death as she always did.

He dressed in white cotton pants, an old blue shirt, and loafers without socks, then walked deliberately out of her view to stand before the tall mirror at the end of the hall. His hair was still wet, slicked into place, but it would fluff up as it dried the way he liked it. He studied the tiny red veins in the corners of his eyes, then backed away to get the full view and stared at himself until the face looked like that of a stranger.

"You're a bastard, Braddock," he whispered, then gave himself the usual reply: "Yeah, I know."

"I won't be gone long," he called into the bedroom. "Take care of Esther."

"You take care of *you*! Aren't you going to shave?"

"Nope. I'm on vacation."

Marie met him in the doorway and kissed him on the lips. She followed him into the kitchen and kissed him again and told him to be careful.

Simon gave a dopey smile and went out the carport door.

Marie listened until the van pulled away. She got the number Simon had left and sat on a bar stool, holding the terry cloth robe with one hand, punching phone buttons with the other. She requested Don Howard's room, then heard the familiar voice.

"Hello?"

"Don? Are you okay?"

"Yes. What about Esther?" he said.

"She's fine. We have her back. It's all over. Let's not talk about it on the phone."

"It's completely over?"

"Yes."

They both waited in the silence, astounded and relieved, afraid to discuss the matter on the open line.

"Why didn't you call me sooner?" Don tried to sound normal.

"I don't know. Don't ask me anything today."

Again there was a pause. "Your husband is full of surprises," he said.

"He surprises me."

"Where is Esther now?"

"She's taking a nap. Simon went by the office."

"What about the guy who hit me?"

"He is no longer among us."

Don said nothing.

"When will you be out of there?" Marie asked.

"The doc says tomorrow or Thursday. Turk thinks I'm over there, so if he calls, tell him I'm out."

"Mom thinks you're over here too."

"I'll have to make up something. The back of my head's shaved, and I have a bandage."

Marie cringed. "Are you sure you're all right?"

"Yeah, the headache's about gone. I've been watching TV."

"Don, I'm so sorry. I was completely concerned about Esther. I know I haven't prayed about you like I should have."

"I'm okay. The BMW's still out at the truck stop. I'll bring it over when I get out."

"No, go back to Charleston. I don't want you driving any farther than you have to. We can pick it up."

"Fine with me."

"Take care of you. I love you," she said with quiet sincerity.

"Everybody loves me." He made a kiss sound and hung up.

Marie was relieved. Don sounded like himself.

She peeped into the bedroom for the umpteenth time, then walked in and sat on the bed, deliberately, to rouse Esther.

The child sat up and leaned against her mother's chest.

Marie held the warm body and caressed her golden head. "Did you have a good nap?" she whispered.

Esther snuggled. She didn't want to be bothered.

After a time, she was up and about in customary pattern. She went outside to the trampoline. Easter was two days past. Snowy patches of dogwood blooms covered the ground under the trees. Late afternoon shadows were long, the air was warm and still.

Marie sat on the patio to keep a close watch, obsessed with their problems but weary with thinking about them. The life-or-death confrontation was not over—first the gangsters, now the FBI. Their unsolved cases probably stayed open forever. How long would she and Simon worry that the dreaded three-piece suits might suddenly appear and flash the heavy, polished badges?

They had waited once before in youthful fear and ignorance. Dr. Elsworth Purifoy. Dreaded instructor of college freshman English. He was a round dark balding man with a small, pointed mustache and quick, penetrating eyes, not physically commanding yet terrifying to the students. She and Simon had met in his class, the only time either of them had entered the old building. They would talk and study and caress in the forbidden upper reaches of the Shakespeare theater. The area was off limits to students, kept sacred as if the bard himself were about to appear on stage. It was during one of those muffled groping escapades that they heard other voices and other sounds of groping from below, backstage. They stood to look, rather innocently, they thought, but the old floorboards creaked, giving away their hiding place. Elsworth Purifoy, Ph.D., stood in a shadowy corner of the stage embracing a buxom coed from behind, each hand cupping a breast, bra and blouse dangling toward the floor. They all four saw each other. The other girl shrieked and fled. Marie recognized her but didn't know the name. She and Simon retreated quickly without speaking to the professor. With all the purity of inexperience, they were repulsed to see one of their contemporaries with a man of that vintage.

For twenty-four hours they had reasoned and worried. Purifoy was married, but they were the ones who were trespassing. How could they know what his anger and authority might do?

The next day they walked into class together and sat together as they always did. The other girl entered and took her place. Dr. Purifoy came in and started to lecture. It was as if the incident had never occurred. Days passed. Weeks. Nothing was said. The quarter ended and they both received the grades they expected, no more, no less. That was the end of it. Purifoy taught them little English literature but much about the power of owning the upper hand. They later laughed about the incident. Simon was disgusted with himself for being afraid, but she reminded him that some good had come of it—they never would have met except for the English lit class.

Marie's memory of that trivial episode suddenly paled against her fear of the FBI.

Simon returned. No news.

Marie made the evening as normal as possible and finally got Esther to sleep somewhat later than her accustomed time. At least she was in her own bed.

It was well after dark when they settled onto the den sofa. Simon was on his third drink. "How's Esther doing?" he asked.

"Okay, so far. I told her that being afraid was normal, that anybody would have been scared, and I promised her it wouldn't happen again. I told her if she ever felt uncomfortable in any situation, she should immediately tell us or tell her teacher, whatever adult is around. She needs to know she has some recourse."

"You're pretty smart. So now what do we do with her?" Simon asked.

"Nothing. Don't mention it again unless she does. Just make her feel loved and secure. She'll be wary of any new situation for quite some time."

He put his arm around her. "I'm glad I've got you. I wouldn't know what to say to her."

"If you didn't have me, you wouldn't have her either. I gave her half a Valium."

There was a long silence.

"Does Norman Cary really run around on his wife?"

"That's what I hear," Simon said.

"Who did you hear it from?"

"I don't remember. I heard it."

She looked at him in the dim light and knew he was drowsy from the alcohol. "How could you hear such a thing and not remember where you heard it?"

Simon sipped his drink. "I don't care if he's dead or alive. Why should I care if he runs around on his wife?"

The anger was still there, she could tell, beneath the surface but incendiary. A two-year-old who needed his nap. She patted his arm and said nothing more.

Marie knew they were both exhausted. The den was their customary place to collapse and drink too much, to drowse through a movie and make love on the large, mushy couch, but this accumulated weariness was not likely to abate so easily. She had turned on no lights, only the TV without sound, remembering other nights of nudity and caresses in the flickering dimness. This would not be one of those luscious times. There were conversations yet unspoken and vows to reaffirm. "Would you like to fool around?" she asked.

"No."

"Do you want to tell me about this morning?"

"No."

"Do you think there might ever be another extortion attempt in Macon?"

"Not likely."

"What would you do if it did happen?"

"I'd turn it over to Li Dao," he mumbled.

Marie regretted her question; she had forced him to lie. She caressed his face with the back of her fingers and kissed his mouth, slight, sweet impetus but enough for the routine to flow from its own momentum. She gave herself to him quickly.

17

Wednesday morning.

After giving a ride to the bizarre kidnaper, Luther Steele had driven carefully to a cousin's house and stashed the money in his garage. Luther was a patient man. It was easily in his nature to let the money sit until the murder investigation was long past. The situation presented little moral dilemma. The cash had come into his hands through no dishonesty on his part, and had been taken from thoroughly evil individuals who had no further use for it. To tell the police the truth would be to give up the money. Besides, the killer might come back for revenge. Prudence and fiscal considerations required that he follow orders.

For twenty-four hours Luther had wanted to call the police but resisted. He had wanted to go in to work earlier but thought he should wait for nine o'clock, his usual time.

At last he drove toward the cottage with unaccustomed feelings of anticipation and excitement. He would discover three dead bodies, not a thing one did everyday. Luther had seen death only at funerals after the professionals had done their work and the deceased was presented in cosmetic perfection. He had never

seen a dead white man. This would be a new experience, three of his acquaintances brutally murdered
and left as they had fallen, open to his unhurried
viewing before the police arrived with technicians and
photographers.

He parked in his customary place and walked to the
cottage. The side entrance was unlocked. Luther stood
in the doorway and looked and listened. All was silent,
but the lights were on. He eventually tiptoed through
the utility room as if stealth or reverence was required,
and peered down the dim hallway. Wexler's body was
there, just as the killer had told him. He walked as far
as the kitchen door and took a long look at Willis Carruth. The room seemed colder and quieter than usual. It
was a shocking, arresting sight, yet Luther took some
satisfaction in viewing the housekeeper laid out in such
an undignified position, the cocky manner silenced forever. There was much spattered blood, but Luther was
careful not to touch anything. For an instant he imagined one of the dead bodies suddenly opening its eyes
and rising up, but Wexler and Carruth could not make
real his fantasy.

At last he entered the den and stood at his former
employer's bedside. She looked the same as always
except for the bloody hole in the center of her forehead. Dead people were mysterious and queer. Luther
had never touched a dead body but finally decided
against it.

He walked back out into the inviting air and sunshine and went into the garage to make the call. The
call itself was exciting. Luther had never made such a
report. His heart rate increased as he waited for the
police to answer. "Yes, sir! I say yes, ma'am! This
here's Luther Steele. I'm the driver for Miz Wexler,
Mr. Heinrich's mother over on Jackson Springs Road,"

his voice trailing off into a question. "I just got to work and everybody's dead here!" he blurted. "She's dead, and Mr. Heinrich, he's dead! And the housekeeper. There's blood everywhere!"

Rachael Brucker was beaming as she entered the cubicle, attractive in spite of the hair that looked like she had slept on it wrong. The pants suit was the color of orange juice. "I see the fibbies are still hanging around," she said.

Lid hung his coat and tried to ignore her, resigned that the relationship was over. "I've told them everything I know."

"What do they want now?"

He pulled at his collar and sat at the desk. "They're still trying to put Braddock at the scene of a crime."

She took a seat.

Lid watched her hands and lips, in spite of himself, as she lit a cigarette and blew smoke.

"You think he's your man?" she asked.

"Not my man. Those smart-asses took over the case, let them figure it out. I still think Braddock chopped up Prather and they do too, but they can't prove it."

"You like Braddock, don't you?"

"Off the record?"

"Everything's off the record between us, Martin."

He was charmed by her use of his name. Nobody ever called him Martin. "Sure, I like him."

Rachael suddenly ignored the answer. "This is Wednesday and I haven't heard from you since Saturday. Are you trying to tell me something?"

Lid was surprised and pleased. "I like you, Brucker, but frankly, I thought you preferred the kid."

She took a moment to understand. "Andy? I told you he's my cousin."

"He looked like more than a cousin to me. Aren't you two . . . well, aren't you?"

"Andy?" She was incredulous. "You think I'm making it with Andy? That's insulting!"

"Well, you hugged him and kissed him."

"Lid, I've known Andy all my life. I hug a lot of people, but I don't hop into bed with them. You think I do that with just anybody?"

"Okay. I thought it looked like more than that."

"Besides, I'm thirty-six and he's only twenty-three. I could never be interested in anybody that much younger than I am. I can't believe you thought that."

Pratt Mimbs stuck his head in the door. "Lid! You and Alex!"

Lid grabbed his coat. "See you later, Brucker."

"My name is Rachael," she complained through the stream of smoke, but he was already out the door.

"Alex is in court," Lid said. "What've you got?"

Mimbs scowled. "More murders over on Jackson Springs Road. Here's a copy of the call. Wexler and his mother are both dead."

Lid took the slip of paper and walked hurriedly away, trying not to smile until Mimbs was out of sight. So Heinrich Wexler was dead. Good. He didn't know the old bastard ever had a mother.

The Macon police were already on the scene when Colish and Presnell arrived. Two black-and-whites waited at the entrance, ready to fend off onlookers and reporters who hadn't gotten wind of it yet. The yellow tape strung widely around elms and hickories, cordoning off the cottage. Luther Steele sat in the shade of the carriage house and told his story to the uniforms.

Presnell nudged his partner. "Go talk to the driver."

Presnell entered from the side and stumbled down

the darkened hallway to the kitchen door. "What a dump! Who are these people?" he asked nobody in particular.

Lid stood in the bedroom. "The little man is Wexler," he called. "The other guy must be the housekeeper. There's another one in here."

Presnell squinted into the room, lighted only by a ceiling bulb and a bedside lamp. He was breathing through his handkerchief. "Li Dao? What are you doing here?"

"We got the call."

"This is our jurisdiction. The extortion case. I hope your people haven't fucked with anything," he said.

"We didn't kill the old lady, if that's what you mean."

The stale air and odor were adding to Presnell's frustration. "Do you have anything useful to contribute?" he snapped at Li Dao.

"Whoever did this was a pretty good shot."

Presnell walked out muttering something Lid didn't catch.

"Always glad to help, Walter."

Lid was enjoying himself. The people who had snuffed out Bruce Murray's life were turning up dead, not one at a time, but in bunches, shot at close range like Condon and Noles. Why would Braddock have done the old lady? Maybe she had witnessed something she shouldn't have seen. He looked at the dead skeletal face and remembered the weak feminine *hello* they had intercepted with the phone tap. Such brutal killing no longer seemed beyond Simon Braddock's capability, yet Braddock had been at the beach when Prather was shot. The fibbies would've checked.

Lid sighed and thought of his own involvement. What he had given away to the dentist was culpable if it ever came to light—*conspiracy to commit a crime* or at least *violation of oath by a public officer.* But Presnell appeared to have nothing. If Simon Braddock was Bruce Murray's avenging angel, he was a maniac and probably the luckiest man in the world.

Lid moved carefully through the narrow hall back out into the sunlight. He met Colish in the yard. "Did the driver know anything?"

"Nothing more than he gave over the phone," Colish said. "He's pretty shook up. Maybe he did it."

"You're thinking of the butler, Harvey."

Colish grunted and walked toward the house.

Lid watched after him. "You need a new partner, Harvey, while you've still got a sense of humor left."

Harvey Colish entered the house and found his partner in the kitchen. He stepped carefully over the body in the doorway and paused, offended at the smell and the scene. The air in the room was stale and held the faint odor of human feces mixed with the aroma of assorted liquors. A wide column of ants made a serpentine line from under the sink to a pool of cream sherry in the center of the floor. The bottle was opened but unbroken.

"The driver's not telling anything new," Colish said. "What do you think?"

Presnell shrugged. "One decapitation, one strangulation, six shootings. All close range, three in the back of the head. Systematic execution. Big-city style."

Colish looked closely at the hole in the plastered wall. "Maybe we'll find some better slugs, maybe match the one that got Prather."

"Maybe we'll find our asses in Siwash," Presnell said. "Where the hell are those lab guys?"

Colish grinned. "The dentist did it, Walter. He drilled them all."

Presnell was not amused. "How the hell could a dentist do this? These people are the organized thugs. You've met Braddock—can you see him doing this?"

"Not really, but he's our only suspect. We still have probable cause. Want me to pick him up?"

Presnell shook his head. "Braddock's not going anyplace."

Agent Guthrie stuck his head in the door with the same look of repugnance Colish had shown. "Braddock's a fucking daisy," Guthrie said. "He didn't do this shit."

"What have you got?" Presnell said.

"Delivery truck driver. Says he saw a guy walking down the driveway yesterday morning about nine o'clock—tall, slender, blondish, had on a coat."

"Can he make a positive ID?"

"Probably not. He only saw him from behind, but he's willing to look at a lineup."

"Don't line him up yet," said Presnell. "First, I want to know *when* these people died. Braddock better have a damn good alibi. Who's the witness?"

"UPS driver. I think you'll like him. He's intelligent, has a good memory."

"Set it up for tomorrow. I want that lab report today! Where the hell are those guys?" Presnell brushed the air aside in front of his face. "Let's get out of here."

They stepped again into the fresh air and sunshine.

Luther Steele was still enjoying the notoriety. He had repeated the account until he believed it himself. The part he was telling, after all, was true. The discovery of three dead bodies would be a Halloween story for his grandchildren.

Ten A.M.
Simon's mental images had taken on a dreamlike

quality, yet an unspoken terror palled over the yard work and other odd jobs. There were fence posts to paint and a kitchen cabinet that wouldn't stay closed. Every object possessed a new innocence and likened itself in inorganic plea to his abject guilt. He brooded in ignorance: had Luther Steele given his report? Had the FBI believed him?

Only Esther's survival of her ordeal overshadowed the withering mental anguish. It was a miracle. Simon offered a prayer of thanksgiving each time he looked at the lanky physique and yellow hair. Marie would spend the whole day with Esther, he knew, watching closely with singular loving attention. The child was still frightened and didn't want to be left alone. How would it be when she went back to school? Marie would keep her out until Monday—five days away. Worry about it then.

By late afternoon, Simon had worn himself out with yard work. His back was sore and he had blisters on both hands, but the physical exertion was good therapy. He showered and collapsed onto the chaise longue in fresh shirt and shorts.

Marie brought a bourbon and water without being asked.

Simon sipped the drink and leaned back against the warm plastic. He tried to remember a dream from the previous night, but couldn't. Mr. Squirrel and Mr. Rabbit had let him sleep peacefully, or perhaps he had drunk his way to oblivion. He would drink his way there again tonight.

Esther came out the kitchen door with two young friends. They skipped toward the trampoline without speaking. Each time she passed, Simon tried to discern something in a look, a gesture. He wanted to take her into his arms and feel his own power and conviction flow into the small, shattered mind. He sat and watched the bounces, the flips. Marie hoped she would be an Olympic gymnast, but Simon knew she was too tall. All the ones he had seen were tiny. Esther should be a model. She had her mother's looks but his personality. It was a sometimes joke, the quiet, moody periods, the scowls and lack of interest in any business except her own. When she overdid it, Simon received his wife's reproving glare: Esther was *his* daughter.

The genetic thread pulled at his soul. No one was better suited to understand Esther and draw that tender, afflicted spirit back from the abyss. He perceived on an emotional level, a knowing of his own temperament, but Marie had maternal right of access, that unique umbilicus. She would ultimately preserve, succor, and reclaim.

Marie brought out the *Macon News*.

Simon opened the paper casually, prepared for what he would see. The story was not the largest headline; the Cherry Blossom Festival took that honor. Still, the report was there on page one and continued on page seven: *Household Murdered in Shirley Hills*. He read the long article slowly, then finished his drink in one swig and rattled the ice cubes.

Marie came out to take the glass. "What's the news?"

"Three people in Shirley Hills were murdered," he said.

"Do they know who did it?"

"Not yet."

His answer made her feel slightly ill and took away her voice. Marie walked unsteadily back into the kitchen.

Five-thirty P.M.

Lucille Li Dao walked across the squad room with

Marty trailing behind. The teenager was taller than his mother but slouched as he walked with reticence and consideration, a certain nodding and downward cast that announced that he was not a menace. Marty didn't look like a cop's kid. He wore denim and a sweatshirt that accentuated his rangy adolescent build.

Lucille was average height for a woman, and overweight, though her friends told her she was pleasingly plump. She carried herself with pride, an almost manly upright gait. Her graying hair had once matched the brown eyes but was stiff now and uncontrollable. Her cheeks had not begun to sag but held that unmistakable waxen density of post-menopausal flesh. She was still considered a handsome woman.

Most of the detectives were gone, but Li Dao's family drew one or two questioning glances. Lucille seldom came by the department.

Lid looked up as they entered. He and Lucille watched each other for a moment as she took a seat. The communication was silent, but old and filled with private meanings, two companions nodding with inevitable recognition.

Marty slumped into a seat with indifference to wait for adult business to be concluded.

Lucille got right to the point. She needed money. The house had to have a new roof immediately unless he wanted them to move back in with him. Lid wrote a check, always a responsible man and spurred now by guilt. Lucille expected nothing less. They spoke and gestured farewells, traditional and unnecessary. She and Marty left.

Lid wanted to finish a report, but the meeting had suddenly released his store of energy. He was done for the day. It was the first time he had faced Lucille since the passionate afternoon with Rachael Brucker.

Through all the flirtation and baloney in thirty-three years of marriage, Rachael was his only infidelity. Cops were tough, or pretended to be, yet they suffered the same guilt as everybody else.

Lid had an sudden thought: he and his son hadn't spoken during the meeting. He tried to remember when that had ever happened before, but couldn't. Marty, who had been fun when he was a baby and a little boy, had grown into that odd creature who was not a child but not quite an adult either, and only able to communicate with his own species. Lid hated the feeling. He was a failure as a father, a failure as a husband. He drew the line at thinking a failure as a cop. He was a damn good cop. He had once been damn good at all of it but lost the way somehow. There was a time he had snuggled and nibbled the fat cheeks and neck when Marty liked it. What was the date, the hour, when that was no longer permissible?

And what of Lucille? What moment did her soft, familiar flesh lose its appeal?—hardly fair that matters of such magnitude be dictated by time. Rachael's younger body had enormous sensual allure, the more so because it was forbidden, but she was an amorous episode, a yielding to lust. There had been an emptiness when it was over. Thirty-three years was an investment not to be squandered for an afternoon of pleasure.

Such thoughts of Lucille and Marty hadn't entered his mind for months or years. Maybe it was the spring weather, warm sun and gentle air renewing life and hope. But Lid was not a romantic and he knew it. Life was basically unfair, or at least random. Lois Murray would attest to that, as would Dr. Guy Bissett.

Lid suddenly understood his infidelity. He had taken Brucker to counter the unfairness of nature, the lack of control that human beings had over anything. Was his rebirth of familial interest simply because Bruce Murray's killers were dead? Lid floated, for a moment, in that puissant, time-honored elation of vengeance. Did the new retaliation mean he would stop seeing Rachael Brucker? A good question, he thought.

Lid found the bourbon bottle. It contained an inch of the clear brown liquid, which he poured into his coffee mug, still showing a ring from not having been washed. He took a swig and grimaced.

The unlawful search of his home had given him occasion to reminisce as he stowed away family items. Some of Marty's and Lucille's clothes were still there, pictures and other effects. They were living only two miles away in a house he was putting a roof on, and for what? Why the hell did she buy rather than renting? The answer was clear and painful. For thirty-three years she had relied on *him* for such decisions. The thought conveyed a moment of pity and tenderness, an urge to protect. Lucille still communicated and came to him for money, sometimes advice. Things were not that different when they were together. Now she was duplicating the entire cost of running a house, a ridiculous waste but when was life ever economical?

Lid took another swig and wondered if she might consider reuniting. At least it would save him the cost of a roof, but he wouldn't mention that. He would never again feel the lust for Lucille that they had once shared. Maybe that was the nature of marriage, a gradual metamorphosis but meant to endure. Lid sighed and drummed his fingers. He knew the mature outlook was one that rested only shakily in the fringes of his judgment, easy to ponder when Rachael Brucker wasn't there to proffer the gentle curve of her belly against his cheek. He emptied the mug in a swig and thought to sleep on it. Memory of the drunken night with Guy Bissett had taught him not to make an important decision on three fingers of bourbon.

18

Thursday. Nine A.M.

Aikman's beagles were excited over something, and other dogs in the neighborhood were joining the lusty primal yelp. Toby was aloof. Simon walked about the yard carrying his second mug of coffee. The sun was above the trees, drying the shaggy silver lawn into a cool haze. He was sweaty from hand-tossing fertilizer. Marie's vegetable garden still needed to be tilled. Simon's feet were cold and his boots were wet to the ankle, yet there was something noble about work, and a feeling of security in the process. No evil could come upon him in the midst of honest labor. Simon had sometimes thought to be working in the soil at the moment of death. Now, for the first time, that deliberate exertion carried new alertness and apprehension, almost a shudder.

He sat on the patio to finish the coffee and try another Band-Aid over a blister, but his hands were too moist for the adhesive to stick. The night had left only one hazy dream fragment that he wouldn't mention— one more thing for Marie to worry about.

At that moment Marie emerged with coffee and sat with him on the other chaise longue. She bent her knees and pulled her long white robe over her slippered feet. As she lifted the cup to her lips, a siren gave a single whoop. Marie's whole body jerked. She tried to control the cup but felt hot liquid in her lap. The startling sound was a personal assault so close to the house, too close to be in the street. She stood and looked toward the driveway.

Simon didn't move.

Two men walked into view on the dewy grass. The dreaded FBI in dark suits, out of season, neither smiling.

"Sorry folks, I didn't mean to hit the horn. I'm Agent Guthrie, and I think you know Special Agent Colish." Guthrie allowed the flat leather to fall open low in his hand.

Colish showed his badge. "I'm afraid we still have questions, Dr. Braddock." He paused. "We'd feel more comfortable in our office if you don't mind, if you'll just come along with us."

The arrival was more frightening than Simon had imagined. His heart was racing, but he maintained a calm face. "Haven't you people solved that case yet?"

The question got no answer.

Colish and Guthrie stood and waited. They hadn't mentioned a warrant, but Simon knew they could always get one. He had no choice but to cooperate. He downed the coffee and got up to give Marie a peck on the lips, then walked away toward the driveway.

Marie sat in numbed silence after they were gone. It was a rude jerk back to reality. She had meant to say something. For twenty-four hours her thoughts had dwelt on the FBI, yet their actual appearance was abrupt and startling. The mental preparation failed her.

Esther came out onto the patio and crawled into her

lap. Marie held her and rocked gently, a giant healing goddess who wielded heavenly balm, diluting and dissolving away all pain. The thought slipped by with almost physical anguish because she didn't actually possess that power. Esther was showing uncharacteristic glances and sudden nervous gestures since the kidnaping, slight movements but enough for Marie to notice.

Marie stifled her own tears. If Simon went to prison, this is the way it would be, mother and daughter clutching each other in unveiled empathy and feminine weakness.

Esther turned her head. "What was that noise?"

"It was just a car, honey. Daddy went with some men in a car."

She twisted and snuggled closer. "Will they kill Daddy?"

"No, honey! No! Don't ever think that. They were the police. The police are our friends." She jiggled the child and patted her shoulder and tried to think of something more to say, but couldn't. "The police are our friends," she repeated and hoped she was more convincing to Esther than she was to herself.

Toby came over and sat against the chaise longue. He nudged Marie with his head and offered a quiet sound with animal discernment—perhaps it was a scent—that told him his master was in distress and needed consolation.

Simon sat in the backseat and hoped his neighbors weren't looking. He was hot and wet, and the coffee had made him hotter. He was wearing his plowing boots and hadn't shaved for three days, but it didn't matter. They had arrested nastier people.

His fear and imagination began to soar. Why would

the feds pick him up unless they had something? Maybe the driver had turned him in; Luther wouldn't do that. What if the Hilton Head alibi had failed? The feds had found Don in the hospital and traced back to the muscle man who had put him there. Simon wanted answers but was afraid to ask questions.

The familiar streets and intersections flicked past. They turned onto First Street, a block away from his own office. Simon waited and watched. At last they turned in at the city hall and started up the parking ramp. "Why are we coming here?" Simon asked.

"Police lineup," Colish said.

Simon panicked as the thought sank in: *He had been seen.* He felt himself flush, but his forehead was already beaded with perspiration. He got out and walked toward the entrance, aware of an agent on each side, but neither one was touching him.

The air conditioning struck his wet face as they entered. Simon heard a ping and the sound of an elevator opening. Somebody held the door and they squeezed in.

Colish spoke in the quiet moment after the doors slid shut. "This is very simple, Dr. Braddock. Just stand against the wall and do what the man says."

Simon cringed in the confined space, hoping nobody knew the words were meant for him.

He was first off, relieved to escape the crowded elevator without those behind seeing his face. It was rare apprehension. He was a professional, one of an elite group in Macon, Georgia. His escorts were cordial because it was their job to be so. Deep down, he knew they were the enemy.

Colish led with small gestures but mostly with nods, down the hallway and through another door. "Wait over there." He pointed.

Suddenly Simon found himself alienated at that vulgar end of the room where three men were already standing without speaking. Two others followed him through the doorway, making a row. Everybody except him seemed to know what was happening, as if they had all been awaiting his arrival. He wiped his brow with both shirtsleeves to make a better appearance before realizing what a foolish gesture it was.

Without warning, spotlights glared into his eyes and cloaked the deep end of the room. "Stand behind a number," came a resounding invisible voice.

It was all happening too quickly. Simon got scarcely a glimpse of the other men in line. He stood at the number 3 marking on the floor, astonished to play out something he had seen only in movies. He was a mannequin among real criminals to keep the eyewitnesses honest. Then it dawned on him with amazement: the others were the mannequins—cops, janitors, clerks on a ten-minute break.

"Face right!" commanded the hidden voice. Simon and the others obeyed. The man in front of him was his height, light suit, darker hair.

"Face the wall!" came the voice.

Simon waited through long moments of quiet shuffling in the darkness behind him.

"You're free to go." The voice was quieter.

Just as suddenly it was over. Something in the bored tone told Simon that he had not been identified. The whole business was too quick and neat. It was a bluff.

The blinding lights were switched off, but Simon could see nothing clearly at the shadowy end of the room. He stayed in line as the row of players stumbled out. His fear surged again when he saw Colish waiting at the door: Special Agent Presnell wanted to see him.

Colish led him down a hall into a large office

buzzing with activity. He indicated a chair where Simon obediently sat, glad to have a moment for his blood pressure to return to normal. The room was bright with windows on two sides, but the atmosphere was sober. It was a cop's world, easy to distinguish those whose job it was to be there from one like himself who would prefer to be elsewhere.

Simon sat, edgy and tense, without his watch to check the passage of time. Now he was a patient in somebody else's waiting room, completely at their disposal. He had heard of being *charged, arraigned, indicted,* but such terms had only vague meaning. Simon deliberately stared at nothing, determined not to let his fear and impatience show. He ignored the movement and conversations around him, the telephones jangling between stabbing fragments of conversation.

Suddenly, a single exchange registered in his brain: "Alex, you take a lot of time off."

"I was only off Tuesday."

Alex caught his attention. His eyes found the big man who had spoken the name. It took Simon a moment to recognize him, one of the FBI agents who had been waiting as they returned from the beach. Then he saw *her,* Lid's partner—Alex *something*—the gal who would give him an alibi. He wasn't looking for her and wouldn't have noticed her except for hearing the name. She was the only woman there. They had talked—joked—about an alibi that day, only three days ago, though it seemed longer. Simon wished he had pursued the matter more seriously. Alex sat at her desk, too far away, not convenient to make conversation. He remembered the perky smile, the way she had leaned her chin against her thumb and wagged a finger. *Just say the word,* she had said. He had responded with a wisecrack—*If I need you, I'll point.*

Suddenly, they made eye contact.

Alex glanced away, then stared at him again with a quizzical look.

Simon froze in the urgency of the moment. He stroked the beard stubble under his chin and held the gaze beyond the socially acceptable limit, then pointed a finger straight at her face.

Alex was wide-eyed. She gave a single nod and dropped her eyes.

Simon looked again at the floor but saw the large FBI agent in the corner of his eye.

"Dr. Braddock, I'm Agent Presnell. We've talked before," he began.

Simon nodded.

Presnell returned the leather pouch without comment. The wide face and narrow eyes leaned closer. "There have been more killings," he continued with the slow voice and deadly serious expression. "We don't mean to monopolize your time. You've not been charged and you have certain rights, you know that."

Presnell paused. Then he was reciting the infamous list. "You have the right to remain silent . . ."

The words faded as Simon tried to understand. Was he being arrested? It seemed a foolish question but one he was afraid to ask.

Presnell finished his speech. "Do you understand these rights?"

"I guess so," he said.

Presnell sat on the edge of a chair. "Where were you Tuesday morning, two days ago?"

"We were at home."

"Was your wife there also?"

"Sure, we're on vacation."

"Did anybody else see you Tuesday morning?"

Simon smiled familiarly and gestured. "Alex was

there the whole time. She and Marie had breakfast on the patio while I worked in the yard."

Presnell's official stance shattered and his voice rose awkwardly. "Alex *Sinclair*?" He looked around toward her desk.

"Yes." (Sinclair! Simon thought. Alex Sinclair.)

Presnell's voice hovered in the high register. "Detective Sinclair was at your house all morning Tuesday?"

"Yes."

The agent pointed at the seat. "Stay right there." He walked away toward Alex's desk.

The business was happening faster than Simon could think. Alex Sinclair was a cop. She knew about murders. She would know what he needed. He had just heard it stated that Alex had had the day off Tuesday. What if that was an inside joke, she had been at the police department the whole time, seen by dozens of people? He barely knew her last name. It was an enormous risk. He wished that he hadn't said anything, but it was done. They had no story straight between them. Even if she attempted an alibi, their accounts would vary. Simon's terror soared. He couldn't hear the conversation but only watch as Presnell's large body blocked his view.

Presnell stood at the desk. "Alex, if you don't mind, let me ask you something."

She waited.

"Would you tell my what you did Tuesday morning?"

"Why should I?"

"This is important."

"Walter, I work here, remember? I'm not one of your collars. Ask me about business."

"Believe me, this is business."

The moment required finesse. "Tuesday?" Alex shrugged. "Maybe I spent the morning in a bubble bath. Maybe I had brunch with Marie Braddock," She gave an ambiguous smile and watched Presnell roll his eyes and press his lips together while he glared at Simon.

Colish walked up. "What?"

Presnell looked again at Alex. "You really spent the whole morning there?"

Alex felt relief. Presnell had no idea where she had been. "Why not?" she asked.

"That's when those three people were murdered."

"Who was murdered?"

"Where've you been, Alex? It was in the papers."

"I didn't see the paper yesterday."

"I never knew you were friends with them." He jerked a thumb.

Alex pretended to notice Simon. "There's a lot you don't know about me, Walter. What's he doing here?" Her tone showed annoyance, but she was panicked again and wondered if she'd gone too far to back out.

Presnell clipped his words angrily. "We had him in a lineup, but he passed."

"Who was murdered?" she repeated.

"Heinrich Wexler and his mother, Ilsa Wexler, and a guy named Willis Carruth. He worked for them. This is old news, Alex."

"I was in court yesterday."

Presnell leaned on the desk with both hands and looked at her, still doubtful. "How is it that the FBI has been investigating Dr. Braddock for two weeks and never knew you were friends? Is he your dentist too?" He raised his eyebrows and looked toward Lid's office.

"No, I don't know him very well. Marie and I are friends."

Presnell sighed. "I didn't know that. The killings took place Tuesday morning, Alex. How long were you over there?"

"About eight-thirty until noon."

"What did he do all that time?"

"We ate on the terrace. Marie and I talked."

"I mean what did Braddock do?"

"Puttered in the yard mostly."

"From eight-thirty until noon, he never left?"

"No."

"Was he out of your sight at all?"

"Not for more than a minute or two. Do you really believe he's involved?" She gave a deliberate look of repugnance.

Presnell stood again and squeezed his lips and waited. "Apparently not," he said. He stalked away and spoke privately to Colish. "Where was Braddock when you picked him up?"

"They were outside in the back, looked like he'd been digging around in the ground."

Presnell squinted his eyes. "Take him home."

Alex sat at her desk, light-headed and stunned. She had perjured herself to an FBI agent. How had it happened? Every moment she had intended to admit it was a joke, but each statement had built upon the last until it was too late. She started to get up even then and detail the truth, but wondered what the repercussions would be. Presnell had little sense of humor. Then she thought of Harry Hall, and her anxiety diminished. She kept her seat at the desk.

After a few minutes, Lid waved her into his office. "Are you all right? You look a little pale," he said.

"I'm fine."

"You don't look fine. What are the fibbies doing here again?"

"They had Braddock in a lineup. Presnell thought he killed those three people."

"He probably did," Lid said. "Did he pass the lineup?"

"Yes. I spent the morning with Marie and gave him an alibi."

Lid looked up and stared at her blankly. "You and Braddock's wife have become buddies?"

"Not really."

"You just said you spent the morning over there."

"I lied." She looked at her partner without smiling, her eyes daring a rebuke.

Lid studied the face in silence. He tried to disbelieve but couldn't. "Uh-huh," he finally replied. "They got any coffee out there, Alex?"

"You got it, partner." She walked out of the cubicle.

Lid watched her cross the room, astonished at the chance she had taken. Alex would probably do time in Hardwick if she was ever caught. In any case, her career would be in the toilet.

For the first time Lid understood her devastation, her willingness to take any risk to assuage the anger and resentment. Her feelings for Harry Hall would protect his avenger, right or wrong. The assignment with Alex was only two months old. She had come to him bright-eyed and bushy-tailed, a stickler for procedure, but she was no longer that person. Lid remembered her words: *Let me know if there's anything I can do to help Braddock.* "Goddamn," he said aloud, "she helped him, all right."

Alex returned with the coffee and stood for a moment, awaiting some reaction. The color was back in her face.

Lid looked into the pale blue eyes that sparkled

when she laughed and saw the steel and resolve for the first time. "I'm glad you're my partner."

Alex didn't smile. "Thank you. I'm glad you're mine."

He watched again as she walked away. Three weeks ago, Alex wouldn't have dreamed of such connivance. Every man in the department knew about her and Harry Hall. How could Presnell not know? Presnell was vain and condescending, but he was a good agent. Maybe he hadn't been around much lately, and none of the detectives talked to him unless they had to. Presnell would put it together in an instant if he made the romantic connection. Otherwise, Alex was law enforcement, above question.

There were obvious clues, Lid thought—the roses, the day off after Hall was murdered. Pratt Mimbs knew about the relationship, but Mimbs knew when to give a damn and when not to.

Lid drummed his fingers. Alex must have gotten together with Braddock and his wife at some point to agree on a story. Such complicity was impossible without planning and consideration. A sane person would have backed out. And how had she gained Braddock's confidence? It went against his nature to confide anything.

Lid felt sudden alarm. If the fibbies shot holes in the story, the string of lies would unravel all the way back to his own conspiracy. At least his aiding and abetting had been circumspect; Alex had jumped in with both feet.

Lid stared at his partner seated calmly at her desk. "I hope you and that maniac pulled it off," he thought out loud.

Simon left the police station without even speaking to Alex Sinclair. He could only assume she had alibied for him—they were letting him go. Special Agent Colish gave him a ride home, but their conversation was sparse and indifferent.

Marie greeted him at the kitchen door with tears. Her relief at the story soon turned to curiosity. Why was this strange woman taking such a risk to help Simon? Marie listened to the details—the code book, the key, Harry Hall.

"Shouldn't we call Alex to get a story straight?" she asked.

"No, she'll contact us."

Simon showered and dressed and went off to the office.

His cold, calculated design was typical, Marie thought. She said a prayer for Esther for the hundredth time that day. Esther had been taking naps since the kidnapping, something she hadn't done in years. It was only accumulation of mental and physical fatigue, she told herself. It would pass.

She checked on Esther, who was watching TV. Marie carried her lunch in on a tray, then cleaned and worried, unable to relax. She talked to neighbors, repeating what little she knew about the police and the man they had shot in her driveway, releasing some of her real fear and anxiety through the sympathetic conversations.

It was late afternoon when a car sounded in the drive. Not the van, Marie saw, but a maroon Toyota.

The young woman who got out of the car was small and brunette.

Marie knew who it had to be. She automatically made a physical assessment. So-so. This woman had saved Simon's life, she thought with strange fascination. She watched to see if Alex would go to the front door or the back. Strangers usually went to the front, but Alex walked toward the patio. Marie met her outside. Toby had already given her a wet sniff.

Alex had a solemn, weary look. "Marie?"

"Yes. Are you Alex?"

"Yes."

Marie extended both hands, but Alex only shook her hand in the traditional manner. "Is Dr. Braddock all right? The fibbies haven't picked him up again, have they?"

"Who?"

"The FBI."

"No, not since this morning."

"They haven't contacted you at all?"

"No."

Alex looked at Marie seriously. "If he's in trouble, I'm in trouble."

"I know."

They each waited for the other to say something.

"I know what you did for Simon. I guess I know."

"It wasn't for him," Alex said with an edge in her tone.

Marie nodded. "He told me about your fiancé."

"He wasn't my fiancé; he was just a friend."

Marie could think of no response. "Would you like some coffee?" she asked.

Alex shrugged with indifference. "Look, I've been sitting at my desk all day watching the clock, cringing every time the phone rang. I took a great risk and it was really stupid, but I thought we should get to know each other since we're supposed to know each other. The feds will ask more questions."

"Sit here and relax. I'll be right back."

Alex followed Marie with her eyes and evaluated in turn—dangling earrings, oversized T-shirt, shin-length leggings, sandals. Alex was happy enough about her own appearance but felt a bit plain in the presence of the tall blonde.

Marie filled the clear glass pot with water and poured it into the top of the machine. She peered at Alex from behind the kitchen curtain. The woman detective had a pleasant face. The pants suit was neat and clean. Her hands were pretty. Then Marie saw the shoulder strap. This was a career cop, yet she had gone completely against her training and instincts. Marie needed to understand. The boyfriend story was all Simon had told her.

She walked out onto the patio. "It takes a few minutes."

"Is that your daughter?" Alex asked.

"Yes, Esther."

They watched her bounce on the trampoline and turn graceful flips in the warm afternoon air. Toby sat nearby, inattentive but allegiant. Eventually, Esther stopped and lay on her back in the center of the nylon surface.

"Is she all right?" Alex asked.

"Sure. She does that. She'll start jumping again in a minute. That's what you meant, isn't it?"

"What?"

Marie bit her lip. "You don't know what happened to her, do you?"

There was a pause.

"She was kidnaped Monday night. Simon got her back Tuesday," Marie said bluntly.

Just then two other children and a beagle came into the yard and ran toward the trampoline.

"Is she all right?" Alex said again.

"She's fine. I'd rather not talk about it."

"Marie, you don't have to talk about any of this. I don't need to know what actually happened. What's important is that we learn something about each other. I'm not here to protect you; I'm here to protect me. We've got to pretend we're friends, just in case."

Marie managed a weak smile. "We don't have to pretend, Alex. We could really be friends, you know. Is Alex short for something?"

"Alexandra."

"Well, Alexandra, I grew up in Charleston. I'm thirty-two years old. Simon and I met at the University of South Carolina. We've been married for nine years."

Alex was still distracted by indecision and regret. She maintained a serious expression, and self-contempt showed in her voice. "I don't approve of what Simon did or what I did. I shouldn't even be here." She paused and sighed. "Okay, I grew up here in Macon, went to the University of Georgia. I'm thirty-two too. I told an FBI agent we were friends."

"What about your boyfriend who was murdered?"

Alex looked with sad, appealing eyes. "Harry Hall. He taught at Mercer. We were seeing each other, and I wanted to marry him. Don't ever mention this. The alibi might be blown if the feds find out about Harry. The extortionists murdered him because he was helping us with the case." Alex averted her face.

Marie excused herself inside to get the coffee.

All three of the children were bouncing. The beagle puppy wanted to play, but the fat, shaggy dog could not be excited. Alex watched the scene with satisfaction, Esther's thick blond hair dispersing wildly with each bounce. The family resemblance was plain. What would life be for the slender blond child if her father spent ten to twenty years in prison? For the first time that day Alex stopped regretting her lies to Presnell.

At that moment Simon pulled the van into the carport. He disappeared inside the house and came out onto the patio only as Marie was bringing the coffee.

Alex was suddenly attentive. She stood, to be prepared for his greeting.

"I believe you two know each other." Marie set the tray down.

Simon only smiled slightly and shook her hand. "I think this is our fourth meeting, Alex."

"Simon! The girl stuck her neck out pretty far for you! She deserves a hug and a kiss."

Simon gave an awkward perfunctory embrace.

Marie's manner was suddenly repellent to Alex, who felt weary of the Braddocks' neat, homey little life. Simon's noncommittal gestures and remarks also left her deflated. She deserved much more from this man.

They took their seats again as Esther and the others came running toward them.

"Don't let her see your gun," Marie said.

The two friends stayed in the background as Esther hugged her father briefly, then pulled away. "We're going to watch TV."

"Esther, say hello. This is Alex. She's one of Mommy's old friends."

Esther turned and stood next to the chair. "Hello."

Alex looked into the tanned face, callow and solemn, and wondered what the child had endured. "Hello, Esther. How are you?"

"I'm fine."

Marie gestured. "These are the Aikmans, Milt and Edie."

Alex nodded.

Marie patted Esther. "Okay, go watch TV."

"Can the puppy come?" Esther said.

Dogs weren't allowed in the house, but Marie smiled and nodded. Esther and friends disappeared inside.

There was a pause as the three adults mused silently. Marie spoke first. "Alex, you and Simon have to be certain your stories are the same. What did you tell the FBI?"

"Very little. I said you and I were friends and had brunch on the terrace Tuesday morning while Dr. Braddock worked in the yard."

"I think you'd better call him Simon."

"Okay, Simon worked in the yard. I was here from eight-thirty until twelve."

"Honey, what did you tell them?"

"Exactly what Alex told me to say—we had brunch on the patio and I puttered in the yard."

The conversation remained shallow and desultory. Alex didn't want the coffee but sipped it politely, secretely surprised and angered at Simon's manner. This was a man who had murdered three people only days before, and she had risked her career to protect him, albeit for personal reasons. She expected open discussion of the day's events and deserved that much, she thought, but Braddock's professional standing made him difficult to approach. Alex herself felt a stubborn pride that wouldn't allow her to demand answers, yet she wanted him to speak on his own.

Marie went inside again.

Alex glared at Simon and tried deliberately to be offensive. "What did Presnell say to you after I lied to him?"

"I didn't talk to him again. The other man brought me home."

Alex sniffed. "Apparently they bought the story. You know, I could go back and tell Presnell I never saw you on Tuesday."

Simon kept the pleasant expression. "Why would you do that?"

"Well, I really wouldn't," she admitted.

They were silent.

Alex knew that Simon Braddock knew her threat was a bluff. Nobody had forced her to lie, and she could never change her mind about the alibi. Alex felt used, the way men always treat women, she thought, until they get what they want. Then they deny all responsibility. She was angry at Simon and angry at herself. Nothing would bring Harry back; she was a fool.

She looked at him until he made eye contact. "You're a bastard, Braddock," she said because she could get away with it.

Simon said nothing.

For all Alex could tell, he really *was* innocent. She wanted to hear it from his own voice: *Yes, when I shot Wexler through the head . . .*

Marie came back out, and Simon took the excuse to disappear inside.

"Your husband is a strange man," Alex said.

"I know. He's very private and doesn't like to rely on people, doesn't like to deal with people at all. Don't let him hurt your feelings. I know him. He appreciates you and would do anything for you now. But he's not verbal. Don't expect it."

Simon eventually returned with a highball and sat with them again.

Alex watched him. His face showed no emotion, neither anger nor appreciation. She made eye contact again. "Lid sends his regards."

Simon nodded gently. "What ever happened to the code book?" he asked.

"We never got it back. The code and the key would be a help to the feds."

"How so?"

"The extortionists killed to get it. It must be important."

She looked hard into his eyes. "Even though the gang leaders have been exterminated, it would be useful to have the code book deciphered. Maybe the FBI could tell how the operation was run. They would know who was paying off."

"So what does the FBI do now?"

Alex's voice was cold. "They'll keep digging."

"Do you think they might discover that we only just met?" Marie asked.

"If they look long enough and hard enough, they will," Alex said. "We have to hope that the fibbies will believe the extortionists were fighting among themselves."

Simon gazed into the distance. "That's probably what happened."

Alex stared at him. He looked as if he actually believed it. Lid was right. Braddock was crazy, but he never fell out of character.

"The police might get the code book yet," he said. "Whoever is left could turn it in. You get anonymous mail and phone calls, don't you?"

"Sometimes we do."

"Maybe you'll get a belated Easter gift, all wrapped in blue bunny paper with Easter baskets."

Alex felt lost in the conversation. Perhaps it was the alcohol. "Yes, maybe we will," she agreed.

Simon shrugged and went inside again.

Alex had reason to like him and reason to dislike him. Marie was a nicer person on the surface, yet spoiled and smug. Her physical beauty was intimidating and kept people at a distance. Alex could sense the usual competitive posture that two women took when both had done something wonderful for the same man.

They talked for another hour and tried to discover

points of mutual interest and experience for the con-
trived friendship. Alex hoped to have another chance to
question Simon, but he never rejoined them.

The sky was becoming pale as Toby ambled over
and sat, looking pointedly at Marie. It was suppertime.

Alex pulled herself up from the chair. "I really
should be going."

"Have dinner with us Saturday night?" Marie said.

Alex was surprised. "Are you sure?"

"Alex, I insist. You and Simon will get to know each
other, and you'll like him. He takes a little time. We're
friends, remember?"

"Thank you. I'd like that."

Marie walked her to the driveway and watched the
maroon Toyota drive away.

Alex had accepted the invitation partly from desire
but mostly to nurture the friendship. She needed all the
contact possible in case the fibbies were looking. Braddock would have one more chance to act like a human
being before she decided he was a complete sociopath.
She didn't wonder that Lid was attracted to him. They
were the same type—ruthless, single-minded, and private. She doubted that Braddock had more than a few
real friends, or wanted them.

Marie went inside. Esther was in her room; the
Aikman kids were gone.

Simon was slumped on the sofa with a drink and a
baseball game with the volume turned all the way
down. The quiet ticking of the Seth Thomas was the
only sound.

Marie mushed into the pillow beside him. "Can you
hear that?"

"I don't need to hear it. I know what they're doing."

"What did you think of Alex?"

"I like her."

"She's coming to supper Saturday night."

"I thought we were going to Charleston to get the car."

Marie shrugged. "Next weekend." She waited. "Is that all you have to say? Alex went through a terrible experience. Do you realize what an enormous risk she took for you?"

Simon took a sip. "What'd you want me to do, go to bed with her? She doesn't really know me. She was just pissed off with the hoods for killing her boyfriend."

Even in the dusky light Marie recognized the physical and mental exhaustion—the two-year-old who needed his nap again.

"Alex is a nice gal," Simon said. "I'll say something sweet to her Saturday night . . . even if it kills me."

"Simon, she wanted to discuss the alibi and the rest of it, and you wouldn't even talk to her. She's a woman. She wants appreciation, some visible sign." Marie squeezed his stubbled cheeks with her thumb and finger. "A woman wants to be told."

"Okay, maybe I will go to bed with her."

"You'd better go to bed with me, Braddock, if you want to do it with anybody." She snuggled closer and reflected again with thanksgiving and disbelief. "We have passed through the valley of the shadow of death."

"Yeah."

"And you need to thank Alex for what she did for you." Marie shuddered. "What if she should change her mind?"

"She lied to the FBI. She can't change her mind."

His lack of concern was harsh, yet Marie knew he

was right. Elsworth Purifoy, Ph.D., had taught Simon well: when you have authority, use it.

"At least you might act like you appreciate it," she said.

"I appreciate it."

Marie guessed he was on his second or third drink. She tried to feel as relaxed as he looked, but had a deep, abiding fear that they had missed something. If the FBI discovered that Alex Sinclair was lying they were all in trouble. A collapsed alibi was worse than none at all—an innocent person wouldn't have needed one.

19

Friday morning.

The Charleston sun felt hot against his arm. Don's Porsche was old, but it was his pride. He drove with the top up, his hair not able to blow in the breeze as usual. He had called his mother rather than stopping by, so she wouldn't see his injury. The original bandage had been replaced with a smaller one, the extent of the laceration less obvious, yet he wanted to put off an explanation. The throbbing had ceased, and the uncomfortable tightness at the back of his skull was not something he would admit.

The takeout pizza shop was a half block from the beach. Don parked in the ocean lot and hiked across dirty white sand up onto the concrete apron in front of the store. The fine powder around the entrance needed sweeping as usual. He paused for a moment and shaded his eyes to gaze at the familiar seascape, then pushed open the heavy glass door.

The aroma of cheese and dough and onions filled his nostrils. It was a warm, comfortable odor that did more to sell pizza than the pictures on the menu did.

Don was wearing his standard uniform—shorts,

shirt, and sneakers with no socks. "Hi, Maggie." He walked past the cashier toward the rear.

She took a moment to recognize him. "Hi," she said.

Turk stood in front of the huge, hot ovens, shuffling a long wooden spatula into the narrow opening. His face was wet with perspiration. He wore a paper hat to cover the long hair. They were the same age, but Don could never have grown the heavy black mustache that made Turk look like a Spanish warrior. He trusted the shop to nobody other than Turk. They were both good short-order cooks and liked the challenge of the rush.

Turk looked up, relieved to see his boss walk in the front door, but turned quickly back to the oven. "I've been jumping. These four go out. Those are pickups." He pointed at the stack of flat boxes on top of the oven. "Toni should be back in five minutes."

"Well, I'm here. Take the rest of the day off."

"Thanks! What happened to your head?"

"I was making it with this guy. His girlfriend came in and hit me with a bottle of Jack Daniel's."

"You making it with guys these days?"

"It's the same thing."

Turk smiled. "Where've you been? You stayed gone longer than I thought."

"I was at the beach."

Turk banged the oven door closed. "You live at the damn beach. What beach did you go to?"

"Hilton Head."

Turk wiped his face on the apron and smoothed his mustache. "You're nuts, Howard. See ya!" He dropped the hat into a trash can, tossed the apron onto a hook, and was out the back door.

Don opened the oven and looked at the edge of the dough. Another ninety seconds.

The heat at the back of the store was smothering and

sweet, completely neutralizing the effect of the air conditioner, which labored throughout the day. Don enjoyed being hot. The pizza was selling.

Maggie came back to marvel at the shaved head, to fondle the bandage and hear the explanation. She knew not to believe whatever he said.

A group of bikini-clad sun worshipers gaggled in the front door, offering up their breasts and fannies for admiration.

Don suddenly remembered that he had the greatest job in the world. He would wait until his hair grew in and he was feeling a little better before toying with the female customers, but it was good to be back in the groove. He walked to the front and smiled.

"What can I do for you young ladies?"

Noon.

Alex dumped the mail on Lid's desk as always and waited.

"What?" he asked.

"I want to watch you open the mail."

"You've never watched before. Let's go to lunch." He buttoned his shirt at the neck and shoved up the tie.

"Look at the mail," she repeated.

Lid made a face and looked at the pile. "What is this?"

"Open it."

"Mailing tape around gift-wrapping paper?"

"I know the jerk who sent it," Alex said.

"How could you know?"

"I'll bet you a million dollars I know what it is."

"I don't have a million dollars. How about dinner tonight?"

"All right, I'll bet dinner tonight I know what that is. If I'm right, you pay."

"Done. What is it?" Lid said.

"I choose the restaurant?"

"Sure." He pulled out a pocketknife and waited.

"It's the code book and key that belonged to the extortionists."

Lid looked at her with a half smile, then cut the tape and tore back the paper. "Well, I'll be damned. I don't suppose there's a return address?"

"No, there won't be a return address."

"You know who sent this, don't you?"

She gave a sardonic smile. "Yes, I know, and you know too."

"Braddock?"

Alex nodded. She picked up the file, which was familiar, and the key she had not seen before. "Harry died because of this," she said quietly.

Lid's expression was solemn. "Yeah, I guess he did. How do you know Braddock sent this?"

"We can talk about it later."

Lid spotted Mimbs and waved him into the cubicle. "Look what we got in the mail."

Mimbs twisted one end of his mustache. "What is it?"

"The code book and key from the extortion ring."

"Really? Presnell will be happy to see that. Who sent it?"

"Anonymous gift, Lieutenant."

"The best ones always are."

"One of Wexler's shithead relatives," Alex said.

Mimbs frowned. "You're getting an attitude, Alex. You been hanging around Li Dao too long. Maybe I should reassign you."

Lid raised his hand. "Nope. Alex is my partner."

Alex grinned at Lid, distinctly pleased.

Mimbs was satisfied. He took the books and walked out.

Alex watched as Lid examined the blue bunny wrapping paper. In typical indirect manner, Braddock had told her to expect the code book and key; he wouldn't discuss it openly. "Don't bother," she said. "Braddock won't reveal anything. He probably wrapped it with rubber gloves on. This was your case, Lid. I don't care if the fibbies did take it over."

Lid chuckled.

"You look good when you laugh. You should do it more often."

"I could do that. We're celebrating tonight, Alex! It's Friday. We'll have dinner, maybe get drunk afterward."

Her blue eyes sparkled. "I could do that."

"How did you know that was the code book?"

"I know a lot about the Braddocks. We're *friends*." She smirked at the word. "I'm having dinner with them tomorrow night."

Lid would wait for her to tell the story in her own time. The painful experience with Harry Hall was not something to probe deliberately. "You're moving in elite circles," he said. "Soon you won't like to be seen hanging around with cops."

Alex looked seriously into the gray eyes. "I hope you don't really believe that, Lid. It's sort of a forced friendship. Braddock is a scoundrel. I'll tell you about it tonight."

There was a long silence.

"You took a hell of a chance," Lid said. He watched her mouth stretch widely, and thought she was about to cry.

"I agonized with second thoughts, but it was already done. You still want me for your partner, don't you? I mean, you don't think I'm an evil person or anything?"

Lid was serious. "Who the hell am I to lecture you? I knew what Braddock was doing. I still don't know how he did it."

"You didn't lie about it."

"Sins of omission rather than commission," he said.

Her blue eyes widened. "I was really terrified that Presnell would show up at my desk again."

Lid gave her a hard look. "He may show up yet. All you can do is wait."

"What about Mimbs?" she asked.

"Mimbs doesn't care who killed that scum, but he *will* keep his department clean. If he finds out about you, we're both in the stew." Lid made a slashing gesture across his throat. "I guess I've been a bad influence. I'm a bastard, right?"

"No, you're a good man." She turned and walked out to escape the intimate moment.

Rachael Brucker greeted her in passing, then entered the cubicle without knocking and collapsed in a chair.

"You didn't kiss me on the mouth," Lid said.

He had to wait for her to light a cigarette and blow smoke. "I didn't think you liked it," she said. "It embarrassed you in front of your fellow cops."

He smiled. "So I'm old-fashioned."

"You've been ignoring me again. This is Friday and I haven't heard from you since Tuesday."

Lid admired the lip turning inside out as she spoke. The effect was better when she was angry. "Yeah, we've been busy. What about dinner tomorrow night?"

Her dark eyes brightened. "What about tonight?"

"Sorry, Alex and I celebrating tonight."

"You and Alex have become very close, haven't you?"

"What do you think? She's my partner."

"Is she good?"

"The best."

Rachael sat while Lid gradually understood. "What? Alex? I told you she's my partner."

"Well, you said she was the best."

"I meant as a partner! You think I'm making it with Alex?"

"You just said you were very close."

"I'm close to a lot of people, but I don't hop into bed with them. You think I do that with just anybody?"

At that point they both remembered the conversation, only it was his turn to finish the speech. Rachael leaned back and took a long drag, watching him through a thin stream of smoke.

What he said was the last thing she expected. "This is a dead-end situation, you and me, I mean."

"What? Am I being kissed off already?"

He shrugged. "We could ball each other's brains out forever and I'd love it, but what's the point? I'm not getting a divorce, and you wouldn't marry me if I did."

"Who said anything about marriage? I like who I like, Lid. I don't make any apologies."

Lid felt again that affliction of human sexuality: guilt if he went on with the affair, regret if he didn't. "At least you could act a little persuasive."

"If you're dropping me, I'm out of here." She smiled.

"You head doctors think you're so smart, don't you?"

"I'm smart enough not to hurt somebody I care about."

It was a sweet, painful remark. Brucker wasn't making it easy. He wanted to hold her, to do it all over again. "Dammit, Rachael. Get your redheaded ass out of here before I rape you."

"Lid, you're starting to excite me. That's the first

time you ever called me Rachael." She stood and deliberately blew a stream of smoke toward his face, then
stubbed out the cigarette. Her smile faded. "Don't hesi-
tate to call if you need me with a case." She turned and
walked out.

Lid watched her out of sight. Brucker was completely professional again. The broad could walk out of
his life and never give him another thought. He would
think about her for a long time, probably forever.
"You're a loser, Li Dao," he said quietly. "Brucker was
a once-in-a-lifetime piece of ass, and you don't have
guts enough to follow up on it. Yeah, you're a goddamn loser, Li Dao."

Romano stuck his head in the door. "Who the hell
are you talking to, Li Dao?"

Lid shook his head. "Sit down."

Romano took the seat. "Who the hell are you talking
to?" He didn't wait for a reply. "There was this old gal
in Parma used to talk to herself. People said she was
crazy, but the local boys liked to fuck her—damn
farmers, sheep herders. She'd talk the whole time they
were fucking her, probably didn't even know she was
getting it, talking about the pine trees or goats or something. Helluva way to get a piece of ass! Who the hell
are you talking to, Lid?"

"Don't you ever talk to yourself?"

"Naw, I talk to stiffs," Romano said. He waited and
tapped a finger nervously, then stared with a long, slow
smile. "That extortion case was somebody local,
wasn't it?"

"Why do you say that?"

Romano lit a cigarette and blew smoke. "Prather and
those guys were nothing but rich lowlifes. I don't know
why any of you give a shit."

Lid was impressed with Tony's assessment. "Some of us don't."

"Don't give a shit?"

Lid nodded.

Romano held the half smile. "You know who blasted those fuckers, don't you?"

Lid respected Tony Romano enough not to lie to him. Romano would see through it anyway. "Yes, I know."

Romano took another drag and blew the smoke slowly. He knew better than to ask. "Some maniac with a grudge," he mused and gestured lack of interest.

In the midst of Lid's mid-life confusion, the weight of Romano's friendship suddenly became more important than anything else. Lid stared at him seriously. "It was a dentist, Dr. Simon Braddock. I think he did the whole thing." Lid could see immediately the self-confidence and acceptance in Romano's dark face. He was glad he had told him.

Romano flicked at his cigarette and said nothing.

"What about Presnell?" Lid asked. "Does he really believe it's organized?"

Romano shrugged. "Presnell never says much to me. Who knows what that guy thinks?"

"You know not to repeat this," Lid said.

Romano gave a lopsided smile. "I'm a humble lab technician."

Abruptly, Romano changed the subject. "I need to see DNA, Lid. If this damn department would get the right equipment, I could tell you if the dick and the head belonged to the same guy. We're way behind big cities! I need to see DNA." He walked out the door.

Lid wondered for a moment if Tony Romano would know a DNA molecule if he tripped over one, yet somehow the lab technician gave the usual pleasant glimmer of correctness and balance in a world full of cheats and pious philosophers. Romano, in spite of his language and manner, was real and earthy, as holy as anything in nature, Lid thought honestly.

Visions of Rachael Brucker still drifted lovingly in Lid's thoughts. He should feel righteous for doing the moral thing, but didn't. That was the unfairness of it. He should either have the woman or have at least a suspicion of chastity, but he had neither.

Lid picked up the phone, muttering *shit*, punched the buttons, and waited. Lucille answered. Could he come by and see them tomorrow? She stammered and finally asked him what for. Lid laughed. He'd have to think about that one. Maybe to check the roof. Maybe because it was Saturday and they could all do something together. It would be a pretty weekend. No, he wasn't drunk, he told her, but he and his partner were going out tonight and get drunk. Lid felt the first tingle of that simple, ancient happiness, but he knew Lucille would not inquire too deeply. She would wait until Saturday.

Five P.M.

Simon stood on the hard-packed ground and waited for Skip to look up.

The older man stopped what he was doing when he saw the van. He carefully lit a cigarette, then twisted the knob until the blue acetylene point vanished with a pop. He laid down the torch and pulled off his gloves, then mopped his brow and walked out into the afternoon sunlight. The long johns had finally been replaced by a shortsleeve shirt revealing more of his dark, hairy arms. Skip tipped his head to see through the bifocals and face Simon at eye level. "And what would you be needing today, young fella?"

They both grinned.

"Dammit, don't you tell me to take you somewhere, Simon. I've had enough of that wild cowboy stuff."

"This is a welding shop, isn't it?"

"That's what the sign says."

"I need something welded." Simon yanked open the van door. "I want this gate put back together. It goes between the patio and the backyard."

"I believe I can do that," Skip said with the cigarette in his mouth. The large, callused hands picked up the heavy wrought iron pieces and set them against the wooden garage door.

"You'll have to come out to the house to mount it back on the hinges," Simon said.

"Well, now, I don't usually make house calls. That'll cost you extra."

"We can work something out. I understand you welders earn a pretty good living."

"Some of us do. And when would you be wanting this, Mr. ah . . . Braddock, ain't it?"

"Doctor."

"Yeah, Dr. Braddock."

Simon got back into the driver's seat and handed a six-pack of Budweiser through the window. He cranked the engine. "Whenever you get it ready. We live out on Marcus Lane South."

"I believe I know where that is." Skip nodded. "You looking mighty pretty. You been bathing and shaving again, ain't you?"

Simon smiled. "It's a hard habit to break." He pulled into drive and eased down the accelerator until Skip was clear and the van was back out on the pavement.

Skip stood in the hot sun with the cigarette and the six-pack and watched him drive away. It had been a bizarre three weeks. The shop had been closed more

than it had been open, but Vashti didn't know. She
never knew how much money he made anyway, and he
hadn't even counted what was left in the seabag.
Maybe he would try one of those little bottles of liquor
that came in the cloth sack.

Skip walked back into the garage, sat on the tractor
seat, and cracked a beer. Late afternoon sun streamed
through the doorway and lit up the layer of dirt and
dust that covered everything inside the shop. Skip took
a drag and a swig. He would have a couple of beers
before he started on the gate.

Seven P.M.

Dusk was settling when Guy Bissett entered his
large, empty residence. It was a two-story brick house,
as they all were in that old, established neighborhood,
the kind of house for a big family that needed room to
grow. The television in the playroom remained on
twenty-four hours a day. He seldom watched it but
liked the idea of something going on in the house.

It had been a long week, and he was tired and
depressed as always, and showing no sign of coming
out of the black mood. He talked daily with his psychiatrist colleague, more out of boredom than hope of reju-
venating counsel. The advice he received was a
loathsome cliche: time is the only healer. Bissett was
tired of hearing it, and his anger wouldn't allow him to
admit it yet. Only in the deepest awareness did he knew
it was true. Weekends were especially difficult, and this
was only the second Friday without Anne, another
Friday night to eat alone, to be alone. Tomorrow he
would work out and jog longer than usual to kill the
time.

The tragedies were too recent for him to have
thoughts of remarriage or selling the property. Every

night he returned to the spacious, empty dwelling, thawed a TV dinner, and dined alone in the silence. He disliked eating out even more. Friends were still having him over, but that wouldn't last forever, and it only reminded him of the sickening disarray his life had become.

Bissett hung his coat on one of the dining room chairs and switched on the kitchen lights. He stood at the stainless steel counter under the bright ceiling and flipped through the mail. Most of it was familiar. He only bothered to open a large brown envelope without a return address. It contained three pictures, grisly photos of dead bodies and a hand-scrawled note: *It's over. Destroy these after you've looked at them.*

He studied each one carefully, close-ups of people shot through the head, two men and a woman. The photos amazed and appalled him. The larger man looked the part of a gangster, but the others were old and harmless in appearance.

It was a cruel gift, but he had requested it. He felt foolish remembering he had wanted to do it himself. The pictures made him know it was not as easy as he thought. Still, he was glad they were dead. These were the people who had taken his son and, indirectly, his wife. He absorbed the images and savored the hideous acts in his imagination, grateful to the nameless executioner. He thought at first to keep the photos rather than destroying them, to examine at his leisure. But these creatures would not have a permanent place in his home; he would burn the prints.

Bissett sat at a heavy antique table and felt the smooth, curved edge of the rosewood. Anne had spent weeks refinishing the wood. He could still picture her leaning over to reach the center and rubbing in the numerous coats of linseed oil. Anne no longer needed a table. The thought astonished him. She no longer needed anything. Life was brief and fragile and pointless. He read the note again with bitterness. How could it ever be over? Anne and Kyle were gone. That would never change. Li Dao was wrong, and yet he was right—it was over.

20

Saturday. Seven A.M.

Simon paced around the backyard in a wide rectangle. The sun had barely broken the horizon, now past those first seconds when he could still look directly at it. Heavy dew sharpened each blade of grass and gave the lawn a green-silver haze. The air was cool and pure. Toby had followed for a few minutes in nosy half interest, then returned to his doghouse. Marie and Esther were still in bed.

Simon was having that unique sensation again of looking at himself from the outside, the alien, that touching, sad image. There was a reason the cave had always settled easily into the deepest reaches: he had never killed anybody before. From now on that fateful reality would find a new home in the sunnier places of his mind, along with the tedium of everyday affairs. In this calm moment of judgment, Simon saw himself with ease, who he was and what he was.

He pushed the idea out of his mind and whistled for Toby. The large white body sidled over, blushing, Simon thought, and bumped himself with clumsy devotion into his master's leg. Simon rubbed and patted the solid flank. "Don't ever kill anybody," he said as the terrifying image of Special Agent Presnell flitted into his mind again.

Marie would always accept him as he was. What else could she do? Simon knew he was sometimes a disappointment, but he was half of her life and Esther's father. Nothing would change that. Their joining had made each the inheritor of the other's liabilities as well as assets.

Tomorrow they would return to Sunday school and church—another bizarre thought. *We have left undone those things we ought to have done; And we have done those things which we ought not to have done; And there is no health in us.* The ancient prayer flowed from rote memory. *But thou, O Lord, have mercy upon us, miserable offenders. Spare thou those, O God, who confess their faults. Restore thou those who are penitent.*

At last one of Aikman's beagles broke the silence with a long, throaty squall. The neighborhood was waking up. Toby shifted and stood and woofed an inept howl of his own. Simon patted him again.

Marie appeared at the back door. The coffee was ready.

Simon went into the kitchen, heavy with bacon aroma, and mixed his coffee. He walked back out on the patio.

Marie got the bacon up before joining him. She still wore her gown and robe. "Esther wants to go to the zoo with Molly and the Kitners," she said. "It's a good sign."

Simon nodded. The Kitners lived a block away. Molly was the same age.

Marie watched him sip from the heavy mug. "How are you feeling?"

He shrugged at the oblique question. Their shared

fear of losing the alibi had remained unspoken. "When are they going to the zoo?" he asked.

"Sometime after lunch."

"Hmm," was all he said.

"Do you love me?" she asked.

Simon smiled. "We just had sex like a couple of wild people."

"Love and sex have little to do with each other."

"Yes, I love you." He looked at her and said it again. "I love you, dummy."

She grinned. "I like to hear it every day."

Simon patted her arm. He never knew exactly what people meant when they said *love*. He understood lust and a certain affection and caring that seemed to focus on the object of that lust. But love? Take away everything that held the slightest taint of lust—the act itself, kissing, touching, exchanging glances—and what was left? That would be love, he thought, but what was it? Simon was wise enough not to share his thoughts with Marie Braddock, a person of exceptional romantic and maternal proclivities.

Simon thought of something he hadn't remembered in days: he wished Marie was ignorant of the killings. Being a murderer was not so distressing as the fact that she knew. That knowledge was one more piece of his private nature for her to possess, a large chunk at that. Simon hated for Marie to see the struggles he went through in order to live. He wanted to be strong and clever and talented, but it had to appear effortless.

He looked at her and patted her again. "I'm sorry for everything, and sorry I made you part of it."

Marie felt a loathsome urge to confess. Simon was not the only person willing to suffer defilement. She placed her hand on top of his. "A girl's gotta do what a girl's gotta do," she said.

Simon looked toward the sky.

"I know that sounds dumb, but I'm serious. We all do what we have to do. You hear about situation morality, and it's really true. Everything in life is situational."

Simon was unaccustomed to hearing Marie philosophize. "What do you mean?"

"We plan our lives like we created the world and everything on it," she said. "Marcus Aikman was mouthing around about how he wouldn't drive anything but a Ferrari. If he'd been born a hundred years ago, he wouldn't be driving a Ferrari."

"So what's your point?"

"Just that. We think we own the earth. We make up rules, then suffer about it when we break one of the rules. Murder. Adultery."

"What about the ten commandments and all of that?"

"Every culture has its myths."

Simon was surprised at her sophistication or cynicism, whichever it was. "You think organized religion is pretty much horse shit?"

She looked at him with a straight face. "Pretty much. At least when it interferes with normal human relations."

Simon had to smile. He had always thought it was horse shit but rather enjoyed being married to a believer. It made sex dirtier and better. But he understood what she meant. Marie had an automatic commonsense alarm, something that took over when institutional dogma or etiquette conflicted with family. He and Esther always came first.

"I appreciate you, Braddock, and I love you," he said. "I really do. You and I have an understanding. Not many women would put up with me."

That was truer than he knew. Marie hesitated. She was not getting any closer to confessing Sammy Self and suddenly realized that she never would. Simon was finely tuned and neurotic but subject to breakdown. His ego would never stand the truth. She had come as close as ever to that vile disclosure but wisely slid back to safer ground.

Esther came out and climbed into her mother's lap. She was barefoot and wore only a summer gown.

Marie set the saucer on the brick deck and held her, rocking gently. "You can wear your Easter dress tomorrow, honey," Marie said. "Nobody will know it's an Easter dress."

"And the hat?" Esther asked.

"And the hat."

"Will you wear yours?"

"I'll wear mine too. We'll look alike."

Esther made a sound of agreement. After a minute she roused and went inside and returned with a bacon strip in each hand. She stood at the edge of the grass and nibbled the bacon until it was gone, then brushed her hands and tripped off through the wet grass.

Simon and Marie watched and admired with inexpressible love and amazement, and with relief. Unspeakable relief.

Simon looked at Marie. "So you think God is a lot of horse shit?"

She jerked away from his glance as if he had stabbed her. "I didn't say God. I said organized religion."

Simon pictured Esther and Marie together in the wide straw Easter hats. Suddenly, the familiar confession from the Morning Prayer flowed again with cataract force and abandon. *But thou, O Lord, have mercy upon us, miserable offenders. Spare thou those, O God, who confess their faults. Restore thou those who are penitent; According to thy promises declared unto mankind In Christ Jesus our Lord. And grant, O most merciful Father, for his sake; That we may hereafter lead a godly, righteous, and sober life, To the glory of thy holy Name. Amen.*

He wondered at the efficacy of those words. Did they still carry power over the centuries? Did he believe? Simon wanted desperately to ask Marie for her opinion but had courage enough not to cloud his own conviction. Every man had to answer that for himself.

Seven P.M.

The sun was still above the pine trees. The noise of Ollie's mower rended the early evening hush and made conversation impossible. Simon sat on the patio and read the *Macon News* while Alex Sinclair mentally closed her ears and waited.

Ollie moved away toward the front of the house.

Simon tossed the newspaper aside just as Marie came out with drinks. She was barefoot. The cycling shoes were set evenly on the brick step, but she still wore pink Spandex pants and a nylon shirt. Her hair was tied loosely back in a ponytail.

Alex shifted uneasily. The new pleated trousers had hung in her closet for weeks awaiting warm weather and the right occasion. She had tried to dress up an old blouse with a new scarf, casual and cute, she had hoped, but Alex knew she was not in Marie Braddock's league. "Anything I can do to help?"

"No, thanks, Alex. Simon will entertain you for a few minutes while I finish up."

Marie deliberately left them alone again to force him beyond the bare civility he had managed on their first meeting. Simon could be charming when he had to be.

Simon picked up the drink and took a swig. "Alex, I'm sorry I was grumpy when you were here before. I appreciate what you did for me."

His statement was a startling surprise. "I understood

why you were secretive in the beginning," Alex said, "but not after I lied to the fibbies. You did kill the Prathers and the Wexlers, didn't you?"

"Yes."

"And the guy with the ponytail?"

"Yes. He was the one who murdered Harry Hall. I'm sorry, I don't know if you wanted to know that."

"How do *you* know that?"

"Don't corner me, Alex. Believe me, I know. He also injured Marie's brother and took Esther."

"The big guy on the table?"

"Yes."

"I didn't go over there, but I saw the pictures. Tell me about it, Simon."

"That's the same thing Marie said." Simon stared into space. "He never saw me. I shot him in the back of the head." Simon waited again, but Alex was silent. "You want to know what it was like, don't you?"

She tasted the drink and nodded.

"I thoroughly enjoyed it. It's eerie to recall how much I enjoyed it. And there was one other guy, Max, they called him. I think he was a butler."

"We never found him. What about Noles and Condon?"

"No, I imagine Willard Prather did those two."

"What about Prather? You were at the beach when he was killed."

"I never went to the beach."

"The feds said you did."

"It was my brother-in-law."

Alex smiled with satisfaction. She was pleased and amazed at the ease of his admissions. "You're a devious son of a bitch, Simon."

"Am I?"

"Yes, you are. Why did you mail the code book? Why didn't you just hand it to me?"

"Being a devious son of a bitch is a habit, I guess."

Alex was finally relaxed around him, able to ask real questions and get real answers. Her curiosity was deep and genuine. "How did you decide to do all that?"

"You may laugh if I tell you." He took another sip and looked into the sunset. "There's this place in my mind, and I get pushed in there sometimes. It's like a cave, and I can see out through a little hole but I can't get out. Anger puts me there, and the only escape is to relieve the anger, but I have to abide by the rule."

"What's the rule?"

"The rule is you can't threaten a person who makes you angry. He either chooses to undo whatever he did or he becomes the enemy. You destroy him."

"You say 'you' as if we all have such a place."

Simon shrugged. "I don't know. I've never discussed this, but I've always had it, as far back as I can remember."

"Why can't you threaten?"

"It's against the rule."

"You've never discussed this with Marie?"

"No."

"Why not?"

"Damn, Alex. I've never told anybody about this."

"I'm not pushing you into your cave, am I?"

"No, but some things need to stay private. Marie is a very curious type too. She wants to be inside me, to feel the same feelings and think the same thoughts. If she ever knows everything I know, I become only an extension of her. I cease to exist. I love Marie, but I have to hold her off. Can you understand that?"

"I think so. If you've never discussed this before, why are you telling me?"

"Because of Harry Hall," he answered bluntly, but Simon knew that was not the whole reason. He could be open with Alex Sinclair; he didn't have to live with her. "This is just between us, Alex. Don't mention any of it to Lid, and I won't say anything to Marie."

"Deal," she said.

They touched glasses and sipped the whiskey.

Alex gazed at the handsome face and sandy hair. Simon was barefoot as usual. He slouched casually and held the glass by the top, stirring an ice cube with one finger. He looked like an ad for the cotton slacks. "You were very lucky," she said.

"What ever happened to that other family?" Simon asked. "Lanier—the doctor whose daughter disappeared?"

"He closed his office and they left town. They moved somewhere in Alabama." Alex sipped her drink and felt a strange admiration, not respect but something akin. "Why did you cut Prather's head off?"

"It was the only way to get out of the cave."

Alex made a face. "Did you enjoy him?"

"I enjoyed all of them," he said.

Marie stepped out of the kitchen. "What did you enjoy all of?"

"All the women I've ever had."

Marie flipped her eyes skyward as she took a seat.

Simon wondered if Marie even wanted her feelings protected. She needed to know everything until he had only a small place left to call his own. Physical love was like that, he thought, an act of total yielding, acceptable with the body but not with the whole being. There was a part of one's self that had less intention than existence and yet was more important. The greater his love for Marie, the greater the danger that she would beguile him out of that ultimate space.

Marie sat and chatted but never picked up her drink. After a while she came back to the question. "What did you enjoy all of, Simon?"

"The murders," he said.

Alex and Marie smirked in unison as if it were a joke, but they both knew better, each according to her understanding of Simon.

Alex took a large envelope from her purse and held it out to Marie. "This is a copy of the FBI report. I thought you might like to have it."

"Thank you. Does it say anything that wasn't in the paper?"

"A lot more. Besides, you can't always trust the media. This is official. Presnell says it was an internal feud, just like I'd hoped he would. It gives them a neat way to put the case on the shelf. That's a confidential file. Don't ever let anybody see it."

Only in that moment did Simon and Marie realize that the risk was truly over.

Simon wondered why Alex had taken so long to break the news. He knew Marie would love the file, final confirmation that the FBI was settled in the matter and wouldn't come after him again. Marie would devour it line by line and relish the details like reading a good mystery, just as she had picked his brain until he admitted he enjoyed the killings.

Simon glanced at the small brunette furtively. Alex had been an embarrassment, a symbol of his own corruption, yet Marie was beginning to have genuine fondness for the woman detective, he could tell. Simon was glad he had talked about the cave, even to a person of such short acquaintance.

Suddenly, the cave stood in clear relief, apart from his own being. He felt its supernormal danger and anaesthetizing effect. Reality became palpable: He was a murderer. It was done and couldn't be undone. How had he gotten away with it? Perhaps it wasn't over. Obie's body would be discovered. Bits of wood fiber would match the plywood scraps. A single hair or a few blood cells would correspond to Obie's type. Just as abruptly, the notion struck him as absurd; he had gotten away with it.

He and Lid would not meet again, Simon knew. They didn't need to know each other. Marie and Alex would have a real friendship, thrown together as they were because of the extortion. Women seemed to enjoy dwelling on a common experience, especially a bad experience.

Simon deliberately tuned in their conversation. Alex was telling Marie about her own guilt and fear, about Anne Bissett and the son, Kyle. Harry Hall wasn't the only reason the woman cop had alibied for him. Marie would eventually tell her side of the story, the fat man with the big gun, the night in the welding shop, and the rest of it. Simon relaxed. Alex might do him another favor without even realizing it. She and Marie could become buddies and discuss the extortion forever. He didn't want to hear about it.

Esther came out and climbed up on his lap. She gave a single squeeze, then hopped down and ran toward the trampoline. Toby wobbled out of his doghouse to shake and jostle his way into her attention. Esther prodded him with the same hasty caress she had given her father. She swung up onto the springy surface while Toby shook and sauntered and collapsed onto the newly mowed grass.

Simon watched her begin, the blond head now almost touching the sun with each bounce as the orange ball settled into the pines.

He loved the extended pale evenings of daylight savings time. The air was quiet in the early summer sky. In two days the sun would perch atop the woodshop before it disappeared. In six weeks it would set completely to the right of the shop—the summer solstice—then begin the long slow trek back to the south.

He closed his thoughts again and listened to their voices. The gist of the conversation was children—one as opposed to several. Alex thought the trend was to smaller families as lifestyles changed from rural to urban. Marie suggested the pendulum effect. Statistically, the U.S. might be moving back toward larger families. It was odd to hear women talk about having children in such clinical terms, like deciding whether or not to buy a second car. Nobody ever said, *My husband and I like to have sex because it feels so good!* Marie wanted two or three, and wouldn't be satisfied until they had at least one boy and one girl. Simon looked at her long legs and flat tummy as lewd thoughts of touching, holding, and licking entered his mind and moved his blood. Maybe she was right; Esther needed a baby brother. They would begin working on it tonight.

At last the mower ceased its distant whine and added a pleasant layer to the silence. The bouncing sound was more distinct now, even and inevitable, hypnotic. The female chatter faded as Simon sipped his drink and drifted again into solitary considerations.